Pure Love,
Or
Is It?

Pure Love, Or Is It?

Sean Gold

An Open Letter

Dear victims and survivors of sexual assault:

First, I would like to thank you for being able to read this book when you've actually been through it. Your experience and traumas caused by it are valid; never let anyone tell you any different. My intentions with this story were never to disrespect, make fun of, or invalidate your story. I've tried my best to study, research, and empathize with you all, and I hope I've done a fair job. As a gay man myself, I have not been through anything like this in my personal life. If something seems unrealistic to you, please forgive me as this is a fictional story from start to finish. Everyone's story is unique in its own way, and so is my character's, Brandon's, which you are about to read.

If you are a male victim, being assaulted at any age doesn't make you any less of a man. If you are a female victim, you're worthy of healing yourself as much as possible. If you are a child victim, my heart breaks for the day that your innocent childhood was ruined forever and transitioned into a nightmare. It wasn't your fault. It's never your fault, no matter what the circumstances were. I advise you to consult with your therapist if this book is right for you to read. Please take as many and as long of a break as you need to with this book. This story goes into feelings very vividly in detail.

I dedicate this book to you most of all. I'm inspired by your abilities to continue with love and life after your trauma. Always remember that you are worth it.

Love,

Sean Gold

Acknowledgements

Mom:

There are not enough words in the universe to say thank you to you. You've done so much for me and continue to do so. It means more than you'll ever know, and I'll spend an eternity trying to show my love and appreciation. I couldn't have made it this far in life without you. I love you so much. Since the day I was born, you've never left my side, and you are the reason I'm the kind of man I am today. You're everything to me, and I'll never let you go!

Brian:

My big brother. Correction, my annoying big brother. Thank you for all of the lessons that you've taught and continue to guide me in life. I did bring many of your big brother protective ways into the story as I know you'd act the same way if it were me. However, that's a compliment! I look up to you in so many ways, and I'm lucky to have you as my brother.

Grandma:

My ninety-five-year-old grandmother. You have always been my biggest cheerleader. For as long as I can remember, you've always been there for me. I have learned so many great lessons from you that I'll cherish for the rest of my life. You have taught many lessons and done so much that I'll never be able to thank you enough for. I pray that everything I do makes you proud of me. I love you with everything in my soul.

Family:

This includes all of my aunts, uncles, and cousins. I am lucky to be part of this family. Thank you for loving me, supporting me, and giving me everything that I need and more. I appreciate the laughs you all gave me and for sticking by my side no matter what. I don't know where I'd be without you all!

Emily:

My best friend and life partner. You're more like a sister to me than a friend. We've been through so much in ten years, and we did it all through social media. I know that you'll be a fantastic nurse, and I'm so proud of you for graduating from nursing school last year! Thank you for being there for me throughout everything. I don't know why you put up with me, but I'm so glad you do. You are braver and stronger than you'll ever know.

Dasia:

My school best friend. Thank you for letting me vent to you whenever I need it. I appreciate you for looking past my disability in high school and getting to know me. I can't say that for many classmates besides our lunch friends and those in the Web and Computer Programming shop with us. Thank you for all your dark jokes, crude humor and for making me more morbid than I ever wanted to be.

Kamille:

My other best friend that's like a little sister to me. I see how hard you're working at your job, and I'm so proud. Thank you for everything you've done for me, and I appreciate your endless support. Life without you would be crazy! I will always cherish that we got to grow up together in our teen years online. The long night chats and endless jokes will never be forgotten. I know that we're busy adults now, but not a day goes by where I don't think about you. You're stuck with me for life, and I'm so sorry for you.

Samara:

I appreciate all of your help with this book. Without you, I wouldn't have known how to write some of these chapters effectively. I thank you so much for your constant opinions and advice on how to improve the story. It's awesome to find someone who is such a fan of the same show as I am, even when it's no longer on the air. You're one of the reasons why I was able to finish this book.

Alyssa:

My first ever fan fiction writing buddy. I appreciate all of your feedback and help throughout the years. You've been there through my WORST writing to now this first book I've published. This would've never happened without you! I enjoy growing and improving our crafts together in both middle and high school. I've truly improved my writing because of you!

Ase and Zoom family:

There are too many of you to name individually! All of you have made my 2020 so much fun despite everything that happened in the world. I love being able to laugh and talk past midnight about everything possible. I thank you all for embracing me since the very first night I joined you all. Ase, I have listened to a couple of your songs as I wrote this book, so technically, you've helped me write this before you knew I existed! It sounds funny even though it's the truth. Your book is terrific, and I hope that my book is at least half as good.

Prologue

College is never an easy time for a student. Especially when they were going to get a master's degree in law. Brandon Andreas happened to be one of those students. He was a twenty-two-year-old man in the middle of his last year as an undergrad. Everything that would happen for the remaining months leading up to his graduation would determine everything for him in law school.

Brandon's best friend Shane was his roommate. The two had been friends ever since they met in their freshman year in high school in 2011. They decided to get a bachelor pad together to live out their best college experience. Just like with any other two friends who choose to live together, it took a while for them to get used to sharing the same space all of the time. At the end of the day, they were glad that they were in each other's corners at all times.

Brandon and Shane were different in a lot of ways when it came to life. Brandon was the hard-working, career-driven guy who put his career and college work first. Brandon was a five-foot-seven, slim, hazel-eyed, and curly black-haired man. He wore his hair in a low cut, and it was often gelled back. Whenever he smiled, two noticeable dimples on his face lit up the room. Brandon made sure to keep up with his appearance. He didn't care to go out to the significant events or made sure his closet had the latest style trend but was always presentable. It was the ambition of making his life purpose a reality. It happened to be his last year at an undergrad college; he was determined to finish strong before going into law school. Since he was gay, it added additional challenges for his everyday life.

Shane Jacobs was more outgoing, and he had a carefree attitude about life. He was a lot more buff than Brandon was. Shane was about five foot nine with dirty blonde hair, and eyes were light gray. He had his hair in a fauxhawk. The gym was one of his favorite places to be besides hanging out wherever his college friends were. Of course, he knew that school was important, but he would instead have spent his free time going to college parties and having dates with the ladies on campus. It also didn't help that Shane had a learning disability. His dyslexia made it challenging for him, but with Brandon and the great professors' help, he succeeded. Shane was a jock in high school who played on the football team and loved working out. So, it made sense that he would want to be a fitness trainer going for his physical education degree. It was important for Shane to choose a career that didn't involve as much critical thinking as Brandon's would.

Brandon and Shane knew just about everything about each other. From favorite colors to their biggest pet peeves, there wasn't much that would shock the other anymore.

Chapter 1: Out of Curiosity

It was evening time in New York, and the sun had set. They had just finished studying when Shane had a particular look on his face that Brandon knew all too well. The kind of look that Brandon knew would only cause trouble for the duo, but he always had to ask.

"What's floating around in your mind now, Shane?" Brandon questioned as he closed his books and placed them to the side.

"Why would this look mean that I'm thinking about something?" Shane asked.

"When has it not meant that?" Brandon retorted, "Whatever it is, that look has always been connected to us doing a dangerous activity. We'll argue about it because I never seem to agree at first. You end up convincing me, and it usually ends up fun. Most of the time. I can recall plenty of times you've suggested something that landed us in the hospital."

"Fine, I am thinking about something I want to try. I want to try it with you, and this activity requires two people anyway. Who else would I feel comfortable with asking?"

"Requires two people? Big word. College is definitely doing some good for you." Brandon smirked and teased, which earned him a pillow to the face.

"No need to be an asshole," Shane chuckled. "This is serious, though! You can say no this time for once."

"I'm allowed to say no this time? That's never an option; now I'm terrified. That option wasn't available the one time you made us try jumping on our pogo sticks while on the trampoline two years ago." Brandon reminded him. "I broke my arm then!"

"You enjoyed it before that happened. Isn't that the most important part?"

"Easy for you to say! You weren't harmed, Shane." Brandon groaned. "Just tell me what it is already!"

Shane sighed and looked at his best friend. This request had been in his mind for quite some time, and he's now brave enough to ask. "I have been wondering what it's like…"

"What are you talking about?"

"Sex…" Shane blurted out nervously.

"I hear you having sex with a different girl every other week," Brandon gestured to Shane's room, "Be more specific, please."

"I meant what it's like to have sex with another guy." Shane clarified as if Brandon was the one being stupid this time around. Yet that still wasn't the case with this one.

"You what?" Brandon questioned with disbelief of his best friend.

"I said—"

"I heard you…That was a different kind of 'what.' Like an 'I can't believe what I heard' kind of what. Just like when I had to tell you the other day that the sun is just a star." Brandon informed him. He often had to do things like this for his friend. Not that he ever minded doing it, but that's a story for another time.

On the other hand, Brandon didn't know how to feel. He'd spent years swallowing his love for that man, and now all of a sudden, Shane wanted sex with him? There were red flags all over the idea.

"You don't have to say yes…" Shane reminded him.

"That's the problem! I want to say yes. Shane, I just…" Brandon stopped himself before his words came out like vomit, and he confessed his feelings in front of a man whom he adored. "If you're sure…" he said after composing himself once again.

Shane looked at his best friend giving him a reassuring smile that melted Brandon's heart as usual. "I'm sure, man. You're my best friend, and I'm just curious." That's what Brandon was scared of; he didn't want to be an experiment for just anyone, and it didn't matter who it was. On the other hand, Shane was his best friend, and if he were curious, in a way, he'd rather it be him than some random.

Brandon took in a big, long sigh as he thought about his options before answering. After so many years of trusted friendship, what's the worst that could happen? "As random as this is, I'll do it. Since you're my best friend, what's the worst that could happen?"

Shane stood up with a smile. "Awesome! I didn't think you'd agree."

"Yes, you did. I can't ever say no to you…" Brandon stood up as well, shaking his head and chuckling a little. "I can't believe this is what you're wanting!"

Shane nodded. "Well, believe it."

"I don't want to hear you complaining afterward, or ever." Brandon playfully warned him in a severe tone, which made him laugh.

The boys went their separate ways into their rooms to change. Shane decided on a shirt and boxers, while Brandon chose something similar. Even though it was shocking that Shane wanted to go through with this, he had to admit he wanted it too.

Brandon rolled his eyes at himself after coming up with scenarios about how that night could go. Like always, Brandon over-prepared himself for all the possible things. However, Shane seemed different from the others; he was right in front of him. Maybe it had to do with him caring about his best friend and wanting the experiment to be worthwhile for him. Or, maybe Brandon saw it as a way that Shane could realize that he was the one for him.

It wasn't the first time Brandon had thought of doing it if he were ever to try to pursue a relationship with him, but it was worth a shot. He went in his drawer, fetching for a condom. Brandon wasn't as big on sex as Shane. Sure he enjoyed it, but the romance part was way better to him. He liked the idea of being swooned over and courted. Brandon was old fashioned in this modern world; if anyone knew that about him, Shane did.

He made his way from his room to Shane's. It was a weird feeling knowing what they were about to commit to doing, but Brandon was ready. If he had to admit it, he was also a little intrigued to see how everything was about to go. He took in a breath turning the knob to Shane's room, and went in. There was no turning back now.

Chapter 2: Just an Experiment

Brandon closed the door behind him, and he felt a little anxious about it all. He was going to be an experiment for his best friend. As much as it hurt him, Brandon knew Shane cared about him. Brandon looked at Shane differently; he has this inner glow about him that radiates off of him. Shane was Brandon's golden boy. The journey that they were about to go on was something they have never been down before. From that night onwards was going to be different; somewhere deep inside, they both knew it.

"You ready?" Brandon asked nervously.

"Yeah," Shane nodded his head, and he moved closer to him. "I'm ready."

"Okay. Whenever it's too much, tell me." Brandon told him as he moved forward and started to run his fingers up Shane's chest. He looked Shane in his dark gray eyes. He looked different in the current setting as if he was seeing him for the first time.

"It won't be," Shane assumed.

"Okay…" Brandon responded.

They both took in a breath before going in for a kiss on the lips. Brandon couldn't help but stare at Shane's bottom lip. Plump and fully ready for the taking. Brandon went in first, nipping at Shane's pink colored lips. They felt sweet, slightly innocent, something he had never experienced before. The only problem besides nerves were their lips, both moving in sync with each other. Brandon decided to go in the opposite position of the kiss, realizing that Shane wanted to lead.

Unfortunately, they both had the same idea, moving in sync, and ended up bumping heads. "OW," Shane whined. They both pulled apart.

"Okay, this isn't working so far…" Brandon rolled his eyes.

"Clearly." Shane groaned. "Is this supposed to be so complicated?"

Brandon sighed. "No, it's just always awkward the first time. We need to, you know, figure each other out."

"What? You know I'm straight, and I know you're gay; what's to figure out now?" Shane was still very oblivious to what Brandon was saying. Brandon had to let out a small chuckle as he heard the question.

"Not that," Brandon started. He already knew that he would have to explain as they went along. "I mean, what do you want to try? Do you want to be on top or bottom?"

"Explain the difference?" Shane requested.

"Oh God, Shane. You don't know anything about this." Brandon chuckled. "Okay, the top gives it, the bottom takes it. Now pick."

Shane took a minute to think about it. He didn't consider that to be an issue. He was always on top with the girls, so he decided: "I'll bottom this time."

"This time?" Brandon raised an eyebrow in question.

"Well, yeah…" Shane answered in an evident tone. "I would like to try both positions."

"This wasn't said earlier," Brandon told him.

"I know, but if I like it, I want to try to top as well…" Shane confessed.

Brandon couldn't hold back his chuckle while wrapping his arms around Shane's waist. "You're ridiculous."

"What else would you expect me to be?" Shane asked rhetorically.

"Good point," Brandon shrugged as he could smell the freshness of Shane's breath, and it drew him in more.

Brandon was the first to press their lips together softly for the kiss. It was slow, with some nervousness from both parties. Even with the nerves, there was a connection between them that neither had felt with anyone else before. It was unique and even a little magical.

They pulled away after a while, speechless from the connection. It had been so powerful that they were caught off guard and lost from reality. Shane and Brandon just stared at each other not doing anything, but there was another feeling building up inside them. Before knowing what was happening, Brandon had pushed him down on the bed and positioned himself on top of Shane.

This time the kiss was more heated and passionate. It wasn't long before moans were escaping each other's mouths with Brandon's tongue touching Shane's lips, asking for permission, which got granted within seconds. They kissed in a rhythm that was still slow but had more emotion in it. Shane's arms wrapped around Brandon's neck while Brandon's wrapped around his waist. Brandon and Shane enjoyed each other and explored each other in ways that hadn't been possible before.

Clothes began being taken off and tossed on the floor. Kissing one last time, Brandon moved down to Shane's neck, kissing and biting down on it, earning him a pleasurable moan, and hearing him turned Brandon on more. It was getting heated, and the room echoed with Shane's sounds. Shane was enjoying everything Brandon was doing to him.

When Brandon got lower to the waist, he looked back up at Shane. He wanted to make sure he was going the right speed for Shane. Brandon slowly started to expose him. Brandon couldn't help but bite his lips at what was revealed to him. Shane was more prominent than he imagined. It only made him crave for his best friend even more. He went down and touched it through the fabric, getting a feel for it. Shane began to beg for more through his sounds. They were sexual sounds that Brandon hadn't heard before, and it brought a good feeling knowing that he could make Shane react in a new way.

"Take them off," Shane whimpered, which Brandon couldn't resist. He slid the underwear off, leaving his best friend exposed and vulnerable. After the clothes were on the floor, Brandon paused for a moment to admire Shane's perfect frame and to savor the moment. He smirked to himself as he witnessed seeing his perfectly chiseled body. It was raw and pure, something Brandon never caught before.

"You're beautiful." He whispered before sucking the tip of the dick. The precum tasted salty and addictive. Brandon teased until Shane was practically begging for more. He was enjoying the action more than Brandon thought Shane would.

Brandon took it back in his hand, going back up to Shane's lips, kissing him harder. Both men were grinding against each other and moaning louder than before. Shane was enjoying it and loved having sex with a man. With his best friend. They kissed for a while before they flipped over, letting Shane be on top. Brandon loved the feeling of Shane's lips on his; it felt like they belonged together, pressed up forever, and for a second, he was hoping that.

Shane was the one who broke the kissing, starting to give the same treatment he had received from Brandon. He kissed and bit on the tender skin. It was driving Brandon crazy unsatisfied and wanting more. The feeling of a man wanting him and the thrill of it all was something he could get used to doing.

He grabbed Brandon's dick through the underwear nervously, not sure if he would do it right. To give his best friend the same pleasure received. Brandon didn't want to rush him, but he started to get desperate for Shane to taste him. To take off his underwear and have at it. He needed more.

"What do you need, baby?" Shane asked sensually. He knew what was wanted, but he wanted to hear it.

"You...I want your lips on me," Brandon breathed out, "Please..."

With that, Brandon's wish was granted. Shane tasted the head slowly, unsure if he would like it. The precum was salty and savory, unlike anything else he had tasted. He took a second to enjoy the precum before going down for more. Brandon thought he was a natural at this, unable to stop moaning out his name. It only got better feeling Shane's hands going up against his thighs and playing with his body; he couldn't get enough of it.

There was a whimper in protest when Shane lifted off and made his way up to kiss Brandon again. It was a sloppy and heated kiss. They stayed kissing and grinding on each other for a while. The moaning got louder for the both of them. Something about kissing your best friend intrigued Shane and Brandon. Neither have expected to have this much of a connection but couldn't say anything at the moment.

Shane got off Brandon and laid down on his stomach. Brandon worked quickly to stretch him out. Shane winced at the uncomfortable feeling that came at first before he could relax and enjoy it. Once he was ready, the second finger followed, and then the third.

"Shit," Shane breathed out. It was a weird feeling that he was liking. Brandon must've been doing something right because it felt amazing. Three fingers up his ass were doing things to him. After taking his fingers out, Brandon worked quickly to get the condom on.

Brandon lined up with the entrance and kissed up his back to the shoulder. "Tell me if it hurts." He whispered and then started to go in carefully. Shane still felt tight with it being the first time. Once he was inside, he allowed time for Shane to adjust beneath him. After Brandon got the okay, he eased his way in and out of his friend.

It quickly turned into thrusts. Brandon moved fast in the hole and got closer to Shane's spot. Shane loved it, making pleasurable sounds as it went in more. When Brandon hit a particular area, he let out a loud yell from the feeling. Shane didn't understand what it was, but he liked the feeling. The pressure was a little painful, but worth it.

"I'm close," Brandon warned after a few minutes. He kept thrusting, going as fast as he could until he collapsed with his orgasm. Shane was already having his orgasm by the time Brandon pulled out. He flipped back around to his back and met with lips pressed against his hard.

They kissed with a sense of passion. Shane pulled Brandon closer, not getting enough of him. They gave their bodies something to remember until they passed out on the bed next to each other. Shane had an arm around Brandon as they eventually fell asleep. Everything was perfect.

Chapter 3: The Morning After

Daylight broke through the windows of Shane's room. Brandon was the first one awake, and he felt safe in Shane's embrace. He didn't want to get up. Would it mean that Brandon had to act as if that night didn't affect him as it did? Brandon also felt uneasy about it knowing that all he provided was like a sex service. Brandon went into his room and took another shower before getting ready for the day.

Maybe he should have said no, but there was something inside him that wanted it. Something that he didn't know that he wanted as much as he did. Now that it was over, he didn't know what to do. After he washed up and got dressed, Brandon went into the kitchen, brewed the coffee, and packed his lunch for the day.

It was the most critical year in college for him. Graduation was around the corner, and making sure he kept that GPA up was crucial. Not to mention, his father had cancer, and he became one of his caretakers. It was a lot on his plate. Even if Shane wanted a relationship with Brandon, he wasn't in the best mindset to be in one. Although his best friend would understand, Brandon would still say yes. He was a people pleaser at heart, always looking for approval. That was the one question Brandon knew that there would be no regrets from answering yes.

It startled him a little when Shane came up behind him, wrapped arms around him, and pressed up against him. "Morning..." Shane mumbled in his ear.

"Good morning to you too?" Brandon greeted; he felt slightly confused. He didn't understand what was happening. Brandon thought that maybe he was in the morning after sex haze and that it was too good to be true.

"It was better than anticipated. Everything was amazing. Thanks for that." Shane told him, his hand grazed Brandon's butt.

Brandon chuckled, not thinking much of it. "I haven't decided if you should owe me for that or not since I enjoyed it as well."

"I'm glad you did." Shane hummed as he kissed his neck, which surprised Brandon a little, even though he liked the feeling of his lips on his skin. Somehow it felt like they belonged pressed against his body. "Whatever you want, just let me know."

"Deal, now wish me luck on my test today. It counts as half my midterm." Brandon nervously sighed.

"Dude, you know you got this. You've been studying hard, don't stress about it." Shane encouraged him. He didn't doubt how smart his friend was, especially when he was going for a challenging degree. For as long as Brandon could remember, all he ever wanted to be was a lawyer. As a teenager, Brandon loved watching the court shows and figuring out who would win the case.

Brandon smiled, "Thanks." He turned around to kiss him on the lips. When Brandon realized what he was doing, he immediately pulled back in embarrassment. "I'm sorry I didn't mean to-"

"It's okay; I don't mind you kissing me," Shane reassured his best friend. Brandon gave a little smile at him, but he was oblivious to what it meant. "Dude, go to class! You don't want to be late."

That's when Brandon's smile faded away. Was he not allowed to show affection back? What was going on? Instead of letting his feelings lead, Brandon decided to let it go and head out for class. That left Shane alone in the apartment with his thoughts. It was a memorable night with no regrets. He wanted more experimenting with a man learning how to please men sexually. To know what it feels like to be in control of a man, and having sex in various places. All of it turned him on. Why these ideas come at random times were unknown, but he rolled with them anyways.

Shane poured the coffee into his mug and took a seat on the couch. Many thoughts flowed through his mind as he sat in silence. What was it that he liked about last night? How could sex with a man feel so different than it did with women? Last night was special without a doubt; Shane couldn't deny that. Whether because it was his first time or the fact that it was with Brandon, something told him that he could get into this.

He began wondering about Brandon and all of the little things leading up to the moment. He never wanted to lead him on. He was confused, or maybe he wasn't. Brandon was there the whole time. Shane was starting to question everything that he knew. He wanted this man, maybe. Shane thought it would be what people call the college experimenting, and no feelings would get involved. No one would get hurt. Except what if someone did get hurt if the magic was lost? How could either of them recover?

Brandon was heading into the Communications building at Kingsborough Community College when he caught up with his friend, Zach. They met at the beginning of the semester and immediately hit it off as friends. There was something about Zach that drew Brandon in, but it never went further than a friendship.

"Hey, Brandon," Zach greeted him.

"Good morning, Zach. Are you ready for the test today?" Brandon smiled at him.

Zach was a twenty-three year old man also In his last year for his undergraduate degree. He was five foot six, had a buzz cut brown hair, blue eyes, and he loved fashion. Zach wasn't a feminine man, but he always had his nails done. On that day, he painted them in fall colors.

"I'm not sure. I studied as much as I could. The laws seem simple to remember but to determine which law goes with which case will be tough. They are so similar." Zach told him.

"I know, you'd think that this would be like a personal opinion, but this isn't acceptable within this career. You have to use your knowledge of the law. Plus, this test is towards the midterm grade! We have to do good on this." Brandon stressed.

"At least the other half will be multiple choice questions, but that's on Friday," Zach smiled. He turned to look at Brandon, and he sensed that something else was bothering him. "Are you okay? You seem a little down."

"Well, your predictions on me would give you an A." Brandon smiled a little for the first time and then sighed. "It's just Shane, my roommate. He's ridiculous at times. Last night just caught me off guard after studying."

"Shane Jacobs? The one who bangs every girl he can get up on this campus?" Zach asked with a raised eyebrow. "I feel so sorry that you have to hear all of that. People in the dorm next to you guys complain a lot already. I can't imagine being in there." He shuddered.

Brandon just stared at Zach for a moment. "Word gets around that fast, even in college?"

"Yeah, everyone has been talking about him and all he does. Haven't you two been at this college for four years?"

"Okay, yes, we have. I guess a lot would know about him."

"You admit that it's true, then?" Zach pointed up his eyebrows in question.

Brandon groaned, "I don't want to call out my best friend, but let's just say they're not all lies."

"Shane is cute, but I don't get the hype. It's unbelievable that you're single." Zach fathomed

"I guess I just want to focus on my degree." Brandon smiled and shrugged. He opened the classroom door, letting Zach go in first. "We do have a long way to go until we are certified as lawyers."

"Tell me about it. Seven whole years and we have three and a half to go. It seems scary." Zach groaned.

"It'll be very frightening. We'll get through it together, Zach. I'm glad we met this year. We seem to have a lot in common." Brandon sat by him like they did most days in class ever since they met. Shane was great with encouraging him that he was choosing the right career path, but to have a friend wanting the same degree comes with better understanding. Not to mention, he adored Zach's sense of style. No matter what he had, it was always interesting. "Another new outfit?"

Zach let out a chuckle. "You noticed! Yeah, I bought it last week."

Brandon sarcastically gasped. "Zach Deanes waits a week before showing off his new outfit? That's impossible. He enjoys showing off his style right away, I thought."

Zach chuckled. "Hey, some things you have to admire on your own before showing up in the world." Brandon laughed and shook his head, turning to face the professor that had just walked in.

"Good morning, class. I hope you studied hard for your exam." Professor Baker spoke when she walked into the classroom. "As a reminder, this is a part of your midterm grade. Best of luck to everyone.

Any questions before I pass out the test?" No one seemed to have any questions, and the professor began to pass out the test.

Brandon took in a breath when the papers were put on his desk. It had a total of ten questions that he had to think and thoroughly write out his answers. He looked at all the questions before starting. After he finished, he took the exam up to the professor.

Brandon and Zach left the class after the course was over, "How do you think you did?" Brandon asked Zach.

"It wasn't as hard as I thought, but oh my God, the examples started to look similar. We got through it, that's all that matters." Zach assured.

Brandon hummed in agreement. "Now to just get through the other tests. This was my biggest one for the week."

"Same here, I don't think my other courses will be as bad," Zach said with hope.

They decided to go to the cafeteria before their next class began in an hour. Zach and Brandon got something to eat and sat outside. The New York weather had a slight breeze in the air, and the sun was shining through the whole campus. It was the middle of October, and everyone wanted to enjoy the weather while it lasted.

"This is pretty good today," Zach commented on the food.

"I know, the cafeteria workers must be in a pretty good mood today." Brandon Chuckled.

"I think you're right." Zach laughed. "On bad days, it looks as if they literally put their feet in the food."

"Yeah, on those days, I run back to the apartment and get my food. Shane and I switch off cooking for the week." Brandon told him.

"That's good, Adam and I do that too," Zach responded. They both continued to eat in silence while checking their phones. When Brandon wasn't looking, Zach would sneak looks up at him. He thought Brandon was a sweet guy, and he liked being his friend. He could tell something was bothering him, but he didn't want to bring it up, assuming that it wasn't his place to be nosey. The conversation continued to be light. Discussing the classes, studying, and the other gossip around the campus that was spreading around.

Brandon was grateful for a friend like Zach. They laughed at the ridiculous rumors floating around, and Zach seemed to know that most of them happened to be true. Some surprised him while others were so obvious. When it got to some of the girls that Shane had been with, it got more interesting for him.

"How do you know all these things?" Brandon asked in surprise.

"Rumors spread like it's Fox News around here. Everyone wants to know the gossip." Zach informed him.

"The joys of a community college?" Brandon chuckled and stood up.

"I suppose," Zach agreed while getting up from the seat. "Don't worry; there are no rumors about you, though." He chuckled.

"Well, thank goodness. I don't hang out around campus much to avoid the lies." Brandon laughed. "I just go to class and work. That's it!"

"I don't blame you." Zach agreed. "I should get going, but we should study together sometime."

"That'd be awesome. See you later." Brandon waved goodbye and headed back home.

He entered the apartment and put his bag down on the kitchen table and went to wash his hands. When he got a paper towel, Shane was coming out of his room with a big grin on his face.

"Hey man, I—" Shane started to speak.

"No." Brandon shook his head, not letting him finish the sentence. "Whatever it is, no."

"You don't even know what I was going to say!" Shane in defense.

Brandon sighed and turned to face his friend. "Okay fine. What's up?"

"Madelyn is in town for the next two weeks, and we're going on a date Friday night." Shane enthused. "I need your help picking my outfit."

Brandon paused for a moment. Usually, he wouldn't mind since he always helped him, plus Madelyn was his friend too. However, his heart was beating fast, as if it was ready to escape his chest. There was something inside of him that wished that he was Shane's date. He decided to stay silent at first.

"Of course, man." Brandon managed to get out with a convincing smile on his face. "You have to look good for a date with Madelyn."

"Thanks, I knew I could count on you." Shane smiled and walked into the bathroom. After he closed the door, Brandon dropped the fake smile on his face and let out a big sigh. Luckily, his friend didn't think much of his pause. He hated that he had to be on board. Brandon has a feeling that it was going to be exhausting. There were no other choices except to keep it cool.

Chapter 4: Reconnecting Old Love

Friday night came, and Shane was ready to go, and Brandon was excited for him. Well, in a way, he was happy. Shane was in his room looking in his closet, still deciding what to wear. Brandon came into the room and looked at him up and down while he bit down on his lips. His friend was covered up in a towel from the waist below, and he liked knowing what it looked like as if it was his secret to keep.

"I have one hour and a half until I have to meet her at the restaurant. Yet, I still have nothing to wear!" Shane panicked.

"What are you talking about?" Brandon questioned, "Everything was put through the wash earlier this week, you have something. Calm down."

Shane sighed and looked through the clothes, finally picking something out. He decided on a tee shirt with a plaid shirt over it, a pair of jeans, and some tennis shoes. Brandon was about to leave the room to let Shane get dressed when Shane stopped him.

"What?" Brandon asked.

"You've seen me naked before. You don't have to leave the room." Shane smirked.

"Shut up, Shane." Brandon just rolled his eyes, not really in the mood.

Shane chuckled. "You didn't want me to shut up when I was moaning your name the other night."

"Shane!" Brandon shouted at him, finally leaving the room. He rolled his eyes, then he blushed and chuckled. "What the hell am I supposed to do with him?" he whispered to himself.

Shane got dressed and combed his hair one last time, making sure he got everything right. Nerves began to go through his body about the date with Ms. Madelyn Rhodes herself. It was the first date back after they took a break from each other. He collected his wallet, keys, and exited the bedroom.

"How do I look?"

"Very nice. Are you trying to get lucky tonight? You know she's still a Christian." Brandon jokingly asked.

"Shut up, man." Shane rolled his eyes holding back a laugh. He gave the finger to Brandon and left the apartment.

Shane made his way to the restaurant that was named The Musket Room. As he drove his way there, he thought about the last time he left things with Madelyn. He wanted tonight to be perfect as memories of his night with Brandon started to creep in. He knew he had to turn off those emotions before walking into the restaurant doors. Shane parked the car, and he couldn't help but notice he was there early. So he decided to wait a few minutes before going in to get a table.

Moments later, Madelyn showed up wearing a pink curve-hugging dress with nude heels and hair pulled back effortlessly. She was a beautiful and curvy black woman; her hair was black and curly in a long ponytail. He thought that he was the luckiest man on the planet. Shane waved her down so she could join him at their table. She walked over as she gave her coat to the hostess to hang up in the closet. Madelyn put the ticket in her purse.

"Hey, Madelyn," Shane greeted.

"Hi, sorry that I'm a little late." She politely apologized as they hugged.

"You're not late at all; I'm just arriving myself." He reassured her, "You look beautiful, like always."

"Thank you! I'm glad you like it. I remember this being your favorite." Madelyn smiled. Shane helped her into her seat; then they began looking through the menus.

"Please, get whatever you'd like. No matter the price." Shane tells her.

"Are you sure?" Madelyn looked up from her menu.

"Yes," Shane smiled at her, "I want us to enjoy each other and not worry about the bill."

The two placed their orders and continued to talk. "So, how are you doing in college?" Madelyn asked him.

"I'm doing pretty good. My classes challenge me a lot, especially the math that's required for my degree. It'll hopefully be the last hard class to take before I graduate in May." Shane tells her.

"That's a good plan, and I'm happy to hear that. I've been doing the same for mine. I managed to get so much of the general education completed. Now I need to complete my studies and graduate in May. I've missed you guys so much, though" Madelyn smiled, "LA is gorgeous, but you are like my family. I hate being apart from you all."

The waiter brings their beverages. Shane ordered iced tea, and Madelyn ordered lemonade.

"We missed you, too! We see Mike and Xavier every now and then. Tori moved to Florida, and Quinn is always busy." Shane exclaimed.

"Yeah, I know! You and Brandon are the only two who, literally, stayed together. Let's be honest, though. You were going to have to go with either him or me. We could never trust you on your own!" Madelyn pointed out. Shane couldn't even protest against it. He knew it was the truth.

"Well, damn, thanks for believing in me." Groaned a sarcastic Shane. "Okay, maybe you're right. I just, I guess I'm dependent on people, or I'd fuck up? Kind of hate that about myself." Shane looked down and rubbed his arm. Not everyone thought that he would be able to make it in college. Some family members and teachers weren't so supportive of him going with Brandon.

"Yet, you haven't. Your family is wrong about you. You're going to be a fantastic gym trainer and be very successful. I don't doubt that." Madelyn told him. They both took a sip of their drink, not saying anything for a moment.

"I hope so. Working out is a hobby that I do a lot. Being a trainer fits me. To my family, I should just be working at McDonald's or some fast-food restaurant." Shane sighed. "I really need to prove them wrong, Madelyn."

"You've been doing that. This is your second to last semester in college; you're already proving people wrong, Shane. You just can't let them get to you." Madelyn told him.

"I try not to. It would just be nice to have my family supporting me." Shane groaned. "They haven't given me too much trouble this year, though. Yeah, I know I fooled around with my high school grades, but I'm taking college more seriously. I don't think anyone understands how much I want this degree except my friends."

"I think you should let that be enough. We believe in you, Shane. All of your friends do, so let that be enough." Madelyn said.

"Well, thank you for that. I'm just starting to believe in myself. I just had a tough time with the 'support' I had at home." Shane admits. Madelyn just gave the nod and placed her hand on top of his on the table. A few minutes went by, and their food was delivered to the table.

"Everything's tasting good as always." Madelyn complimented the food after the first bite.

"Yeah, it is. I always love eating here." Shane smiled as he began to eat. He had ordered steak, green beans, and mashed potatoes while Madelyn ordered fried chicken, corn, and black-eyed peas. They both ate silently for a while, chewing their food and listening to the soft music playing above.

"Do you have your classes picked out for next semester yet?" Madelyn asked.

"I don't. I'm thinking about continuing the English to get that out of the way, and I think the science credit. Why do I have to take science in college? It's so annoying." Shane expressed his aggravation.

"I know! I hate that so much. I got science over with the first year-round and history. History wasn't too bad, though." Madelyn told him.

"Do I have any competition with any 'cute LA boys'?" Shane jokingly asked.

Madelyn let out a chuckle and shook her head. "Hey, you know me. I'm focused on my career path before any guy. That doesn't stop me from looking, though. How about you?"

"Well…" Shane began to blush and play with his fork.

"Tell me, Jacobs," Madelyn demanded with a smirk.

"I've never been with anyone for more than two weeks besides you." Shane laughed.

"Oh Lord, Shane." Madelyn laughed. "Are you at least clean?"

"Yep," Shane confirmed. Madelyn raised an eyebrow questioning that fast response. "I know that sounded suspicious, but I'm serious."

"Shane…" Madelyn warned.

"Oh, that's how you feel?" Zach asked, trying to keep an offended look on his face.

"Definitely, and for the record, I could be better than your man." Brandon chuckled. "Jason is not all that impressive with his accent."

"I think someone's jealous…" Zach teased.

"As if! I have my eye on someone else that isn't Zachary Deanes." Brandon stuck his tongue out.

"Then, who is the lucky guy?" Zach questioned.

"I can't say because I know you'll judge me. Plus, I don't know if he's still single or not." Brandon sighed.

"Why would I judge you? We can't help who we fall for, Brandon." Zach told him.

"I know, but it isn't that easy. Not with him." Brandon shrugged.

"Well, please tell me who it is. I could maybe help you—"

"No…" Brandon sounded unsteady, "I can't get help with this. I just need to get over him. Plus, I see this guy every day."

"That has to be tough. Is he in one of our classes?"

"No, he has a different major than us. We have taken a couple of general education courses together." Brandon informs, "Also, a few high school classes."

"Oh, you've known him for a while. Is he not into guys?" Zach asked.

"I could swear on my life that he was always straight. A ladies' man. Not one sign of being into males." Brandon explains." Just multiple girls from school loved him, and he could get any girl he wanted. Only one kept him grounded. Madelyn. I remember just wanting to be her. Wanting that chance to know what it's like to be the one that had his undivided attention more than just as a best friend."

"Was he like a jock?" Zach asked.

"Yeah, he was on the football team, and he was pretty good." Brandon took in a long sigh and chuckled sadly. "I had the biggest crush on him. A crush that I had to bury deep within me, never to ruin one of the best friendships of my life. Anyone who would question it, I would deny it as if my life depended on it."

"Why did you feel the need to do that?"

"I was afraid of him finding out about it and then wanting nothing to do with me. He was always there for me when I needed him and still is to this very day. Just a phone call away, I mean, we're that close. I couldn't risk losing him then, and I still can't now."

"So, you still feel that way," Zach spoke.

"Yeah, I just can't imagine him exiting my life. If that means suppressing my feelings, then I am okay with it."

Zach reached over between their laptops and grabbed the tissue box between their laptops on the table, giving them to Brandon. "I have a feeling these will be needed."

Brandon gave Zach a weak smile before continuing. "Probably, but I felt so guilty having this damn crush on him. Yes, I knew it was normal, but I just couldn't get over him, and it got better with time. All was good up until this week."

"This week?" Zach raised an eyebrow.

"Uh-huh, I saw something that changed dramatically in him. All due to one request from him." Brandon continued.

"What did you see that changed?" Zach urged gently.

"Everything. He asked me something that came out of nowhere, and it caught me off guard..." Brandon closed his eyes, looking away from his laptop when he felt tears forming. "He wanted to know what it felt like to have sex with a man, so he asked me to...You know."

"Shane asked you to have sex with him?" Zach asked, surprised. Brandon didn't say anything at all. He didn't know whether he should be surprised or feel disgusted and just break down.

"Yes, he did. How'd you guess?" Brandon whispered as he began to feel paranoid.

"It had to have been him. If anybody else were to ask; you'd probably spit in their direction. I'm not wrong, am I?" Brandon just looked at his hands again, which Zach then grabbed. "I am not judging you at all, Brandon. I am curious as to why you agreed."

"I can't say no to him. First off, I never had the option to say no. This was the first time to have the option to, and I didn't even want to. Somewhere in my heart I said, 'This is your chance, Brandon. Take it.' Then I just ignored the logistics from my mind and agreed. That's why." Brandon confessed.

"I see..." Zach said, "I'm guessing you regret it now?"

"It's not that I regret it, but now that Madelyn is back for like a couple of weeks, I think it brought back the high school feelings and emotions that I thought I'd left behind." More tears came rushing down Brandon's face as he talked to Zach. He never had anyone he felt comfortable talking to about this.

"I am so sorry that you have to go through this. I can't even fathom how you feel. Let me tell you, though, your feelings are not worthless when it comes to this." Zach stood up from his seat and went to the other side and sat next to him. "I think this indicates that you feel as if you need to shut up and act like everything's fine, and it didn't affect you like it truly did?"

"That's what I have to do. Zach, I hate it so much to the point where it's breaking me. I don't know what to do about this." Brandon whined.

"Set yourself free, Brandon. This definitely should not be happening to you. I can't tell you what to do, so you have me to talk to if you continue. Alright?" Zach grabbed his hand, and Brandon looked at him, upset.

"Okay, thank you so much," Brandon said. He wiped his eyes one last time and smiled weakly. "Come on, let's finish these assignments and go get something to eat."

"Sounds like a plan," Zach tells him.

Chapter 6: Surprise Visitor

A few days went by without Brandon and Shane having much time to talk to each other. It was nothing unusual, though. They both had responsibilities, such as maintaining jobs to keep up with the apartment bills. Shane worked at the local gym as a front-desk receptionist while Brandon had a student-intern job at a local legal internship. Neither paid much, but with the two of them, they made it work. Brandon walked in the front door yawning and taking off his coat. He was heading to the kitchen when he recognized something unusual.

"Care to explain, buddy?" Brandon asked Shane, who was apparently on the floor looking up at the ceiling. "Can't be sit-ups because your arms aren't crossed over your chest, and I'm positive that's not even your workout clothes."

"I'm just staring at the ceiling. "Shane simply stated.

"Why?" Brandon questioned. Did he ask Madelyn for sex and got rejected? He didn't want to ask that question at all. It was like a pain in his chest that would cry in defeat if she'd said yes to him. Brandon had finally gotten Shane to become open-minded. Well, maybe he did that on his own from being curious, but now it'd be harder to find out if Shane had feelings for him now. Almost as if Brandon was close to coming out all over again. He wanted this man so bad to become his. To have him stay forever in this apartment so no other girls could ruin it. Nobody else deserved to be with Shane as much as Brandon did. No matter how good any female would treat him, Brandon could do it twenty times better. Everything about his friend was a craving. From the way he moved to how he breathed became a desire, Brandon began to want more.

"Take a guess…" Shane mumbled. The look on his face was perplexed, and Brandon noticed how all the goofy spirit in his voice was gone. Whatever it was, it had to be worse than Madelyn.

"Oh no, not your parents again…" Brandon groaned.

"Yep," Shane confirmed.

"Hey, look at me…" Brandon starts, taking a seat on the loveseat at the other end where Shane's head wasn't. "You can't keep listening to your family; you're doing good—"

Shane shook his head. "I can't help it."

"I know it's hard. Remember, I deal with it too from my parents, but we have to be strong." Brandon tried to encourage.

"I can't help it, man." Shane groaned. "It's bullshit. After almost three and-a-half years they still don't believe in me."

"That's true, and I know you want nothing more than their love and support for you…" Brandon stopped for a second before continuing, realizing he was about to be talking about him and Shane. He knew it wasn't the time for that. "Just don't let them get to you, okay?"

"I'm trying not to. It's just that I have so much to prove, and I don't know how." Shane sighed.

"I understand that one hundred percent. My mom has been trying to get in touch with me, as well. I just keep declining the calls." Brandon explains, "She had the nurse's help last week. I don't have to help this week either, so it's like let me have my break."

"Why can't we just have supportive families?"

"I don't know, but we're becoming too busy to care. Get up," Brandon instructed as he pulled Shane up by his shirt. "How the hell did you end up on the floor?"

Shane shrugged and stood up. He sat on the couch next to Brandon, and they looked at each other in the eyes. Neither spoke a word as they faced one another and stared. Brandon still had a hold of the collar of Shane's shirt. Brandon was the first to lean forward halfway, which Shane met the rest of the way connecting their lips with a slow kiss. One thing led to another, and Brandon ended up lying down on the couch with Shane on top of him as they made out. Small moans escaped from each other when things got heated between the men. Shane wrapped Brandon's legs his waist as they began to grind slowly on each other.

The soft lips of Shane traveled down from his lips onto the tender skin of Brandon's neck. Brandon opened his mouth, expecting a moan to come out but all he could do is let out a satisfying breath. The coolness of his moist, soft lips was driving Brandon crazy, making him fade away from the world around him. Kisses were getting more massive and more erotic from Shane as Brandon felt his friend's bulge become thicker through his pants. Brandon began to unbutton Shane's shirt when they went back to kissing, but the moment was interrupted by a knock on the door. If was like everything got frozen in time, and Shane groaned, getting off of Brandon.

"Hurry…" Brandon instructed impatiently.

Shane got off the couch and went to the front door. "Who is it?"

"It's Madelyn."

"Shit," Brandon muttered, jumping up fast to straighten his clothes before Shane opened the door. He sat back down and got a weird feeling in his stomach. Shane figured that they weren't doing anything wrong cheating, but that wasn't how Brandon wanted to greet his old friend, who happened to be the ex-girlfriend of his best friend. His best friend that's straight yet wants to make out with him. It's not like there's anything wrong with that.

Sure…

"Madelyn!" Shane greeted enthusiastically and hugged her.

"Hey, sorry that I didn't call, but I had to come by and visit my friends." Madelyn smiled.

"It's never a problem. You know you're always welcome here." Shane told her. "Come on in; I'll take your coat."

"Thank you." Madelyn took her coat off and went into the living room, smiling more prominent, seeing Brandon. "Well, hey, stranger!" She laughed and hugged him.

"Me?" Brandon playfully questioned, "You're the one who's going across the country to sunny Los Angeles to study engineering. Forgetting to call and everything." Madelyn looked even more beautiful than when he last saw her. He would never stand a chance against her for Shane's heart. From losing weight to her new hairdo, Brandon had nothing in comparison to his friend. He wanted to give up right then and there, but something told him to keep going. Ever since she left, he's been there for Shane, not her. Why would she have a better shot at getting Shane when she hadn't done anything?

"Boy, please. I'll never forget about you. I did tell you guys to come with me, so don't even complain, Andreas." Madelyn chuckled.

"I know, I just couldn't afford it. I needed an undergraduate college first…anyways." Brandon said.

"Yeah, all three of us were trying to get into a college in California," Shane said as he came from the other room, "Madelyn was the only one that got accepted." All three took a seat on the couch. Brandon on one end, Madelyn in the middle, and Shane on the other end. Just the same example as always. The main thing getting in the way of the man he loved was in between them. "We miss you, but I miss you more."

Madelyn laughed and sat closer to Shane when he opened his arms for her. Brandon tried hard not to show that it was bothering him and to keep the smile on his face. On the other hand, Shane looked normal as if nothing had happened between them before she knocked on the door. Somehow he knew how to turn it off like a light switch. That killed him.

"Very sweet. Honestly, though, you guys were my two close friends in high school. I hate being so far from you." Madelyn said.

"The weather is a great trade-off, I bet." Brandon pointed out which Madelyn nodded in agreement.

"It's gorgeous." She hummed. "I couldn't possibly want to come back home during the summer. That weather is so lovely out there."

"I think we should visit for Christmas. That'd be a nice treat for us, Brandon," Shane thought out loud.

"With what money, Shane?" Brandon chuckled at his friend's crazy idea.

"Hey! I could have enough money in my savings that I might be hiding from you!" Shane said in defense.

Brandon started to laugh, but then he thought for a second, which brought a glare to his friend. "I swear if you do when I'm paying most of the bills—"

"I'm just kidding, man!" Shane put his hands up.

Madelyn laughed at Brandon's reaction, saying, "I see that I've taught you that face well?"

"Yes, and it comes in very handy with this one." Brandon motioned his hand to Shane.

"Maybe I'm going crazier because I've been missing your beautiful face." The blonde man said smoothly and pressed a kiss on Madelyn's cheek.

Affection…

Shane was very affectionate towards Madelyn in high school, and Brandon was uncomfortable at times with it. Now, it was unbearable witnessing it while Shane already flustered him.

"How sweet," Madelyn awed. The way that they looked at each other as if they were back in high school in love. Brandon remembered them always holding hands in the halls, forever linked with each other, giggling and talking as they waved at Brandon walking past him. That's the one thing Brandon hated. He held a grudge towards Madelyn for winning Shane over, but he also disliked that he felt that way in the first place.

"He's still smooth with the compliments," Brandon said halfheartedly. He just sighed and let it go. Their actions were similar to high school. Brandon tried to stay in the conversation while the two lovebirds eventually drifted off to compliment each other, forgetting he was there. Why couldn't Brandon catch Shane's undivided attention the way Madelyn did without effort? It didn't seem fair then, and it didn't seem any better now. Shane had his back to Brandon almost leaving no room on the couch for him.

"How long are you in town for?" Brandon asked in a dry tone. He was over it. Shane might have forgotten what was going on before Madelyn knocked, but he didn't. It wasn't fair at all how one person, in particular, could ruin his time with Shane. Couldn't she notice the wrinkles in their shirts?

"Until the end of next week," Madelyn said. "I resume classes on Monday." A full two weeks of Shane gushing over Madelyn and not paying attention to him. That was going to be dreadful for Brandon. The couple just went on and on gushing over one another. Brandon's face grew more annoyed while the other grew in love.

"Why don't we get a fall break?" Shane complained.

Brandon shook his head. "Shane, we go to a community college; we get most days off. Only for holidays do we have actual breaks."

"I know it's just still discriminatory!" Shane protested. Brandon and Madelyn just looked at him in surprise.

"New vocabulary word…" Brandon said.

"College is definitely for you," Madelyn added.

"Isn't it?" Brandon agreed, "I just really—"

"Thank you, babe," Shane interrupted again, "I'm trying to do my best to keep up with you."

"Well, so far, it's working." Madelyn blushed. They were still all over each other, as Brandon suspected. They were ignoring the rest of the world as if no one else mattered. Brandon eventually rolled his eyes, aggravated, and stood up going in his room. He slammed the door behind him and laid on his bed with a groan. It was going to be a long two weeks.

Chapter 7: Into The Dark

"Brandon?" Shane called out when he walked out of his room.

"I'm in the kitchen." Brandon hollered back. He was looking in the cabinets, preparing to make them lunch. Their kitchen was reasonably small. The room was in the shape of a perfect square. Both the top and bottom cabinets were white as well as the appliances. The floors were light brown tiles in the kitchen and bathrooms that neither of them liked, but they made do. On the other side of the wall to where they would walk through the front door to the right, and the living room to the left. The bedrooms were down the hall and each bedroom had its bathroom, which was a bonus when they found the apartment.

"You okay?" Shane asked. He immediately got distracted by Brandon. With Brandon looking down at the food he was preparing, it gave Shane a clear view of what he desired so badly to see undressed. Something about having Brandon's body pressed against his was so thrilling. He was craving for that pleasure again.

"Yeah, why wouldn't I be?" Brandon responded a little too fast. He was still clearly upset with what happened yesterday and how he got treated.

"Well, you kind of disappeared on us yesterday. You didn't say goodbye when Madelyn left." Shane said. Brandon had to pause before he could decide on what to say to that. Was that all he noticed about it, or was he beating around the bush?

"I know I heard my phone ring, and I had to answer it. That was an important call." Brandon lied.

"Oh, okay. We heard you slam your door, and we were wondering what happened." Shane told him.

"I thought nothing could ruin your 'perfect moment' with her…" Brandon bitterly whispered to himself.

"Huh? I didn't hear you."

"Nothing, don't worry about it. What do you want on your sandwich?" Brandon asked. He still hadn't turned around to face Shane. How could he? The annoyance wasn't about leaving him flustered but how Shane completely dismissed his presence after Madelyn had arrived.

"Lettuce, tomato, and do we have cheese still?" Shane requested.

"I think so." Brandon nodded his head, going to look in the refrigerator. He found the cheese in the back and got it out. "It's the last slice."

"I hope my luck continues with my date with Madelyn tonight."

That made Brandon stop in his tracks. He was determined not to let Shane see him sweat or entertain anything about her. "Bologna or ham?"

"Ham," Shane ordered. His friend finished making the meals and handed Shane his plate. Brandon then picked up his food, grabbed something to drink, and then took a seat at their table. The other male joined him, sitting on the other side of the table with a drink eating in silence. "Was it one of your parents?"

"No, it wasn't," Brandon flatly answered before taking a bite of his food. Shane wasn't picking up the negative energy that was coming from him. That was where he was a little oblivious when it came to his best friend—always knowing when he was mad at anything else except him. Sometimes Brandon spoke up, then other times he wouldn't.

"How are your grades?" Brandon asked to break the silence.

"Physics is kicking my ass, man. I'm really struggling with that class, but Sociology is going fine, and so is Injury prevention." Shane explained.

"Well, remember to ask for help if you're struggling." Brandon reminded him.

"You sound like my parents; I will. Right now, I want to spend all my time with Madelyn as much as I possibly can." Shane couldn't have said a deadlier sentence to Brandon. Once again, Brandon stayed quiet about that subject.

"Hey, does one of our shows come back on soon?" Brandon asked in an attempt to change the subject.

"I think Law and Order next Friday night. I'm so ready for that!" Shane enthused. Brandon took mental notes on what could make him smile like that. Seeing his face light up like that made his day as long as it wasn't about Madelyn.

"I know! The last season ended on a cliffhanger." Brandon agreed.

"What if your brother was the secret guest celebrity for the season?" Shane chuckled.

"I thought I told you he is! You know that mother fucker likes to brag on his success. I can't shut him up." Brandon laughed, thinking about his crazy yet successful older brother.

"Have him tell us secrets about the upcoming season! You have to!" Shane begged.

"No! I don't want spoilers, and neither do you!" Brandon laughed.

"You are so lame," Shane playfully insulted and shook his head.

"Shut up, that's not true." Brandon rolled his eyes. Shane chuckled, and they continued to finish their meals. Brandon couldn't help but think about ways to keep Shane from going on that date later on. He could say that he should study. Or how about tagging along and sitting purposely in between them? Sighing, he knew that wouldn't work at all and would be too obvious.

Deciding just to relax his mind, Brandon sat on the couch, got on his laptop, and turned on the TV. He thought maybe a game would distract him from thinking about Shane's date that should be with him instead of Madelyn. Their relationship couldn't last long, though. There was no way a long-distance relationship between her and Shane would work out. That's the reason why they initially broke up anyways. For them to try a relationship again sounded ridiculous to Brandon. Two whole weeks! That's nothing to worry about; however, Brandon knew how fast Shane could fall for someone. He's seen it with his own eyes.

Perhaps he should get out and date other people. Get his mind away from Shane and find a relationship of his own. The problem is that Brandon couldn't imagine spending his life with someone else. Brandon needed and loved Shane, and he was sure Shane loved him back, but it wasn't the way he wanted. Groaning, he laid back on the couch watching TV until something blocked his view.

"Why are you in front of me butt naked with your dick out?" Brandon questioned.

"Which shirt do I pick?" Shane asked as he held up two shirts.

"Why are you in front of me butt naked with your dick out?" Brandon repeated.

"I need help picking a shirt!"

"The blue one!" Brandon chuckled, "What the fuck is wrong with you?"

"Don't ask, just love me." Shane joked and went back to his room. Brandon watched him go back from the corner of his eye. The way his body moved with those muscles was a turn on. Why did Shane have to go out on a date that wasn't with him?

"I think I love you more than I should…" Brandon whispered to himself. His friend eventually came out ready to go a half-hour later. Shane collected his keys and jacket. Brandon couldn't stop looking at him from the corner of his eye while trying to watch the TV. It didn't seem as impressive, though.

"Wish me luck, man," Shane said while putting on his coat.

"When will you be back?" Brandon responded. He was not going to wish him luck with Madelyn. If anything, he hoped that the date would be terrible.

"I don't know," Shane shrugged, "The movie is two hours, and we may go eat afterward."

"Alright, what movie are you going to see?" Brandon tried to ask casually.

"We're seeing Black Panther."

"I thought we were going to see it together Saturday night…" Brandon questioned, he tried not to sound hurt.

"I know, but she wanted to go see it. You know I can't say no to her." Shane said.

"No spoilers," Brandon said disappointedly. They waved goodbye to each other, and Shane left the apartment. That's when Brandon sprung up from the couch to get ready to spy.

Shane made his way over to Madelyn's parents' house and knocked on the door. He held a bouquet in his hand and smiled, waiting for the door to open. When Madelyn opened the door and came out, Shane thought he was the luckiest man in the world.

"You look so beautiful," Shane awed as he gave her the flowers.

Shane came out in flannel pants and a t-shirt. Madelyn hoped that he didn't hear any of that. She didn't want to crush him and his hopes.

"I hope you didn't miss me too much while I was away. I know you don't have your luggage with you; I figured you would want my shirt to sleep in for old-time sake." Shane offered.

A sense of relief washed over Madelyn. She loved that naive blonde boy but was that enough for her. Meanwhile, Brandon looked at the shirt; it looked all too familiar to him. It was the same shirt he stole the night they first had sex together; he guessed it wasn't special anymore.

"Thanks, babe, you know I like wearing your shirt. I've always felt like you were a part of me. Also, I felt safe wearing it. It's sweet that you remembered." Madelyn smiled at him before standing up, "I'm going to go wash up and change." She left the room, leaving Shane and Brandon alone.

"I thought you said you couldn't fit that one anymore?" Brandon questioned.

"I can't," Shane confirmed while taking a seat on the couch. He then let out a chuckle, "I kept it because of her. It reminds me of the fun days in high school with just Madelyn and me at my house sneaking in a sleepover. We would have to get up so early not to get caught."

"Do you have to rub it in my face? I thought you were done with those other people. Do I need to start to record everything you say when we—?" Brandon blurted out. "I need some air; I can't be here right now." He took his coat and left the apartment.

Brandon raced down the stairs and out into the cold. It felt like someone shoved a knife down his throat. He kept trying to catch his breath; all of his feelings, piling up just slowly oozing out. This only fueled the fire in him even more than before. He didn't care how Shane reacted to his outburst; he just needed to get away from them. If she was staying in his apartment that night, he sure wasn't going to.

Shane was taken back by what Brandon said. He had to shake it off before Madelyn entered back into the room. The truth was that he felt something for Brandon, and it scared him half to death. That was why he went back to Madelyn when she came. She was familiar to Shane. He loved her, but this was something he couldn't control.

"Alright, guys, let's make this a fun night!" Madelyn enthused, "Where's Brandon?"

Shane had to think before he could speak, "His mom called and said she needed him to help with his dad. He'll be back in the morning."

"I thought that he didn't get along with his parents. Are you telling me the truth?"

"He doesn't get along with them. You know, not any better than the situation with my parents. Yet we have to listen to them still. Any chance for their acceptance, we take it," Shane explained.

Meanwhile, Brandon had made it to his car and drove out the apartment complex. He was beyond furious at that point, and he needed to drive without any particular destination. All of the red lights were driving him crazy. He didn't want to stop because when he did, it just got him angrier. Why was Shane so inconsiderate whenever she was around? It had never been this bad before. What was it about Madelyn that Brandon didn't have?

He eventually came to a stop once he was at the college dorm rooms. After Brandon got out of the car, he ran inside to get out of the cold fall weather. Brandon eventually found the dorm he was searching for and banged on the door, not caring what time it was.

"I told you for the millionth time, Lewis, stop—!" Zach shouted through his phone before he saw that it was Brandon, "Brandon? Are you okay; what are you doing here?" He asked, concerned.

"I need a place to stay tonight, and I'm sorry for bothering you guys. I just—" Brandon started to say.

"It's okay, come in. You can definitely stay here," Zach assured and opened the door wider for Brandon to go in. Brandon went inside and immediately crashed on Zach's couch, letting out a frustrated groan. "Lewis, that doesn't make any sense!" Zach said, returning to his phone conversation.

"Honey, who's at the door?" Jason asked, coming out of their bedroom.

"Babe, you remember my friend Brandon I was telling you about. Brandon, this is my boyfriend, Jason—No, Lewis!" Zach tried to introduce the two. He went into the other to finish the phone argument with their friend.

"Hi, sorry I don't need to intrude. I just had to find somewhere to go," Brandon said apologetically to them and shook Jason's hand.

"Nice to meet you. Don't worry; you're welcome here anytime. Zach says you're a nice guy," Jason smiled, and Brandon returned it slightly.

"Babe, let me talk to him. I'll be in bed in a few minutes," Zach told his boyfriend. Jason nodded his head before kissing Zach on the cheek and went back to bed. Zach then sat down next to Brandon. He looked at him, concerned, "I take it that things got worse?"

"How can he act like what happened didn't exist? He is rubbing it in my face now. She is over there probably in the bed we fooled around in. How could he be so curious yet so fucking blind?" said a furious Brandon.

"So, you've only had sex once, right?" Zach asked.

"One and a half."

"What?"

"I didn't tell you? We were making out one day this week on our couch, and all of a sudden, Madelyn is knocking on the door. He fucking changes immediately and forgets all about what was happening!" Brandon exclaimed, "I had to act normal even though she distracted my man!"

"So, you're mad at him, right?"

"I am, but I'm more upset at her," Brandon huffed.

"Why? Does she know he's been a dick?" Zach questioned.

"No, but I'm tired of her distracting him! She needs to fucking go. I love her as my best friend, but I hate competing with her."

"Alright, now you're making no sense. You're mad at Madelyn for his actions?"

"I don't think it's fair. Madelyn had him all this time in high school. Why can't she just back off?"

"I know you're frustrated, but I think you have anger towards the wrong one. I suggest you try to talk to Shane after Madelyn goes home," Zach opposed, "Until then, you don't pay them any mind unless they speak first. You're a great guy, Brandon. If he can't see that, then forget him. Okay? You deserve better than that."

Brandon sighed and gave a small nod, "Thanks, Zach."

"You're welcome."

"What's wrong with Lewis?"

"Test anxiety."

"Again?" Brandon groaned and shook his head at their friend.

"I know! He needs to chill. Anyways, the guest room is all ready, and there is a clean towel and everything in the bathroom," Zach informed as he stood up. They hugged each other and left the living room. "Good night."

"Good night," Brandon said back. He went into the guest room and got in the bed, actually feeling pretty tired. It didn't take long for him to get to sleep as he continued to think about all the ways to get Madelyn to leave.

Chapter 9: I'd Lie For You

Brandon woke up in the morning and groaned. He looked around the room, confused. "Wait, where am I?" It didn't take long to remember where he was and why he had been in an unfamiliar place. Brandon sat up and rolled his eyes as his mind replayed everything that happened from the previous night. He felt disrespected by him, and he didn't know what to do about it. How could Brandon possibly face either one of them that morning? Brandon had to go home and get ready for class and work, but he couldn't find the strength of catching them making out or something worse.

He eventually got out of the bed and went to the guest bathroom. Since he didn't bring a change of clothes, he just splashed his face with warm water and brushed his hair. He saw Zach and Jason already in the kitchen eating. They were feeding each other, looking so in love, and just enjoying each others' presence. Brandon hated to have to ruin the moment by walking in the room. He could only wish that he would eventually have that for himself and Shane.

"Hey, Brandon," Jason smiled when he noticed him.

"Hey, thanks for letting me stay." Brandon yawned, "I just couldn't take it. Not last night."

"What are you going to do about that situation?" Zach asked.

"I don't want to deal with him this morning. If I'm lucky, he will be gone to class, and I can get ready in peace." Brandon guessed.

"Well, if not, just ignore him?" Zach suggested. Brandon sighed, knowing that it wouldn't be comfortable with them, but he had to try. He made his way to his car and started to go back home. If he focused, he would have a half-hour to get ready and be back on the campus. Upon entering his apartment, he saw that Shane had already left, and he sighed happily, knowing he was alone.

He took off his coat, set it on the couch, and headed to his room while he checked his texts. Brandon didn't look at where he was going, which caused him to stumble when he bumped into someone.

"Shane, why are you still here? You should already be gone..." Brandon paused mid-sentence when he looked up to see Madelyn standing there. He was confused as to why she was still there. He wondered if Shane gave her a key without talking to him about it first. Shane shouldn't have done that.

"My bad, I didn't mean to run into you," Madelyn apologized, "I couldn't get dressed in time, so he said to wait for you to come back."

"Oh, yeah, no problem. I'm just here to get ready for my class." Brandon told her.

"Alright, I'm just finishing, so I'll try to stay out of your way. Oh, hey, is your dad okay?" She asked. Brandon was completely confused by the question, not knowing what she meant by that. When she saw his expression, she felt terrible for bringing it up, "I'm sorry Shane told me that's why you had to leave. I understand if you don't want to talk about it since it's personal."

Brandon just stared in surprise. Shane was lying to her about what had happened, but was he shocked? Brandon wanted to expose the truth and ruin it all for them, but he didn't have the guts to out Shane even though he deserved it.

"No, it's fine. His health has been slowly declining due to cancer, and we don't know how much longer he has to live. My dad still hates me so much, but the 'favorite son' is in California, so they have no choice," Brandon scoffed. The unfortunate part of what he said was that it wasn't all a lie. The last time he went home was for that reason. That whole night Brandon had to deal with the inappropriate name-calling, the guilt shaming, and the ungrateful attitude from both of his parents.

"What does Richard say about this?" Asked a concerned Madelyn.

"He always argues with them saying they need to respect me more. I appreciate him trying, but one day I just told him to let it go. The old man doesn't have much longer to live so I can take it," Brandon shrugged, "I've spent this whole time since coming out trying to get back on his good side that I just eventually said fuck it. It's the same with my mom."

Brandon hated Madelyn for being such a distraction to Shane. It was never supposed to be like that, but she had won him over. On the other hand, he loved talking to her as friends. If she would just leave Shane alone about wanting to be in a relationship with him, everything would be alright.

"Do you think it'd get better between you and them?"

"I don't even care if it will ever get better or not. At this point, I just do things for them because I have to, not because I want to. They never appreciate it either way. We always end up arguing over stupid shit, and I'm just over it." Brandon sighed, "I want the impossible to happen. To be okay with them and to mend shit with him before he...You know. Except that it's not looking possible."

"I will be hoping that it happens for you both. Please let me know if you ever need anything from me. I'll help in whatever way I can. I mean it." Madelyn assured him. They both hugged and went their separate ways in the apartment. Brandon sighed as he went to his room and got his clothes. Shane was full of shit to cover himself by putting Brandon in the hot seat. He took a quick shower and got himself dressed to go. Madelyn had her things packed, and she was in the kitchen on her phone just waiting for him.

Brandon took in a sigh, realizing what he was up against; perfection. This woman was so perfect in Shane's eyes that Brandon could never top. A badass woman who received a scholarship to go to a California school to become an engineer. He was proud of her, but why would that draw Shane to her more?

"I must say you're lucky, Madelyn," Brandon spoke up when he finished brewing them both a cup of coffee.

"Why is that?" Madelyn asked as she started to drink from her cup.

"You only have one more semester after this to go until you graduate. I have another three years to go!" Brandon exclaimed playfully, making Madelyn laugh, "I mean after next semester, I'll have to go to either New York Law School, CUNY School of Law, or Brooklyn Law. Shane only has one semester left to go as well."

"He's going for his physical education degree, right?" Madelyn questioned.

Brandon nodded his head, "Yeah. He already passed his certification after high school, but I'm glad he still wanted the degree even if he doesn't necessarily need it."

"Do you think it'll be enough for his parents to believe in him?"

"His parents are assholes. I probably shouldn't say that, but he's said it himself before, so I think I'm allowed to. He has a different situation," Brandon started, "With Mr. and Mrs. Jacobs, they only look at his past. Seeing the immature kid who rarely finished his homework and it's not far."

"For God's sake, he has dyslexia and dyscalculia!" Madelyn exclaimed.

"Thank you! That's where I have my problem with them. He would always complain about needing help and them not willing to give him time to receive it." Brandon scoffed.

"Are we his true parents?" Madelyn said sarcastically.

"Oh absolutely, I've already figured that out. Especially since I now live with Shane. I should sue you for child support," Brandon joked, and they both laughed. They both stood up, and Madelyn got her coat on while Brandon washed the cups before doing the same. "So how much longer do you have left in your semester?"

"Four more weeks to go. What about you guys?"

"It's the same for us," Brandon groaned, "I am so ready for Christmas and the holidays to be here. I think Richard is planning on coming this year." He turned out the lights and opened the front door allowing Madelyn to exit first, and he locked it behind them.

"I don't miss this cold weather!" Madelyn groaned when she snuggled in her coat, trying to keep warm.

"The weather must've dropped from when I left my parents' this morning," Brandon said back. They hugged one last time before going to their separate cars.

"Text you later!" Madelyn hollered out the passenger window when their cars were next to each other, headed in opposite directions.

"Okay," Brandon shouted back. He made it to the campus with five minutes to spare and went into the building. On his way in, Zach caught up with him, and they smiled at each other.

"I'm surprised at how fast you were able to clean up and change," Zach complimented.

"I am too. Especially when somebody was at the apartment when I got home." Brandon replied.

"You're kidding me," Zach exclaimed.

"Only her! I thought he gave her a key. I was about to go fucking crazy. She just couldn't get ready before he had to go to class." Brandon explained to him.

"So, how did that go?" Zach asked quizzically.

"I have to be honest and say that it went well. Maybe it's only Shane that pisses me off, but Madelyn still plays a part in it." Brandon groaned, "I just hate this. Ever since we slept together, I've been playing this cat and mouse game, and I've been coming up short every time."

"Then stop playing his way, and you create your own rules in this. If this is a two-player game, then you show your moves," Zach suggested.

"I guess, but how?" Brandon asked.

"You have to figure that out yourself, Andreas," Zach shrugged, "I can't help with everything."

"I know I just need guidance," Brandon sighed, "I'm ready for her to leave. I'll tell you that." They made it to the classroom and sat in their usual seats. Brandon's phone lights up, Shane's name flashes across the screen. Brandon's skin flared with goosebumps, seeing his name got him off like some kind of high.

"Can you meet me in fifteen minutes? I'm horny," read Shane's text. Brandon rolled his eyes at his immature choice of words. He waited to answer back because he didn't want to sound desperate. He tried to slip out unnoticed; he didn't even want Zach to know that he went missing. Brandon waited five minutes to send him a reply.

"Yeah, I'll be there. Let me just slip out of class," Brandon replied in a text. Just like Brandon was a ghost in the night and he was running back to Shane, he wanted to get under his skin and his sheets.

Brandon gets to the door, there awaited Shane at the door frame with a hunger in his eyes. He wanted Brandon right then and there. He pulled in Brandon by his shirt. Brandon was in his glory to have his sweet naive blonde boy back in his sights. He put aside his jealousy just for a few moments.

Chapter 10: Finally Gone

After Shane locked the bathroom door, he pushed Brandon against the wall capturing his lips in a heated kiss. His tongue immediately dipped into Brandon's mouth, deepening the kissing and pressing up against him. Shane's lips were frantic against Brandon's while his tongue explored every inch of his mouth. Moans escaped from Brandon's mouth as he hungrily kissed back. He wrapped his arms around Shane's neck, pulling him in closer, not wanting to let go.

Shane was the first to break the kiss going to attack the tenderness of Brandon's neck. The way that his desired lover bit down and sucked on him like a starving vampire made his hormones go crazy. Brandon started to grind against Shane for the added friction he desperately needed causing them both to moan. Before he knew it, Brandon's shirt had been taken off and thrown on the floor with his bare back up against the tiled bathroom wall. They resumed kissing before once again, breaking the human connection to let Shane remove his shirt. He desperately wanted to see him free from the fabric.

Having Shane's exposed chest pressed against Brandon's was all he desired. The kisses got sloppier, and the sinful hands of his went further down, pinching his friend's sensitive pecks that were his weakness. Brandon growled against his mouth as he continued to do that. "Fuck," He huffed.

"Shut up, or else someone will hear," Shane warned sternly before going back to working on his neck. Brandon didn't give a damn if he left a big hickey that everyone would see. He needed Shane, and that's all that mattered to him. It didn't take long before the belt got thrown off, causing the jeans to drop to the floor. Although it was only the previous week that was Brandon's first time seeing his dick, it felt like years.

Shane was touching all of his sensitive areas like a master. Everywhere his hands went on Brandon's body did things to him. No one else knew how to make love to him like that. That was everything he'd wanted, and he didn't care about anything else—no other man or girlfriend.

He heard Shane rip open the condom and forced Brandon to stand up while he rolled it on his dick while kissing fiercely once more. He turned Brandon around and pinned him against the wall again, going in his ass. One finger went in his ass hole to stretch him out before two more fingers followed behind. He fucked Brandon at a steady pace that rewarded sexual moans from him.

"Fuck me already," Brandon desperately begged. He didn't care how much it could hurt. Stretched out or not, his body demanded Shane's touch. Upon hearing his command, Shane stopped his actions and grabbed the condom from his pants, rolling it on. He pushed in and leaned over his body. Shane began moving his hips back and forth at a steady growth pace with the sexual heat building up by the minute. His thrusts became rapid and out of control. It made Brandon gain a high he never experienced in his life. He was in the best pain he had ever felt and at Shane's mercy, letting him do whatever the hell he wanted.

Brandon was in his heaven. He imagined what it'd be like with no one there to interrupt them—obeying to each others' sexual needs and desires—making him realize that Shane belongs to him and nobody else. Both of their orgasms were strong. Shane immediately pulled out of him, threw away the condom, and came all over Brandon's chest as Brandon released his load on Shane.

"Make her leave," Brandon demanded and looked straight into his eyes while trying to catch his breath.

"Her plane leaves tomorrow morning." Shane confirmed, "When she's gone, it's going to be me fucking you all the time in that apartment of ours."

Brandon saw the lust take over Shane while he talked. It was so hot; if it weren't for the class, he would go for another round. They both collected their clothes scattered around the bathroom floor and got dressed. He looked at his watch and saw he had two minutes to make it back before the lecture began.

Zach was faced the other way talking to other students when Brandon entered the class again. He got out the textbook and turned to the chapter that they were studying for the day.

Nobody noticed he was missing, not even Zach himself. He was too busy in the conversation beside him to see anything about Brandon. The only thing that caught his attention was the professor walking in the room, starting to write on the smartboard.

"Good morning, class," The professor began, "I have graded your assignments from last week, and I'm very impressed with how well everyone did and the theories you all came up with. Please open your textbooks to the chapter written on the board, and we will begin."

On Friday afternoon, Shane agreed to take Madelyn to the airport. He picked her up from her parents' house and drove.

"I can't believe you already have to leave, babe." Shane complained, "I feel like you just got here, and it makes me sad." It was sort of a lie. The truth was that he did want her to stay, but the thought of having Brandon to satisfy his needs whenever he demanded was an immersive craving than to be with her.

"I will be back this summer, I promise." Madelyn told him, "I was lucky I had time to come now. As soon as I get back home, I'm studying nonstop for my finals."

"I need to study too, but it's hard to focus and compre— Something?" Shane groaned when he couldn't think of the word. Having dyslexia made him feel stupid at times. This was the worst time for his brain to fail him in front of his girlfriend.

"Comprehend. You were close, Shane." Madelyn smiled. Shane just let out a sigh continuing to drive.

"I'm scared…" Shane admitted.

"What do you have to be scared of?" Madelyn questioned when she looked up from her phone at him.

"Of failing this class. I'm barely at a C, and it's dropping with each test I take. What should I do?"

"I think you are going to be okay. It's not the end of the world if you can't pass it this semester, but keep trying. Pick classes that are easier next semester to keep that GPA up so you won't suffer in the end when you're ready to graduate. You can do this," Madelyn advised, "Do not give up on yourself."

"I'm not trying to pity myself, although I couldn't stay focused. My fucking disability messes up at bad times."

"All you can do is your best."

Shane parked his car at the baggage drop off and kissed Madelyn on the lips. "I love you," he whispered.

"I love you too..." Madelyn replied before pulling him in for one last passionate kiss. She got out of the vehicle and rolled her suitcase into the airport. She looked back at Shane, gave him one last smile, then kept walking, disappearing in the crowd of fellow travelers.

On the way home, his mind kept going back to Brandon. To his naked body and everything that he wanted to do to it. He couldn't get enough of him as if he was on a high, and Brandon was the drug. Shane was almost racing up the apartment staircase to get inside to claim the body once again. He got into the house and went into Brandon's room, where he found him.

Brandon took one look at Shane and saw the fire and lust in his eyes that captured him in. "She's gone?"

"She's gone," Shane confirmed in a mysterious tone. Brandon recognized the weird way that he said it, but with the fire and determination that he saw in his eyes made him too turned on to care.

The next thing he knew, Shane was attacking his lips again in a hard kiss with mainly teeth and tongues. Clothes began flying off, and Shane gave him no mercy with how hard he pressed against his body. He found the same place where he'd left the last hickey and attacked it again with his lips. Brandon had no time to comprehend what was happening as if his brain exited the room. When Shane kissed him again, his tongue immediately shoved into his mouth, exploring every inch of him and pulling his head closer.

It wasn't about love; it was about the devilish desire that he had for that man. To make his own body feel good and provide him the sex service, only Brandon could do well. He showed Brandon no mercy this time around, being tougher than before with every touch he made. His bites were harder, his hands held him down stronger, and his movements were faster. Brandon couldn't control the moans flowing louder and louder out of his mouth. As if with every move, Shane's hand just got faster and better.

Brandon was pulling on Shane's head and moaning like crazy, feeling his mouth all around his dick, sucking long and hard. Shane pulled off once to swallow and to give attention to the rest of his body.

"Shane…" Brandon moaned out. He was trying to get his attention to tell him something, but he wasn't listening. It was getting more aggressive and harsher that was no longer enjoyable for him.

"Shut up!" Shane snarled at him with lust-filled eyes. It scared him so much. What was going on? Brandon had no explanation for what had changed in Shane. He tried to push him off, but his grasp got stronger. Brandon felt weak and useless. Shane aggressively flipped Brandon over to his stomach and got the condom on. He didn't waste time trying to stretch him out and immediately began to thrust into him. Brandon wasn't feeling any pleasure about what was happening. He pounded hard despite hearing the wails from his mouth. All he could care about was getting his fix.

Brandon knew it was never about love for Shane. He only wanted it for the thrill of it all. It was just a shock that Shane would hurt him this way. It was no longer fun, and he desperately wanted it to end. Tears came rushing down his face, and his body started to get weak. It was the worst sex experience he ever had. Brandon tried hard to get him off. There had to be an end to that horror. All of his innocence and joy that he had for Shane vanished at that very moment.

It didn't feel like sex anymore. His body registered it as danger.

Shane came inside of Brandon and fell on top of him. He caught his breath, pulled out, and threw away the condom. While Shane gathered his clothes, he saw Brandon shaking but didn't say anything. He left the room satisfied that he got what he craved.

Brandon couldn't rationalize what he just went through with his body shaking and his emotions out of control. It felt like torture. He wanted to move around and shake it off, but he couldn't. All his mind could do was play one burning question on repeat:

What just happened to me?

Chapter 11: Avoidance

The next couple of days felt like a blur. Brandon had stayed in his room with the door locked for most of the day. He would only come out of his room to use the bathroom or to eat. Even then, he didn't feel like doing that. His eyes were bloodshot from the lack of sleep, life around him was still going, but it was like his world froze. Any free moment alone with his thoughts flashed back to the night Shane took away his sense of self. He felt gross and used. His skin crawled at the thought of Shane ever touching him again. His apartment doesn't feel like a safe place to land anymore.

Brandon began to gather up the strength to get his work clothes out and shower. Usually, he would have time to go home between class and work to change, but he didn't feel safe there. The worst part was Brandon knew he had to put on a mask through all of it, especially with his mom and dad. Brandon felt disgusting even after all of the showers he had taken daily throughout the weekend. No matter what he tried, he couldn't feel clean. As if the water washed over his skin that was covered with the hands of Shane.

Somehow it was Monday morning yet again. Brandon knew it was going to be a long day. He had class, work, and going to his parents' house to care for his dad. He'd been avoiding their calls when Madelyn was in town being too preoccupied with her and Shane. So he had to prepare for what was coming next.

After the shower, he decided not to stay for breakfast. He went to a McDonald's drive-thru for breakfast. It was mostly because he didn't want to face him at all. He was barely keeping it together as it is. He tried to detach his emotions; Brandon was torn between staying or leaving, giving up his dream of living with Shane. Why did Shane have to go and taint that dream? Brandon was now scared to be around him. It wasn't his fault that all he wanted was love but felt violated instead.

As if Shane would have followed him, he looked around the parking lot before getting out of his car once he reached the campus. He took one final bite of the food and exited the vehicle. Brandon couldn't stop checking his surroundings as he walked with his book bag. He felt so paranoid thinking Shane would come out of nowhere to harm him.

His phone started to go off, and Brandon jumped. He didn't know who it would be on the other end. Every single little sound made him feel paranoid, and every look made him feel unsafe. He was that far gone. He looked at the caller ID. Brandon felt semi relief, knowing that it wasn't him. It was too early for who was calling, but he had to pick up. Despite how much he wished that he could decline as he had been for two weeks.

"Good morning, mom," Brandon answered flatly.

"Why the hell haven't you been answering my calls?" She snapped.

"School and work have been keeping me busy. I was studying all week for finals," Brandon lied, "How are you?"

"I've been all alone taking care of your father because our ungrateful son has been ignoring us!"

"I wasn't purposely ignoring you guys," Brandon defended himself, "I thought that the nurse helped you last week. That's what you told me. You said she came to the house to help and do the checkup—"

"It doesn't matter! Don't give me that 'I'm a college big shot' bull shit. You should have been there for us, regardless!"

Brandon tried his hardest not to crumble on the concrete ground. It usually didn't get to him, but she was winning him over this time. That was only his mom, and he couldn't imagine how much worse his dad would be when he got over there.

"Yes, mom, I understand," Brandon obeyed as he tried to hold back the tears from bursting down his cheeks and not let his voice crack, "Do you guys need anything before I get there?"

"His medicine refill is ready, be helpful for once and pick it up before your sorry ass gets here!" She shouted for the last time.

"I will—mom?...Ma?" She had hung up on him. Brandon angrily put his phone away and ran into the building before the rain began to pour. His eyes were burning from the silent tears falling from his eyes; he let them flow down, not caring who saw that he finally hit his breaking point. He made his way upstairs to his class and saw that he was early. Only a few of his classmates were standing outside of the professor's door, waiting for him to come and unlock it.

His mind kept replaying the incident like a movie on repeat. The images were vibrant in colors as he remembered the way that Shane touched him. He kept thinking that everyone already knew what happened to him based on what Zach had told him. Rumors get around the campus fast. They were probably whispering about him before he even walked up. Brandon desperately needed to get away from those people. He practically ran to the bathroom; he went in there, slammed the stall door behind as he broke down entirely. He couldn't be numb anymore and suppress his feelings. His chest started to cave in; his breathing got heavier. He had a full-blown panic attack. He felt the stall was closing in, and he had nowhere else to go.

He felt his mind replaying the terrible event that happened on Friday afternoon. The way Shane shouted at him, the scary look in his eyes, and how he held him down, preventing him from moving one muscle, just began to haunt him. He looked around, and another memory came to mind: Brandon had run to where Shane asked him to meet him. The last time Brandon agreed to have sex with him. He slid down the wall and shook more than before, landing into a fetal position. Brandon couldn't stop the sobs that came from his mouth, the more demanding screams of tears coming down his cheeks, and how often that memory replayed in his mind like a song on repeat.

Why did he agree to that stupid ass text? That text was like a damn booty call people get in the middle of the night. The thrill was no longer existing in Brandon's system. It had died the moment Shane told him to shut up and then aggressively flipped him over. This is his best friend— correction, that WAS his best friend. Whoever he turned into after Madelyn left was this damn monster. Somewhere deep down, he knew it could only get worse from there. In a way, he would still take his chances to have him eventually see that he was the one for Shane. That was all he wanted, but he wasn't sure if it was all worth it.

Brandon stayed on the floor for a few more minutes before he finally stood back up. He went to the sink to look in the mirror while he dried his face to make himself presentable again and headed back to class.

Seeing that the class was now open, he took his seat and got out what he needed from his book bag. He tried to stay focused through the class period taking detailed notes, listening to his professor, and asking as many questions as possible.

People were surprised at how often Brandon was getting confused. He was usually the one helping others, but he just couldn't that day. Zach was concerned the most, noticing that Brandon acted strangely that morning, but Brandon refused to discuss anything. It was all still so raw for him. After class, when he was walking out, Zach caught up to him.

"Brandon, wait up." Zach called after him, "Are you okay?"

"I'm fine," Brandon lied to his face, "I just have so much to do today. Class, going to work, and I have to go help take care of my dad. That's why I'm already in my work uniform. I won't have time to go home."

"Oh wow, you're busy," Zach nodded his head, "Is there anything I can do to help? Anything at all?"

"I appreciate it, but no. You can't do my job for me, and I don't feel like introducing someone to my parents. They're not my biggest fans." Brandon sighed.

"I am sorry to hear that," Zach said, "Can't Shane help you with him?"

Brandon could've almost crumbled when he heard his name. On the inside, hearing his name was the worst thing ever, and it made his skin crawl. On the outside, he kept a straight face. It was like knives stabbing at his chest. "He does most of the time, but today he has a double work shift. I'm going to be okay, though. I've done this many times alone."

"If you would want me to come help, I will," Zach offered.

"Thank you, but no. Today is the only day I'll do it by myself. My brother will be in town next week for the holidays to help," Brandon tried to smile genuinely, but it was more of a forced one. Brandon felt at ease, having Zach beside him. Not that he would be able to do much, but if Shane were to pop up, he wouldn't have to face him alone.

"I didn't know you had a brother?" Zach asked.

"Yeah, my brother is the famous Richard Andreas, popular for his many roles in TV and movies," Brandon chuckled, "Are you going home for the holidays?"

"He isn't that famous if I haven't heard of him." Zach jokes. "I'm trying to. It'll be great to see my family again after having been away for a few months. The flights to Ohio are expensive, though."

"I hope you get to see them, send them my best please," Brandon smiled at him while he put his coat on, "I'll see you Wednesday."

"Okay!" Zach waved goodbye before going their separate ways. Brandon got to his car and drove off the parking lot to his first destination: The local drugstore. It was only ten minutes from where his parents lived.

He got to the pharmacy and waited in line. It was longer than he had hoped. There were about ten people in line, and Brandon groaned. He didn't have time in the day to wait around. Brandon had to have enough time to bathe, feed, as well as the other medical care that his father required.

"Hi, I'm here to pick up a prescription for Harold Andreas," Brandon told the pharmacist.

The worker went and searched for the name and came back, entering some information into the register, "Will you be paying in cash or credit, sir?"

"I'm sorry?" Brandon questioned, confused.

"The copayment for the insurance this month was not met, and you have to pay for the remaining fees. It's one hundred and fifty dollars." The worker informed him. Brandon just stared at the worker, mentally screaming at him for a couple of seconds. So far, his day just wasn't getting any easier.

"Credit, please," Brandon sighed, taking out his wallet and handing the man his credit card. The man rang him up and gave the medicine and card back to him.

He got back in the car and drove the rest of the way.

Shane didn't feel much different from the other day. He thought that Brandon just couldn't handle his new thrill for sex. All of his desires slightly flared up while being with Madelyn. There wasn't enough time in the day to love on her then go back home to get his high from him. Shane didn't care if Brandon wanted more of him or not; he was going to give it to him no matter what.

Shane woke up later than usual that morning. Brandon usually would've been yelling inside of his room to get up, and he wondered why he didn't do it again. He relied on Brandon more than he wanted to admit at times, and he figured that he was paying him back with his newfound pleasures. Shane quickly got dressed for work and got out his phone to text Madelyn the best he could. She was the one who he wanted for the rest of his life; Brandon was just temporary. He wasn't into men, after all.

Right?

He made his way to his vehicle and began driving into the city. Flashes of Brandon's body came into his mind, and he smirked. That night was amazing, even if the back of his mind was trying to tell him that something was off. He chose not to believe it and shrugged. It was his body that he craved. Shane wanted to ruin that ass no matter what the price would be. Something about his body drove him insane, and he questioned why he didn't ask Brandon sooner than he did. To him, it would've been much better than going from girl to girl around college just so that he could get laid. His heart was with Madelyn as he figured that she would eventually become his wife.

She was the only woman in his life that was patient with his dyslexia. Madelyn never made fun of him when he couldn't spell some words correctly. Shane didn't understand how he got so lucky to get someone like her. That's why he had to get rid of the need to want fun with Brandon. They were the best of friends, and he figured that having sex was a way to show his appreciation. He arrived at the college campus and found a decent parking spot. Shane wasn't going to lie to himself; being loyal to Madelyn was a challenge. Ladies craved to get into his pants, and he loved getting into theirs. He was going to have to decide: did he want Madelyn or desire sex more? This made him groan.

"Shane!" A voice behind him called out.

Shane turned around and smiled, "Suzie!"

They both hugged, and Shane's hands went straight to her butt. He missed the touch of a woman whom he didn't have to be romantically involved with. He wanted her to be his next one night stand, but he had to get Brandon out of his system. Whatever Brandon was doing for him turned into a craving. It was a newfound pleasure that he didn't want to keep. He was straight. That's what he had to keep reminding himself. Brandon was great in bed, but he didn't want any relationship with him. He figured that Brandon was the same way.

"How are you doing?" He asked.

"I'm great. I just broke up with my boyfriend, and I remembered your offer. Is it still available?"

"As much as I'd love a good time with you, I have to decline. I'm in a relationship again with my former high school girlfriend, and I do not want to mess it up,"

"Damn, another new relationship? You know you're too much of a manwhore to commit."

"Anyone else I'd gladly cheat. I just really want to make this last. She's the one." Shane meant every word. Madelyn had his heart. He never planned on getting back together with her until they finished their degrees in the spring. Suzie was hot. He had given that nickname to her. Her real name was Susan, but it didn't sound cute enough.

Suzie rolled her eyes and walked away, "You're missing out on an amazing night with me."

Before Shane could respond, his professor caught up with him. "Hey Shane, may I speak with you before class?"

"Yes sir, is there a problem?" He asked his English professor. Professor Williams led him to his classroom and got Shane's essay from his bag.

"Your essay was great; I just need a few clarifications on some words."

Shane sat down and groaned. His dyslexia messed him up again! All he could think about were his parents. They didn't think he was cut out for college. If they knew about all of the essays that he had to correct, he would be convinced to drop out. Shane and his professor worked through all of the mistakes in less than ten minutes, and the professor graded it as a B.

"Thank you for understanding," Shane mumbled.

"Hey, you're doing your best, and that's nothing to be ashamed about."

"I'm just so close to graduating, and I feel as if I'll mess it all up!"

"Don't think about it so negatively. You will graduate, look at how far you've come." Professor Williams encouraged, "Just study as much as possible for your final essay, alright?"

"I'll try to. I know my friend will help me."

"I do not doubt that you'll get through the semester and graduate on time. Just believe in yourself."

Shane sighed as he left the classroom. That was embarrassing to have to do that again and again in each class that involved writing. He decided to walk outside until his class began. The thought of graduating was something he wanted to accomplish so badly, and he was ready to focus on his future. Shane felt like he owed that to himself. However, it frustrates him. His parents were conditional love. At least, that was what it felt like. Shane's family was always surprised when he made it through each semester in high school and college. He hid countless papers from them, but they knew that their son barely made it through the cracks of graduating high school.

Shane walked around, noticing many guys that had nice bodies. He was not attracted to men at all; he was straight! Ever since he and Brandon fooled around in that bed, Shane had a desire to want more. No matter what it would cost, it was going to be worth it. He began to feel like he no longer needed to ask Brandon.

"That's it..." Shane smirked to himself. Forget asking Brandon if he wanted to have sex; he figured that walking up to him and starting to please him would be good enough.

Meanwhile, on the other side of the city, Brandon used his key to get inside his parents' house. He paused to prepare himself for the bashing, "I'm here."

"What took you so long?" Janet Andreas asked sternly.

"I had to wait in line. The pharmacy was pretty busy this afternoon..." Brandon told her carefully.

"Why are you in that fancy outfit? Are you trying to say you're better than us?"

"What? No. I'm going straight to work after I leave here. I have to be there in two hours, and it's a long drive from here than where I stay..." Brandon reminded her.

"Your father is ready for his shower, hurry up." Janet snatched the bag from Brandon and went to their kitchen while he took off his coat.

"How is he feeling?"

"How cute that you're pretending to care," She fired back, "He's not getting any better. I'm afraid to lose him because then I'll only have Richard, and he's in California."

"I am only thirty minutes away!" Brandon shouted out of anger and pain, "You're really just going to throw me the fuck away after he's dead? After I've been busting my ass for the both of you throughout this whole experience?"

"You threw out our relationship when you chose that lifestyle of yours."

"Mom, I—" Brandon started to say. He was interrupted by the food tray shoved into his chest that he had to take upstairs.

"I don't want to hear it. I'm running late to work because of you. Go, do your shift, and get out. The only thing I'm looking forward to after your father's death is never seeing you again." Janet walked away and got her purse and jacket; she slammed the front door behind her.

Brandon made his way upstairs to where the bedrooms were and looked around. So many memories started to run through his mind. There were many good ones as a child, but he experienced a whole lot of hell after coming out in his teens—so many smiling family portraits on the walls of the four of them. Looking at ten-year-old Brandon could've brought more tears to his eyes. He had no clue that he felt a little different from most boys because he would come with what felt like a stab in the back. The only one who he still had a strong relationship with was Richard. He stopped and looked inside the doorway to his old room, seeing that nothing changed. Usually, he was happy that not everything got thrown out.

The day he could only imagine was what happened on Friday with him. It was as if the room changed from his childhood to his room in his apartment. He could see Shane holding him down on the bed, resisting him from moving and just giving him pain just for his self-pleasure all over again. Brandon just stood there watching it like a horror movie reliving it all. He finally went into the master bedroom to find his dad wide awake, glaring at him as if looks could kill. Even with him in his condition, Harold Andreas still scared Brandon. Harold had stage four brain cancer and couldn't talk anymore. He had to write on paper or point.

"Hey dad," Brandon greeted him cautiously, sitting the food tray on the end table, "How are you feeling?"

He let out a grunt as his response.

"I know, we were all hoping it would have gotten better by now. Look at you sitting up, though," Brandon said with a forced smile on his face.

"Shut up, you can't wait until I'm dead," His dad wrote on the board and glared at him.

"Oh, come on, dad, that's not true. I wish they could still cure it. Who knows, it might still be a chance to." Brandon put a napkin on his father and began feeding him. He kept talking to him about things as he fed him. There had to be a new way to communicate since Harold had lost the ability to do so verbally. After feeding him, he went into the bathroom, started the shower, and put the shower chair in place. He wheeled him in, carefully transferring him from the bed to the wheelchair, then from the chair to the shower. Brandon got him washed up, put clean sheets on the bed, and put clean pajamas on him.

In a way, he knew his mom was right. He was just their maid helping with chores and nothing more. Brandon took out the trash, cleaned up the messy kitchen, vacuumed, and washed the tub out. He was exhausted after doing his responsibilities; it surprised him that he had extra time to lie down in his old room. That's when the flashbacks came to his mind of the abuse, rape, and the scary eyes of Shane. It wasn't easy to relax his mind entirely as he kept tossing and turning on the bed. His thoughts were suffocating him like hell. No matter how hard he tried to block them out. Brandon said goodbye to his father after the care attendant arrived and left the house.

Brandon drove away from the house, drowning in his pain and suffering, wondering: *was this ever going to end?*

Chapter 12: Drowning

He felt his life shatter into pieces right before his eyes. No matter how hard he was trying to catch everything, it all managed to slip from his fingertips. Brandon was at the point of questioning everything all over again. Why did everything change so quickly? How come he had to be so scared of him? It was like a complete stranger was on the other side of the wall he was living with. Nothing on his body seemed sterile anymore. As much as he wished for his body to go back to normal, Brandon felt like the grip of his hands was still grabbing at him. He felt him all around him; he couldn't shake him off. Brandon was drowning and losing his purpose. Shane stripped him of everything that he knew. Brandon stopped caring about everything and everyone around him. He had gone numb. Shane broke down Brandon for all that he was worth. It didn't feel safe anymore. His emotions came in so many waves that he didn't know what to feel or how to feel. When was he ever going to feel at ease again?

He wanted to curl up in bed and cry; his pillows were so soaked from his tears. Most nights, Brandon only got three hours of sleep. He went into the kitchen to start the coffee and to turn the heat up. Brandon leaned his back against the counter and let his thoughts get to him for the millionth time since it happened. He was trying to figure out what he could have done differently. He wanted Shane but not like this. Shane's door was closed, which meant he would have to face him.

As if on cue, Shane walked out of his bedroom, making his way to the kitchen. He saw Brandon leaning up against the countertop. Shane was unaware of how Brandon felt; he didn't see that the man was falling to pieces. He was only acting on how he felt and didn't care that he hurt him in the process. Shane snuck up on Brandon, pressing him up against the plain white counter, capturing his lips in a hard kiss and held his body down so he couldn't move. His hands explored down his back to Brandon's ass, squeezing it hard and earning him a fake moan.

Shane pulled away, satisfied, and growled softly in Brandon's ear, "If I didn't have to go to work right now, I'd undress you right here and bang you." There was so much hunger filled in this man's voice that made him a completely different person. Shane nibbled on his ear slowly and hummed while Brandon's body had chills. He desperately wanted to be free from his grasp. Shane then walked away, put on his coat, got his keys, and left the apartment.

It was his goofiness and oblivious personality that made Brandon fall hard. That's who he fell in love with. In no way was that moan filled with any pleasure, more out of habit; that had been more of a whimper to get free and push him off. The only problem was that Brandon didn't have any energy to do that. Brandon started to shake but not enough where anyone but himself would notice. He rushed to the other side of the kitchen to turn the heat up. Even with the room temperature already above eighty, he needed more warmth. There was no way in Hell that Brandon could feel safe anymore, but where would he go? The apartment turned ice cold on him. He was trapped in the apartment, with him being this sex toy of the other man's mercy.

With his hands trembling, he tried to pour coffee into his cup carefully, but instead, the coffee spilled all over the countertop. It was like this metaphor that everything that's going on in his life. His parents, his previous relationship, and now with Shane. As if he needed a new reason to feel small in this world. To leave him feeling empty with no refill. He just wanted to feel whole again.

He set the cup down to clean up the mess before pouring more into the cup and taking his seat on the couch. Brandon booted up his laptop and quickly typed in the web address to his college. He had to distract himself somehow, and he had plenty of work to turn in the next week before finals. Seeing that some work was due brought more relief to him than usual. Usually, it was the opposite feeling knowing he waited until the last minute, but he would try anything to get his mind off of Shane. Also, he wasn't sure how much he would focus on his work with Shane being around.

Brandon started to relax, the more he got into his assignments. It wasn't much, but with the projects being more complicated than before and having little to no time to do everything, it kept him focused. It didn't keep Brandon from the uneasy feeling that Shane had trapped him in. He took many notes and went over definitions until drained himself. Brandon didn't want to stop knowing this was what helped him take his mind off of things even though it wouldn't last. He tried to block the bad out by fulfilling it with knowledge. A few hours went by, with him working on every assignment completing over half of his to-do list.

Shane's words kept replaying in his mind the whole time, no matter what he tried to do to block it. The voice was like an echo in his mind that wouldn't shut up. No matter the thoughts that he wanted to counter it with. Brandon's mind felt like the words were earring him up.

"I'd undress you right here and have my way with you." repeated like a song that people couldn't get out of their heads. Shane no longer cared about what Brandon could've been doing. He made it very clear that he gets what he wanted for the sinful thirst, regardless of how it hurt Brandon. It was certain that Brandon was more of a sex toy to him than a human being. Was this forever going to be his way or pain? He desired love as a human, not to be used and thrown away afterward.

Brandon looked around the room and instantly started to clean up. He didn't have time during the week, but that day seemed perfect to do so. There'd been dishes in the sink, the trash needed to get taken out, and his bedroom could use some straightening up. Brandon felt like a maid all over again for his own home; if he could call it home anymore. He couldn't find a place to call home anymore. Brandon started to reorganize his drawers and closet to distract him from the time. He paid no attention to how the day passed by fast, and the sun was already setting. That meant Shane would be home soon.

Brandon went into Shane's bathroom, starting to clean the sink off. It was filled with the clutter of opened tubes of toothpaste, brushes, combs, and hair all over the sink, which not only looked like his but Madelyn's as well. That burned him even worse than just being in his space. Yet he had to occupy himself from thinking about facing him. Brandon got the sink organized again and cleaned the bathtub out. When he was about to stand up to turn off the water, he heard footsteps coming in the bathroom, making him freeze in position.

Shane must've gotten off a little early, he figured. With his body starting to tremble, he glanced at his watch and realized it was his usual time to be home. He didn't know that time had slipped away from him. His hands began to sweat as he stood up and waited for the door to open. There was no way out of it. Shane was going to take over his body again, leaving him with no way out. He was trapped in his own place.

"Hey Shane," Brandon greeted in a shaky tone, "How was your day?" He turned the water off and faced him with fear. There he was with those lustful eyes scanning his body like it was his possession. Shane moved forward, making Brandon go against the shower wall in fear of him. Of his touch that he once would do anything to have. The next thing he knew, Shane was pinning him against the wall, kissing him harshly before he could protest. His tongue immediately slid into Brandon's mouth, exploring the back of his throat. Whimpers came from Brandon that got misinterpreted as moans.

Shane ripped off Brandon's T-shirt throwing it away along with his. He held Brandon down while he quickly searched for a condom in his medicine cabinet and placed it on the counter. He resumed kissing Brandon harder with his hands grabbing at the pajama pants Brandon had on exposing his member. Shane stroked him as hard as he could as they made out, more like as Shane forced them to stay kissing while he touched it all over. They remained in that position for what felt like hours to him. No matter how his body needed to push him off, Brandon couldn't find the strength to do that. Shane eventually broke the kiss to taste that precum that needed his attention.

Once all the clothes were off and out of the water, he focused on Brandon's member. The only thing Brandon could do was shed tears with all energy drained from his body. Shane sucked him so hard, filling his mouth with his cum and swallowing it all. He loved that salty feeling inside taste buds and could never get enough of it. It was making Brandon feel weak and as if his legs would give out on him. Shane stood up, opening the condom package, rolling it on his member, and roughly kissed Brandon one last time.

Shane turned Brandon around and held him so he wouldn't move and started to play with his hole. Pretty soon, he was lining his member up with the hole and charging in him as hard as he could despite the cry from Brandon. He fucked him slowly to feel around him first. He wanted to handle all the tightness of Brandon's walls around his member as the water was still coming down on them. The pace started to pick up as the minutes went by. It got to the point where Brandon was in full-blown tears and hollering out for help. That didn't feel good. The man he once loved taking away everything he had in him all over again.

Soon, his mouth was covered once Shane had enough of the crying. He thought Brandon was so selfish to be hollering when he wanted to get his fix. According to Shane, it was no big deal, and it was benefiting both of them. His hips were rapid, and his moans filled up the room in an echo. Shane put all of his energy into this because, to him, every time had to be better than the last no matter what it could cost him. This was only about him regardless of how he thought it was helping both of them. Brandon was feeling miserable with this man doing things to him that he no longer wanted. He desperately wanted out but felt like he deserved it. Brandon did come into his room without permission. Shane owned him, and it seemed like he couldn't do a damn thing about it.

Shane came intensely inside of Brandon, experiencing the best climax he ever had. Louder moans escaped his mouth as he caught his breath and pulled out of Brandon. He turned him around and ignored his scared expression kissing him roughly on the lips. Shane felt completely satisfied while Brandon kept reliving his nightmare. Brandon never even kissed back the whole time. It was all Shane.

"What a pleasant surprise for you to already be in my bathroom when I got home," Shane growled lustfully, "It's like you knew where I wanted you." He turned the water off and got out the shower collecting his clothes. Brandon somehow found the strength to exit the shower to get his clothes even with his body feeling dead. Right when he was about to escape the bathroom, Shane gripped his arm tight. He looked at Shane, who still had lust-filled eyes that frightened him so badly.

"What?" Brandon asked fearfully. He couldn't stand looking at him any longer and desperately needed to get to his room.

"No one can ever know about this. Do you understand me?" Shane warned with a devilish glare. Brandon vicariously nodded his head yes in response, but it wasn't enough for Shane. "I said, do you fucking understand?"

"I understand," Brandon spoke softly with his stuttering. At that moment, he realized that his best friend had left the household, and he was now living with a master who had complete control over him. All of this because he said yes over two weeks ago to be his experiment, his little sex toy.

"Good. Now get the fuck out of my room until I need my high again." Shane ordered him.

Brandon immediately got his clothes and ran into his room, locking the door. He was finally free for the time being. After getting on a clean pair of pajamas, he crawled into his bed, brought his knees up to his chest, and let all his sobs come out. The rest of the night, Brandon stayed awake, not able to fall asleep. As much as he didn't want to admit it, it was clear that he was in danger while living with him.

But he had nowhere to go.

Chapter 13: Finals

Another week had come and gone faster than Brandon had thought. It was now the last week of the semester, and he had been studying like crazy. Between Shane, work, and his ungrateful parents, Brandon had his hands full. On top of all that, he no longer had control of his own body. It was now Shane's. The deep black marks that he kept leaving on his body just gave more clarity to that. He resulted in long-sleeved shirts to hide it all. Luckily with the excuse that it'd been snowing in New York, no one would question him about it. Brandon didn't know if it was all made up, but he felt like more people were starting to see through him, looking at his deepest and newest scars, and judged him more for them. He couldn't wait to go into a hibernation state for the next three weeks.

He had gotten up early while Shane was asleep to get ready and leave quickly. Of all days, Brandon couldn't let Shane hurt him any more than he already was. He couldn't bare anything that'd cause him to lose focus and fuck up. He was on the way to the campus when he received a text message from him. No matter how bad he wanted to ignore it, something inside of him needed to know what it would say. His finger was already opening up the notification.

"I guess you had to leave early. Don't be late tonight. I've been horny all night."
Brandon shuddered just by looking at the words on that screen. This was who he was, no matter how he wanted to deny it. There'd been no way to escape from his desire to abuse him whether Shane knew that he held him in one or not. He told himself if it didn't get better between them in the next semester, he would move out. The only problem was he needed Shane and couldn't imagine being roommates with anyone else or living alone. He was starting to realize how dependent he had been with Shane. The real Shane. Did he even want that one to return at this point? What if this rapist was the real him and the one he thought he knew was a lie?

Another thing was, where would he go? The other apartments in New York were expensive no matter where he could look, and his mother had already disowned him. No one seemed to love him anymore, and he only existed to become a servant to others. Brandon became a maid, a human sex toy, a punching bag, and a wastebasket. His heart and soul became homeless in his body, feeling like they should've never been there in the first place. If he decided to no longer be on Earth, would anyone truly miss him for the right reasons? Or even know he's gone? Shane only would care because he wouldn't feel comfortable being up anyone else's hole. Brandon began to think it was the only reason he hadn't thrown him away too.

Brandon made his way to the testing lab and gave his phone to the instructor before sitting at the computer. Zach waved at him from the other side of the room, and he gave a forced smile in return. Even though he knew he could tell Zach anything, he still felt distant from him. Someone could sit next to Brandon, looking at him dead in the eyes, and he would still feel as if they were on the other side of the damn room. There was nobody to lean on who understood him like a book as he did. Nobody whom he could open up to like he could with Shane. If anything, Shane's friendship was missed.

"Good morning, class," The instructor began, "Today is the final exam. For some of you, it will determine if you are going to transfer to Law School next semester, be one step closer to going to Law school, or, unfortunately, set you back one semester. It will be multiple-choice questions and comprehensive questions. Please read the instructions carefully for each question; it is timed for two hours if needed, so do not rush. Any questions?"

Nobody raised their hand, and the professor gave them the okay to begin. Brandon pushed all thoughts about Shane to the side and focused on the exam. No matter how much some memories would try to creep in, he didn't allow them to take over. Every thought of him, of Madelyn, of the rape, or his parents were trying to rule over his mind, desperately trying to break him down, but he didn't let them. The test was far too important. Now and then, he would only take a drink of his water to calm him down. Everything seemed to go fine.

Two hours later, he was the first to finish the test. Even though he was scared to click the "Save and submit" button, he felt satisfaction in his answers and was eager to see his score. Upon completion, his eyes closed as the web page loaded, and he said a quick prayer to the God he hesitated to believe in. Once he opened his eyes, he looked at the percentage and didn't believe it at all. Brandon's mouth went wide open, and his heart dropped.

"Oh my God…" Brandon whispered to himself. He knew he worked hard, but never did he think it would pay off so much. He raised his hand, and the professor came over and looked at the score in amazement.

"This is the highest I've ever seen, Mr. Andreas," The professor grinned, "Congratulations. Can I share it with the class?" Brandon just nodded his head, not being able to speak anymore, still processing it all. It didn't matter how high the score was anymore. With this low and deep hole that the pain and suffering buried him in, nothing could heal his internal wounds. It could only last for the time being. The professor handed him his phone back, and Brandon just tried to relax. He was ignoring every text message from him, with there already being twenty unread all from him. Brandon would take a glance every once in a while that would break him down even further. Eventually, he saw something that just put him over the edge.

"I wanted to try something new, so I bought some toys."

Brandon just couldn't believe it. Shane was in so deep with his craving that nothing else mattered. Brandon began to breathe heavier than he had wanted. Every new picture came with a bigger worry that made him crumble. Everything he looked at was very sharp. He was no longer looking forward to this long damn break. He wanted to run away and hide from his own life. What was going to happen when they got snowed in the apartment with nowhere to hide? Brandon could only fathom what was awaiting him at that apartment. Shane was stronger than him. He couldn't fight him off as he worked out way more than Brandon. Physically, Brandon felt so weak.

After everyone completed their tests, the professor passed everyone else their phones back. From what Brandon could tell, most seemed to be satisfied with their scores. The only difference between him versus everyone else was he was drowning on the inside, begging for help, and just pleading for someone to save him from his life and Shane. Someone whom he never imagined in his wildest nightmares that he would need to get protected from. His professor cleared her throat to get everyone's attention.

"I would first like to say that I've enjoyed getting to know everyone in these last four and a half months. No matter what the test says, I know all of you will be amazing lawyers, judges, and attorneys in the future," She smiled. "I am very proud and honored that I could work with every one of you."

The class all smiled at her mumbling their gratitude for her. Brandon had to admit that before this shit with Shane, he loved getting to go to the class and learning from her. He was lucky that her class hadn't filled up when he finally picked his schedule for the semester. To have passed the course with the highest final score gave him validation for his career path.

"I would also like to give a personal congratulations to Mr. Andreas. He had the highest score of the class, and the highest I've ever seen in this course for a final with a ninety-six percent. Let's all give him a round of applause." She announced. Everyone started to clap and cheer for him; It made Brandon blush and feel flattered. However, it still couldn't make his life feel worthwhile. After the end of the day, he would still have to go be with Shane having to do shit with him forcefully. There was no rush returning to that hell hole. He desperately wanted to stay right there with those smiling faces than to see him or his objects.

"Thank you! I've loved being in this class. Professor Baker, I thank you for making my time in this class worthwhile, and because of you, I've scored so high." Brandon forced a smile on his face. It didn't feel right to smile anymore, but he still had to. He saw Zach cheering the loudest, and seeing him proud made it better for him.

"I hope everyone has a safe and wonderful holiday with their loved ones. The class is dismissed." Professor Baker ordered for the final time. The entire class packed up and congratulated Brandon personally on the way out. Zach and Brandon were the last two out of the room walking together.

"You deserve it, you know?" Zach nudged him, "I knew you could do it, but wow. What's your secret?"

Brandon paused, trying to think of an answer. "I don't know. Shane has been…He's been busy, so what else is there to do in my free time?" He sighed, "I've hardly gotten a chance to hang out with him, and that's with us living together!"

"I guess college is like that." Zach smiled, "You'll get sick of each other over break now." Brandon sighed, realizing that wouldn't be true for Shane in all of the wrong ways. He needed time away from him to try to enjoy his break, but Richard was coming home for the holidays. That would've been his only escape. Not that he was lying to Shane about them not having any money to save to travel, but if he asked Richard to fly him out to California, he already knew the answer would be a yes.

"I know we definitely will," Brandon tried to laugh even though it was forced. "I will probably end up escaping from his craziness!"

Zach laughed along with him. "I think that'll be my sisters and I once I'm home after the first week. I'm bringing my boyfriend to meet everyone, and that's a little nerve-wracking!"

"They'll love Jason, are you kidding me?" Brandon chuckled.

"I know, but I'm still scared. It's my first serious relationship, and we've been together since May." Zach Shrugged then blushed, "I think he's the one already."

Brandon smiled happily for his friend. "I think he is too. I see how you smile every time we talk about him."

"Do you think it'll be like that for you and Shane?" Zach asked, which made his heart sink.

"I don't know anymore. He's been sending these…Mixed signals, I'll call it for now, and I'm not entirely sure what to expect." Brandon told the narrowed truth. He couldn't dare tell anyone the guilt and shame he had, even if it wasn't his fault at all. At least he hoped that it wasn't. Brandon often thought back to when he had first said yes almost four weeks ago and thought he deserved it. Nothing came easy for him, so why would a best friend?

"Is he acting weirder now?" Zach frowned.

"I guess you can say that, yeah. Not entirely sure where he's at in his mind right now." Brandon paused and sighed, "I wish he would talk to me, but he won't." Zach patted his shoulder as they went into the cold, snowy weather of New York. The two men carefully walked to their vehicles, trying to be aware of the ice that hadn't melted yet.

"I will see you next year, I guess?" Zach asked as they hugged.

"We'll see each other before then when you're back in town, but yeah," Brandon said to him and hugged him. "Happy holidays."

"You too," Zach smiled as he headed to his car. They drove off the campus, going in different directions honking at each other as their final goodbyes.

Brandon decided to stop at the park just to look around and prepare himself before seeing Shane again. Once he parked, the tears and sobs couldn't be held back any longer. He undid his seatbelt, lying his head on the steering wheel, just letting it all out. Brandon was close to rock bottom only with no rock down there to accompany him. There was no room for being happy that he completed all of his classes getting straight A's because who gave a fuck? If no one was trying to use Brandon for their own benefit, then his needs were irrelevant.

This was not a silent cry, but a hard and ugly one.

Chapter 14: Brother

The following week, Brandon had to be at work earlier than usual. He figured since his boss knew his class schedule, he knew when Brandon would become available for the last week of work. Brandon didn't mind at all; he would've done anything to get away from Shane. That made him groan just thinking about it. He went from always wanting his undivided attention to wanting to have as much distance as he possibly could from him. At his reception desk, he was working on the computer and taking calls, as usual, trying not to think about what happened over the weekend. Those toys were pure hell once Shane started using them on him. They were cutting his bare skin while Shane was just in his own world, getting even more turned on by the scene. The worst part? There was nothing he could do about it.

One of Brandon's bosses, Daniel, came up to him holding papers. "Hey, my printer is acting up. Will you make copies, please? I'll be back after lunch."

"Yeah, sure, Daniel, I will. Enjoy your lunch." Brandon said with a weak and forced smile on his face. He took the papers putting them on his desk while he finished typing something up. When his phone rang, he didn't even look at who was calling as he was concentrating. "Hi, this is Brandon Andreas."

"I know your name, ass hole." The familiar older voice said that made Brandon laugh. It felt like his first genuine laugh in months.

"Oh, hey, Richard! I answered without looking at the number. Shut up." Brandon laughed at him.

"You probably shouldn't do that, you know?" Richard teased, making Brandon roll his eyes.

"Oh, really?" Brandon asked, heading to the copier, "Why is that?"

"What if you're ignoring somebody, and they're the one who's calling?" That was all Richard needed to say to make Brandon scared all over again. He was right, even if it was said in a joking manner. Brandon couldn't let him be a distraction like he was in class, almost breaking him into bits and pieces.

"I've never thought of that…" Brandon tried to sound normal, "Damn, you…You bring up a good point." He tried to focus on the printer to get it up and running before he could start to crumble on the outside.

"I try to. How were your classes?"

"I did good, actually. In the Social Sciences, I got a B, Psychology and Law an A, and in the criminal justice course, I scored the highest on the final that my professor has ever seen." Brandon tried to sound happy and proud of himself. Even though he could pretend it in his voice, on the inside, there was no room to be happy.

"I knew you could do it!" Richard enthused, "You were always the smart one."

"Oh yeah? Try telling that to *them*." Brandon hinted at.

"Don't get me started. Last night he tried to talk to me, and I just ignored it. I did feed him and bathe him, but I took away his board, not letting him talk." Richard laughed, making Brandon think all over again.

"I've been taking care of his ass all year. Why the fuck couldn't I think of that?" Brandon whined, not caring if anyone was around. He forgot how his brother thought with logic instead of emotion, to which Brandon did it the other way. It always had gotten him into more shit.

Clearly…

"Let's not start pointing out the obvious just yet, baby bro. I just got in town."

"Whatever. How's mom treating you?" Brandon wondered.

"I guess she was surprised to see me. I know I told her I was coming. She's so fucking fake." Richard groaned.

"I would rather fake than what I've gotten all throughout my teenage years. I'll tell you that." Brandon seriously stated.

"Tell me it's gotten better since you're busting your ass running around this damn city for them?"

Brandon paused for a second. He could lie and say she had, but his brother needed to know the truth about that. "Oh, of course not! Why the fuck would I be deserving of that?" He started to get furious thinking about it but realized he couldn't get upset at work.

"Are you serious?" Richard sounded angry, and Brandon could tell.

"Richard, a couple of weeks ago, I had to go to class, stop at Walgreens Pharmacy for the medication, go take care of him and be on time for work all in a two-hour window. Oh, guess how much that fucking medicine cost?"

"How much?"

"One hundred and fifty fucking dollars. She didn't pay the insurance copayment, Richard. I had to use my damn credit card." Brandon huffed.

"Dude, what the hell! You should've called me, and I'd give you my card." Richard told him, "That pisses me off. I'm so sorry."

Brandon sighed, "I was in a hurry and just said fuck it." He turned his attention back to the completed printed copies getting them from the copier, and went back to his desk. Brandon placed them by the computer, so he remembered where they were and continued his conversation. "Richard, you there?"

"Yeah, you just sounded busy. I was waiting," Richard spoke.

"Oh, I just had to make some copies for one of the lawyers. I can still talk. Nobody's here really; it's lunchtime for some." Brandon told him as he went back to typing on the computer, "Also, you know they wouldn't accept it over the phone."

"Why do you still deal with them?"

"I have to; they're my parents." Brandon knew it was a weak but honest response.

"Okay, that's the B.S. answer you give to friends who don't know you. Or even to your best friend, because we know he's not bright. I fucking lived with your ass. Fuck that; I changed your diaper, getting your baby shit on my hands. Answer the question." Richard demanded.

When he heard the phrase 'best friend', Brandon could've broken down instantly. That was not his best friend any longer. It made Brandon shake throughout his entire body, causing him to blurt out: "What else am I valued for?"

With his whole body just wanting to expire in that very moment, everything just went silent. His hands stopped typing on the keyboard; one went to the desk to hold his posture, while the other gripped the phone tighter. Brandon looked around as he felt a whole crowd of eyes staring at the back of his head, but no one was there when he turned around. What felt like ages for anyone to say something, Richard finally spoke in a soft tone.

"What?" Richard asked in confusion.

Brandon froze, realizing that it came out of his mouth. His body began shaking all over again. "Nothing, Richard, forget that I said that, please..."

"Absolutely not. You're talking. I know it's been a minute since we spoke, but you're talking."

"Richard, I—"

"What was that about?" His brother asked, concerned.

"I promise it was nothing."

"I don't believe you. That was clearly something with deep meaning behind it. I just want to know." Richard tried again.

"I can't tell you," Brandon desperately whispered.

"I care, Brandon. I'm not the idiots whom we call mom and dad. Whatever that was, I need to know."

Brandon tried not to burst out in tears. No one had shown this type of care for him in so long. Everyone else just ignored or couldn't see his pain. Somehow over the phone, his brother could. With this being the very first person to see through his pain, even though his outburst did state it loud and clear, Brandon couldn't say no.

"Can we meet up this evening and talk?" Brandon asked.

"Six-thirty at our usual restaurant, you show up, or I'm picking you up," Richard warned him. Brandon knew he had no way out after that slip-up. What the fuck was he going to say, though?! He couldn't tell the full truth because he still loved Shane. Part of him still hoped that the real Shane would return. However, the other half knew it was way too good to be true.

"*Only* for the two of us. That's my exception. Also, you can't tell me what to do...because I'll still be scared either way." Brandon whispered the last part.

"I will try my best to respect that, but by the way that you're sounding, I'm not making promises. Please show up. You know I only want what's best for you."

"I know, thank you. I promise I'll be there; you won't have to go looking for me."

"I will see you tonight," Richard told him before they hung up. Brandon had to look around one last time before letting tears fall down his face. He had to tell his brother. This was his sign of being able to escape it all. He knew he needed this and that he had to ignore his heart that yearned for the man he once knew existed. If his brother could save him, then that's the ticket out he'll take.

Brandon finished his workday at his usual time and headed back home. He again took the long route to prepare himself for what he now wanted to be the final time he had to be alone with Shane. Brandon took a deep breath realizing his car was in its usual spot on the lot. This wasn't going to be an easy way out tonight. He got out of the vehicle and headed inside. It was only an hour before he had to meet Richard.

Brandon slowly went inside, trying to carefully not be heard. After looking around, he went into the bedroom, getting out regular clothes for the evening. By the time he turned back around, Shane was there on the bed, and he jumped in shock.

"Shane!" Brandon shrieked. The next thing he knew was his owner grabbing him and pinning him down on the bed against his will. Brandon wailed out loud for help even though he knew they were alone. Shane's body was pressed against him, holding him down hard as he reached around to unzip Brandon's pants. He kissed up Brandon's back, making him feel filthy all over again. No matter how much Brandon was fighting, it wasn't enough. The next thing Brandon realized was his bare behind exposed from his underwear.

"Fighting it will only make it worse, man," Shane spoke normally. Almost as if he didn't know what he was doing to Brandon. That's when it hit him: this demon inside still had the oblivious ways of Shane Jacobs. He was too occupied by the need to *experiment with a man* to know how this made him feel. He didn't give a shit anymore. Shane went in him with a hard thrust making Brandon wail with tears. Moans immediately came out of his mouth, and he acted like it was the only sound that could be heard. As if this toy of his was silent and not a real human being. With every moment, his hips sped up, making the sensation louder and more demanding.

Brandon couldn't take it anymore even though there was nothing he could do about it. He just laid down on his stomach crying hard. Shane eventually seeded his mark inside of Brandon, pulled out, and zipped his pants back up. He left the room without a word spoken, leaving to whom he believed was still his best friend alone to drown in his tears.

Brandon curled up in a fetal position and cried for what felt like an hour before getting up to wipe his face. Looking in the mirror, all he could see was an ugly man who couldn't stand up for himself. The man he saw let others use and walk all over him without a second thought, someone that was holding all blame for his misery. A person that didn't let anyone see his pain because it'd only make shit worse for him. It was also the man who probably had to lie to his brother that night out of being ashamed.

Shane didn't think much of Brandon screams or cries for help. He was only aware of his own needs and desires. Once he sat on his own bed, he let out a satisfied sigh. Who knew that another man's body could bring so much joy? It was such a thrill that he had to continue with self-pleasure. Brandon was way too annoying to keep pounding inside of him. It didn't make sense to him, shouldn't he be able to take it without him crying like a bitch? Shane didn't realize that he had Brandon in a dark hole that left him with no escape. He didn't see the way that Brandon's eyes no longer lit up, or how he didn't seem as confident anymore. Shane was too far gone.

He shook his head, realizing what he had missed all long. Shane was so caught up on a woman's touch even to consider a man's. Yet, attending college had brought him new sexual desires and questions. Shane lost his virginity in the middle of his freshman year of college. It was with his first college girlfriend back in 2015 after parting ways with Madelyn. He was proud to see her get excited to attend her dream college in California, but his heart had felt empty. His mind played a slideshow as he pleasured himself of Brandon's body as well as all of the women he had been with. Shane began to get annoyed when Brandon kept popping up on repeat. Yes, his body was giving him such satisfaction, but he didn't want to become gay! What they were doing—or what Shane was doing—wasn't going to be forever.

He lost all sense of his surroundings; It was only the imaginations inside of his mind that mattered. A loud moan escaped his lips once he reached ejaculation. Shane had become this sex machine, and it took over

Chapter 15: The Truth is Out

"Hi, my name is Amanda. I will be your waitress this evening. May I start you two off with drinks?" Asked the waitress.

"I will have a sprite." Richard requested.

"Water for me, thank you," Brandon says. After the lady walked away, Brandon took a sigh before talking. "I hate this."

"Hate what?"

"I feel ashamed and stupid because none of this stuff would be happening if I'd said no." Brandon was trying to keep his voice from cracking, but he felt weak. How was he ever going to say this without breaking down?

"I'm here; talk, and take your time."

"I feel like I'm losing everything, Richard. I just don't know what to do."

"What's going on, man? You can trust me." Richard comforted.

"I would tell you, but I'm afraid of what you'll do." Brandon sighed.

"I need to know Brandon. Have you told Shane?" Richard asked.

Brandon looked down and tried to think of an answer. The shame that he'd bottled up and drowned into had him screaming for help. He just shook his head, not making eye contact with his brother.

"Why not?" Richard questioned, and sounded more concerned, "Does it involve him? You usually tell him before me."

"He's the main problem of it all," Brandon admitted. He could feel his hand shaking with his nerves coming back to him, wanting to flee away. Brandon knew he had two choices: suffer internally forever or get over the shame of letting someone in. The biggest fear wasn't what Richard would do to Shane; it was instead what Shane would be able to do to Richard. Even though he knew that his brother was taller and more robust, his now traumatizing life made him think that his abuser was capable of anything.

Richard sighed, "Okay, we already know that I don't like him. Also that I think you could so much better even if he ever comes out. Now you're telling me you're having problems. Is he an awful roommate?"

"He wasn't at first. The first year and a half were amazing. We were getting along, and I loved living with my best friend because he could cheer me up and everything. I told you this when I decided to give it a go." Brandon started.

"Yeah, and what did I say?"

Brandon groaned, "'Even though it's your best friend, it doesn't mean it'll work out in the end. He may use you, you might pay more than half of the bills,' which I am not afraid to say you weren't wrong about that part, 'He may turn into something you regret ' and once again you were right…Mostly"

"So, where was I wrong?"

"I haven't regretted it. At least not completely…"

"Why have you begun to regret it?"

Brandon sighed. "So, Shane always comes up with random crazy-ass ideas for us to do. You know, breaking my arm from pogo jumping on the trampoline, making me run into the fucking ocean when there was a big wave coming in, and a lot of other shit that ended us in the hospital."

"Another reason why I don't understand how you're best friends but keep going."

"Right," Brandon mumbled and looked down at the table for a moment letting a sigh come out of his mouth, "Even though I enjoy most of the activities, I'm the one that suffers the repercussions. He just got out of hand with this one."

"What is he doing?" Richard asked, already sounding like the protective brother he always was.

Brandon just closed his eyes, shaking his head back and forth. It was going to be the moment that he'd let the words come out of his mouth. With another deep breath, the sentence was finally free from his mouth. "Shane has been raping me…"

Silence filled the area with guilt and despair. He finally admitted to the truth. Not only to Richard but also to himself.

"What?" Richard sounded heartbroken and in disbelief. How could he do this to him? Brandon spent so many years trying to prove to him

"I was humiliated!" Brandon admits, "I was the one to leave the apartment not being able to take it anymore."

"I'm sorry, you pay eighty percent of the bills, and you left?" Richard groaned, "Fuck no. Mistake number one."

"I didn't care, Richard. The disrespect and the humiliation I just couldn't care. I went to the college dorm rooms and stayed with a friend from my class."

"Okay, so, you stayed there, went back home the next day. Then what?"

"I got mad because she was the only one in the house when I went to get changed. Also, this was all in a time span of two weeks. I'm barely seeing him due to the usual college and work schedules, which is normal."

Brandon finally let it all out. He told every detail and the emotional rollercoaster that came along with it, from the first rape to the one that happened an hour before they met at the restaurant. Although it was hard saying everything, he had to let his brother know. By the time Brandon told everything, he had collapsed in Richard's arms, crying harder than ever. The overwhelming feelings were hitting Brandon as if they were a bunch of baseballs hitting his face.

"I am so sorry, Brandon." Richard pulled him into an embrace, holding him tight. For the first time in so long, Brandon felt utterly safe and comfortable with someone. Both brothers decided to ditch their meals altogether and went outside after paying. They sat in Richard's truck, and he continued to hug Brandon letting him cry hard.

"I am such an idiot. All I needed to do was say no!" Brandon sobbed, trying to catch his breath. His breathing became hitched, hard, and puffing at a fast pace.

Richard was so heartbroken and angry at the same time. How could this have happened? It didn't make sense. Although he wasn't fond of Shane by any means, this was the last thing he ever saw coming. He hurt his little brother, practically destroyed him. This bitch took away every ounce of happiness that Brandon had. All because of curiosity. Well, he could get curious as well. He could get curious about killing people and have Shane become his first victim. As far as Richard was concerned,

Shane better had hoped he'd never have to run into him because he wouldn't be alive for another day.

"Please promise me you won't go find him," Brandon begged, "I don't know what he's capable of in this mindset."

"I can't." Richard admitted to him, "I can't promise that at all."

"Richard, please!" Brandon begged through his chokes, "I'm so scared."

"Brandon, look at yourself," Richard tried to reason with him, "You're expecting me not to do anything when he's close to killing you? I can't promise you that."

"I need you to listen to me, that's it! Plus, you've worked so fucking hard to get to where you're at in your career. I can't let you jeopardize that for my troubles."

"I don't give a fuck about my career if I'm close to losing you. None of this shit is more important than you in this situation, or any situation. Everyone we know is using you, and I'm just supposed to shrug it off?" Richard asked, "Why haven't you gotten the cops involved or thought about suing?"

"I know how this system works; I'd lose!" Brandon told him.

"I think you're overthinking it," Richard sighed,

"Oh please, haven't you seen the Me Too shit online? Fucking strangers are blaming the victims!" Brandon groaned, "My story? I'd get dragged all over that court case!"

"Alright, here's what we're about to do. First, wipe your face," Richard opened up the glove compartment getting out a box of tissues handing them to Brandon. After Brandon calmed down, he spoke again, "Now you follow me home to our parents' house. You're not going back to him. If anything, you ignore them too because they're all noise, and we're figuring out what to do. Alright?"

Brandon hugged his brother once more, feeling beyond thankful for him. He'd finally told someone, and there was so much weight lifted off of his shoulders. Talking to Richard gave him hope that he could live to see another day.

Chapter 16: Holidays

Brandon sat down on his parents' couch after helping Richard with their father. The past couple of days were both relieving and terrible all at once. He was heartbroken, confused, and ashamed. The only safe place he could be was there in that house, getting daggered looks from his own mother, who had no idea what he was dealing with. If she knew what was going on, then Brandon would get non-stop nagging of how it was his fault for being gay in the first place. Not that it would matter since he felt so empty and weak already. All he would do was stare and tune her out. Brandon would somehow consider it progress, turning numb for everything instead of crying all over again.

This made Brandon reevaluate his life. At the beginning of the year, he had a crush on his best friend who was straight, a bright future headed towards his last full year as a student going to a community college, and he viewed the world with so much joy and happiness. He could almost laugh hysterically at how naive he was about it all—thinking that it was going to be "his year" and that nothing was going to go wrong. Most people would say that they didn't know when their lives took a wrong turn, but Brandon knew the exact moment when it happened.

"Why are you here?" His mother snarled at him.

"I would say that you could want to spend Christmas with both of your sons," Brandon fake reasoned with her, "Instead, we can say that I'm here for free food since I'm the unpaid nurse for your husband. Which would you prefer, mom?"

"My real son is in town. The hell would I need you around here for?"

"I guess that works, too." Brandon shrugged.

"Get out," Janet demanded at once as she tried to keep up her scary personality that she knew always scared Brandon. Only this time, he didn't even flinch. "You did your shift for the day, now leave."

"If he goes, I go, and you won't be able to reach either of us when Harold dies and goes to Hell," Richard spoke up as he came out of the bedroom.

"I don't want you to go, baby. I've missed you so much, and you're a joy to be around!" Janet said to him in a loving, mothering tone that made Brandon roll his eyes. He was just over it all. "Especially on Christmas day!"

"So, you're not grateful that both of your sons took time out of busy schedules to be with you?"

"I think he fucking fakes being busy on purpose. Probably does all sinful things with other disgraceful men just like him!"

"How can you—!"

"Richard, it isn't worth it. Not today," Brandon mumbled. "I have to admit that it's unfortunate how none of this would be as it is if I'd stayed in the closet."

"Yeah, so why didn't you?" Janet shouted,

"I don't know at this point, but I'm glad it showed how your love is fake. Faker than the wigs on your head, Janet." Brandon could see Richard's proud look from the corner of his eye, but that didn't matter at that moment. He realized that Brandon was only able to do this with him there. Other times he would be so quiet not to have all hell break loose. Janet just stood there, surprised but angrier, and Brandon could see it all written across her face. She was used to verbally abusing him and him continuing to kiss her ass. This was all a new game for her that Brandon could tell she didn't know how to play. Janet just walked away while Richard gave a big grin sitting next to him.

"The bitch in you is coming back; I love it!" Richard enthused.

"Oh, please, you know good and well if you weren't here, I'd stay quiet." Brandon groaned, "He's not back."

"Fine, but still! That's what should come back. Come on, Brandon, you deserve this as a Christmas present to yourself."

"I want him back," Brandon admitted, "He's been gone for over two months almost. I know I need him back, but he'll run away the very next time I'm in his sight."

"Why are you worried about the next time? It's not happening as far as I'm concerned." Richard dismissed that idea quickly.

Brandon sighed and pulled out his phone again. He opened up texts that notified him when he woke up that morning. It was all from the same number, but with mixed messages.

"Merry Christmas, man. Guess you went home and spent it with your family. Enjoy." From Shane.

Then the rapist came back right after with a naked selfie with a caption: *"I'm alone and so horny for you, though."*

"So what, he's bipolar now?" Richard sounded annoyed.

"I don't know what to think, man. All of this is just so scary, and I can't seem to focus. To be fair, it's not about being focused at all, but about being distracted. My work in class was the perfect distraction for me. Seeing these texts just scares and confuses me even more."

"Why would you go back to that?"

"I would go back based on that first text. Look at it, Richard; it's Shane. My best friend. The one whom I fell in love with. The real Shane.." Brandon expressed as his voice began to choke up, "I need him, Richard. His friendship means the absolute world to me. The Shane Jacobs that I know has been the reason I'm able to keep taking care of that bastard."

"I hate to break it to you, but that is not the real Shane." Richard sighed.

"Yes, it was. It had to have been! Eight years versus two months? You can't tell me that I've been friends with a fake for eight years. That first text is him, and the other one isn't!"

"I know for a fact that it is."

"Richard—"

"This is Shane Jacobs on his fucking sex addiction! Come on, man, admit it." Richard insisted as he pointed to the last message, "Accept it and get rid of him."

"I've just never seen him like this."

"That's because you've never been the woman on the other end."

Brandon opened his mouth to speak and then closed it back in confusion. "Come again?"

"All you know is that he's never been able to keep a girl after a couple of weeks, right? Maybe this is why. You don't know if this is how he's tried to keep having sex with the same girl or not. I believe it is, though."

"I don't believe this; it can't be why. If so, Madelyn would've never agreed to be his girlfriend again. Something is going on with my best friend that's trapped, and I always figure it out!" Brandon expressed, getting angry. He thought that this time away would help Shane calm. That maybe things would get back to normal once he would return after the new year. He knew Shane at the core of his heart.

"Okay, you and Madelyn have been either lied to or manipulated at this point. Hell, probably both. The difference is he is so fucking stupid that he doesn't realize it himself."

"Why do you keep calling him stupid?"

"Why are you trying to color a black area into gray?" Richard questioned back. Brandon hated how he would get so much smarter in conversations like this. Everything he was saying, Brandon knew, was right. No matter how much he hated to admit and face reality. What started as a pleasant conversation an hour ago turned into this debate. The younger brother both loved and hated times like these, mostly when the older one was right.

"Fine! Some of this is not due to his disability. Shane is a little stupid! Are you fucking happy now, Richard?" Brandon yelled at him out loud. Angry tears were streaming down his face as he was starting to shake. "No one, and I mean fucking no one, has been there for me like he has when you're not. No one has fucking kept me going as he had been. Not a single mother fucking person on the entire planet can break me more than him because he knows shit that even you don't! As my brother, you are my rock, but he is my stone. I'm trying to give him up. I'm trying to put myself first. I just never thought that the man who always preached that to me would turn around to give me the perfect example of his own lesson. I'm not coloring anything black into gray. How can I do that when I see nothing except gray?"

Brandon started shaking uncontrollably with tears streaming down his face. He wanted to shut down and curl up into a ball after raising his voice at the one man who wasn't judging him. Brandon felt like the worst person in the world that no longer deserved help from Richard. He thought that his brother was going to give up and walk away from him. That he would get mad when all he had done the last couple of days was be patient and empathetic. Everything that Brandon needed in his life right now was right in front of his eyes, trying to comfort and love him. Brandon was only pushing him away further without meaning to.

Richard just embraced him in his arms, protectively letting Brandon cry harder. Of course, Richard wasn't angry at this outburst whatsoever. It was what he wanted Brandon to do. To allow himself to sob like never before because he knew it was what Brandon needed. Whether he realized it or not, his brother had to have that safe person to cry to. Richard was glad that Brandon had that much trust in him. Brandon shook, cried, screamed, and hollered in that living room for what felt like hours to him. What he had planned on being the best Christmas day for both him and Shane was all ruined earlier that month by becoming someone's sex toy. Only to allow somebody to experiment on him; use his body as an ongoing science project without caring about his feelings that lowered his worth.

Once Brandon had calmed down, Richard wiped his eyes for him. "Come on," he whispered, "We should go get some fresh air outside. What do you say we drive around town for a while?"

Brandon nodded his head before getting up to go clean up his face in the bathroom. He felt so ugly, looking at that reflection of the new unattractive person that he turned into. Even though he knew Richard was right, Brandon still thought he caused all of this shit to occur. From his swollen eyes to the way he shut down to the world, Brandon blamed himself for all of it. The ugliest man alive was his new face in the world. He didn't feel right in his usual bright clothes anymore. They still screamed "happy, healthy, with a bright future!" when he didn't know anymore if he would even see tomorrow. It was the complete opposite. Plus, he only had a limited number of items at his parents' house. Brandon wasn't planning to stay long after Richard left, anyway. Shane would be back to his usual self after the new year.

Right?

Shane put his phone down after he tried to text Brandon for what felt like the hundredth time. He didn't understand what was going on with Brandon and why he was ghosted. Were they best friends or not? Were they roommates or not? He'd looked forward to ignoring his family and spending time with him. To say that Shane was annoyed was an understatement. How could he betray him like that? Shane sighed and figured that maybe he wanted alone time with Richard, but it had been over a week. He wanted answers to the point that it drove him crazy. After he scrolled through his other texts, he finally gave in and replied to his family, saying that he was going to the family gathering.

Shane got out of bed and took a shower. His mind kept thinking of Brandon's body. The demons inside of him lusted to do things to him against his will. It didn't feel right somewhere inside of Shane, and he was questioning why he wanted it so badly. It infuriated him to know that he couldn't shake off the thoughts of him and not be able to focus on Madelyn. What the hell was going on? Shane leaned against the shower wall and groaned. His holiday wasn't going as planned. Once he got dressed and collected his items, Shane got in his vehicle and drove to his aunt's house. He parked on the cul-de-sac and went inside the house.

"Hey, everybody!" Shane greeted with a smile. He hugged his mother first, "Mother."

"Hey, honey, glad you made it." Cindy Jacobs smiled and kissed her son's cheek.

"Merry Christmas," Freddie Jacobs grinned as they hugged next.

"I didn't want to stay at home alone this year. Brandon went to his family's house, I'm assuming." Shane told them.

"We're about to bring the food down. Go wash your hands and help us." Cindy said. Shane nodded his head and went into the half bath down the hallway. Once he carried the food down with his father, Shane greeted his cousins, who were playing on one of the card tables set up.

"Hey, Shane!" Victor grinned.

"We didn't think you were coming," Raven laughed.

"Why wouldn't I? This is the only holiday I'd fuck around with you bitches." Shane fired back jokingly.

"We all know you'd rather be fucking one of your hoes."

"I had to get rid of them for my lady."

"Carly?"

"No."

"Olivia?"

"No, she was horrible in bed."

"Catrina's dumb ass? I told you she was up to no good!"

"No, but since when have I given a damn about personality when she's good in bed?" Shane laughed.

"Shane!" Cindy scolded him.

"Sorry, ma!"

"You told us that you were going to prove us wrong about you graduating. Yet, I hear that you're focusing on your sex life as a priority?"

"I didn't mean it like that!" Shane blatantly lied to her face, "I'm a grown man who's dating, but I'm working really hard for my degree."

"You better be. I still cannot believe that you've made it this far. Surely your English classes will make you drop out." Cindy shook her head as she returned to set up the food table.

"Thanks, mother, you're my biggest discourager." Shane scoffed, "I work so hard to please you and dad, even in middle school, when my dyslexia was very noticeable. You made me ashamed to have to go through the disability office at my college for accommodations. So what if I focus on sex? At least I know it's where I never disappoint!"

"I'm your mother; I don't want to hear anything about your sex life."

"You weren't even a part of this conversation, Aunt Cindy," Raven spoke up. Shane just let out a frustrated sigh. There had to have been something else for him to do, but nothing was open on Christmas Day. At least, nothing that would interest Shane. He felt small with his parents and useless. Everything else about the relationship with his parents was perfect; however, when they talked about his academics, the mood went left.

"I promise I'm doing the best that I can. I'll be honest and say that it was a hard semester trying to get these English credits out of the way. I didn't enjoy struggling this semester; I won't enjoy it in my final semester. All I'm asking is for some respect for how hard I've worked these last three years."

"Your father and I just want what's best for you, Shane," Cindy spoke empathetically.

"Then act like it, mom. Come on, you should have been proud of me a long time ago," Shane then got up from his seat and went over to her, "I didn't just do these last few years to prove you wrong. This is my dream to be a fitness trainer. You know how much I love working out; that has not changed. I'm not even working at some McDonald's; I'm a receptionist at the gym membership, not fifteen minutes from here. That includes reading, and I love how it challenges me with my dyslexic ways. You think I'm illiterate!"

"I never said that!"

"You and dad act like you believe it!"

"Is it so bad that your father and I worry about you?" Cindy sighed.

"It is when you guys make me feel like I'm some dumb ass that doesn't know what he's doing."

"Your high school report cards—"

"That's not my final college grades! I'm doing much better. I've only failed two college courses in four years, which I passed on my second try without cheating, and you still focus on my failures."

"Can you blame me when there've been so many setbacks?" His mother asked as she got back to organizing the food.

"Yeah, I can," Shane told her in all honesty and decided to help her, "You're supposed to encourage me to keep pushing when I fail, not tear me down more."

"What would you know about parenting?"

"I'm not saying that I know anything about being a parent, but I know what I need as a son. As your son, fighting a hard enough battle with his inner demon named Dyslexia. I know plenty of successful people, both famous and everyday people who have this disability."

"Oh yeah?" An older man's voice challenged him as he came from the backyard. "Name three right now from the top of your head."

Shane couldn't help but smile and laugh, "Hey, uncle Timothy." Shane was grateful that his uncle came down to the basement. He gave a glance to his mother, who had a look on her face indicating that the conversation wasn't over yet. Shane sighed and shook his head as he continued to help to get the food ready. Cindy knew how to make her son feel uncomfortable and out of place. Shane had to keep his posture to not crumble in front of her. The last thing Cindy needed to know was she could still tear him down quickly.

"Hey—now name three celebrities."

"Tom Cruise, Cher, and Whoopi Goldberg."

"Well played," Timothy laughed and hugged him. "How have you been?"

"I'm doing good, Uncle Tim. How about you?"

"I'm alright; I haven't seen you in a while!"

"I know work and school has me pretty busy. I'm almost done with my requirements."

"That's good to hear; I, for one, didn't think you'd make it."

Shane sighed, "Not you too?"

"Hey, now we know never to doubt Shane Jacob's brilliance!"

"I guess."

"Go back over with your cousins. I'll help your mother from here." His uncle told him.

"Are you sure?"

"Yes, go enjoy yourself."

Shane nodded his head and went back to the table. He was unaware of how tensed up he got from being next to his mother. Every encounter with his parents went the same way. The conversation would start right on a positive note and somehow left him feeling useless and dumb. It was the worst feeling in the world for Shane, the feeling that was uglier than him earning bad grades for his assignments. Luckily, that was the only bad encounter of the gathering. He enjoyed getting to laugh and goof around with his family again. Shane caught up with all of his cousins, uncles, aunts, and grandparents. He had to admit that he missed all of his family members. Ever since he began college and his part-time job, Shane couldn't come around as often as he'd like. He enjoyed all of the conversations, food, and shenanigans that he and his cousins got into that day.

At the end of the day, Shane and his cousins decided to go to a bar for a drink. Despite not hearing from Brandon, Shane had to admit that he had a pretty good holiday. His only hope was to get to see Brandon before their break was over.

After straightening himself the best way possible, Brandon met Richard in his truck. They both buckled up, and Richard drove off down the roads of New York City. Taking a big sigh, Brandon had started to relax for the first time on Christmas day. The city was at below-freezing temperatures, but the road wasn't bad at all. No sign of ice on the streets; to Brandon's surprise, a lot of people were still out doing things. Many buildings and shops had hundreds of Christmas decorations all over in celebration. Usually, Brandon would be all excited, loving each unique decorations and lights, but that couldn't make him happy with everything going on. He was preparing to lose an ungrateful father to aggressive cancer, his home situation was currently unsafe, only one person could see through all of his pain, and Brandon had to go to work and school to push through it all.

"I mean, at least something good came from this holiday. Getting to spend time with my big brother is what I needed. More than I realized." Brandon slightly smiled. For the first time all day, it wasn't a forced one.

"That's the spirit! I just want you to be okay, but I know it'll be a long time to get through this. What will you do once I leave?" Richard asked in concern.

"I don't know because I can't find a way out, no matter what way I go. If I stay with mom and dad, I'm a twenty-four-hour manual labor slave, but if I go back home, then I'm a sex toy slave. All of this is just bullshit."

"Why not move with me after you finish community college?"

"I could do that, but I have a great chance of getting into CUNY Law. You know it's one of my dream universities, and if I'm accepted, then I wouldn't want to leave. Two more years at this community college, then I'll have to see." Brandon explained to him, "Not to mention that the acceptance rate is only forty-one percent. That's not even half; it would be an honor to get in. I'm working my ass off these last two semesters, and I can't give up because I'm close to losing my mind. If anything, this is what's keeping me from going bizarre."

"Do you understand this is why I have so much respect for you? You're not giving up, no matter what life has thrown at you. From doing college full time, working full time, and taking care of two of the most ungrateful people on this earth, you are not letting it stop you. If no one else tells you this, let me be the first." Richard told him as the car came to a stop at a park. "I am so, so proud of you. You're doing shit that I could never in my wildest dreams. If you want to stay for that college, I support you one hundred percent; however, you will get a new place to stay. I don't care how much you need my help. You're going to get through this and survive, Brandon. I've got your back."

Brandon nodded his head feeling grateful for his brother. Out of all the people whom he could have let in, he made the right choice. If anything, that was the best Christmas gift he could have ever asked for.

Chapter 17: Goodbye Father

It was after the New Year's, and Brandon was back to work. He was still at his parents' house for the time being, and Richard was still in town. Their father was admitted into the hospice, and honestly, Brandon didn't know how to feel. This was his verbally abusive, ungrateful father who still had nothing nice to say, even with Brandon doing his care most days. The man was still the same one who told him that he didn't love him anymore because he was gay. Did he really need to be sad? He didn't want to.

As a matter of fact, Brandon didn't want to do anything. His body fought him more than usual to return to his routine. Every inch of him felt like he was in flames. Taking a bath didn't work. Eating cold cereal didn't help much, and no amount of water bottles did the trick. Brandon was hopeless and still had to continue with life as if nothing was wrong.

One of Brandon's bosses, Daniel, who had been a great mentor and friend to him, walked over to his desk. He had let Brandon know more information about a lawyer's life giving him many tips on what the process was like per case. Brandon looked up to see him with a concerned look on his face. "What's wrong, man?"

"I'm wondering why you're at work today," Daniel stated, "Didn't your father go on life support over break?"

Brandon shrugged and kept typing. Of course, he was concerned about his dad. No matter how shitty he became after Brandon came out after so many years prior, as well as ungrateful, Harold was still Brandon's only father. He and Daniel had gotten close through always working together, and he knew how Brandon had a rough relationship with both parents. That's how they both connected, by being gay and disowned by their parents.

"I get it; you know I do more than anyone else you probably know. Yet, Harold is near death. He may be sorry and regret how he treated you."

Brandon gave a sarcastic laugh at that before responding. "That is the last thing I need to hear from him. An 'I might as well apologize because I'm dying' apology? Screw that, man. That's what he would do as a joke; he wouldn't be serious. Plus, he can't even talk anymore."

Daniel just nodded his head and sighed, taking a seat next to his desk to relax. "I can't fight with that logic. You know, my father actually called me faggot the whole on Christmas day. My husband, Isaac, just had to bite his lip with me the entire night. He doesn't understand why I still want to go, but my grandma is a sweet ninety-seven old lady. I go for her."

Brandon sighed and leaned back on the chair, facing him. "I don't know if either of my grandmothers would have accepted me, to be honest. They both loved me so much, oh my gosh. It was the best, but my parents also loved me before I came out. New York wasn't always so accepting either, as you know. At least you have your husband and his family."

"I know, but it's not the same. You want your own family to come around to accept you. To love you and apologize sincerely for all of the shit they put you through," Daniel frowned, "I'm much older than you, you're nearly twenty-three, and I'm forty-nine, so you've been around to see the country come to acceptance. On the other hand, I go back to the 'Don't Ask, Don't Tell' bull shit. I was kicked out of the military after serving from 1991 until the ban in '94. After that, I just said fuck it. Why go back?"

"How did you get found out?" Brandon questioned him.

"I was having sex with another soldier." Daniel laughed, and Brandon laughed along.

"That has to be the best way to get caught!"

"The revenge is even better; I'm married to him!" Daniel exclaimed happily, and they laughed, giving each other a high-five.

"I would love that to happen to me." Brandon sighed.

"Not even a boyfriend yet?"

"Not since high school when I got cheated on. I don't know if I was fully into him anyways, which is why he cheated," Brandon informed him, "Now it's complicated, to say the least. Kind of cliche to use a damn Facebook status option, but I guess I could call it that."

"I get it. You're here, in college, and taking care of a parent. You don't have time to breathe, do you?" That hit home for Brandon. As if Daniel saw directly through Brandon at that very moment, he could let tears fall from his eyes. However, he already had his cry for the day. Brandon had left his parents' house early to go be alone for a few minutes before work. The broken man had gone back to that same damn park just to let it all out. He was tired of being that way. Just sick of all the tears, fear, and nightmares taking over his life. The redness in his eyes never left him for too long of a time before returning.

"I think I'm close to drowning under this water. That's saying something because I never complain." Brandon admitted.

"Anything that I can do to help, please let me know. I mean it, you're my friend. Not just a boss, alright?"

Brandon smiled at him slightly with a nod. "Thank you, Daniel. You don't know how much that means to me."

Just as Daniel was going to talk again, the phone in his office rang. They gave each other a nod for goodbye, and Brandon went back to work. Another three hours went by when Brandon's phone went off, and Richard's number popped up. Taking a shaky breath, he answered the call.

"It's time, Brandon. Get here soon." Richard told him.

"I'm on my way," Brandon confirmed as he saved the last bit of work on the computer. He kept his brother on the phone as he collected his stuff going to clock out. "Daniel, I'm leaving!"

"Good luck. Let me know if you need anything!" Daniel called out from his office.

"I will, thank you!" Brandon shouted back before he entered the elevator. "I'm in the elevator, so I may lose you, Richard."

"That's fine," Richard sighed, " I've just never seen mama like this. She's crying so hard right now. I just don't feel the same. I'm sorry for her, but I just…"

"I know, it's just all so shitty. We shouldn't be emotionless right now, but what can we do?" He drove out of the parking lot and took the quickest route to the Bellevue hospital.

"Please don't rush and get into an accident. The doctor is saying he has about fifteen minutes max."

Feeling anxious, Brandon decided to put the phone on speaker to have both hands on the wheel. This was going to be his very first death he would witness in person. Was he going to cry? Could he handle it without his best friend by his side? Brandon kept talking to his brother as he drove to get as many updates as possible. There wasn't any traffic on the highway, which Brandon was thankful for. He made it there in eight minutes, and Richard had said that everything was getting worse by the minute. He made it to the hospital in seven minutes flat, then rushed into the building.

Brandon made it through security, got his name tag, and went up to the ninth floor. The aspired lawyer found his brother right outside their father's room, pacing around. As soon as they made eye contact with one another, they were embracing each other tightly.

"You alright?" Brandon mumbled quietly.

"I don't know," Richard responded in the same tone, "What about you?"

"I don't know either."

Brandon took a big sigh looking at the door to the room that their parents were in. He didn't know what to expect to see once he'd walk into the room. Richard patted his shoulder as they went inside to witness the last minutes of their father's life. In that room, Brandon saw what he considered was the most heartbreaking scene to be entering. Harold's breathing was at an irregular pace with a mixture of gasps, and fast, loud inhales. The heart monitor was speeding up by the second showing his rate of well above one hundred and his oxygen below fifty. Both of the brothers just sighed as they went closer to their mother. Richard and Brandon stood on opposite sides of her, both kneeling and placing hands on her shoulders. Janet startled at the unexpected touch looking at them both. She turned her head towards Richard, gave him a sincere look, then turned to face Brandon, and gave a hard look before focusing back on her husband.

Brandon and Richard just looked at each other rolling their eyes. It wasn't the time to confront her about anything. Brandon looked around at all of the machines that Harold Andreas connected to keep him alive for as long as possible. The gasping breaths, static body, and the closed eyes would be Brandon's last image of him. Everyone stayed quiet for the last minutes of the life of Harold Andreas, letting only the sounds of a beeping heart monitor fulfilling the room. With one last final straining breath, Harold's eyes shut for the final time, and all of the monitors went flat.

"January 18, 2019, at 2:09 PM," Richard announced after what seemed like an eternity of silence.

"Are you okay, mom?" Brandon asked softly.

"This is all your fault…" Janet spattered through tears. Brandon could have burst into tears after hearing that. He didn't believe she had said those words, let alone it being the first thing out of her mouth. Not only did his mother no longer care about his being, but there she was putting an entire death, something Brandon had no control over, on his shoulders. He looked over at Richard, who shared the same disbelief to what they just heard. All his fault. Doing all that he possibly could, and that was the 'thanks' he got.

"Excuse me?" The next response came out of anger. Brandon and Richard both stood up, moving away from their mom. Even in the midst of her husband being dead, Janet Andreas still found a way to blame their son, just like Harold would want her to.

"How the fuck is that his fault?" Richard shouted.

"He knew he could've done more to prevent this. Brandon wanted me without my husband as payback," Janet argued.

"Okay, you're not even thinking logically with your hate at this point," Brandon screamed at her, "I wanted my father to die? I took care of him because I wanted him dead? You'll find anything to blame me!"

"If you had really taken care of him, he would have been cancer-free."

"What the hell? He had stage four brain cancer, Janet," Richard shouted, "There wasn't anything that Brandon or anyone else in this world could have done differently."

"I only had two people in this world, which were him and Richard. You have plenty of people," Janet continued to yell at Brandon.

"If I had plenty of people, then I would be happy right now. You don't know a dammed thing about me," Brandon hollered with angry tears falling from his eyes, "If you knew the fucking truth about me, you'd be so happy to know that I'm miserable. Only Richard knows me at this point, and that's all I need. All I know is he better not tell you anything about my life right now."

Brandon turned to look at Richard, "We both know it won't help, anyway. I'm not even sure why I'm still alive."

"Brandon, don't say that." Richard calmly spoke. Brandon could see how heartbroken he was about everything that was said. He was sorry that his mother could do this at the worst time, but he had been close to the breaking point for far too long. Everything was tumbling down, and he had nowhere to go. No other shoulder that he could cry on would ease the pain. If this wasn't Brandon's rock bottom, he was close to it.

"What's going on with you?" Janet asked, annoyed.

"You won't care!" Brandon shouted.

"Brandon, just fucking tell me!"

"Why? I can't let you have anything else against me."

"I am your mother, and I have a right to know. You're a pathetic little bitch, and this isn't to use against you."

Brandon took a look at his brother and then at his mother again. His heart began pounding hard out of his chest, telling Janet was going to be ten times worse than Richard. Every part of his body wanted to abort the mission, but his heart longed for her support. Harold Andreas may not have gotten the chance to hear out his son's problems, but at least his mother will. Everything around Brandon began to disappear from his eyes, and his vision became blurry. That wasn't how he wanted his day to go, standing in front of his mother and deceased father telling his darkest burden.

"Shane..." Brandon tried to get out.

"Shane, what?" Janet rolled her eyes.

Brandon took one last look at Richard, and he gave Brandon a nod to proceed. He could tell that Richard was afraid for him, too. His heart pounded faster, and felt like throwing up all over the room. Part of him wanted to back out be the second person dead in the room than to tell Janet. He could only imagine what would come out of her mouth. For the second time in his life, Brandon allowed the sentence to come out: "Shane has been raping me..."

Janet looked at her son, who was breaking down in front of her. She could not believe what she had heard. She chose not to believe it at all.

Janet viewed her son as many things; weak, smart but a disgrace, a drama queen, and in that moment, a liar. "You are truly the living version of the boy who cried wolf, huh?"

Brandon's heart shattered more than he could have ever imagined. Janet didn't believe her own child. Hearing those words was like someone taking the sharpest knife that Janet could ever find in the world and stabbing his body all over. No matter how much physical pain that Shane had caused him could ever top it. Brandon looked at his brother, who had the meanest, and ugliest face he could ever give a human. His stomach turned, his hands were cramping and hurting. All of his childhood was officially a damn lie. Brandon had turned to see his dead father's body, just lying lifeless in the bed. He couldn't have imagined death being any worse than what he felt in that room. His mother had sucked all of the air out of his system, and it took forever for him to recover.

"You did not just say that," Brandon said in disbelief.

"You're such an attention whore making up such a ridiculous lie! A straight man, Brandon? Do you know how stupid you sound right now? The love of my life just died of brain cancer. You're so damn desperate to make this all about Brandon."

"All about me?" Brandon shouted.

"Was this your last attempt to try and make me love you again? I can't believe you'd do this. Richard, this is why I say you don't have to care for him anymore."

"Janet—" Richard started to defend his brother. He wanted to tell her off for good, but Brandon wasn't allowing him to fight his battle for him.

"You have shown true colors leading up to this point," Brandon said with tears that scrolled down his face, "I now know why blood doesn't mean a damn thing."

"Brandon—"

"Don't...Don't 'Brandon' me right now, Richard. I can handle her. I'm fighting my ass off every day to get to that finish line and graduate from CUNY Law or wherever I attend. I'm fighting, bleeding, screaming, almost selling my soul to get that degree. You don't believe me, Janet? Fine, fuck you, I don't need you. I'm not that fifteen-year-old scared for my life; I'm that twenty-two-year-old with grown-ass man problems, you wouldn't understand. If I'm going to Hell for my sexuality, then by the time I get there, you better already be in ashes with Harold. So after the funeral, never call me again. You are no longer my mother. I'm done."

With that, Brandon stormed out of the room, face full of tears down the hall. That was the last straw for him. Throughout everything he'd been through, it was officially broken. His personality, dignity, and self-love were all drained from his system. The first person to not believe him was Janet; his own mother chose not to care. He immediately started to question the funeral, whether or not he should go. His pride was telling him to skip it, and his heart wanted to have a sense of family still. Everything felt as if he was homeless.

Brandon got out his phone without thinking and called that familiar number that he'd known by heart, praying that the right version of him would be on the other end.

"Dude! I haven't heard from you in weeks! I've been worried." It was Shane. He had returned at last.

"I need you. Please, I need you so bad, Shane." Brandon begged through choked up tears.

"Brandon, are you okay? Where are you? What happened?" Shane was back to normal; it sounded like. Brandon was right; all they needed was a break apart to clear their heads.

"My father just died. I'm at the hospital; please come!" Brandon begged.

"I'm coming right now," Shane made it to the hospital in thirty minutes flat, and Brandon had gone down to the lobby to meet him. He didn't want his brother to find out at all. As soon as Shane came up to him all worried, Brandon fell into his arms, letting out the most heartbreaking sobs.

Chapter 18: Is He Back?

Brandon couldn't think anymore, and nor did he care. The man who he thought was his future was back in his body and had fought that monster away. People were walking by, glancing looks at them, but he couldn't have cared less. The way that Shane smelled, his hairstyle, just everything about his best friend, was terribly missed. If anything, Brandon had been mourning the loss of Shane way long before his father.

Brandon eventually calmed down and forced himself to step back from Shane. He needed to see him. See his eyes, dirty blonde hair, and all of his features once again. Brandon gestured over to an area in the lobby where a few seating areas were, and they went to sit there. Even though he was just in his arms, Brandon knew to keep a certain distance between them to feel safe. They were in public, but at that point, anything could happen.

"What happened?" Shane questioned.

"There wasn't anything that we could do anymore. His health just kept declining to the point beyond recovery. It's been hard." Brandon explained, still wiping his eyes. "I have Richard here as well, so I'm not totally alone."

"That's good that you aren't alone. You know you could've called me, man." Shane sighed, which made Brandon go completely silent. He didn't know what to say to that, considering that Shane never realized what he did to him.

"I didn't want to burden you with my family's stuff." Brandon lied

"I don't understand that, though. We live together, and we've always told each other everything. What's the true reason?" Shane questioned.

"We are not discussing that right now," Brandon sternly told him, "I don't know when or if we will ever. All I know is you have so much fucking explaining to do, Shane. Right now, I don't care because my dad is gone"

"I feel like you're not explaining your problem. Are you mad at me?" Shane asked.

"You really don't know what you did?" Brandon questioned back.

"I'm lost here…"

"Are you joking with me? Some kind of mind games you're playing with me?"

"I don't know what you're talking about, Brandon. What happened between us? I haven't even talked to you since before Christmas!"

"I need you…I need you back for good, Shane!"

"I never left!"

"You did!" Brandon shouted. He looked around to see many people had glanced at them and groaned. It seemed like people were staring at him everywhere he would go. Both men remained silent for some time, not making eye contact. Looking down at the floor, Brandon took a big sigh of exhaustion. He decided to keep the conversation about his father.

Brandon looked at him with tears in his eyes. "He died, not loving me. Harold thought that I couldn't wait for him to die even though I spent the last year helping him with everything. Why did he never realize that I—Why did he not love me anymore?"

"We always talk about this, Brandon. It isn't you at all; it's because he was scared. I think he appreciated it."

"He loved and appreciated Richard, not me." Brandon sighed.

"I think he just didn't know how to deal with it." Shane tried to reason why it would be that way.

"I'm done with my mom after the funeral. She's the absolute worst."

"I understand that; you came here from work?" Shane guessed as he noticed his work uniform.

"The first day back after the holidays was today."

"Oh, you had a nice amount of time off."

Brandon shrugged, "I guess I needed it. Richard coming home was a great help. I don't know what I'd do without him."

Shane smiled and placed a hand on Brandon's shoulder. He missed his busy best friend and hoped that they could hang out soon. There were quite a few things he wanted to catch up on, including his feelings. It wasn't like Shane didn't want to talk about them; he didn't know how. He had a desire that he wanted gone, but on the other hand, Shane wanted to rip his clothes off right there and screw Brandon in public without consequences.

"You'll get through it all, including law school. Alright?" Shane encouraged.

Brandon gave a half-smile, "Thanks, Shane."

His eyes eventually met with Brandon's, and they gradually leaned into each other. Before Brandon knew it, his lips were attached to Shane's in a slow kiss. All of the sparks had returned, the comfort was there, and the way Brandon felt about that oblivious man was back again. They kissed for a few seconds until Brandon pulled away slowly with a soft smile. It wasn't long before he realized what had happened, and he could feel a panic coming on.

"I'm…I'm going to go back up. Thank you for coming." Brandon told him shakily.

"What? I just got here, and I want to see Richard!"

"No!" Brandon shouted without realizing, "No, you know how he is about, uh…About letting others see him cry. I'll call you later."

"Why are you shaking Brandon? What's going on?" Shane questioned worriedly.

"I have to go!" Brandon explained briefly as he stood up, "Thank you for coming." With that, Brandon took off, trying to walk normally when in actuality, he was running away. His stomach was turning into knots with his heart speeding up to rapid paces. Even though the hospital was cold, he felt so hot and nauseous that he could throw up.

Shane raised an eyebrow as he saw Brandon runoff. He didn't understand what had happened. One minute Brandon was upset because of his dad, and then the next, there was arguing that led to a kiss. The cravings for that man were back in full force, which scared him. His mind desired to have Brandon naked under him again. Of course, Shane was concerned for Brandon but somewhere inside him said to disregard that and get his sexual needs taken care of by him. There had been an ongoing battle inside Shane's mind whether or not he should focus on their relationship more than the sex. Brandon made it seem as if they were falling apart, which he hated. All he needed was one conversation to get through his confusion, and Shane hadn't gotten his wish granted. There was a worry that he never would.

Brandon ran into the nearest bathroom, locking the door before darting to the toilet, trembling to the ground, barely missing it as he threw up. He let out the loudest sobs he could imagine, leaning his back against the cold wall.

They kissed. Somehow their lips met, and it felt nice. Brandon became so disgusted with himself all over again. All of his complaints wouldn't mean shit anymore if anybody ever found out.

"Who kisses their abuser? No one does that. Well, no one except me." Brandon bitterly thought out loud. He swore that the monster was all gone, though.

When he looked back up, he was met with another man standing in front of him, which made him startle.

"Are you okay?" Richard asked.

"Yeah, I just needed some air to calm down from her. I'm used to keeping it together, and hearing her not believing me was the final straw," Brandon explained to him. "You know that you don't have to end your relationship with her just because I am?"

"I lost all respect for Janet after what I heard in there. For her to not believe her son in desperate need is unacceptable. Honestly, I can't wait to get this funeral out of the way!" Richard groaned, "I'm so glad you let her have it. She deserved every word you said. Do not feel guilty."

"That is the last thing I feel about her. Tired is the simplest way to explain it right now. When it comes to everything she's put me through, I'm tired of it all."

"I understand," Richard nods, "Anything I can do?"

"You've done so much already. Stop that." Brandon mumbled, "Where is she?"

"I think she went into the bathroom. They were about to roll him away, and she couldn't bear to watch. Maybe I'm morbid for this, but I still don't care."

"We just have to get through two days. Cleaning up that house with her, and the wake and funeral. We can do this, right?" Brandon asked.

"I believe we can. As a matter of fact, we have no choice. As much as I hate it." Richard sighed.

"True, I would rather be at work doing other lawyers' work than to be here helping. At least we took care of the funeral arrangements already. Now, that's really morbid. We did it while he was still alive." Brandon exclaimed.

"I know, but she was already grieving him. For anybody, it's much worse when you know it's about to happen because you see them suffering. There's nothing that a person can do to…To make it better, then you just feel horrible watching them suffer. You just…" Richard sighed, looked away, and Brandon knew what was happening. He wrapped his arms around him and led them to a seating area nearby. Richard had finally allowed himself to cry about everything that was happening, and Brandon was glad he could be there for it to return all of the comforts he had received from him.

Richard let out a hard cry that Brandon had only heard from himself. It was as if a dark cloud appeared over his brother's head like a curse making him cry. He was breaking heavily in his arms. It was more like hitched breaths that could only have been from an emotional shock. It was hard for Brandon to not cry along with him. He needed to be strong for Richard in that moment. For Richard, the denial was finally becoming real. He was gone. His father was gone; no matter how horrible he was to Brandon, he couldn't believe it. He refused to accept that his father died from brain cancer.

The bittersweet memories and sadness engulfed his soul. As a child, his father had loved him, but not since he found out who he was. How can he cry for someone who despised him, hated all that he stood for? What good would that do for him? He held his brother tight in his arms, letting him cry it out no matter how long he needed. Looks were being sent their way from time to time, but Brandon tried to ignore them. Neither of them seemed to care. Richard finally looked up with red eyes that killed Brandon's heart.

"I shouldn't be crying like this. It's unfair to you after what he put you through and—" Richard started to say.

"Richard, stop that now. This is what I expect you to do. No matter how bad he was to me, Harold is still our father. I get it because I didn't want to cry either. Just want to say fuck it and just be so hardcore about this, but we can't," Brandon sighed, "We are obligated to love them. You know I'm close to crying at a simple gesture of a middle finger sent my way by a stranger on the highway. Do not feel bad crying in front of me."

"You're going through so much more than this, though."

"So what?" Brandon shook his head, "I'm a grown man who should suck it up. I'm too afraid to tell anyone else. Doesn't that mean I somehow must like getting raped?"

"Don't say that!"

"Exactly my point. It's not the truth about me as much as the voice in my head says it is, and it's the same for you. Maybe I am carrying triple the weight than you are, if not more, since he died not loving me. That doesn't mean you talk your pain down. I need you to be as authentic with me as I am with you. Okay?"

Richard sighed, looking up at his younger brother nodding his head. "Alright," he looked around for the box of tissues on the end table next to them, wiping his face, and Brandon did the same.

"We're going to go get her, take her home and stay with her, then clean up the master bedroom with her. We can do this, okay?" Brandon calmly spoke to him.

"Okay," Richard echoed as he calmed down as much as he could. They went back to their mom and checked on her. They managed to get Janet to leave the hospital for the night.

The next couple of days seemed like they flew by. Richard and Brandon were helping out with everything they possibly could around the house. The smells of Harold were still all over the master bedroom and the rest of the house. Janet hadn't shed a tear ever since they left that hospital room, and it was making them concerned. She was still acting so cold to Brandon as usual, and he had to let it happen. There wasn't anything left to say to her anyway. The wake was a couple of days away, with the funeral following right after. Brandon walked back into the bedroom after taking out the third bag of trash, seeing them on the floor with a box of photos.

"The room is cleared up, and she wants to go through pictures," Richard informed him. Brandon sat down on the floor by Richard as they started to go through the boxes. There were pictures of them growing up together. He and Richard did everything together just about. They were taught to always be there for each other no matter what. Maybe that was why Richard was angry at their parents the most. Neither practiced what they preached as they got older. There were birthday photos, family vacations, and yearly school pictures. Brandon came across one specific photo that surprised him.

"Mom, you kept this one?" Brandon asked, surprised. It was a photo of him and Shane after school studying. His mom had taken the picture without them knowing and showed him after Shane left the house.

"Yeah, you can take it. I don't care," Janet replied flatly.

Richard looked at the picture and sighed, "I don't know if that's a good idea, man."

"Why? I should give up my lie like mom said and make up with Shane."

"You really want to go there right now?" Richard warned in a quiet mumble, and Brandon just continued to glare at him.

"I fucking hate you," Brandon mouthed to him and rolled his eyes. They continued to search through the photos, actually smiling at some of the memories. Brandon had to admit that he even loved his childhood before coming out, but that was what made it so hard. All of the smiling faces as a child with his parents. Him playing basketball and baseball with his father cheering him on. Was his father's love ever real, or was it all conditional? Everything Brandon would do was to please them both. To get those happy smiles and praises that every kid yearned for.

"Either cut yourself out the pictures or take them," Janet ordered Brandon.

"You're kidding me, right?" Brandon looked at her with disgust.

"You can't stay nice for a damn day?" Richard angrily asked.

"Why the hell are you always by his side anyway?" Janet glared at him, "I know you're the good son, but we gave you permission to hate him as well."

"Do you not realize that he's the one doing the most for your ignorant ass?" Richard shouted, "I don't think you realize, but I wouldn't have done half the shit he did for you two. I'm selfish."

"Richard..." Brandon warned.

"The reason why your husband was able to stay alive from July to January was that Brandon was the caretaker. Where's that nurse you hired? Paid the bitch the other day and haven't heard from her since." Richard then laughed sarcastically, "Karma served his ass exactly what he deserved."

"Richard!" Brandon shouted in shock, "You're going too far right now. Even if you're completely right, this is not the time."

"We did the best we could with both of you. This is the appreciation I get?" Janet yelled back, "Your brother is awful doing what he does. It goes against humanity!"

"I'm just going to say it. For all you know, I could be way worse than him." Richard shrugged

"Wait; what?" Brandon questioned. "Tell me you're not on drugs?"

"What—No!" Richard rolled his eyes. "I'm ignoring you. All you need to know is that I have done worse shit. You would be devastated."

"It's against the Bible!" Janet exclaimed.

"Not going to Church is against it as well, but you haven't been in five years." Richard was used to shutting her down, especially when it came to religion. Brandon just shook his head as he continued to look through the photos. He picked out a couple of recent pictures that could be used for the funeral portrait setting them aside. Everyone stayed quiet after Richard had won the argument again. Once they were finally all done looking through pictures and cleaning, the two brothers left the house. They had to get suits for the funeral, and it was the perfect time to get away from her.

"I'm so sick of her!" Brandon exclaimed as they drove down the street.

"I know, only a few days away." Richard reminded him.

"Luckily, it's all in one day," Brandon nodded his head, "I'm going to work right after."

"What? Brandon, you deserve a break."

"I don't care, Richard. What the hell would I do? I'm not interacting with any family afterward, and I'd feel useless doing nothing but that funeral. You can't change my mind." Brandon told him.

"Fine, I understand. You're used to it, anyways."

"Yep, I did college, took care of dad, and went to work all in one day. Then I'd go home, do my homework, eat, and go to sleep. Only now there's no more him, I need a new place to live, and I have no best friend." Brandon sighed.

"You have me…" Richard comforted.

"Thank you," Brandon commented, "Really, I appreciate it, but it's not the same, and you know that."

"I do understand what you mean. Let's get these suits, and we can go do something to relax, alright?"

"I like the sound of that." Brandon agreed as they arrived at the shop.

Chapter 19: The Funeral

It was the day of the wake and funeral, and Brandon was in the shower getting ready. He sighed and leaned on the shower wall as he thought about all he had to do. All of his friends flew in to support him, including Madelyn. He just hoped that she hadn't called Shane because he was the last person who needed to show up. Whether it was the rapist or his best friend, it didn't matter; it wouldn't go well. He also realized that he needed to tell Madelyn the truth. If Shane started to do the same to her, then it'd be all his fault. How many times would he have to tell this story? Telling Richard was shameful enough for him.

Brandon got out of the shower, still feeling the hands of Shane all over. No matter how long ago that the last incident had happened, his body always felt like he had just grabbed him, restraining him on that bed. The tears in his eyes desperately wanted to roll down his face while his mouth needed to let out sobs. To make matters more hectic, he still had work afterward, and he couldn't ruin his suit. His boss even offered him a paid day off instead of just coming in, but he turned it down respectfully. Well, he turned down, taking the day off, but he still wanted the money. It didn't look like Brandon was going to get a real break anytime soon. After the day was over, he would start making a new budget to get a new apartment. Of course, he didn't want to move, but he had to in order to be safe from Shane. How he hated to come to terms with a sentence, he never imagined he'd say. He had to move away from his best friend to feel safe again.

Brandon put his suit on and searched Richard in his old room and hugged him. "Good morning."

"Morning," Richard sighed, "How'd you sleep?"

"Awful because of the nightmare. I woke up in the middle of the night to throw up again because Shane chased me in my nightmare. Everything's getting worse; it seems like," Brandon sighed and sat on the bed, "Also, all of my friends will ask where he is, especially Madelyn!"

"I say you have to tell her first, Brandon. She needs to get away from him," Richard rubbed his back, "No one is going to hate you. If anything, they'll all hate him and defend you as they always have. I'm not leaving your side today so that you won't be alone. You know, I'm dreading having to see the family."

"We still call it 'family'?" Brandon asked with sarcasm.

"Barely," Richard rolled his eyes as he finished putting his suit on. The two brothers helped straighten each others' ties before looking at the mirror. "I'm serious about never seeing Janet again after this."

"I am so done with her after today. Expecting her to care about me when I told her was my last big mistake with her. I've already packed whatever little belongings I had here, and I'm going to a hotel close to my college." Brandon sighed, "It's one of the hotels where you can pay weekly. Not ideal, but it will do."

"Why not apply to Concord University in California, or Abraham Lincoln University as well? Both have higher rankings and ratings." Richard suggested.

"I was going to apply to those, too. Moving is going to cost, so I might as well consider it? I just really want CUNY." Brandon explained while looking in the mirror.

"I say follow your heart unless it leads to him."

"I'm trying," Brandon mumbled. It wasn't long before a lot of people were arriving at the funeral home. He and his mother and brother decided not to have the funeral cars and to drive themselves. This worked out best for Brandon having work afterward. Once he had arrived, there was already a parking lot full of cars. He saw many familiar faces going into the building as he got out of the car. Brandon was greeted with judgmental looks from his relatives as he expected while going to Janet, who was by the open casket.

"I can't believe how peaceful he looks." Janet sighed through her tears.

"They did an excellent job," Brandon spoke softly, "I mean, it isn't exactly like he was but very close to it."

"I have to admit that it's surprisingly good," Richard agreed as he walked up to them. There Harold Andreas laid in that casket looking lifeless with his eyes closed, unable to open them ever again. Harold was being buried in his favorite suit that he loved to wear to events along with pictures of his wedding, two sons, his own parents, and some best friends. A picture-perfect family. That's what they had to pretend to be in front of all his parents' friends, and Brandon hated it.

"My brain keeps replaying his last breath. It sounded really strained."

"I can't believe I'm saying this, but that moment was so beautiful," Janet recalled, and they looked at her like she was crazy. "Oh, you two are fucking stupid, it was! There's nothing morbid about what I said."

"I just find it weird to call it beautiful." Brandon shrugged.

"Yet, you think your lifestyle is beautiful?" Janet had to take a hit at him. For some reason, she couldn't resist the urge to insult her unloved son. Richard and Brandon just walked away to avoid any arguments.

"She has to be the devil." Brandon bitterly mumbled to himself. He went to get a drink as more people started to arrive, looking around. Some people made it through the crowd, and he recognized them, trying not to burst into tears. Xavier, Tori, Madelyn, and Zach were walking towards him, and he panicked. Richard was on the other side of the room, talking to friends, not paying attention. He promised to always be by him. To not leave him alone when it was time.

"Hey…" Madelyn was the first one to greet and hug him. All of the guilt feelings just bottled up inside him, but he struggled to hold back the tears.

"Hey guys," Brandon greeted, not making eye contact with Madelyn, "I really appreciate you coming and flying in."

"We do this for each other; you know that," Tori told him as she hugged him last.

"I know," Brandon sighed and looked at Zach, "Oh, this is my college friend Zach, we met last semester, and he's studying the same thing. Zach, these are my high school friends Madelyn, Tori, and Xavier." They all adequately greeted each other and said hello.

"How have you been through all of this?" Zach asked him.

"I survived, I'll say that." Brandon answered, "I think I have…"

"Where's Shane? I thought he'd be here?" Xavier questioned, and Brandon's body started to feel weak just from hearing the name.

Just then, his brother walked up to them. "Did somebody ask about the whore?"

"Richard!" Brandon groaned, "Can I at least start explaining before the name-calling?" All of his friends looked at them, confused, wondering what was going on.

"Name-calling? I thought that was his new name." Richard shrugged and saw Brandon's glare. He then sighed. "Fine."

"Shane isn't coming because I refused to let him," Brandon started.

"Why?" Madelyn asked in a concerned tone.

"I don't know who he is anymore…" Brandon let tears fall from his eyes, "I…I haven't been safe with him for so long. Not since Madelyn went back to California in November."

"What happened?" Tori questioned cautiously.

"I guess I'll start from the beginning…" Brandon sighed as he told the full story for the second time in his life. Explaining every detail from the first time he asked, to the whole deal with Madelyn and every traumatic experience after she left. Everyone had surprised and devastated looks as he told the entire truth. He had to hold onto Richard as he began to sob between each sentence. It was getting harder to look at any of them in the face, afraid of laughter and judgment that could come his way. They made sure that nobody else in the room could hear him as they'd pause now and then when people walk by. Once he finished, Brandon was embraced in a group hug with all of his friends.

His true friends.

"I don't know what to say, Brandon," Madelyn choked through tears.

"I'm so sorry, Madelyn. I've been such an idiot." Brandon sobbed, "I should've told you what—"

"Stop…You don't need to apologize for anything." Madelyn soothed, "I don't care about him or that you were jealous about it. You don't deserve this, Brandon."

"I want to murder him," Xavier mumbled.

"Xavier…" Tori tried to say.

"No! He's a real damn fool. He didn't even ask if you were hurting?" Xavier exclaimed, "Fuck that! He needs to die. Richard is right; he's no longer Shane; his name is now Whore. Oblivious Whore."

"He's so sick," Zach shook his head.

"I used to think 'why would anyone stay so long with their abuser,' you know? Why wouldn't they leave?" Brandon then laughed sarcastically, "I completely understand now because I'm right there in that perspective. You think they'll change back and realize how they hurt you. That he will swear never to do it again, and you two work it out. I'm still there...In the back of my mind, I'm still hoping that. Then I sarcastically laugh because I'm such an idiot. I don't deserve any better or to be saved because clearly in my heart, I still want to stay!"

"You want to stay? Why?" Madelyn asked.

"I still believe he can come back, and we can work it out," Brandon mumbled.

"Absolutely not. Even if he does change, you are not staying with him. We are all losing all contact with him." Madelyn told him, to which Xavier and Tori nodded their heads in agreement, "It felt so weird not texting him that I was coming, but something inside of me said I shouldn't."

"Richard, how long until the funeral begins?" Brandon asked.

"Another ten minutes." Richard guessed, looking at his watch.

"I need a minute with them, please. Thank you," Brandon requested, and Richard nodded, walking away. He needed to tell them about the hospital, but he didn't know how Richard would react. "There's a little more to the story that Richard can't know just yet. Please don't say anything? At least not until I understand myself."

"We promise," Everyone agreed, and Brandon told what happened in the hospital. How Shane seemed back to normal and didn't know what Brandon was referring to. Every word felt like vomit coming out of his mouth. He still felt Shane's lips on his and how warm they felt on his. As if Shane was standing behind him, Brandon had to take a look behind him every few seconds for precaution. More of his secrets were revealed, and it felt like he was butt-naked to them. There still wasn't a clear explanation as to why Shane was the first person to call. He could've picked Daniel or one of his other bosses, but no, it had to be Shane.

"I still don't know what happened. Is Shane back? Does he really not understand, or is he playing games with me?" Brandon sobbed, "How could I have kissed him?"

"I don't want you to beat yourself up because of it, Brandon." Xavier comforted.

"I'm such an idiot, though!" Brandon cried, "I still feel so sick from it. That's why I know I don't deserve to get saved from this situation. Just let me rot in this hell."

"Listen to me," Tori stated, "As much as you hated it afterward, know that you didn't necessarily do anything unexpected. That was a normal instinct."

"He's right; you had no one else that could come to you. More importantly, you have this connection with him that you just can't get rid of easily. After the rape, the human connection is as strong as sex. Believe it or not, it's a similar connection." Zach went on to explain.

"Oh great, now I'm stuck forever because of that." Brandon gave a sarcastic laugh.

"Untrue because you caught that early. You're in deep, but you can stop it before that's your addiction." Madelyn added.

Soon after, everyone went into the chapel as the funeral began. It wasn't any different from a regular funeral. There were scriptures, beautiful music, and going to the cemetery. Brandon then headed straight to work as planned, despite his brother and friends insisting him not to. His father wouldn't have stopped working if the roles were changed, and it was him in that casket.

Why would he do any different for him?

Chapter 20: Moving On From You

This was it for Brandon. Mr. Andreas had checked into his extended stay hotel room and had moved all of his belongings he brought from his mom's. He had said goodbye to Richard, who had to get back on the plane to California for his job a week after the funeral. All of his friends had to fly back as well but promised to keep checking on him. Madelyn informed Brandon that she sent a breakup text to Shane and that she was disgusted with him. She told him that it was all of Shane's fault and she couldn't trust him. Afterward, she blocked his number. Zach tried to convince him to move in with him instead, but he politely declined. Brandon knew it wouldn't be fair to his boyfriend, Jason. However, Zach had a funny look on his face when he said his name. Brandon just figured not to ask any questions about it.

Brandon sat on his new temporary bed and sighed. Work wasn't so bad when he went after the funeral. There were many things that he had to do, but he got everything done. His boss was impressed with him so much that she gave him a raise. Brandon needed that in this time of getting his life back in order. He was shy of his twenty-third birthday and already wishing for a rewind button. Was this it for him and Shane? Part of him didn't want it to be; maybe it could still be a way to mend everything despite what everyone tells him. He knew it was all foolish talk at this point, but something kept telling him to give one more chance.

Like every past beginning of a college semester, Brandon would get his materials needed for classes. Coming up was the most important semester of his undergraduate years. He had worked so hard over the years, and now he was hoping that everything would be worth it by the time he would graduate in May. Graduation wasn't what he was looking forward to; it was the opportunity for an actual break. Two full months to do nothing except getting his life back to the way it was. Well, it was

more like getting used to a whole new normal. Whatever that may lead
to. He was over everything at that point. One more blow, and Brandon
felt like he would die. After disinfecting everything, he took a shower,
trying to relax. There was no hope in getting rid of the feels of Shane's
lingering grasps off his body. He came into the acceptance to never feel
completely clean for the rest of his life. He felt like crying, screaming,
and sobbing nonstop, yet what would be the point? The best thing he
thought to do was try to move on. After getting dressed, Brandon
collected his items and headed out for the day.

"I'm running errands today; meet up on campus?" Brandon texted Zach.

"Yes, definitely. I'm heading out now." Zach replied. That brought a tiny
smile to Brandon's face. He no longer had to hide his feelings from him.
They'd been texting nonstop since the funeral, both about Shane as well
as other things. It was great to have a friend in Brandon's life again finally.
He'd just have a hard time learning to trust again.

He arrived at the campus in no time, parking his car. Once he got
out, Zach walked up and hugged him. It felt great to have a safe touch
from a man again. At times he would tense up even from a hand grab,
and other times he would be completely fine. That happened with
Richard, Zach, even his co-workers, and he couldn't explain why it was
like that.

"Good morning Brandon. How are you today?" Zach asked in the
hug.

"I finally got out of my mom's house, so that's progress, I suppose.
The hotel is pretty nice and cheap, so I'm able to work on my savings. I
appreciate you coming on Monday." Brandon responded.

"Of course. I wouldn't have been anywhere else except supporting
you."

"I would do the same for you." Brandon smiled. They went inside
the student center, making their way to the bookstore. On the way, they
were stopped by other classmates from the last semester greeting them
with hugs.

"Hey, Stacey and Lewis!" Zach greeted them, "How was your
break?"

"So relaxing and needed. It was great to see my family." Lewis
smiled.

"Same here. I did nothing until Christmas and went over to my relatives. Always good to see family, you know?" Stacey expressed happily. Everyone seemed to agree. Everyone except Brandon, who stayed quiet. "Not you, Brandon?"

"Not really," Brandon mumbled, "My father died over the break, and his funeral was this past Monday."

"Oh my God, I'm so sorry." Lewis sounded shocked.

"That's terrible," Stacey expressed, giving him another hug.

"Are you serious? I'm so relieved right now." Brandon answered, honestly. That made everyone stare at him, confused, and Brandon understood why. It isn't something people would expect someone to say.

"Wait, huh?" Zach asked.

"I don't get that, not at all," Lewis stated.

"Brandon, that sounds morbid..." Stacey commented.

"Doesn't it?" Brandon sighed, "Yet it's true. I never understood it either until it happened to me. No, you don't realize how much stress, anxiety, and pressure you're under until after you're done being a caretaker. You're just sitting and thinking like: 'This is my reward for all of my hard work?' It's crazy, I know."

"No, it makes sense now that you've explained it. Now you have this free time that you didn't before." Lewis nodded his head.

"Free time to remember my regrets?" Brandon mumbled, looking down.

"Do not regret anything; you needed to find out." Zach placed a hand on Brandon's shoulder, and they made eye contact in a way that Brandon felt like only the two of them understood.

"Maybe I never needed or wanted to find out." Brandon hinted subtly.

"I can tell you right now that you needed to find out," Zach affirmed to him. Lewis and Stacey just looked at them with confusion. Brandon knew that they wanted to know what he and Zach were referring to, but he knew if he had to tell the story one more time, he would vomit.

"Can we not talk about this here?" Brandon asked Zach politely.

Brandon looked at Zach, and he could tell that he had forgotten that other people were around them and felt ashamed. "That's right, I'm sorry."

"We take it that we can't know what's going on here, and I understand completely. I'm going to work right now, anyway. See you guys in class in a few weeks." Stacey told them as she left the conversation after everyone said goodbye to her.

"Are you guys headed to the computer lab? I'm about to look up information to study for the admissions test!" Lewis excitedly spoke, trying to change to an enlightened conversation.

"I think we are after we get the textbooks!" Zach grinned.

"Let's go, guys," Brandon replied with his forced smile. All three men decided to go to the computer lab first to figure out what textbooks were required. They found three computers next to each other and signed in using their school IDs.

"How are you feeling?"

"I think I'm good," Brandon sighed. He could tell that Zach knew he was lying. They weren't in the right place to discuss anything that had happened. It was also unsettling to think that Shane could show up at any second. He wasn't ready to face him. Chills took over his entire system with the thoughts of that happening. Part of him still longed to be next to him, and the other just needed him gone for him to breathe.

Brandon took his time to search the web. He didn't have his laptop with him, and there were many emails to sort out. It took twenty minutes for him to get through every one. He then went to search for something on Google, and an article caught his attention. It happened to be about a court case that occurred before the new year. A woman was in a trial to prove that her co-worker sexually assaulted her for many years. Brandon's heart sunk but continued to read on. There was plenty of evidence both parties had given to the court. In the end, the defendant was set free.

Brandon immediately opened up a second tab in the browser to look up the case. His hands began to cramp up, and his fingers typed at the speed of lightning. Sweat began to pour down his face, and his breathing got heavier. It couldn't be right. There had to have been information that the judge or jury overlooked. Brandon didn't want to accept the truth as if it were his case. Zach noticed that Brandon was looking with such worry. He couldn't tell what he had on his computer screen, but it concerned him to see Brandon in a frantic rush.

"Brandon, are you okay?" Zach asked.

"I'm fine," Brandon snapped his head around in an instant and gave his friends a discreet smile. A smile that caused unsettling chills to go through both Zach's and Lewis' spines like a lightning bolt.

Zach could tell that something wasn't right by that response or smile. However, he was clueless about what to do. He knew that Brandon had to be breaking on the inside. Brandon's eyes were almost like a different color than before. Zach could tell that Brandon hasn't had any quality sleep all break, and it made him feel awful. By the way that Brandon's body shook, he knew that Brandon was about to run away. Something had triggered him. Once he got up to look at his screen, it all made sense.

"Brandon, this won't happen to you." Zach tried to talk in an unalarmed tone.

"You don't know that," Brandon said audibly.

Lewis turned to look at the two in concern, "Is everything okay?"

"This is why I can't report, Zach! I'd be the joke of the town." Brandon whined in fear.

"I promise never to let that happen to you. Brandon, I need you to relax," Zach worried.

Zach tried everything that he could to avoid Brandon from having a panic attack. He told him to try to breathe, think about something else, and nothing was working. Brandon's body tensed up worse, unable to hear anything from Zach or Lewis.

"What do we do?" Lewis asked as he tried to help, "His heart rate is up to one hundred and ten beats per minute."

"Deep breaths, Brandon. Think about something calm," Zach tried to tell him. However, Brandon was too far gone.

The two of them tried everything they could to get Brandon to relax. People started to overhear the conversation and looked in their direction. Zach looked directly into his eyes that were registering fear and anxiety. They were losing Brandon, and it only made Zach furious at Shane.

Brandon ran out of the room without warning and ran to the nearest men's restroom going in one of the stalls. Lewis and Zach chased behind him without caring who they knocked down. Their friend's health was more important.

"Stay out here; I'll go with him," Zach told Lewis.

"Okay," Lewis agreed. Lewis held all of their belongings outside of the door.

The sobbing noises that came from his body as he threw up were awful. Zach ran inside of the stall behind Brandon and locked the door. He held Brandon's head so that he wouldn't accidentally bang his head on anything. He felt awful yet angry that his friend had to go through something so traumatic. Zach wanted to take away all of the stress, hurt, anxiety, and guilt that Brandon was holding in his body. Nothing was fair about it.

"Let it out, Brandon. It's okay; I'm not letting you go. I'm never letting you go," Zach whispered in his ear.

He didn't know how long that he sat on the floor before another man walked in, sighing.

"Here goes another semester." The male cried out, and Brandon froze in Zach's embrace. It was Shane. His footsteps made squeaky noises as he went to the stall next to him. Brandon could hear his pants fall down, the belt jiggling being undone, and him peeing in the toilet. He just sat there on the floor, hoping Shane wouldn't hear him. Brandon's heart sped up again, and Zach had to grab his attention. As Brandon looked into Zach's eyes, Brandon felt a sense of comfort like Shane couldn't get to him. His body still shook in fear as he paid close attention to Shane's every move. Nothing was scarier than the possibility of being caught. It seemed like Shane was in the bathroom for over an hour before he heard him finally leave. He let out a sigh of relief, glad that nobody saw or heard them.

"Are you okay?" Zach asked him.

"That was so close, but I think so. I'm sorry for scaring you," Brandon apologized.

"I think you need to report, Brandon. He can't get away with what he did."

"I'm too scared to!"

"Please, trust me that it'll be for the best."

"Zach—"

"I can't let him get away with this."

"I understand that, but I'm going to end up just like that case online!"

"I promise you won't."

"You don't know that!"

"We're going to be lawyers ourselves. All this will do is start our law school journey a little earlier."

Brandon still had fear in his eyes, but he knew that Zach was right. One day, he needed to say that he at least tried to get justice for his own case in the courthouse. They both knew that it was a long journey ahead that required real commitment, no matter the outcome.

Brandon then got up, flushed the toilet, and went to wash his hands. Before leaving the bathroom, he made sure Shane wasn't around then went back to Lewis.

"Are you okay?" Lewis asked, concerned.

"I think so, yeah," Brandon sighed, "I am sorry for scaring you guys."

"No, it's alright. Do you still want to go get the books today?" Lewis asked.

"Yeah, let's go." Brandon nodded his head. He got his books with his two friends, and then he and Zach went back to his temporary home. Zach looked around the place before sitting at the small dining table with him, "You like it?"

"I still don't understand why you won't just move in with me." Zach insisted again.

"I appreciate the offer, but you've done enough for me. I promise I'll be okay. Like I've said, I can't mooch off of you and your boyfriend." Brandon explained, and he noticed how Zach uncomfortably shifted in his chair. "What's wrong?"

Zach sighed, looking down at his hands, "Nothing, but you wouldn't have to worry about him."

"What do you mean?" Brandon cautiously questioned.

"We broke up right before the holiday. We were arguing so much," Zach paused and tried not to get emotional, "Our situation hadn't been good. He moved out and back in with his parents, and that's that. It's over."

"Zach, I'm so sorry that's awful." Brandon hugged him.

"No, it's not; it's for the best. Jason wasn't the one for me. I'll be okay, I have a busy semester that I must focus on as it is important, and a great friend to go through this with," Zach half smiled, "I will get through it."

Brandon went around to the other side of the table next to Zach. He pulled him into a warm embrace letting his friend cry into his chest. Everyone had been, so understanding letting him have his moments when he needed it. It was now time to return the favor.

Chapter 21: Pleasure For His Body

Brandon was a few days into his new temporary apartment, and he was still getting used to it. There was nowhere else to call home; to claim as his safety. Where he used to reside was no longer an option, but he still had belongings at that location. Part of him wanted to let go of it all; another part regretted that he didn't get Richard or his friends to help him retrieve all of his things. The funeral and witnessing the death had taken up his remaining time with his brother. Not only that but telling people puts them in danger of Shane. Especially Zach, since he lived in the same city.

He had the day off from work so he could take his time getting his items. Brandon started his car, heading down the streets. He had moving boxes with him, just enough for him to get everything he needed. Whatever he didn't get that day, he told himself he would have to part with it. To try to relax on the way there, he turned on the radio. It was on a commercial break, but he didn't mind as it was his favorite radio station. Everyone in the world seemed to be so happy around him, even with it still being so freezing cold outside. He missed that feeling of the joys of wintertime. It was as if someone took it all away from his heart and soul, and now he could only feel the heaviness of his despair. Brandon's body tensed up the closer he got to the apartment building. He was praying that he remembered Shane's work hours and that he'd be gone. However, there was also the hope that the old Shane was still there, and maybe they could talk. This was all just wishful thinking.

His heart sank into his stomach once he parked his car in his usual spot that was no longer going to be his. With his pounding heartbeat and wriggling fingers, he got out of the vehicle with a couple of boxes, making his way into the apartment. Everything had Shane's scent in it. The couch, kitchen, even the table, and chairs. Brandon sighed, looking at the messy kitchen and living room. It was always his job to keep it all clean. Without him seemed like a hurricane came through. He made his way into his bedroom, setting the boxes on the bed.

"This is ridiculous," Brandon mumbled to himself quietly. His official move out date had finally come. He started with the bathroom, getting everything he needed from the medicine cabinet and bathtub. Flashbacks came to him, hitting hard while he moved around carefully. His bed where it all went down the first time; the confusion that Shane left him with was brutally returning to his mind. He moved quicker to go through the drawers packing as many items as he could. He found small baggies to put little things in, throwing them into the boxes. Since he was feeling paranoid, Brandon would often check his surroundings to make sure nobody was there. When his phone rang, it startled him before realizing what the sound was. The caller ID showed Shane's number making him almost throw up. Without even thinking about it, he thumb pressed the answer button.

"Hey, I'm on break just wanted to check on you." Once again, it was Shane on the phone, making his heart melt.

"Hey," Brandon greeted nervously, "Thanks, I'm just trying to get my stuff back in order, man. It's so hard."

"Anything that I can do?" Shane asked.

"We need to have a conversation. Will you be at home at your usual time tonight?" Brandon was beating himself up as he was talking. He knew better than to agree to sit down with him alone. Staying away is what he had to do, but it was his heart that made it hard to commit to.

"Yeah, I will."

"I'll see you then," Brandon confirmed.

"Okay," Shane replied before they hung up. No matter what happened, Brandon had to promise himself not to stay afterward, as it was still unsafe for him. He finished up the remaining items and took the boxes back to his car. Once he got back to the hotel room, he brought his things inside, trying to get settled. Brandon had also stopped to get groceries from the store to start him off. There were only two things to focus on: talking to Shane later that evening and getting ready for the new semester starting the following week. This was going to be the last easy semester of his community college career, making him nervous.

Was he going to do well? Would he be able to keep his grades up like he did last semester? Brandon knew that he did so well due to trying to distract himself from the serious issues he had to face, and still had to in a sense. He didn't know what meeting with Shane would do to him. The kiss seemed too promising the last time, but that was because he was in a weaker place. Maybe at the lowest that he'd been in his whole life. All he knew was that he needed to relax before then. In a way, Brandon was trying to heal. It was too embarrassing to go to any therapist because his situation was too out of the ordinary. What would he tell them?

He turned on the TV, trying to find a show that could distract him for the time being. Brandon landed on a movie to watch and relaxed. He also decided to text Zach what he was going to do just in case something went wrong.

"*What? Have you lost your mind?*" Brandon could sense Zach yelling at him through the text message.

"*Something inside of me has to hear him out, Zach,*" Brandon sighed, texting back.

"*Brandon, he has nothing valuable to say! If anything, you should be trying to get a restraining order against him.*"

Brandon's heart dropped, reading the last text from Zach. Even though he was right, it was unexplainable as to why he wanted to go. This could easily be a conversation through the phone, if anything. His problem was that he had already told Shane that they would meet up in person. To make it more complicated, Brandon was a man of his words and always committed to everything he was going to do. Going to see Shane wasn't going to be any different.

Seeing that he still had the full day ahead and had nothing planned, Brandon got a pen and paper. He wrote down all that he needed to say to Shane. How he felt, why he felt that way, and the only possible way they could be friends. All of it seemed ridiculous to him. Did he really think Shane was going to listen to him or understand him? Brandon started to cry as he wrote the list. There was so much to try to put into words. The worst part was that Brandon would most likely have to read it to him.

"I shouldn't have to do this." Brandon cried out to himself. He paced around the room as he thought about what to say. He eventually got tired after a full page worth of things to say. Brandon took a picture sending it to Zach, asking for his opinion.

"I'm still completely against this plan. At least let me come with you. I don't want to lose you, and you're scaring me." Zach sent in another text.

Brandon thought for a minute before replying. *"If I go and don't text back in five minutes that we're talking, please come. Is that better?"*

"I shouldn't agree to this, but know that I'm going to be pulling up right behind you," Zach replied.

"You don't know how much I appreciate you. I'm just afraid of you getting hurt, as well."

"You can get seriously hurt if not killed. What time are you going?"

"Six-thirty, He usually gets home at six."

"Do you need anything before then?"

"No, I have everything that I need. Thank you very much." Brandon appreciated how much Zach cared for him. As he waited, he decided to take another shower to try to feel clean. He was hoping that talking with Shane would get the horrible sensation of having his grip free from him. Memories flooded his mind of when they first began college, how they were so thrilled to get away from their parents' houses and having to abide by their rules. It was like Brandon became a free man the day he moved away from his folks. Brandon didn't bother to visit them on holidays. In fact, he hardly talked to them. The previous year brought so much trauma to his life, and he thought that his best friend would be his safety net once it was all over.

That was what he wanted to get out of this. Brandon didn't want a relationship with him, but the safety net that was previously always there to catch him. Brandon never wanted to see Shane naked ever again. He didn't want to be his boyfriend or have a fairytale ending with him, only his very best friend. Was that too much to ask for? He didn't think so. It was easy for him to reminisce about them being in high school together; how they'd always skip study hall to waste time and relax. Of course, being the nerd that Brandon was, he'd sometimes make Shane go to class. Those were the days he wanted back. Where he'd be jealous over Madelyn having his full attention and then going to Richard to complain, at lunchtime, she and Shane would be all cuddled up together as they ate. Brandon would get so jealous about it all over again each day but never said anything. That was when he decided to get a first boyfriend, and well, that just brought him heartache. Obviously, he still had Xavier and Tori to talk to about it, but he didn't want to annoy them.

Once the time passed by, Brandon got his things and headed back to the apartment. Zach was already in the parking lot, and Brandon went over to his car and got in.

"This is the last chance I have to convince you not to go in there, Brandon!" Zach begged.

"I have to, Zach. I need closure at the very least." Brandon sighed.

"I know we're gay, and this is going to sound very sexist, but what are you, a woman? Closure? Shane isn't about to give you that." Zach told him.

"I have to try!" Brandon defended himself.

"Fine," Zach gave up even though he knew he shouldn't have, "Give me your phone first."

"Huh?"

"Give me your phone, Brandon and unlock it," Zach demanded. After Brandon did as he was told, Zach went to get all the information he could use later on. From phone logs, texts, and emails from the past few months, Zach put his lawyer-brain on getting all evidence. After he finished, the phone was back in Brandon's possession.

"If something goes wrong and you have time, 9-1-1 is on the emergency speed dial. You know, just hit the lock button repeatedly, and they'll be called. If they come, I'll know you're in danger," Zach informed, "I'm calling in five minutes anyway, but if you can call too, then the more, the merrier."

"Thank you," Brandon hugged him, "I don't know what I'd do without you. It looked like you were doing more, though?"

"I will explain that later."

"Well, his car is right there. I don't know what's going to happen, but …" Brandon let out a shaky sigh, "Here I go."

Zach hugged Brandon tight before he left the vehicle. Zach's arms felt just as safe as Richard did, and he never wanted to leave. Once Brandon was near the door, Zach's nerves shot through the roof. He hoped that it would go okay, but knew it wouldn't.

Brandon unlocked the door to the apartment and went inside slowly. The lights were on, and he saw Shane's items on the kitchen table. "Shane?" He called out to receive no answer. It was uncomfortably quiet throughout the whole place, making it uneasy for him. Brandon went into his room feeling confused, thinking maybe he was in the bathroom.

The moment he sat down on the bed was when the attack began. Brandon's mouth was covered, and a human's body was on top of him, strangling to keep him still. Brandon struggled to get free from his grasp, already crying hard. His clothes were ripped off, kisses pressed against his skin, and the lust in Shane's eyes was beaming on him. Brandon was hopeless as he was kissed hard on the lips to silence his sobs. Shane managed to tie his hands up to the bedpost, successfully being more muscular than him. His lips were disgusting as he tried to make him kiss back. The abuser was getting frustrated with him, and Brandon was afraid of what would come next as he begged to be free.

A hard slap came across his face as Shane shouted at him. "Shut the fuck up, and take it like a man!"

Take it like a man...

Those words echoed dangerously in his mind as he cried harder. Shane hadn't returned at all. He just knew how to get Brandon back under him, making him his bitch again. The way Shane did sinful acts to his body was a living nightmare. Nothing about it was enjoyable. He needed a way to break free. He prayed that it wasn't much longer until Zach would be in the house with police officers to rescue him.

He didn't know how much longer he could take it.

Chapter 22: Save Me...Please

Zach began to panic as time went by. Brandon hadn't texted anything in the last four minutes, and he was starting to dial the police. He hated himself for letting his friend go into the house, and now Zach knew that his friend was in trouble.

"9-1-1, what's your emergency?" The lady answered.

"My name is Zachary Deanes, and my friend is in danger! Please send help!" Zach cried out.

"Try to stay calm, sir. Can you tell me where you're located?"

Zach gave the lady the information she needed and stayed on the line with her. He told her what he knew was probably happening in that apartment building, begging to come to save Brandon. Brandon wasn't answering his phone calls, either, which made it worse. No matter how many times he would dial Brandon's number, there was no answer. Useless. That's how he could explain what he was feeling. His friend that he cared so deeply about was being harmed, and all he could do was wait for other people to come help. He decided to get out of his car and go closer to the apartment where Brandon went in. Brandon was inside that place being ripped apart again. The policemen arrived moments later, and Zach waved them over frantically.

"Are you Mr. Deanes?" The cop asked.

"Yes," Zach answered desperately, "The door is locked, and he's not answering my calls. Please save him!"

"Stand back, sir." The other officer instructed while the partner started to break into the place. Zach watched from the sidewalk, afraid as other neighbors gathered around to see what was going on. It wasn't much longer until the door was finally broken down, and Brandon's loud cries were heard from all the way in the back. Zach could hear as the officer shouted.

"Police! Back away from him, now!" The officer shouted.

Shane was startled out of his sick fantasy as he pulled out of Brandon putting his hands in the air, scared. The gun was pointed directly at him, and he backed away to the wall, "Officer, what's going on? It's not what you think!"

"You have the right to remain silent. Anything you say can and will be used against you in a court of law. You have the right to an attorney. If you cannot afford an attorney, one will be provided for you. Do you understand the rights I have just read to you? With these rights in mind, do you wish to speak to me?" The officer stated as protocol.

Brandon hollered out as the other officer untied him. He felt weak, ashamed, exposed, and scared all over again. Shane hadn't changed at all as he'd hope. It was still the devil trying to get satisfied no matter what could cost him. He didn't care, and Brandon saw it in his eyes. Looking at Shane was too hard for him. Why did he agree to see him? He should've known it'd end up like this again. This Shane was impossible to communicate with. He never wanted to reason anything; he just wanted his high, as he called it. Even though he never wanted anything to do with Shane again, Brandon didn't want to see him get killed. All he wanted was to be free.

"This is crazy! I didn't fucking do anything," Shane shouted, which caused Brandon to jump in fear. With one last eye contact with each other, Brandon saw the demon that never left his body. It made him sick to his stomach, knowing that he allowed himself to get played all over again. His entire body was shaking in the officer's arms as she tried to calm him down.

"Where's Zach? I need him," Brandon whispered desperately with a nervous stutter.

"Garrett, go get Mr. Deanes. He's outside still," The female officer instructed her partner, then turned back to Brandon, "We're going to help you through this process, alright? My name is Officer Linda Jones. I'll be one of the officers there for you if you need anything."

Zach walked into the room with tears in his eyes. He immediately went over to Brandon, holding him tight as Officer Jones moved away. That's when Brandon cried harder—letting out his loud sobs. His breathing got heavier, and his body shook. Zach pulled the blanket over him to protect Brandon's dignity even if Brandon didn't think he had any left in his system. They were soon left alone for a little while, and Brandon held onto Zach. It was still noisy in the house as they could still hear the police sirens outside and the policemen in the living room. Zach felt awful for Brandon. He couldn't fathom having his very best friend turn on him in one of the worst ways.

"He ripped off all of my clothes, Zach," Brandon spoke in a broken tone, "He didn't care. He never cared. I'm such an idiot."

"You are not. Please don't say that," Zach cried softly, "He is so nasty and disgraceful. That man doesn't deserve you at all, Brandon. He won't hurt you ever again, I promise."

"I have to go to court, do I?" Brandon questioned, scared.

"Yes, we will get you a restraining order against him, and he's going to serve time for this."

"The judge will never believe me," Brandon stated.

"Yes, they will. You have all of these police officers and me as witnesses. Not to mention, there was plenty of evidence on your phone that I sent to my email. You're going to win. We will get through this." Zach assured. Looking around, Zach found Brandon's torn up clothes on the floor, and it boiled him up. That bitch destroyed Brandon little by little, leaving him with a heavy heart in tears and regret.

"I think there are some clothes left in one of the drawers. This is— was my room." Brandon explained.

Zach's heart broke, having to hear Brandon talk that way. Looking in Brandon's eyes, he then understood some of the signs he'd overlooked before. His eyes darted back with hopelessness and fear. Zach saw so much of the pain, humiliation, and fear that made him angrier at Shane. How could he do this? Why did he think it was all okay to just prey on Brandon like that? All of it infuriated him. He moved away to the Chester drawer as Officer Jones came back in the room.

"May I have your name, sir?" She asked gently.

"Brandon Andreas," Brandon stuttered to her quietly.

"Mr. Andreas, we need to take you down to the station to question you for the investigation. You will receive a lawyer of your choice if you know one, or we can provide you one. Do you know of any?"

Brandon nodded his head, knowing who he wanted to represent him in court. If he was going to do it, then it had to be with Daniel as his lawyer. "Yes, ma'am, his name is Daniel Hart. I can get in touch with him either tonight or in the morning."

"May we still question you tonight?" The officer asked.

Brandon glanced at Zach, who gave him an affirming nod. He was so afraid of doing this process, not knowing what the outcome would look like, but the urge to defeat Shane was urgent, "Only if Mr. Deanes stays with me the entire time."

"I can arrange for that to happen. Do you need clothes? We are going to take the ripped ones in as more evidence."

"I just found some in the drawer, Officer Jones. This was his room." Zach informed her.

"Do you also live here?"

"No, I live on my college campus. He goes to the same college as I do."

"We will have to question you, too." Instructed the officer.

"Yes, absolutely." Zach agreed.

"Can I drive myself to the station? I don't want to leave my car out front." Brandon requested.

"I don't know if it's the best idea, sir." Officer Jones stated, concerned.

"I've been through this before..." Brandon tried to say, but Zach talked over him.

"I think she's right, Brandon. You're not in the best condition." Zach agreed with the lady.

"This isn't the first time—" Brandon tried again.

"We can come back for it tomorrow, I promise." Officer Jones promised again.

"This was not the first time!" Brandon finally shouted to get them to listen, "I don't mean to yell, but please. This has unfortunately gone on for two months. As a matter of fact, last semester, I'd go to class, come home to be raped against my will, and fix myself back up to go to work. I never want to leave anything that's mine in this complex ever again. I can't come back here, and I'm giving up this apartment. Please, just let me drive myself; I'll be fine."

Officer Jones nodded her head as she jotted down notes as Brandon was talking, "Wow," she said to herself, "You are very strong. Okay, just follow me, and we will head right to the station."

Brandon and Zach followed her out to their cars and drove away from the complex for what was hoped to be the last time. He was alone in his car, which gave him time to think.

"I knew better," Brandon sobbed to himself, "I am such an idiot."

He arrived at the police station, parking where the officers instructed him to. Zach, Brandon, and Officer Jones made their way through the building into the interrogation room. Zach and Brandon sat next to each other on one side of the table while Officer Jones and another policeman sat on the other side. They all exchanged looks between one another, not saying a word at first. Brandon wondered where they held Shane at. The thought of still being in the same building as Shane sickened him. He knew that it was all over, but he felt as though it was all beginning. This scared Brandon, not knowing what the outcome would be. Part of him wanted to run away and lock himself in that hotel room to sob, but the other half wanted to make sure that Shane couldn't get to him any longer. It didn't help that everyone in that room saw him exposed and vulnerable on that bed, shaking uncontrollably.

"Mr. Andreas, this is Officer McKern. He is my partner." Officer Jones introduced the other policemen.

"It's nice to meet you," Officer McKern greeted. Brandon just looked at them, not ready to speak just yet, and they understood, "I hope this room isn't too cold."

Brandon shook his head as a response. He looked over at Zach, who held his hand firmly as if he was saying that it was okay to speak to them. The warmth that he felt when they made eye contact was indescribable and safe.

"Was it hard finding a parking spot out there?"

Once again, Brandon shook his head. Only this time, he allowed words to come out of his mouth. "I was able to park close to the door."

"That's good," Officer Jones nodded her head before proceeding to the following question. "I understand that you did not want to be intimate with Mr. Jacobs this evening?"

"No, I did not. I was there in hopes of having a conversation with him." Brandon informed them.

"What happened when you saw him?"

"I didn't see him at first," Brandon started, "When I entered my old room, the lights were on, and from what I could tell, nobody else was there."

"Did you think he was at home yet?"

"Yes, I was able to find his car in the parking lot before I went in."

"What did you want to talk to him about originally?" Officer McKern questioned.

"I...I wanted to talk about how I was feeling. Mr. Jacobs was my very best friend before all of this began. The reason I came back was due to the last time I had a conversation with him over the phone, he was normal. It was the man that was my roommate."

"Can you take us back to what you think started it all?"

Once again, Brandon told the entire journey of how it all happened for the third time. He made sure not to leave out any information or details that occurred between him and Shane. It seemed like every time that he had to tell, it was ten times harder. Brandon gave every detail, every feeling, and every thought that he experienced. Some questions hit him worse than others, and he tried his hardest not to sob. This was hard and painful for him. He thought that having to face Madelyn would've been the worst, but being at that police station with Zach made it surreal.

He was about to press charges against his best friend. To ask for a restraining order in hopes of keeping himself protected. Zach had his arms around him as he began to cry for what felt like the millionth time. The room went silent so that Brandon could have a minute to get himself together. This was so difficult to see any good outcome happening from it all. Why would a judge ever be on his side? He was a victim, a male victim with that. Shane Jacobs was mentally gone for good. The demon won over his soul, and it was time for him to exit Brandon's life forever. All he ever wanted out of this was an honest conversation. That idea landed him at the local police office, getting ready for what will be the most prominent and hardest battle of his life. This was going to be over for Brandon for good, even if he'll never be the same again. Brandon had a new body to live with, work with, and take care of. At least he didn't have to do it alone.

Officer McKern sighed as he wrote the last of Brandon's words down and looked at Brandon. "Please know that no matter what, we believe your entire story. Every detail you just gave will help your case and have a ruling in your favor."

"Okay," Brandon quietly mumbled, "I really appreciate it so much. I guess my story will be an example of why it's not a good idea to go after a straight guy."

"Unfortunately," Officer Jones agreed, "How many times did this happen?"

"I haven't made an official count, but I think it was four times rape, actual sex happened twice before that and almost one other time, and two kisses," Brandon confirmed.

"That sounds right with the information you've provided, son," Officer McKern nodded his head, "Did you tell anyone about the incident or behavior?"

"I had told a few friends, Mr. Deanes being one of the friends and my older brother when he visited over the holidays."

"What about your parents or his?"

"Oh, God, no. My parents never accepted my sexuality after coming out. I was almost kicked out of the house when I told them. My brother had to argue in my defense to let me stay. They would've thought that I deserved everything that was happening. To be honest, that's why I didn't report right away. Their words were in the back of my head as if I knew what they would've told me," Brandon looked down, "I was also taking care of my father until he passed away a few weeks ago. He had stage four brain cancer, and even with me being a primary caretaker helping out, they never appreciated me. Mr. Jacobs' parents weren't fond of him, either. So we connected and understood each other deeply when it came to that."

"Do you know whether the subject of the allegation has been involved in any other incidents like yours?"

"No, not that I am aware of. The women all gave consent."

"Okay, and you are the only male he's been with?" Officer Jones asked.

"To my knowledge, yes. If I know the old Shane, he wouldn't have asked another guy." Brandon confirmed.

"Out of embarrassment?"

"I guess you can say that. We were best friends who trusted each other with everything." He sighed.

"Alright, we may ask more questions later. Mr. Deanes, can you follow me so you can be questioned?" Officer McKern asked him politely.

"Of course," Zach stood up, placed a hand on Brandon's shoulder, and Brandon touched his fingers before Zach walked away.

Brandon sighed as he looked up at Officer Jones after they left, "Do I have to do anything else tonight?"

"You do need to do a sexual assault forensic exam—better known as a rape kit. You need to do it either tonight or tomorrow morning. It's best to collect the data before you shower or even go to the bathroom." Officer Jones informed.

"I guess we're heading to the hospital after Zach is questioned," Brandon sighed.

Zach followed Officer McKern to another investigation room, taking a seat. He wanted Shane to get so much hell from this process, and if he could help, then he was willing to go through the process with Brandon. There wasn't anything that worried him more than Brandon possibly losing this case. It was some concern about that being the outcome, but he knew better than to worry so soon.

Officer McKern sat down across from him just like they did in the other room, looking him in the eyes. "This is going to be a difficult case to win, you know?"

"Unfortunately, but I'll do whatever it takes to get Mr. Jacobs to pay for his crime," Zach stated confidently.

"When did you first find out about the incidents?"

"He actually told me at the wake of his father's funeral. It was his old high school friends that were told, and me. I never anticipated anything like this to happen ever. Shocked is an understatement as I didn't know Mr. Jacobs on a personal level, but I always hear about the women he's slept with from college. Honestly, I just hope that Mr. Andreas doesn't have any STDs from this." Zach explained.

"Were they all mutual high school friends of Mr. Jacobs and Mr. Andreas?"

"Yes, they were. Including the ex of Mr. Jacobs." Zach confirmed.

"Did you say anything to the party involved in response to what you witnessed?"

"No, not at all. I was actually too scared of him after that. Mr. Jacobs was on campus a few days prior to tonight, and I just didn't give him any attention. To be honest, I'm still scared." He mumbled the last part.

"I understand that, and it's for the best." The officer agreed, "Do you have evidence that we can use?"

"I have screenshots of the texts from Mr. Jacobs to Mr. Andreas that were unwanted sexual messages," Zach confirmed.

"Can you email them to me?" The officer asked Zach after he showed him everything. Zach sent them to his email and copied Brandon in the conversation so he could have all receipts.

"I hate that he has to go through this. He's such an amazing man, and he wouldn't lie about any of this." Zach made sure to tell the officer.

"I think we can tell. You guys have been cooperative while Mr. Jacobs has only screamed for the past hour. It's so pitiful. We may have one thing left to do with you and Mr. Andreas, and tomorrow make sure he contacts his lawyer." Officer McKern informed.

"I will, thank you." Zach stood up once the officer did, and they went to find Brandon. He was just finishing up with the other officers thanking them for all their help before hugging Zach tight.

"Thank you so much," Brandon whispered.

"Come stay with me tonight. Tomorrow we have things to do after the hospital." Zach told him, to which Brandon obeyed. Neither of them knew how hard the road ahead would be, but Zach wasn't going to give up on him.

Chapter 23: Lawyer in Need

It was bright and early when Brandon woke up in Zach's guest room. Just when he thought the initial filthy feeling of him was gone, it came back again like a pile of heavy bricks. He ran into the bathroom, lifted the toilet seat, and threw up for the third time since the previous night. If he needed one more reason to get over Shane, then last night was it. He let out more sobs as he threw up again, feeling as if Shane was still on top of him. He tried to fight it. To get rid of the nightmares, self-hate, and shame, but it was only the beginning.

After he calmed down, Brandon opened the bathroom door and called out for Zach, "Do you have a new toothbrush I can use?"

"Yes, I'll bring it to you," Zach told him and showed up at the door, giving it to him. Brandon took the toothbrush, opened it up, and brushed his teeth with him still there. "I guess it'd be foolish to ask how you feel this morning."

Brandon shook his head after spitting out the toothpaste, "No, it's not a stupid question. Honestly, you're the first to witness my process of 'post-rape self-clean-up.' I throw up in the morning or right after it happens, but I clearly had no time last night. Then I act as if nothing happened and internalize my feelings in public. I didn't have the energy to get straightened out after the rape kit."

"You had every right to crash in bed once we got here. At least I convinced you to do that rape kit before you showered," Zach sighed.

"I guess that was the right thing to do. The test should only show his DNA," Brandon sighed and looked at his phone for the time, "Good, I have plenty of time before I have to leave."

Zach then looked confused, "Before you have to leave? Where are you going?"

"I'm going to work. It's my last full day of work before the semester starts," Brandon informed him before he gargled with Listerine.

"After last night, I thought you would—"

"Stay curled up in a ball sobbing all day? No, the world doesn't have that much sympathy." Brandon gave a sarcastic laugh.

"No, I was not going to suggest that…Yet, that rape kit took hours. We were at the hospital until two-thirty in the morning." Zach expressed concern in his voice.

Brandon sighed as he wiped his mouth, turned the water off, and looked at Zach. "I'm sorry that came out rude. Hear me out, though. I'm like a front desk secretary and assistant worker at my job. That's what I do for the lawyers. So, I can see their schedules and enter their appointments for the day. I keep track of the days they need to be in court, when their client set up a last-minute appointment, all of that and more."

"Okay?" Zach listened to him and tried to see where he was going.

"If one of the lawyers has a free hour, I'll make myself an appointment today. I'm hoping that one of them will agree to represent me in court for this long process," Brandon explained.

Zach thought for a second before responding. "I can't be mad at that idea. Are you hoping a particular one is available?"

"I'm hoping for Daniel Hart, Gina Tam, or Destiny Quortez. They are amazing, and sometimes let me shadow them as they do paperwork or talk to their clients."

"That's cool. This is off the subject a little, but I love how focused you stay through it all. It's truly admirable."

Brandon smiled a little for the first time in the past twenty-four hours at Zach. It felt good to have someone recognize how hard he works despite all the problems he had to deal with. "You don't know how much it means to hear you say that."

Zach smiled back and hugged him, "I'll let you get ready. Coffee is in the pot. I just made it."

"Okay perfect, I definitely need it, and it's never ready when I get to work." Brandon chuckled. He then went back into the guest room and got dressed for the day. There were already headlines about the incident on his phone. Only Shane's name had been mentioned, and Brandon was grateful for that. However, it was still bittersweet to see his once sweet and honest best friend be in the news for something so awful. Letting out a groan, he went through his texts seeing his friends were checking on him. Brandon was thankful for all of them. Ever since the funeral, they made a group text talking almost every day again.

Brandon went into Zach's kitchen, pouring himself a cup of coffee, and sat down at the table with him. "I have to admit that I've been lucky so far."

"What do you mean?" Zach asked.

"As bizarre and unimaginable my situation has been, everyone believes me. That rarely happens with these cases," Brandon sighed, "I just still can't believe that I'm a part of another big ass statistic. One out of every seventy-one men are victims of rape. Every one out of ten are men raped by another man. I'm in both categories; this shit is ridiculous."

"Please know you're doing the right thing by speaking up. No matter what the outcome is, your voice is needed." Zach encouraged him.

"All of that is great to think about until you realize that if the court doesn't believe you, you're looking at possible prison time." Brandon looked down.

"Brandon, that is the last thing that'll happen to you. As someone studying law himself, you know how to make sure you're believed." Zach explained.

"I'm so scared, and I never thought in a million years that I'd have to sue him of all people in the world," Brandon mumbled, "This showed that anything that you think wouldn't happen could happen, Zach."

"I understand that. I'm empathizing with you as deeply and authentically as possible. You didn't deserve this at all."

"Thank you; I just hate that you have to be involved."

"I will be here for you any way that I can. I'm so thankful we met." Zach gave a smile, to which Brandon returned.

"Let's hope this court shit won't interrupt me in law school so much." Brandon sighed.

"It'll be a slow process. These cases hardly get picked up fast, even with so much evidence." Zach groaned.

"That's true," Brandon agreed as he took his last swallow of coffee. He stood up and put the cup in the sink to wash it when Zach stopped him.

"I got this. You go to work." Zach told him.

Brandon smiled and nodded his head as he grabbed his items and headed to work. It took him a shorter amount of time to get there. He went into the break room, clocking in where he saw two of his bosses, Gina and Daniel, talking. They both waved at him, to which he returned with a small smile and went to his usual place, turning on the computer. He sat back in the chair, sighing as the computer booted up, and looked at the messages on his phone.

"I can't handle this alone," Brandon thought out loud to himself, "Please, someone, have a free slot today." He looked through the schedule, praying for an available hour. Everyone seemed to be packed throughout the morning as usual, with clients to be coming in an hour.

"Do we have busy schedules?" Gina asked as she walked by when she heard him. Gina Tam was a forty-year-old Asian American woman with light-brown eyes, short black hair, and a curvy figure. Gina always wore black suits and a pair of heels, which meant business.

"Yeah, all of you guys do. I'm trying to find an available slot somewhere; there's someone new that wants to be in today. They said it's an urgent need." Brandon casually foreshadowed.

"Block out my lunch hour and put them in," Daniel commented as he walked up to them. He was a six-foot black man with brown eyes, a low haircut, and the beard was an extended goatee.

Brandon just gave a small nod and entered in the least amount of information that was required. He hated that it needed his real name as he wanted to keep it secret from everyone else, but he would have to deal with it.

The hour went by fast, and the clients started coming in one by one. Brandon got called at least a dozen times to do something for the lawyers. He barely had time to sit at his desk. From making coffee trips to having to make copies of everything that was on paper, Brandon felt like he was always on his feet—not getting a second to think about what he'd say to Daniel. All of this was worrying him more. What if he didn't believe Brandon? Would he get fired? Brandon's anxiety wanted to be through the roof. If he loses this case, he would have to watch out for Shane for the rest of his life. His legs began to shake as the time got closer.

Daniel stepped out of his office and went to Brandon's desk. "Meet me in my office; I'm going to use the bathroom."

Brandon gave him a nod as he watched him walk away. He got up from his seat, picked up his copy of the police report on his desk, his phone, and went into the office sitting where clients sat. He was about to be both an employee and a client to his boss. His case would be filed into the system.

Daniel came back into the room a couple of minutes later, shutting his door and sat back down at the computer. "I was looking at what you entered, and it was very minimum."

"I'm embarrassed, Dan," Brandon sighed, "I just didn't want the whole office staring at me and gossiping this early."

"Dude, you know everyone here! We're all too busy to stand around gossiping about random bullshit; you do not have to worry about that. Shane Jacobs sounds familiar, though. Haven't you talked about him?" Daniel asked.

"Yeah, he was my roommate up until all of this went down." Brandon nodded his head.

"How did you meet?"

"Freshman year of high school in 2011."

"When did you move in together?"

"Almost four years ago in June of 2015 immediately after graduation. We were going to the same community college and still are if he signed up for the semester." Brandon informed him.

"Okay," Daniel said to himself as he opened a new client file on his computer, trying to type out all the information as he listened. "Don't worry, only you, me, Gina, and Destiny will be able to view this file. We won't share any information with others."

"I appreciate it, man," Brandon told him gratefully.

Daniel and Brandon talked for an hour, trying to get through all the necessary information he needed. Brandon told every fact, detail, and feeling of what went on. It was getting harder every time he had to give a better detail of a specific event that occurred. He thought that he had everything memorized, but some of the questions were harder than anticipated. Daniel had an unreadable facial expression as he listened. It was some look that Brandon was familiar with, though. It wasn't the first time he saw or experienced him interviewing a new client; it was just the first time that the client was him.

"Do you have a copy of the police report?" Daniel requested.

Brandon nodded his head and handed it to him. "I should've scanned it, but we were crazy busy this morning."

"No, don't worry, you're fine. We did get swamped. I hardly saw you take a seat."

Brandon gave a small chuckle, "It was like every time I tried, someone else needed me, or the phone was ringing."

"On a Thursday nonetheless," Daniel shook his head in agreement, putting the paper in his scanner. "Did he get a lawyer yet?"

"I actually don't know. I'm assuming Shane did, and I just haven't been told. This is crazy, Daniel. I never thought this would happen." Brandon mumbled the last part and looked down.

"I have to think about this logically. Even though I completely believe you, the court will be a different story. Unless he admits to this shit, we're looking at a jury case."

"So, two to three years maximum?" Brandon groaned.

"I would say so, yeah."

"I'm afraid of this. What if the court doesn't give him the proper punishment? A restraining order would work for me, but he could still hurt other people."

"I hate to say this, but as long as we protect you from this man, you can't worry about future victims. As you know, all cases, and not just rape, are dealt with individually. Unless it's about child abuse, you can't fight for future victims. You can't fight for him to never sleep with another man again. You can only assure that the man won't be you."

"I know that when I think about it logically. Yet, emotionally it seems so unfair. This can't end with Shane in prison?" Brandon questioned.

"That would be the best and ultimate outcome. He can get up to fifteen years maximum. If this had killed you, he'd get up to thirty." Daniel then rested his arms on the desk and looked at Brandon in the eye. "We're more than co-workers, right?"

Brandon nodded his head, "Of course we are. You know we joke around calling each other work husbands." He already considered him like a mentor as he went through this long college journey to get to where Daniel is. This was his dream job.

"Then please take what I'm going to say from one work husband to the other," Daniel started, "I can't promise you a win. As simple and as logical as it might seem for you to win easily, it isn't the case. Magic isn't part of my job description, and it won't be in yours either. You're going to quickly learn that yourself when you get through the next three stressful yet rewarding law school years and you get your own clients. Also, no matter what happens with this case, please do not let it scare you away from going to your law school. You've come too far, man."

"Daniel," Brandon looked him in the eye, "If anything good came out of the last six months for me is that I realize that I am a fighter. I dealt with a busy class load, this job, him, and an ungrateful father that's now dead. Mind you that I'm never seeing my mom again either. If I can graduate in May after all of this hell, I'm ready for law school. Maybe I'm being naive and whatnot, but I am ready."

"That's the Brandon I know." Daniel smiled and gave him a firm handshake, "Let's get to work."

On the other side of New York City, Shane sat in his new cold bed in his cell, angry, disgusted, and confused. He tried to replay the incident over in his head again and again like a movie scene. Nothing added up in his view. What went wrong? Shane was scared to have ended up in jail, and he didn't like his cellmate. Whenever Shane tried to look at him or make conversation, all he would do was look at him as if he had the eyes of a devil. Everything in the cell was gray, and there weren't any windows.

Shane sat up in his bed and sighed. He was on the bottom bunk since the other cellmate had the top. When he first arrived, Shane tried to introduce himself to him and had no luck. He was taller than Shane, more muscular, and gave off a vibe that Shane knew not to mess with. He felt more alone than ever before. From Shane's guess, the man was six feet tall. He was a white, muscular male with green eyes, brown hair, and hundreds of visible tattoos. His odor had been the smell of weed and cigarette smoke all over.

"What are you looking at?" The inmate shouted at him.

"Nothing," Shane mumbled nervously.

"Good!"

"Can I at least have a name?"

"My name is Shotgun."

Shane looked at him, confused, "Are you a child of a celebrity?"

The taller male aggressively punched the wall hard, which made Shane startle. "Fuck, no! I'm from the hood, and my name is Shotgun because I've killed many enemies with one bullet to the head. They got my ass locked up because I couldn't outrun the cops. My trial is next week."

Shane nodded his head nervously and stepped back. As if being scared wasn't enough, he became terrified, knowing that he was with a dangerous being. He couldn't possibly belong there; it had to be a mix-up. Maybe the police went into the wrong apartment. All Shane thought that he was doing was just having sex with his best friend. He thought back to the previous night before giving in and answering questions to the policemen. Shane didn't understand why he had to go through it all. There was much anger and hatred that he formed overnight. Shane had gone towards Brandon, Zach, and of course, at the police.

The more that he thought about Zach, the madder he got. Was he in the neighborhood and decided to drop by? Why would he call the cops? Brandon should've told them that it was all some misunderstanding and that they were having fun. Shane didn't understand how anyone could have viewed that night as something gone wrong. If anything, Shane thought that the lady cop would've gotten turned on. Nothing made sense to him, and he demanded answers.

Another two hours went by, and Shane got bored. There wasn't anything to do except look at the wall and hold onto the cell bars getting the tiniest glimpse down the hall. The hallway seemed to have much more light than inside his cell. Finally, a guard made her way to the cell, and Shane took a few steps back. He could only hope they were letting him free.

"Jacobs, you are allowed one free call," Officer McKern informed.

"My first name is Shane. Did you forget?" Shane questioned bitterly.

"I'm allowed to call you anything I want, and you can't do a thing about it." The officer shouted. He then proceeded to lead them to the call area.

Shane looked confused as they arrived at the phone booth, "This area looks completely different than what's shown in Orange Is the New Black."

"Just make a damn call! You have up to twenty-one minutes."

Shane groaned as he punched in the number of his father's cell phone. He would've chosen Brandon, but his gut was warning him not to. It felt like ages went by while he waited for him to answer. Shane hated the way that the environment felt. The room had cracked walls all over, and there wasn't much light. He made sure that he still had a view of Officer McKern; Shane didn't know who he should've been more afraid of—the guards or his inmate.

"Hello?" The familiar voice finally spoke through the phone.

"Dad," Shane responded, afraid.

"What the hell is going on? Why are you calling me from a collect number?" Freddie Jacobs questioned.

"I'm in jail," Shane explained, nervous about his reaction.

"Excuse me?" Freddie yelled out.

"I can explain!"

"That was you ass-naked getting arrested last night on the news?"

"This made the news?" Shane asked, devastated.

"What did you do, Shane Eugene Jacobs?"

"Why am I on the news? I wasn't doing anything wrong!" He cried out, scared and frustrated, "I don't belong in here, dad. Come bail me out!"

"Tell me what you did!"

"I swear this is some kind of misunderstanding. I haven't committed any crime!"

"I'm surprised you used committed correctly in a sentence," Freddie complimented.

"Focus, Fredward!"

"Who the hell said you could call me by my first name? Let alone my government name!"

"Sorry," Shane mumbled. He took a look at the guard that was still standing intimidatingly. The smell in the room finally caught up with his senses, and it wasn't appealing at all. He felt small and afraid. There was no guarantee that the bail money would be accepted. The judge had considered letting him stay in jail for a while. Why was this happening to him?

"If we're lucky, you should be able to get a bondsman."

"What does having to make a new friend have anything to do with me in jail?"

"Shane—"

"I don't want to trust anyone else with my life, dad!"

"Shut up and listen to me!"

"I'm locked up in jail, and you want to force a new friendship on me?" Shane shouted.

"Shane!"

What started out as a confession, to clarify, turned into a shouting match. Freddie desperately tried to get Shane to understand what a bondsman was before their time was up, but he had no luck. The time ran out before they could say goodbye or that they loved each other. Shane was out of control, and he couldn't help him.

Shane was sent back to that forbidden cell until lunchtime, where he had to continue to face that scary inmate. Somewhere deep down, Shane knew his jail stay was going to be longer than he could imagine. That was only the first day of many more days, weeks, and months left to go.

Chapter 24: Life Goes On

With a blink of an eye, winter break was officially over. Not that Brandon could call it a break, but it was what it was. He was back in the hotel room, cooking himself breakfast in the kitchen. Now with Shane temporarily out of his life and no more parents to obey, he could finally start to heal. The problem was that he didn't know how. His nightmares had gotten scarier, and he still didn't get a full night's sleep. Daniel gave him two weeks of paid time off to settle into the semester and adjust to the start of his new life. Whatever that would intel, he and his brother hadn't had the chance to talk about what happened, but Brandon understood that he was busy in California.

Brandon dreaded the first day back. Not because of the papers and assignments that awaited him, but he knew that his incident had made local news stations all over town. He was now going to get stares in college if he hadn't gotten them already. He turned on the TV and ate his breakfast on the couch. Being in the hotel room wasn't ideal, but it was indeed better than living in that apartment or staying with his mother. There was so much to do, and he wanted to get it done right away to free up his mind.

He smiled as his phone rang, looking at the caller ID before he answered, "Hey Madelyn."

"Hey," Madelyn greeted, "I wanted to see how you've been since I left. Have you stayed away from Shane? I know it's hard to."

"You'd think I'd learn my lesson, wouldn't you?" Brandon sighed, "This made the local news. I'm overwhelmed; I don't know what to do."

"What made the local news?" She questioned, "That doesn't sound good at all."

"I went back twice, Madelyn," Brandon explained to her.

"What?" Madelyn asked, confused, "Why? Did you get hurt? Was he there?"

Brandon began explaining how Shane had called him while he was at the house packing, how he'd gotten fooled by a single phone conversation all over again that led him to be violated. Only the last time ended with him being saved but exposed to both Zach and the policemen. It felt so shameful. He desperately wanted to be better for his friends. To pretend like Shane never affected him and that he could be stronger than that. For Brandon, that just wasn't the case. Brandon was fighting against the tears that begged for release from his eyes. He just couldn't cry anymore.

Shouldn't he be happy?

"Brandon, I'm so sorry. I think I'm going to take this semester off to come to help you. You can't handle it all alone. It's not fair to you." Madelyn expressed, "All of this goes on right before you enter the next three biggest years of your life?"

"Madelyn, don't you dare drop out. I'll be furious at you—this time for a legit reason. You're graduating in May with a degree in engineering. Listen, in May, you're coming back home, and we are celebrating by getting so drunk. It'll be great, and maybe I'll be able to have Richard send me to attend your ceremony." Brandon told her, "I can handle it. Just take away the factor of my father and him, then replace it with law school and a slow court case. I've dealt with worse, right?"

"I just feel awful that I never noticed the signs," She sighed.

"You and I both. However, dropping out allows him to still win even in jail. We can't have that at all," Brandon took a big sigh, "I'm scared, Madelyn. He could get bailed out. A fucking document on paper isn't going to keep me safe!"

"You're right," Madelyn agreed, "Yet, you know better than anyone else that the restraining order is more powerful than we think. Don't lose faith in it."

"I was lucky enough to get it in four days. Zach and I went back to the police station the next day. I did everything and got it done. Officer Jones, who's been amazing, has given Shane the orders in jail. That's going to be the easiest process out of this whole case." Brandon sighed.

"Good, make sure you scan it and have it in your email ready to open on your phone. Just in case," Madelyn informed him.

"I will do that today. I'll use the library scanner at school," Brandon promised her.

"Do you need me to do anything?" Madelyn asked.

"Hurry up and graduate so we can get drunk together?" Brandon joked with her.

"I would love that after this crazy semester," Madelyn chuckled, "Except I'm not letting you drink for a long time."

"Oh, come on, why not?" Brandon groaned.

"Dude, you need to do so much recovering from this. Unfortunately, you can never completely heal, but you have to get better. You will not be drinking for a long time."

"Fine," Brandon sighed, "You know what's embarrassing about this?"

"What's that?"

"Everyone at my college will be staring," Brandon mumbled, "Wanting updates and all of that."

"Just because someone asks doesn't mean they have a right to know. What could they possibly have to say directly to you about this? It's none of their business." Madelyn spoke with sass.

"Yeah, I know you're right. I'm paranoid about everything now since the policemen and Zach saw me exposed like that. Even if it'll help my case in the long run," Brandon admitted, "I just hate that people will obviously ask about him. Are we positive that the general public can't read minds?"

"Yes, Brandon, we're positive about that. You know, you sound like you and Shane know everybody on that campus," Madelyn questioned.

"All I know is he knows way more than me. I know most of the people primarily because of him, besides Zach and others studying the same field." Brandon explained and groaned, "God, we were going to graduate and then visit you in LA this summer."

"Which would've only made you hate me more." Madelyn reminded him, "We would have still been together."

"Funny how life will work at times," Brandon shook his head as if his friend could see him.

"Are you looking to get therapy?"

"I don't know if I have the time," Brandon answered honestly, "I want it so bad."

"You have to make time, Brandon. You know that Tori is studying psychology. Want me to get her on your head about it?" Madelyn warned.

"Alright, alright! You have a point. Plus, my boss told me that I need it just like you're telling me now. I have Zach to keep me on track, so don't worry."

"Zach seems very nice. I'm glad he did this for you. Did you have any feelings for him as well?" Madelyn asked, "I understand that it's not happening anytime soon. Probably shouldn't even ask."

"No, please ask me any question. To be completely honest, I don't know how I feel about him. The thought of love, dating, and intimacy has been torn away from me. Shane ripped out those desires from me, and I have no intention of getting them back ever."

"You'll get through this. You've made it through the worst part. Not many people can say that they've won, or ever got the courage to step forward about their experiences."

"I wouldn't have if the police weren't ever called that night by Zach. My plan was to talk to him that night, get him to understand the issue, and go from there. My heart doesn't deserve to be trusted anymore. If I ever find a good guy, I'll just talk myself out of it," Brandon whined and went to wash the dishes that he ate out of.

"I have to say that I'm torn about that. Yes, you should definitely be a lot more careful about men in your future. I do too if we're going to be honest," Madelyn admitted, "Yet the past can't determine what our love lives will look like in the future."

"Easier said than done."

"Most definitely without a doubt," She agreed, "You have to make sure that a guy is an actual gay man that's not just looking to experiment. I have to make sure that my boyfriend is actually straight."

"You mean we can't give bisexual or pansexual guys a try?" Brandon joked.

"After what we just went through, or should I say going through? No."

"Damn," A groan escaped his mouth, "You're right again. I really should start thinking with logic about everything and not just for college."

"I think that would help, yes." Madelyn chuckled.

"I'm really trying to!" Brandon promised her. He then grabbed his book bag and headed out to his car. Once he got in, he searched inside of the glove compartment to get his school ID and ended up finding a particular picture as well. It was a photo of him and Shane that his mother let him take when they cleaned out her bedroom. His heart immediately dropped, and the phone nearly slipped out of his hand. Everything just went silent for a moment while he just looked at it.

"Brandon, are you there?" Madelyn asked, which startled him.

"I'm sorry, I was looking for my badge, and I found a picture that caught my attention," Brandon sighed and started his car up.

"I would throw it out," Madelyn suggested.

"You don't know what I found, though!" Brandon defended himself.

"I know it's of you and Shane. You paused for too long for it to have been anyone else."

"How come everyone else can understand my emotions, but he couldn't?" Brandon exclaimed.

"Brandon, I don't believe that he cared about my feelings either!" She reminded him.

"I beg to differ," Brandon sarcastically chuckled as he started driving.

"I don't know because when someone is addicted to sex as much as him, that's all they care about."

"He never asked you for sex, though."

"Actually yes, he asked multiple times, and we argued a few days because of it."

"I just thought that he was a complete gentleman with you like normal," Brandon sighed to himself, knowing that he thought that Shane behaved like a perfect gentleman towards her. The jealousy took control of so much to the point where he thought Shane had treated her like a queen.

"It wasn't him asking for sex, he begged me. It was so pathetic, and it irritated me!"

"That means it never happened, right?" Brandon mumbled as he felt embarrassed.

"Hell no, never did. Shane never saw me naked."

Brandon groaned to himself, realizing that he was so stupid to have thought that months ago, "I should've asked you! I'm such an idiot to just assume that about you."

"Brandon, it's okay, I understand. Don't beat yourself up over everything. I've lost my virginity, but not to him. I assure you." Madelyn promised.

"I don't know if I wish that I hadn't slept with him. You'd think it would be easy to say that and mean it, but I don't know. Why do I want to say that it was for the best that it happened to me than some other guy or girl, or you for that matter?" Brandon thought out loud.

"Simply because you wouldn't have believed me," Hearing Madelyn say that broke Brandon's heart. He'd like to think that she was wrong and that he would've stood up for her, but he realized that jealousy had made him hate Madelyn.

"You think that would've been my attitude? Thinking that you'd cry wolf because he didn't satisfy you?" Brandon's eyes watered up as he drove.

"I think we both have to face that truth, Brandon. Yet, that doesn't mean you deserved it because you didn't."

"It just seems like the ultimate backfire. If Shane isn't found guilty, it will serve me right." Brandon expressed through his tears. "Why am I crying again?"

"You're hurting, babe. It's okay to cry right now. Please do not stress about the case that's so far away." Madelyn soothed him. Brandon sighed as he made his way to the campus and parked in the nearest parking lot to the building he had to go in. He saw his friends Zach, Lewis, and Stacey going in, and he caught up with him.

"Hey guys," Brandon tried to smile when he walked up to them. He still had Madelyn on the phone as well.

"There you are!" Stacey smiled, "Looks like we all showed up at the same time."

"Yeah, perfect timing," Brandon gave a forced smile, which Zach could now tell wasn't genuine. He now understood the pain behind it all, "Madelyn, I'll call you tonight."

"Okay, please do. I love you," Madelyn responded.

"I love you so much," Brandon sincerely replied before hanging up, "Sorry, that was one of my high school friends. She called me this morning. How are things, Lewis?"

"The past week was crazy for me," Lewis groaned.

"You and me both," Brandon sighed, "What was happening with you?"

"I just got home from a mini trip. My family member went into the hospital, but they're fine now." Lewis told the group.

"I'm sorry to hear that. Glad they're okay, though." Zach responded.

"I did see the news, Brandon. May I ask how have you been?" Stacey asked.

"I'm okay," Brandon lied straight through his teeth, "It's just good now that he's in jail for the time being."

"If you need anything, please let us know," Stacey told him.

"I will, thank you. This is just so embarrassing. Everything that I do reminds me of him." Brandon sighed, "It's so hard just to erase him from my memories. Really impossible at this point."

"Yeah, I can't imagine." Lewis fathomed.

They made their way to the designated classroom and sat down. All of a sudden, Brandon began to feel his anxiety kicking in as his mind made up scenarios. What if Shane was able to escape without getting caught? Did he really go to jail, or was it all a dream? He could still be free and show up for his revenge at any given minute. Brandon couldn't shake it off of his mind no matter how much he wanted to. This anxiety was in control of him. It was miserable.

Zach noticed that Brandon wasn't a part of the conversation anymore but didn't want to draw any more attention to his situation. It worried him that he got so quiet all of a sudden. He knew that something must've triggered him talking about that horrible man. Zach saw Brandon's forehead was beginning to sweat, and he was looking pale in the face. While trying to keep in the conversation not to have the attention on Brandon, he paid close attention to him.

Brandon's body started to get chills all over. It started with his shoulders all the way down to his toes. Shane was near, and he knew it. Even though logically, he knew that he was probably being transported to prison, it still felt like he could jump out and attack at any moment. His chest started to tighten up, with his breaths beginning to get hitched. He looked around the room as others started to show up, and it made him feel claustrophobic inside. He needed an escape. To get free from his skin and leave it behind. Brandon had no way of knowing the difference between reality and delusion at that moment. All he knew was that he needed to escape.

Without realizing it, he had gotten up from his seat and ran out of the classroom. It alarmed everyone there, especially Zach, who ran after him. It felt like a mile's run to get to the nearest bathroom.

"Brandon!" Zach called after him in concern. He followed him into the bathroom and saw him on the floor, curled up in the fetal position. He locked the door to make sure no one could get in before trying to speak to him, "Brandon…"

"No! Get away from me, Shane! No!" Brandon cried out. It was like feeling his devilish hands all over him again, pinning him down. Flashes of his angry face were engraved into his mind haunting him. His whole body shook with fear and shame as the scene replayed in his mind. Even though his logical thinking knew that Zach was in the room with him, his fears made him think otherwise. The room started to close in, spin around uncontrollably, and everything got dark. His mind had turned out Zach and replaced him with the man he didn't want to envision ever again.

Shane was there standing right in front of him, smirking as he watched him suffer. He didn't love Brandon as he'd thought. This version of Shane loved to see him like this. To see Brandon get deeper into his pain and sorrow. Brandon was trying so hard to run away from him, to escape his grasp and become free. That just wasn't happening. He couldn't see anything else besides Shane. No matter where he tried to go, Shane was there laughing.

"Leave me alone; I don't want you near me!" Brandon sobbed out desperately. He couldn't look away, and he heard muffled voices that weren't Shane's.

"Brandon! Brandon, it's okay he isn't here!" Zach panicked and embraced him tightly. Brandon was trying hard to slow his brain down with something that would get him in focus and settle down.

"He's gone?" Brandon asked. He was still breathing hard and in full panic.

"Yes, Shane is gone forever," Zach told him. At least that was the hope.

"I see him! Zach, he's here. I see him!" Brandon cried out.

"No, he's not, I promise you. Try to calm down, Brandon. Please calm down!" Zach pleaded.

Brandon still had his eyes closed as his body shook. Shane was slowly fading away as his body started to come back to reality. Tears came rushing down his face as he began to remember where he was. He held onto Zach as he began to feel weak and numb all over. Brandon thought that he would be able to heal. To block out the world and focus on his last undergraduate semester, but it wasn't going to be that simple. He was being controlled by his PTSD and anxiety, no matter how bad he tried to fight it.

"Shane isn't here," Brandon stated once he started to come back to reality, "He...He can't attack me?"

"No, he's not here. He'll never return for you," Zach tried to stay calm as he reassured his friend.

"I'm at college getting...Getting ready for the next semester, right?" Brandon asked with his voice hitched.

"Yes," Zach nodded his head while still holding onto Brandon. It was a freaky experience for him as well, but he understood that he needed to be there for Brandon. That made him feel awful not to be able to do anything besides calm him down the best he could. His body also shook slightly in fear. Zach didn't know what to do besides to try and calm him down.

"What do I do?"

"Just relax and take deep, slow breaths," Zach instructed, "Don't worry about anything else. Just get your breathing back to normal."

"What about class?"

"Don't think about that. You need to relax and get your heart rate back to normal. The last thing you need is a heart attack," Zach explained to him, "I need you to take a deep breath in."

Brandon obeyed, doing what Zach told him to. He tried to calm down as much as he could. It was hard to forget him and all that he put Brandon through. The fight ended while the war had only begun. Brandon had entered the darkest tunnel of his life with the world still going on like everything was fine. Nothing was fine to Brandon. He'd lost his best friend, his freedom, and his dignity.

"I didn't mean to scare anybody; it was just so sudden…" Brandon spoke in a shaky tone.

"It doesn't matter, Brandon. It's okay," Zach comforted.

"I need help. God, I need serious help with this."

"I know, and I promise we'll get you that help. Try to relax."

"I want to go to class," Brandon told him.

"It might not be a good idea—" Zach tried to say.

"I can't let him win, Zach. I can't let this PTSD or whatever the fuck just happened to ruin my degree. I'm going to class," Brandon demanded. He stood up slowly and dusted his pants off with his hands. Zach assisted with getting his clothes back in order before they washed their hands in the sink. With one final look at each other, Zach led the way out of the bathroom and back to their classroom.

Their professor was in the room now talking about the course when they entered. She gave them a small nod before continuing with her introduction. Brandon felt the other students staring at him as he and Zach sat back down. It was so embarrassing to know that everyone saw it happen. Surely there was going to be gossip around campus about him now.

"I would like for everyone to introduce themselves and give one interesting fact," The professor smiled, "I will go first. My name is Professor Marnet Flynn. I've been teaching here for nine years, and a fun fact about myself is I love to play the piano and guitar."

One by one, everyone introduced themselves and gave their fun facts. Brandon took a big exhale before taking his turn, "My name is Brandon Andreas. This is my last semester as an undergraduate student.

I hope to attend CUNY Law here in New York, hoping to be a lawyer. Also, I'm sorry if I startled anybody earlier. I had a panic attack."

"Oh no, are you okay? I wasn't in the room yet." Professor Flynn asked, concerned.

"I've been going through a lot, and my mind can't seem to settle down," Brandon answered truthfully.

"Let me know if I can assist," Professor Flynn sincerely offered.

"I will, thank you." Brandon nodded his head.

The professor looked at Zach, and he introduced himself next. "Hi, my name is Zachary Deanes, and this is also my last semester. Very excited and anxious about my upcoming admissions test coming up. I've been studying so hard. I'm originally from Ohio, but I didn't want to stay in town even for my undergrad. So, I came here."

"Well, this course is designed to prepare you guys for that big test whenever you decide to take it. Happy to have you here, Mr. Deanes." She smiled, "Were you with Mr. Andreas just now?"

"I was, yes," Zach told her.

The processor smiled as the rest of the class introduced themselves, including Lewis and Stacey. Zach kept his eye on Brandon just in case anything were to happen. He felt awful not to be able to do much except comfort him the best way he could.

"Okay, class, we are going to go through the syllabus and class expectations. Please know that I am rooting for each and every one of you and helping prepare you for the biggest test you'll take to determine the next three years of your lives. As a reminder, This standardized test, which takes about a half-day to complete, is offered four times per year. You can take it in June, October, December, and February," Professor Flynn stated, "It takes up to four weeks to receive your results by both mail and email. Whenever you take it is up to you, but the sooner, the better. Let's get started."

Chapter 25: Unwanted Dreams

The first week of classes flew by, and Brandon was already back at work. While everyone else was getting excited about graduation, he was alone in his misery. He was sitting at his desk as Daniel walked up to him.

"What's up?" Brandon asked.

"Do you realize how stupid Shane Jacobs is?" Daniel questioned.

"Please tell me he wasn't released on bail. I swear I'm leaving this fucking state." Brandon told him.

"That's just it. The dumb ass denied the bondsman."

"Come again?"

"I have right here the statement from the police department," Daniel stated before he read the paper to Brandon, "Shane Jacobs refused the bondsman because he didn't want to 'bond with another person and make a new friendship.'"

"What the fuck? There's no way he's that stupid now," Brandon sighed, "I mean, knowing this crazy system that doesn't sound right. I was ready to skip town until the hearing."

"Excuse me; you're the best secretary we have. I'm not letting your ass leave us." Daniel smiled at him, "Speaking of leaving; my husband wants me to take a week off to relax. He says I'm working too hard."

"As your work husband, I'll have to agree with that. You deserve it, Dan. Nothing's stopping you," Brandon agreed.

"I just feel like everything's going to pile up fast if I'm gone,"

"That's a typical morning for all of us. I swear I clock in and get to running for you all." Brandon laughed.

"Yeah, that's true. Also, you have a restraining order that's valid for one year. You'll be fine."

"Oh, a fucking piece of paper is a shield, and he's automatically going to pause when he sees me. I forgot that it has magical powers," Brandon exclaimed with sarcasm.

"Believe me; I understand your point. I really do. You should still be aware of what it can do." Daniel reminded him.

"I know, and I'm doing all I can to stay positive. Just so difficult to do so." He groaned

Just when Daniel was going to respond, they heard his phone in his office rang. Brandon gave him a small nod as he watched him leave. He leaned back in his chair, feeling bored since there wasn't anything to do at the moment. Brandon took his phone out, looking at his text messages. Every time he saw his name was like a stab in his heart. He badly wanted to delete them but wasn't sure if he should.

Brandon reached into his bag, getting out his big school binder. He and his friends had finally started to study for their Law School Admissions Test that he had to take in the summer. Throughout the rest of the morning, Brandon had plenty of time to study and take notes. There weren't many calls, which he was grateful for as he took advantage of it. The thought of this big test coming up made Brandon nervous. He was having such great luck with his classes over the past year; he couldn't get distracted now.

After a couple of hours passed by, Brandon's lunchtime finally arrived. He placed his items on the desk and made sure there were no crucial messages incoming. Then he made his way into the break room where he saw Gina and Destiny also starting to enjoy their lunches.

"Hello, ladies," Brandon greeted with a forced smile as he went to the refrigerator and got his food.

"There's our favorite secretary!" Gina smiled, "You never realize how much you need your front desk co-worker until they're gone."

Brandon gave a smile, knowing that all of the lawyers appreciated everything that he did for them. That was one of the reasons why he loved working with the law firm. They were mostly all his friends. Brandon needed all the friends that he could get, whether it was a close friendship or just casual.

"I know, yesterday I came back to a whole pile of work to do. Did everyone take off with me? It felt like it," He joked.

"We wish that was possible. Everyone did get a long Christmas break, so we shouldn't be complaining." Destiny shrugged.

"I guess not. It seems like you just finished a big case?" Brandon asked as he took his seat.

"Yeah, the last of the paperwork finished two weeks ago. Now I'm down to three clients. That's if we don't get more for at least a few weeks. We're growing, at least." Destiny replied with hope.

"I'll keep my fingers crossed that it doesn't get hectic right away with new people just yet," Brandon told her.

"Dan took the newest inquiry I saw. Is everything okay?" Gina hinted at him.

Brandon's heart skipped a beat, trying to think of a response. He wished that the subject didn't have to be about him. It was hard enough not to let Shane cross Brandon's mind as much as he already was. After swallowing his food, he sighed and answered.

"I'm taking it a step at a time. A lot is happening in my life right now, and I need a lawyer," Brandon confirmed.

"We all have your back. You picked Daniel as your official lawyer, but you know all of us will be working on it. You're our priority case." Destiny assured him, "Whatever you need."

"Thanks so much. I'm just trying to figure everything out. My semester is starting; I need a new place to live, the LSAT is going to be early June," Brandon listed, "I just hope it'll all be worth it."

"Hey, don't worry about it. You're going to do great!" Destiny grinned.

"Thank you," Brandon slightly smiled at her.

"Why can't you stay with your mom?" Gina asked. Brandon just gave her a knowing look that said everything that he didn't want to communicate verbally, "Got it."

"I'm never seeing her again in life until she's either dead or in critical condition like my dad became before dying," Brandon sarcastically laughed.

"Damn, it's that bad for you?" Gina asked.

"I've been burning in Hell for so long," Brandon shook his head and took another bite of his food, "You guys have no idea. They hate me for being gay. I'm surprised that she hasn't called to say 'I told you so' after everything was on the news."

"You don't think she'd finally be understanding because of this?"

"I'm done giving her the benefit of the doubt. If she couldn't appreciate me becoming the full-time caretaker for her dying husband, then this wouldn't do shit." Brandon bitterly commented.

"I know it's just words, but I promise it'll get better." Destiny comforted him.

"Yeah? Just tell that to my now daily panic attacks. This PTSD is stressful within itself." Brandon groaned as he drank his bottled water, "I'm sorry we're here to eat and to get away from any cases while on break. Here we are discussing my case that hasn't even begun."

"What? No, Brandon, I'm the one that got on the topic. It wasn't you. We don't want to pressure you into talking about it if you're not ready or just don't want to." Gina assured him.

"Yeah, please don't feel like a burden. We really care and want to make sure that you're okay!" Destiny added in, "Have you looked into therapy for yourself?"

Brandon shook his head, "When would I have time for that while studying for this admissions test? Look at everything that life threw at me. My dad is now dead, a busy college semester, which is my last semester as an undergraduate, figuring out unexpected finance adjustments, and just now getting Shane literally out of my ass."

"Which is why you need counseling, honey," Gina told him and placed her hand on top of his, "You need to talk about it all with a professional therapist too. It'll help you some, I promise."

"Thank you, all of you are so amazing to me to care about me this much when you don't have to," Brandon sighed, "This shouldn't be about me when you have other serious cases to tend to."

"We all care about one another in this company. It's what we do." Gina assured him with a smile. The three co-workers finished their lunches talking about lighter topics for the remaining time.

The rest of Brandon's workday was uneventful. He made it back to the hotel at his usual standard time and felt tired. It wasn't even a busy afternoon, and he was still wiped. The first thing he did was a change from his work clothes into some pajamas. He had gotten some fast food on the way home as well. Even though he had homework to do, it wasn't due for a couple of days. All of his running around caught up to him, especially when his body could finally relax after being sexually abused for two months with no rest. Brandon's arms felt tired; his legs and back constantly ached at night. Shane never gave a damn about his physical wellbeing, and it rubbed off on Brandon.

Brandon looked through his texts seeing many unread messages from the day. He was too busy studying when he didn't have to do anything for the lawyers. It was weather alerts from his college campus canceling classes due to weather, encouraging messages from Zach and Madelyn, and tons of emails that needed to be deleted. Talking to anybody was the last thing that he wanted to do that night. He hated to leave his friends worrying, but he couldn't be bothered. Brandon put the phone on the charger and walked away from it, not planning on touching it again for the rest of the day. He sat on the comfy hotel bed, looking outside the window. New York's streets were covered in snow still, and some cheerful Christmas decorations were still up. Many buildings lit up the area around him, and the full moon was out. Everything seemed so peaceful.

He began to doze off without realizing while sitting up. It startled him when he almost fell over on the floor. Brandon took that as the final sign to go to sleep. He got under the covers and turned out the light on the side table, finally falling asleep.

Brandon didn't know where he was. The room was dark, with no one else around. He started to look around for a light switch. When he finally turned on the light switch, Brandon realized that he was back in the apartment. He figured that Shane must've put a blanket on him since he fell asleep on the couch. The TV was still on the news. They must've been watching together before Brandon fell asleep. He thought that it was strange to have fallen asleep on the couch since he rarely did that. Since he was still sleepy, he was just going to go to his bed.

He figured that Shane had already gone to sleep and had forgotten to wake him up. As he passed by his room, he noticed that he wasn't asleep in bed. However, Brandon didn't think much of it.

"Must be in the bathroom," He said to himself. He made his way into his room and felt someone tap him on his shoulder, making him startle. "Dude! Don't sneak up on me like that."

"Oh, I'm sorry for scaring you. I just wanted to talk."

"Talk? Isn't it too late to just talk? Go to sleep, man." Brandon sighed and shook his head. He couldn't imagine what Shane would want to talk about that late at night. He didn't have a clue what time it was. It had been a long day for him, even though he couldn't remember what he did.

"Please? It's important, Brandon." Shane asked. Brandon could tell by the look on his face that it was serious. He hardly ever saw him with that face, which meant that it would be hard for him to discuss.

"What's wrong?" Brandon questioned and sat on his bed.

Shane sighed and went to sit next to him. He took in a breath before starting to speak, "We're best friends before anything, right?"

"Of course," Brandon confirmed. He felt something weird going on with the way the conversation started. It was like an uncertain feeling that made his stomach go into a knot.

"I've had feelings for someone. He's my best friend, and he hasn't dated anyone in so long. Maybe I've been blind for so long, but I finally realized my feelings for him." Shane admitted while blushing.

Of course, Brandon knew who he was talking about. They both knew, and it had Brandon blushing harder than Shane. After all of the years of hiding his true feelings for his friend, it was finally becoming a reality. Brandon was at a loss for words trying to figure out what to say. His cheeks began to blush as he tried to think of a response. The love he had for Shane was unmatched by anyone else in his life. From his blue eyes to his blonde hair, everything was perfect.

"He?" Brandon questioned, "I didn't think you were into guys."

"I didn't either until recently in the past few months. If I'm honest, I know I'm not straight. Especially not when I'm thinking of him." Shane explained. It was evident just how nervous he was. He wasn't looking Brandon in the eyes, fidgeting with his hands. Brandon placed a hand on his back as a sign of moral support and to try to relax him.

"How does this guy make you feel?"

"He makes me feel worth it. Brandon, he is so amazing and special. He deserves nothing but the best. I'm not sure if I can be what he needs. I want to try, though." Shane admitted.

"I can tell you're afraid of something, though. What is it?" Brandon asked.

"I'm scared of losing the most important friendship of my life," Shane told him with sincerity. That was when Shane made eye contact with him that sent chills down Brandon's spine.

"I can assure you that he wouldn't trade your friendship for anything in this world. What's he like?"

"He's just the best, you know? Caring, loving, funny, and he's so patient with me. I'm just so confused, and I don't want to hurt him if we don't work out."

"I think that'd never happen. Friends before anything else, always." Brandon assured him.

Shane nodded his head, repeating the last sentence, "Friends before anything else."

The two men stopped talking and just stared into each other's eyes. It was everything that Brandon longed to hear out of that man. They gradually got closer to one another until their lips were inches away from their first kiss. Brandon could feel Shane's slow breathing hit his lips. This was the very moment that Brandon always wanted, and he was going to make the best of it.

Brandon was the first one to connect their lips in a soft kiss. He didn't want to scare Shane off by being too forceful. Since Shane was new to it, it took a moment for him to relax in the kiss. It was a soft, loving kiss with the man he loved beyond words. Brandon then wrapped his arms around his friend's neck to pull him closer. He desired more and hoped that Shane felt the same. Shane responded by deepening the kiss and gradually made his way on top of him. Brandon laid on the bed, and Shane pressed his body against him while they kept kissing.

Shane pulled away once to take Brandon's shirt off, and another time to take his off. Brandon admired Shane's muscles and how strong he was, each muscle was perfectly placed along his chest and arms. They resumed kissing more and harder with their lips moving up and down against each other. Shane's hands traveled down his friend's body, feeling everything he could to get Brandon moaning. They eventually parted lips, and Shane trailed his lips down Brandon's body, making sure Brandon was responding to every move how he wanted. Soft moans escaped his mouth as he was being cared for. It felt like love. Shane loved him. He was everything that Brandon looked for in a man, and there he was, making love to him. Before he knew it, Brandon was completely naked under the love of his life being pleasured by him in all the right ways.

Brandon woke up the next day feeling disgusted with himself. He desperately wanted to forget all about the dream. His tears came rushing down his face as his entire body shook. He hated that dream. It was the worst thing that his brain could've cooked up. Brandon never wanted to see Shane ever again. He wished that he could burn those dirty thoughts that he ever had and forget about him. However, it wasn't possible. Before he knew it, Brandon's legs were moving out of the bed, rushing to the bathroom. He lifted up the toilet seat and gagged. Luckily, nothing came up. Once again, the sobs started. How could he? Denial wasn't even the best way to explain it. After having a calming evening, Brandon had to dream about that bastard. Shane was still in his mind and heart whether he liked it or not. It didn't matter if he wanted to admit it; there was nothing that he could do.

He finally got up from the toilet and flushed it. Brandon went into his room and turned on his phone. After not talking to anyone the previous night, he desperately needed to that morning. Brandon called the first contact he saw and prayed that they would answer.

"Brandon, are you okay? You haven't talked to me in three days since class. I've been worried about you." Zach immediately asked when he answered the phone.

"I'm sorry, I just needed the night to myself. I ended up having a nightmare, but I'm fine." Brandon admitted.

"About him?" Zach wondered, even though it wasn't a hard guess.

"Yeah," Brandon mumbled as he felt a wave of guilt flowing through his body, "A sex dream. I don't know what to do!"

"That's natural, Brandon. I'm sorry that you had to have it, but it was eventually going to."

"Why, though? I'm trying to get rid of him from my mind and my heart," Brandon asked in defeat, "How come it has to be this hard?"

"He never leaves your mind. The more you try to get rid of him, the more you'll actually think about him."

Brandon sighed as he listened to Zach's rationalized answer. He despised how it made sense. As much as he wanted to get rid of Shane, he understood why he couldn't. "I don't know what to do."

"You need a therapist. I'm going to come over in about thirty minutes, and we're getting you someone professional to talk to." Zach told him.

"I don't have time to see a therapist, Zach," Brandon complained.

"Do you want to heal the best way you can?" Zach asked.

"Yes, I do. I want to heal so bad," Brandon admitted.

"Then we are finding you a therapist," Zach repeated, "We're doing it today."

Brandon shifted in his seat at the thought of letting someone in, a complete stranger that will judge him. Didn't he have enough people doing that by now? It was hard for him to agree to it as he desperately wanted an alternative. That just let another person get into his business regardless of what for. After contemplating his options, he gave in.

"Alright, I'll do it," Brandon spoke out, "Therapy it is."

Chapter 26: Talk About It

Brandon looked at Zach as they pulled up to the building. They'd found a sexual assault help group in New York, and Zach encouraged him to check it out. To say that Brandon felt scared was an understatement. He didn't want to go into that building to just cry in front of complete strangers. That was what he'd been avoiding the whole time. Now that he was with his friend pulling up to do just that made him hate life more.

"I just think it's going to be a waste of time." Brandon groaned.

"You don't know that, Brandon. I know it's scary to talk to people who you've never met about something so vulnerable, but I promise it'll be worth it." Zach assured him. Brandon looked at Zach in the eyes with an unconvinced expression on his face. There was also embarrassment deep in his heart that he had to be here. Surely Shane had shown him a sign that he'd be like this. Maybe he looked past that as his friend and didn't realize it.

"Don't leave me no matter what," Brandon whispered in a desperate voice that broke Zach's heart. He was so damaged and lost out of his mind, and it was visible. Zach wanted Brandon to be better so bad and hated that it was a long process ahead to get there. This group was only going to be the start of that.

"I promise," Zach replied, putting his hand on top of Brandon's, "I will be here for whatever you need."

Brandon took in a breath and looked at the building. They got out of the car and went inside, holding each other's hands. It wasn't intentional, but Brandon was glad to be holding it. They went to the name tags, each getting one, and wrote their names before placing them on their shirts. Upon entering the main room, Brandon was quick to realize one thing. He and Zach were the only men there. His heart sank into his stomach and gripped Zach's hand firmer. It was already embarrassing to Brandon, even though nothing terrible started.

"You've got to be kidding me," Brandon whispered in hopeless defeat.

"I know, but it'll be okay. Try not to stress." Zach told him. He empathized with the way Brandon felt. To be the one feeling like he wasn't supposed to belong had to be the worst. Even in a room filled with people who had similarly traumatic experiences! Brandon felt outnumbered.

Brandon sighed as they found a seat in the circle of chairs. All of the women were still in coats, some talked to one another, and others sat in silence. Zach decided to sit behind Brandon since he wasn't exactly there to participate and would only help Brandon when needed.

"First time here, too?" The lady beside him asked.

"Yeah," Brandon mumbled, "I'm scared about it. Also unsure if this will help me."

"I feel the same,'" The woman agreed, "I just hate feeling like this."

"Me too," Brandon nodded his head, "I'm the only man which makes shit that much worse."

"Is this all of us?" Another lady asked as she took the last seat, "Full house this morning." Brandon assumed that the lady was the therapist. She was an African American woman with brown eyes and glasses. Her hair was braided and into a ponytail, and she didn't wear makeup. There was also a noticeable southern accent in her voice. "I welcome everyone to the first sexual trauma support group meeting of the year. My name is Sharon Halt, and I am a certified therapist. We will be spending a lot of time together, hopefully. Both like this in a group, and I would also like individual appointments. There are no limits on how many times you can come to the meetings; you're always welcome back whether it's next Thursday evening or a few years from now. You decide what you need for your healing process."

"I will go over the rules since this is the first meeting. This is a free space to share whatever you feel is comfortable for you. Please leave time for everyone to speak as we only have exactly ninety minutes a session. I ask for everyone not to share any information on the medications you're taking and not saying the doctors' names that you go to. Everything we also discuss never leaves this room. We abide by HIPPA. All of that is confidential to you, alright? Why don't we stay by saying our first names only."

"Hi, my name is Tracy," The first one spoke.

"I'm Mary."

"Hello, I'm Pamela."

"Kylie,"

"Audrey'"

"My name is Brandon." He was the last one in the group.

"Who are you, sir?" Sharon looked over at Zach, who sat a few feet away.

"Hello, I'm Zach. I am not a part of the group at all. Brandon is my friend, and I'm here to support him as this is his first time doing anything like this." Zach introduced himself.

"That's perfectly fine. I appreciate you being here as well," Sharon gave him a smile to which he returned. She then put her focus on the group that sat before her. "Alright, so for our first week, we are discussing how we are currently coping with our experiences. Also, if there are any suggestions on how it can be a little easier, everyone has their own story, and each healing journey is different because of it. No way is a wrong way except for self-harm, non prescribed or illegal drugs of any kind, and alcohol."

"Not even wine?" Kylie jokingly asked, and everyone chuckled.

"Unfortunately, that is included. The same with beer because it'll only make things worse in the long run. Avoiding tobacco and gambling is also recommended. This is about your healing in the best way possible for you. I understand that there will never be complete healing as it is a forever burning scar, but you don't have to suffer in your pain."

Everyone gave a nod as she continued, "A little about myself is that I've been doing this for over fifteen years. My specialty is in helping victims who have experienced some type of sexual assault in their lives. I went to college in Miami, Florida, and got my master's in counseling about sixteen years ago. I met many clients throughout the years who I've helped, and this is my passion. Not only will we be discussing what brought you to being here today, but I also want to know about you as a person. Who you are or who you used to be."

"I'd love to be back to who I used to be," Mary sighed, "I feel as though he took that away from me."

"Who was that person? What was Mary like?" Asked the therapist.

"She was fearless. She had to work for everything that she ended up earning in her life. Her degree, house, and her car were all earned by Mary and only Mary. The only thing left for her to earn was a leading position in the job field she was working at."

"Why was this job title so important to you?" Audrey asked.

"I found it to be an important goal because it was why I went to college all along. What would be the point of going through all of that schooling just to let it sit on the shelf, not doing anything with it? I needed that as it meant the world to me." Mary explained.

"Does this career bring you happiness?" Brandon asked her next.

"No, not like I'd hoped. How could it when I had to be abused and used just to please the men who had power over me?" Mary bitterly stated, "I had to go through so many tricks and jump through hoops just to please him and tire me out."

"Men and not just one man?" Kylie questioned.

"There were four men. At one point, I would just go from penis to penis just so they can get their satisfaction. I was held down," Mary began to explain as her eyes teared up, "Tied up, I couldn't have my phone or tell any co-workers. Each month I was an employee of the month and received so many raises. It was all for show, and my colleagues would hate me for not knowing the meaning behind it, not the true and dark meaning. They didn't understand that they didn't want that title or the money. Not for what I had to do in exchange."

"Oh my God," Pamela mumbled as she hugged herself.

"Do you relate to this, Pamela?" Sharon asked.

"I do relate and empathize so much. Except it was three professors at college instead of bosses. How did you escape?"

"I quit my job a year later and never looked back. At the time, I didn't have money, and I had to save up. Including the blame and endless guilt that came with it. I told myself things like 'you're a bitch if you leave. You're getting paid, so why even be upset?' Just so much internal abuse to myself." Mary explained.

Brandon looked down at the floor as he related to those thoughts wholeheartedly. It was so similar to what he'd been feeling about him and Shane.

"As if you're foolish for complaining, right?" Brandon questioned, "You might not have wanted everything that came with the job, but the biggest part was the job, so why would you complain?"

"That's exactly how I feel." Pamela agreed.

"Yeah, same here." Mary nodded her head.

"I didn't mean to interrupt you, Mary. It was your turn." Pamela sighed.

"I apologize, too. I usually have better manners." Brandon then spoke.

"No, it's alright. It makes me feel better that I'm not alone. All of our experiences differ from one another, but we connect on that pain and guilt." Mary sighed, "I was tied down so good. Breasts and other private parts were all exposed to them like it was a piece of meat. They became such dogs who were all drunk, laughing hysterically, and made fun of my body. I wouldn't be surprised if there are videos somewhere online."

"Did you ever see cameras?" Sharon asked, and Mary nodded her head. That broke Brandon's and the rest of the group's hearts. At that moment, Brandon realized that there were worse experiences than his. Even he knew that Shane never recorded anything that he did to him. He felt like throwing up at how much it made his skin crawl. To think that anyone could find it and make this lady a laughing stock of the internet is something he could not fathom.

"I could be on multiple porn websites and never know it. Shit, I'm not looking that up ever!"

"You know that it could make your case stronger if you ever decide to file a lawsuit," Brandon spoke from a lawyer's perspective. As much as it pained him to be a part of this horrible statistic, he was able to put his feelings aside at times to look at the laws regarding his matter. Between the TV, the internet, his job, and all that he read in books since his freshman year of college, he had more information than most.

"How could my lawyer find it if I don't know what sites to look at? There's so many."

"I hate to say it, but that's going to be hard. YouTube doesn't allow those explicit content, luckily, but there are hundreds, maybe thousands of porn sites that do." Brandon then mumbled, "That's the unfortunate part."

"It makes me sick just thinking about it," Tracy spoke for the first time since saying her name. "I was raped by seven different guys as a teenager in high school. There probably is one video of it."

"How long ago, Tracy?" Sharon questioned.

"This was five years ago in my senior year. You never heal from it at all. At least I haven't." Tracy sighed.

"I figured we were around the same age." Brandon sighed.

"Yeah, I did too."

"Are you going through with a lawsuit, Brandon?" Sharon asked him.

Brandon took a glance at Zach, who gave him a reassuring smile. He took in a deep breath before answering, "Yes, I am. It is the hardest decision to make in my life, but for him to understand what he did to me, I have to."

"It was a male assaulter with you too." Sharon hummed.

"A straight male that wanted to experiment, as he called it. The only problem was that he got addicted to the point where he no longer cared about me as a human being. Let alone not caring that we were best friends," Brandon mumbled, "The crazy thing is that he's straight and I'm gay. You'd expect it to be the other way around."

"There are no expectations in sexuality even with the same gender, Brandon. Before you continue, I need to point out that there's no way to know who's a rapist or not. No man or woman can be identified just by passing by somebody on the street. One in three women are assaulted by other women, but it's never talked about."

"I hate to say it, but I understand why. Especially being a part of the community. We need to keep this good reputation for this big movement," Tracy explained, "I think Brandon will agree when I say if we show any signs of same-sex sexual assault of any kind as a trend, that ruins a lot for us all."

"I absolutely agree. A lot will get questioned whether or not we should be able to adopt if marriage equality should be rolled back, or even serving in the military will be questioned. We can't say anything because it'll ruin the good more rather than help fix the bad." Brandon added on.

"If I may ask Brandon, why are you going through with it if you feel like this?" Sharon asked.

"I don't know…" Brandon shrugged as he didn't want to share any more that day. His head was beginning to hurt, and he could feel his anxiety wanting to take over. He didn't want to embarrass himself at the first meeting. Sharon must've realized that as she didn't want to push him or any of the ladies to the point where they could shut down.

This was difficult for Brandon in a new way. Talking about what he'd been through and was still going through was hard on him. It was like letting more and more people in his darkness would allow people to have their own judgmental opinions. He was still feeling brave for going to it, even if Zach had to force him out of bed. Literally. Zach had to go to the hotel to make him get up from the bed and get ready. Brandon knew that he wanted to get help, but it was a drag that morning, not knowing what to expect.

"I would like to thank each one of you for coming out this morning. Even you, Zach. I hope I'm saying your name, right." Sharon looked over at him.

"You are, and I appreciate you for helping my friend," Zach smiled at her.

Sharon then passed out her business cards to the group. "I would hope that you all come back next Friday morning to continue our work together as this is the beginning. As I stated in the beginning, it is at your own pace, and you are welcome back anytime. However, to participate in this healing process, you must come back each week. Please try to make the group sessions and private sessions as this is a program that will work if you commit to these meetings. You have the number to my office and my email address. I sincerely encourage everyone to reach out to me about private sessions as soon as possible as I do have other clients. Also, you are not allowed to get in contact with each other. Your first assignment for the week is to think about how you've been coping with your anxiety and other post-sexual assault emotions. You all come to group therapy to no longer feel as if nobody else understands you when in actuality, thousands of people do. However, no one else can do your healing work except for yourselves. I hope everyone has a safe evening."

Everyone in the group thanked the lady and then got up to move around. Brandon went to Zach and hugged him. "I couldn't have done this without you."

"I'm so proud of you. I was worried you'd run out seeing that it's all women, but you can still relate to them. As she said, it's a long process, and it'll take work, Brandon. You have to do the work. I'll be here to help, however way I can." Zach smiled.

"I know, and thank you." Brandon nodded his head.

The ladies were all still standing around talking to each other, and Brandon went back to them. They all shared a long, deep sigh and then chuckled together. No one else understood what they were going through on the deepest level possible. It didn't matter the variations of stories.

"Thank you, ladies, for not judging me being the only man here. I was so scared walking in; I had no clue." Brandon smiled politely.

"It was interesting to see a man be in this group. I know that we're all brave by just coming to this, but men never speak out. It was amazing." Pamela gave kudos to Brandon, and the others agreed. Everyone said their goodbyes and left out of the building one by one, with Zach and Brandon being the last two out of the door.

Zach pulled out of the parking lot, and Brandon looked out of the window. He was proud of himself. Therapy would be a longer and harder journey than expected, but he had to do his best.

Chapter 27: Reality Sets In

It was a Monday afternoon, and Brandon was at work getting ready for his lunch break. He had made his way into the break room to warm up his food. After that first group session, Brandon had been decisive as to whether he should continue to go back. It was just so daunting to be the only man in the group. He thought that maybe private sessions were a better fit for him as he liked the therapist. That night, Brandon was finally able to sleep more peacefully without a nightmare. He didn't remember the last time that had happened.

Brandon was still willing to do that assignment. He couldn't think of the ways that he'd been coping with his anxiety. If he was honest, maybe he was allowing the panic attacks and anxiety to freely rule over his body just like the lingering hands of Shane still were. He knew that it wasn't healthy for him and needed a way to control them better. While warming his food up in the microwave, he felt stares at the back of his head. When he turned around, Daniel, Gina, and Destiny sat at a table looking at him.

"If this is either about firing me or killing me, please do it fast and painless." Brandon simply stated.

"Sit down, Andreas," Daniel instructed him.

"Oh, this is not going to be good." Brandon groaned as he grabbed his food from the microwave and took his seat.

"We just have your best interest in mind, is all." Destiny opened up the conversation.

"I know that, but what in particular?" Brandon questioned.

"This is about law school. We were all surprised that you are planning on attending immediately after grad school." Gina started, "With everything that you've faced these last few months, wouldn't you like some kind of break?"

"Well yeah, that's why I'm not doing anything this summer. I'm going to be working and sleeping." Brandon told them, "I'll be ready by the time August comes."

"I can assure you that it won't be long enough." Daniel shook his head.

"We all took that year in between the two to regroup and mentally prepare for law school. Hell, I took two years off, and that was still crazy!" Gina explained.

"I was still living with my folks when I finished undergrad. I spent my year off finding an apartment and getting a steady paying job to support myself. You need to do the same. You're living in a hotel, Brandon. We understand that it was a last-minute change and everything, but come on. You know you need a better living situation." Daniel added, "Not to mention that you don't look like you've slept in months. This semester is close to killing you next."

"I just feel like I'd be allowing him to win if I do that. That's the worst thing I could do." Brandon groaned.

"Are you attending because you want to be a lawyer, or are you doing it to prove him and your parents wrong?" Gina asked in all seriousness, "I need you to think about that before you answer."

Brandon didn't have to think about it as he gave the simple response, "My answer is yes."

"I'm just going to guess that means both. Those are not reasons for you to go to law school, Brandon." Destiny told him.

"Okay, okay, they are not the real reasons, I promise. They're more like my emotional reason," Brandon defended himself, "I want to go to law school because it is my passion. Spending four years in community college to earn my undergraduate degree just made me want it even more. I've told you guys that I stay on top of every supreme court case there is. Then all of the civil court cases with Judge Judy, Divorce Court, and Judge Mathis, to name a few. I love them all. I'm not interested in being the actual judge, but representing the plaintiff or defendant means so much to me. It's what I'm supposed to do in my life."

"There's the lawyer in you that we needed to hear," Gina smiled while the others agreed, "We needed to see that fire still lit in you. You have it, no doubt."

"What type of lawyer do you want to be?" Destiny questioned.

"That's an interesting question because, before my situation, I was leaning towards a divorce attorney. Bankruptcy lawyers may be the highest paid, but that sounds so boring to me," Brandon chuckled, "I chose a criminal law firm to work at, so that's appealing to me now. There are so many choices, and I'll have to narrow them down eventually."

"Law school will definitely help you with that," Daniel informed.

Brandon nodded his head and took another bite of food, "I come in here for lunch and get an intervention to go with it."

"You got a two in one special today. You're very welcome." Daniel responded with sarcasm.

"Free of charge," Gina added and went to warm her food up.

"How was the first group therapy?" Daniel asked Brandon.

"I actually liked it a lot more than I thought I would. The only thing is that I'm the only male in the group." Brandon sighed.

"That had to suck," Destiny chimed in.

"When Zach and I first got there, it was, but they were all so welcoming. I have to thank my friend for encouraging me to go."

"Will this be a weekly thing?"

"Yeah, it's every Friday night after work, so it's perfect. We already have our first assignment to think about for the next one, and I'm going to have the private sessions as well." Brandon explained to them.

"What is the assignment?" Daniel curiously asked.

"The assignment is to talk about the ways I'm coping with everything. Something so simple and yet so hard for me to think about. I'm not sure if I have one yet." Brandon shared.

"Then that's what you write down to tell them. You can get help with that, too." He informed Brandon.

"You don't understand how helpful this is going to be, Brandon. We want you back just as much as you want yourself back. Also, ignore social media for now. That's damaging to your mental health, which is already so fragile." Gina spoke before she took another bite of her food.

"I try to. A few nights a week, I've been shutting off my phone once I get to the hotel room. It's just all noise to me. The unnecessary and mean spirited noises that I don't need in my life. I need them not to bother me. I've been so close to deleting all of my social media pages." Brandon shook his head, "It's only a bunch of family and cat pictures anyway. I have Google for that."

"Just have a balance and don't shut down to the friends you see face to face," Gina advised.

"I also recommend that you get used to your body again. Go dancing and do yoga or something. It might help you. Get your body moving as much as you can." Destiny suggested.

"I think we were planning on celebrating at some club in May. The only thing is I can't drink now? That's fucking ridiculous that he was able to take away so much joy from me by doing this," Brandon cried out.

"Were you a big drinker?" Daniel asked him.

"No, more of a social drinker. I rarely got drunk, and I've never done drugs or anything. Maybe beer every now and then," Brandon explained, "Shane liked drinking more than I did, but still wasn't often."

"I think he was drunk the night they arrested him. It was in the police report," Daniel shared.

"No way," Brandon looked at him in shock. Maybe that explained his behavior for attacking him out of nowhere. He obviously didn't give any attention to him showing any signs of being drunk. His heart dropped as he thought about all of the other times. Maybe that was the cause of the abuse, and he didn't realize it.

"Did you not read the full report? It says clearly that at least his breath smelled like alcohol, if not drunk."

"Well, excuse me, I was too busy trying to break free to notice!" Brandon murmured.

"How much is his bail again?" Destiny asked Daniel.

"Just ten thousand dollars. It really isn't a lot, and I'm surprised a family member hasn't done it yet." Daniel shrugged.

"Do not speak that into existence, Daniel," Brandon glared at him.

"I'm not! I was just saying." His boss held his hands up to defend himself.

"I guess I would like to know what Ms. Jacobs thinks about this. It's her only child." Brandon sighed, "Should I talk to her?"

"No!" All of his bosses said at once.

"Who would talk to their rapist's parents, and what for?" Daniel questioned.

"Well, I just thought since we were friends—" Brandon tried again.

"No!" They repeated.

"Stop with the emotional thinking, Andreas. No one should call her, especially not you." Destiny warned him, "Stay away from everyone with his last name."

"Well, back to you and the law school situation, I say consider the break," Gina got back to the point, "We'll support whatever decision you make, and you know that. I'm just concerned that you're damaging your mental health if you go right away."

"Just focus on yourself, studying for this last class load, and graduating. Law school will come when it's time. Also, do not stress about this case that's so far from now. I got your back." Daniel told him, "Calling her is dangerous because if he's around, that could void your restraining order. She could put him on the phone, and they'll be able to use it in court as an incoming call from you."

"They could use it as evidence against you that you called him even though you just wanted to speak to his mother. You won't be able ever to get another restraining order." Gina reminded Brandon.

"Well, fuck!" Brandon groaned, "I guess that's true. It feels like anything that I might want to do would immediately make me lose my case."

"Welcome to being the plaintiff in a possible jury trial case," Daniel patted his back.

"I'm just glad that I have all of you guys to help me through this." Brandon slightly smiled, "Fine, I'll focus on school and this group therapy. Law school I'll think about, alright?"

"Good!" Destiny rubbed his back, "We're still proud of you."

"No calling his family!" Gina instructed.

"I won't," Brandon promised.

The co-workers finished their meals while talking about a lighter topic and headed back to their offices. Brandon was thankful to have people who cared about him during this endless living nightmare. Every time that Brandon would scroll past his text messages, it made him want to vomit all over again.

Chapter 28: Holding On

Brandon walked inside the therapy building, feeling anxious. It was his first private session, and he was all alone. Zach had insisted on going with him, but he really wanted to do it by himself. Brandon didn't want to seem like he couldn't do anything on his own. He hated that he had become such a "dependent bitch" because of his traumatic events. None of it seemed fair that Zach had to carry so much of the weight with him.

"Hi, I'm Brandon Andreas, and I am here for my private session with Ms. Sharon," Brandon told the gentleman at the front desk.

The man at the front desk looked disorganized as he was going through a lot of files. Brandon sympathized with the struggle so much having the same type of job. Some days felt as if nothing was where it needed to be, even though he swore he knew where he placed everything.

"Hi, Mr. Andreas, please excuse my mess this morning. I'm just getting here myself." The name tag on the desk said Raymond ManHock. Brandon took a glance at it before responding.

"Don't worry, Raymond, I understand completely. Having a front desk job can get ridiculous," Brandon chuckled with a smile, "I do the same thing."

"It gets crazy, doesn't it?" Raymond laughed slightly, "You think you have everything, and then the next minute, so much is missing."

"Oh my goodness, tell me about it. People don't really realize just how much you are in charge of."

"No, they really don't get it. It's so much more than just smiling, sending emails, and checking people in. There's always something thrown at you unexpectedly!" Raymond shook his head, "I'll let her know you're here."

"Thank you," Brandon then took a seat and picked up one of the magazines on the end table beside him. He texted Zach and Madelyn that he'd made it safely to the place before he began to read.

"Tell me how it goes. Love you!" Madelyn replied.

"Meet for lunch afterward," Zach responded.

Twenty minutes later, the therapist was ready to see him. Once she called his name, Brandon put the magazine down and went to where she was. He smiled as he shook her hand, "Hi Sharon, nice to see you again."

"The pleasure is all mine," Sharon smiled as she led him to the private room in the back, "I have to say, it was courageous of you to come to join the group session and to speak some. I rarely get men joining since it's a sensitive topic to deal with. Especially with the stigma around men and sex."

"I was so uncomfortable at first. Being the only man just made it weird. Of course, no one ever thinks that they'd be a victim," Brandon sighed when he took his seat, "Especially not from a man who was a best friend."

"More often than not, it is done by people they're closest to. You heard the stories that were shared in that session on Friday night. We obviously can't discuss any of the ladies, but they never thought it would happen to them either. The main thing that you need to learn is not to put any blame on yourself. You didn't cause it to happen," Sharon started.

"Everyone keeps saying that, but I did!" Brandon groaned and looked down.

"Why do you think that?" Sharon asked.

"I could have said no to him wanting to experiment that first night. If I had stopped thinking emotionally and talked to him about it instead of saying yes, I wouldn't be here. I wouldn't have to do this lawsuit where there's a slim chance of the jury believing me."

"I don't know if that's so true, Brandon. I understand how you'd believe it to be the case, but I don't think you triggered him to act like this. For all you know, he could have already been planning for this to happen."

"Shane isn't that clever with his thoughts and ideas, trust me." Brandon shook his head, "At least not the version of Shane that I called my best friend."

"Shane is his name?"

Brandon sighed once he realized that he'd said his name, "Yes, I'm sorry, I probably wasn't supposed to say his name. I hate saying it, anyway."

"Normally, I wouldn't want my clients to say their names because it's a way to stay in the past. The reason being is that he no longer deserves to have his name come out of your mouth," Sharon explained, "However, this is fine as it is good information for me to have. I want to start from the beginning, leading to the first incident, if that's okay with you?"

"Yes, of course."

"How long were you friends?"

"I met him in my freshman year of high school, so eight years."

"Did you have a crush on him then?"

"I did; it was actually bigger than it was in college. I definitely wasn't ever over the crush, but growing up and maturing calmed me down." Brandon sighed.

"What made you attracted to him?" Sharon then asked while she took notes.

"I loved how he didn't make my sexuality a big deal, unlike every other straight guy in high school did. We connected on just about everything from sports, music, TV shows, and cars. We got the same type of first jobs as a front desk receptionist at different companies, moved into our first apartment together as roommates," Brandon began to list, "The same hobbies, group of friends, all of that."

"Even in college?"

"I've been too focused on my studies to make as many friends, but he definitely stayed the life of the party whenever he had the chance."

"During the first few years, were there any signs of him liking you affectionately?"

"No, which is why I was so afraid of ever saying anything. I respected the fact that he was straight, and he didn't mind that I was gay at all. Of course, we joked around about the possibility, but I never took that as an opportunity."

"Are you thinking that if you did, you wouldn't be here?"

Brandon looked down, "I don't know anymore. If he really has this addiction to sex, then this situation could've still happened. If I'm honest,

I wanted to move on from him. Having one crush for so many years seems immature."

"Would it be safe to say that you were in love with him? Expressing something far beyond a crush?"

"Yes, definitely with the years going by. I think maybe it was because he kept doing things that made me fall harder for him. He just knew me better than anyone else except for my feelings for him. Maybe I hid it so well like I wanted to." Brandon explained.

"Yet, this entire time, he was never once uncomfortable with you being gay?" The therapist clarified.

"That's correct. He would willingly talk to me about the guys I liked. I mean, the other guys, I would like to try to get over him. That doesn't mean that I wasn't into them; it wasn't just as deep with them. Then I, of course, talked about girls with him. Despite my jealousy at times, I would even help with getting him ready for dates and such."

"Do you now wish that you could've stayed with one of the guys that you went out with?"

"I don't think so. They were all so awful and mean. Considering my crush with him, my friends who knew would think that I wasn't trying hard enough, but that was never the case," Brandon sighed as he started, "One cheated on me, the other was a hysterical liar, a few were just out for sex, and others just wanted money. I don't even have a lot of money. Four boyfriends and a lot of first dates, actually. They were still months apart from each other. Never going from boyfriend to boyfriend."

"What were you looking for in them that they didn't have?" Asked the therapist.

"Shane," Brandon answered honestly, "Nobody was like Shane. Now I hope they didn't end up like him."

"I would hope not either."

"They couldn't understand me as he did. With Shane, I could have a huge smile on my face, and he would still know when it wasn't genuine. I've tried so many times to be happy around him when I wasn't actually happy. He would just look at me and go, 'I can tell something is bothering you. Don't lie to me.' He was never wrong except for how I felt about him."

"Were you ever close to saying anything?"

"Countless amounts of times. I just knew better not to. So when he asked to experiment, of course, I said yes. That was my chance to get him to become vulnerable and open up to me. Instead, it did the opposite, and I never saw him become so cold like that towards me. He was definitely a completely different man."

"That's how most sexual relations between a rapist can start. Even if we want to believe that he didn't know what he was doing, there had to be some indication inside of his mind that knew what was really going on." Sharon explained.

"He had to have known. I was constantly trying to get free," Brandon told her as his tears began to fall, "Now I can't get his grip off of me. Everywhere I go, no matter what I do, I can feel that tight ass grip around me."

"How many times did it happen?"

"Four times total, even though it feels like a million times. The way he would grab me, yell in my face to shut up, ignoring my whimpers to be set free. He became this monster that no longer knew me, and I certainly didn't care to get to know him." Brandon started to shake as he talked, "He knew how to make me his bitch."

"What did he make you do?" Sharon asked.

Hearing the question made him go weak instantly. That was something no one had asked him, and he dreaded the moment when he had to answer it. No one knew. Not Zach, Daniel, even Richard didn't have this information yet. He was eventually going to, but he had to process it for himself first.

"I remember the day that he texted me the toys he had bought. There were so many, and he used every one in one fucking night," Brandon sobbed, "There were ropes, dildos, fleshlights, and one other thing that I couldn't identify. I was sure that I was going to die. Hell, I didn't even want to live after that night. He'd let me know what he bought through text when I was finishing up a big final last semester in class. It took away my joy from having the highest score on a final that the professor had ever seen. Nothing mattered after I saw those pictures."

"How did that make you feel, Brandon?" Sharon asked and gave him a box of tissues that were on her desk.

"Alone and trapped. As if Shane destroyed so much to the point where I can't appreciate the good I still have in my life." That was the moment when Brandon broke down. He couldn't take any more pain, hurt, or misery from the past. The desperate need to be free became vital to his life.

"Let it out, Brandon. Cry, scream, let all of your emotions free." Sharon told him and embraced him. Brandon let his life shatter right before his eyes. The legs attached to his body couldn't move, his arms suddenly became weights of steel, and the tears in his eyes were so strong like a dam breaking in a river. His mouth was wailing out desperate sobs that he held back for so long. He hated living with a burning ache inside of his heart. The darkness was frightening, and every time it kept closing in on him suffocated him. Brandon's chest began to tighten up with his heart pounding out of it. That was his best friend who had done him horribly. It was the sex addiction that got in the way of what was the best friend of his life.

Brandon didn't know how he was ever going to move on. The thought of loving anyone else again was out of the question. He missed Shane. He hated Shane. He loved Shane. Brandon knew everything about Shane, but he was this complete stranger all over again. His wrists could still feel the pressure of the tight ropes that held him down. The scars from the sharp dildos were still visible on his butt and back. They were sensitive to touch, and sitting down was hard to do.

"I'm never going to heal! I'm stuck like this," Brandon choked out after about ten minutes of not saying anything.

"You can, Brandon. It's going to be hard and take some time, but yes, you will heal from this." Sharon soothed.

"I don't know how to cope with any of it," Brandon shook his head, "I basically just let the panic attacks take over me, and I don't know how to avoid them. They just randomly start and end whenever they want. I can be at the hotel, my job, or in class; it doesn't matter. The last time, my body just darted out of the room, and I ran into the bathroom. It's like I'm blacking out, and my body gets to running."

"Do you want ways to control them? You can try, but it may not always be successful," Sharon asked and then continued once Brandon answered with a nod, "There's meditation, breathing exercises, yoga, and the most popular in many aspects in life is music. Music can help so much more than people realize. Would you like to get a pamphlet that suggests many techniques?"

"Yes, I would like to." Brandon sniffed and wiped his eyes. Sharon gave Brandon another pamphlet that was on her desk. Brandon read the title of it, which was: Anxiety and depression: How to get through it all.

"You're going to have to work on everything I've given you in order to heal, Brandon. You are a strong man for so many reasons that you don't realize," Sharon looked into his eyes, "I believe in you. You can get through this, okay?"

"Okay," Brandon nodded his head, "I really want to get better. Hopefully, I will."

"Does the same time work for next week to meet?"

"It's perfect, yes," Brandon confirmed as he stood up. Even though the situation was still haunting him, talking about it to a professional lifted some weight from his heart. He collected his items, said goodbye to the therapist, and walked out of the room feeling a little better. It still hurt that he had to go through a lot to get over his ex-best friend, and he desperately wanted to be at the end of the long road that awaited him.

He made it back to the car and texted Zach to meet him for lunch. Two minutes later, Zach replied, saying that he was on his way to the restaurant. Brandon started his car up, got his seatbelt on, and headed in the direction that he needed. What scared him the most was not knowing what was getting ready to happen in his life. Nothing seemed to go as he planned, and he was sure that his heart couldn't take any more hits.

Chapter 29: Bad Luck

Nobody likes Monday mornings, especially not Brandon. The beginning of his week was off to a bad start. With a terrible nightmare that felt so real, an alarm clock that didn't go off, and a phone that barely charged, it was bound to be a hassle. He groaned and dragged himself out of bed and into the bathroom. Brandon got his shower and put his work clothes on in a hurry. He decided to skip breakfast and leave his job to eat on his lunch break since he hadn't had time to get new groceries.

Brandon also felt down because of the particular date that it was. March Twentieth: Shane's birthday. He could've just called off that day. There were no classes, and the next private therapy session wasn't until Wednesday. However, Brandon had to remind himself that he could be in worse situations. Over the last couple of weeks, Brandon had finally fallen into a routine for his semester. He was passing all of his classes, he had plenty of time to study at work, and the therapy sessions were going fine. There had to be light somewhere soon in all of this chaos for him, and he desperately wondered when that would be. His heart felt a sense of loneliness that no one could fill. Each day that void was growing and expanding twice its size to which he couldn't do anything about.

Once Brandon was inside his car, he tried to start his vehicle. The problem? It wouldn't start.

"What?" Brandon questioned out loud. He started shaking his head in disbelief as that couldn't possibly be happening to him. To be fair, it was an old 2007 car that he was lucky enough to get from one of his uncles as his high school graduation gifts. Not that his uncle accepted his sexuality, but he knew Brandon needed some transportation for college. His deal to Brandon was that if he stopped being gay, he'd fix it for him whenever there was a problem. That was clearly dropped as Brandon couldn't just automatically start liking women because of a car. He had hoped to have it last until he completed grad school in May. Well, that was before his life turned upside down. The oil was changed in December, he recently got new tires in January, and had just passed the inspection.

"Okay, nice joke, universe. You can let my car start now!" Brandon called out, feeling desperate. No matter how many times he tried to start it up.

Ten minutes passed by with no luck being on his side. Brandon then got out his phone to see when the next bus would be near the hotel bus stop headed to his workplace, and the earliest wasn't for another three hours. He couldn't call Zach because he was gone to work himself, and he wasn't sure if he felt comfortable enough asking any other classmates, especially when he didn't know where anyone else lived. Without having any other options, Brandon decided to take an Uber to his job. It wasn't hard to set up an account, connect his payment option, and request the ride. He was relieved that his first ride was free.

Brandon made sure to check the license plate on the car before getting into the backseat. "You're Elizabeth?"

"I am," The lady confirmed. Brandon gave a small smile as she started to drive. He remembered to lock the doors of his car with the key fob as she drove away. He had everything he needed; his bag, wallet, as well as his school and work ID just in case. He sent a text to his bosses that he could be a few minutes late due to traffic and tried to rest for the ride's remainder. Brandon was trying so hard not to burst into tears in the back of the vehicle. He was not looking forward to the day that his luck ran out, and he certainly wished it hadn't been on a day that was usually celebrated. It was early morning, so the streets of New York were filled with cars in traffic. He was used to it, but it seemed like he couldn't catch a break.

His mind kept stressing about that car. How was he going to afford to fix it? What exactly could be wrong with it when he just had everything checked not too long ago? This was not the day for life to add on additional frustrations to his life, yet at the same time, it was the best day to do just that. The pattern had to continue. His best friend, his dad, his mother, the place he once called home, and now his only reliable transportation. Brandon was dying to get his break from something, but instead, his problems kept piling up one after the other. He was still thankful that his health was able to sustain, and nothing had gone wrong. It was the first winter that'd gone by without him getting sick.

Brandon rushed into the building once the vehicle finally arrived at his destination. He clocked in, got a cup of coffee, and got settled at the front desk booting up the computer. Just as he was signed in, Daniel came by, setting a stack of papers on his desk.

"I need copies," Daniel told him with a grumpy tone in his voice. That caught Brandon off guard; he hardly ever saw his boss upset. His boss turned to walk away, but Brandon needed to understand this mood of his.

"Everything okay, Dan?" Brandon questioned cautiously.

"Why were you late?" Daniel snapped at him and turned back around, "I can't remember the last time your ass was late to work! What the fuck, Brandon? Are you taking this job for granted now?"

Brandon looked at him with total disbelief, "What? No, of course not. I texted you that I was running late. Then there was some traffic on the way on top of it."

"Then you should've woken up earlier!"

"I know, my alarm didn't go off this morning. I was rushing to get here, but then—"

"I don't want to hear it!" Daniel shouted, "Not everything is about you, Brandon!"

Brandon stayed quiet as his boss just glared at him. He didn't know why Daniel was acting so harshly to him of all days. That's where Brandon started to shut down inside. He couldn't react to anything as he didn't know what would happen. He felt his nerves begin to flare up inside of him. His system went back to what it felt like when he was being yelled at by Shane.

By his rapist.

Brandon was turning back into the trapped mindset that his rapist wanted him. It was frightening to him, and he didn't know what to do. The sensation of his grasp began to linger around him again. Flashes of Shane's face took over his boss's going back and forth between the two. With no other words spoken, he watched Daniel as he walked away and slammed the door to his office behind him. He figured that it was no use in fighting with Daniel that morning. Not that he had the energy to do so anyway. Brandon was imagining Shane laughing in glory in all of his pain on his birthday. This had to be the karma of him getting arrested. To think that it would be smooth sailing until their case got picked up by the court system was laughable. He also figured that if there was a way for his deceased father could see him, he was laughing too.

He made his way to the copier making at least three of each paper. Since he wasn't told how many to do, he had to guess. Brandon put them in Daniel's mailbox before he went back to his desk. He checked his email to see if there was anything significant that he had to do. Brandon decided that he didn't have any time to study just yet. In the Google search engine, he immediately entered in "used cars for sale" and got to looking. He wasn't sure if he wanted to spend more money on that old and rusty vehicle that betrayed him. It made him sick and tired of being so reliant on something that was hardly reliable anymore.

He made sure that he drank his cup of coffee throughout the morning. The lawyers barely had anything else for him to do, and it was overwhelming to figure out which cat to try out. Obviously, he knew not to decide based on one day. Brandon had to admit that he hadn't had the time to figure out the bills and how they'd adjusted. Everything he had to spend money on was done without much thought. He made sure that he wasn't overdrawing on his bank account, and he knew that he had three credit cards in case of an emergency. It was clear to Brandon that the emergent moment had come. His friend, Xavier, understood car sales better than him, so he decided to give him a call.

"Hey, Brandon," Xavier greeted, "What's up?"

"Definitely not life, I'll tell you that." Brandon groaned.

"I can't imagine what you're going through; I'm so sorry, man." Xavier empathized, "Is there anything that I can do? I mean it."

"That's why I called you. Didn't you say you knew someone in the car dealership business?" Brandon asked.

"I do, yeah. You need a new car?" Xavier questioned, "I can have my aunt call you this afternoon."

"Yes. I'm tired of the piece of shit that I have to drive. Of all days, this was the day that my car wouldn't start. Why did I think that everything was going to be okay on this day? You know what today is, right?"

"No, should I?"

"I'll give you a hint. Today is usually celebrated, but I'd rather have slept through it. There's no longer a need to celebrate."

"Oh, it's his birthday, isn't it?" Xavier sighed, "I haven't had time to think about it this morning. I'm sure it would've hit me eventually."

"It definitely hit my ass hard. I'm trying not to complain, but it isn't looking possible. I'll call you tonight to tell you about it." Brandon mumbled the last part.

"Definitely, I'm not doing anything tonight. Give me ten minutes to call my aunt, and I'll have her call." Xavier explained.

"Thanks, Xavier," Brandon replied before they hung up. He placed his phone back on the charger and continued to search online. His phone was going off with an unknown number in seven minutes, and he figured it was his friend's aunt. "Hello?"

"Hi, is this Xavier's friend Brandon?" The lady asked.

"I am yes. Hi, how are you?" Brandon greeted.

"I'm fine, and please call me Joanna," She introduced, "Xavier told me you are going to be in the market for a vehicle?"

"I am. Thank you for calling so fast. I haven't looked at a lot of options yet as I've only begun today, but I need something quickly."

"Okay, I understand. Are you trading in a vehicle?"

"I don't know; I'm pretty sure that my car should go to the junkyard. It's really old and in bad condition."

"Is it still running?"

"As of this morning, no, it isn't. I had to uber to work."

"I'm very sorry to hear that. We can probably get you in a new car by the end of the week, if not today. How does that sound?"

"That would be amazing," Brandon smiled.

"When can you come in?" Joanna asked.

"I think tomorrow will be best, please?"

"Of course, I'll have you in my schedule."

"I really appreciate it, Ms. Joanna. I'll see you then."

"Have a great day." She ended the conversation and hung up.

Brandon placed his phone back on the charger and texted Xavier his appreciation. He saw that it was his lunchtime and headed towards the break room, getting his wallet out for the vending machine. When he walked up to it, he noticed that it was out of order and groaned.

"Yeah, it's been down all morning for some reason," Gina told him.

"Of course, it would be. We still have the snacks in the refrigerator?" Brandon asked as he went to it.

"Yeah, there's like a couple of yogurts, and I think cheese sticks or leftover pizza."

"Eating as if I'm back in the high school's lunchroom, huh?" Brandon grumbled to himself. He got his drink, warmed up the pizza, and sat down next to his other boss, "I see someone else is having a bad day, too."

"I don't know what the fuck is up with Dan today. He's never like this at all." Gina rolled her eyes.

"I don't get it. He usually tells us what's going on. I'm not going to say much, but of all days, today was not the day I should've been yelled at."

"What's going on with you?"

"I don't want to talk about it," Brandon mumbled, "I feel like I complain too much that I'm sick of myself. Surely everyone else is sick of my shit."

"Brandon, you know it's unhealthy to keep your feelings inside. Especially since you started therapy." Gina stated.

"I get that. Believe me, I understand that better than anyone else, but I fucking refuse to be a cry baby about everything that's going wrong in my life. I just can't, Gina. Life just decided that I was getting too comfortable with my misery, and it had to become worse. Can we leave it at that?"

"Brandon…" Gina sighed.

"Gina, I cannot continue to be a waterfall of tears because of him. I'm at the point of wanting to die for real. Fuck life."

"Brandon!" Gina sternly said his name.

"Gina, I'm gay, and I have doubts about a god. I'm going to be burning if these religious people are right. So why live?"

"Wait, you never believed in him?"

"You're telling me that a God makes a rule to hate gay people and then makes me gay? As if he created me just so I can burn in an afterlife? No, I'm good, thanks."

"All I'll say is that's only the noise of religion and not the faith of God. However, I completely understand where you're coming from. I'm not going to push anything down your throat." Gina promised him.

"I trust you." Brandon nodded his head and continued to eat, "I'm definitely going to the store tonight. This is completely ridiculous!"

"Alright, well, you know my office is always open to talk," Gina then finished her meal and went to wash her container out.

"I speculate it, Gina." He told her as she left.

Brandon finished his food and went back to his desk shortly after. He searched the internet for the rest of the afternoon since no one else needed him to do anything. After he clocked out at the end of the day, he decided to pay Daniel a visit.

"May I help you?" Daniel asked him.

"Daniel, I'm not doing this with you again on Wednesday. You're going to tell me what the hell is bothering you, man. I need to know." Brandon demanded as he sat down.

"You're really going to talk to your boss like that?" Daniel darted at him.

"Nope, I clocked out ten minutes ago. You're not my boss right now; you are my friend. We're talking man to man with no bullshit." Brandon demanded.

Daniel let out a big sigh in defeat, "I didn't mean any of it. My husband and I got bad news."

"Why couldn't have you just said that? You have everyone confused and concerned about you. I certainly didn't need to be attacked on a day like today."

"I'm sorry, alright? What happened to you?" Daniel genuinely asked.

"I don't have to give you a reason anymore. I clocked out," Brandon shrugged, "You didn't want it this morning. I'm not giving it to you now. What's the bad news?"

"Our bills are getting ridiculous at home. The cable bill is increasing, the house payment didn't go through, and there's the burden of this business. We're barely getting new clients."

"Oh wow, that's way worse than me living in a hotel right now. Especially when I now have no transportation either. I have it lucky compared to you," Brandon sarcastically told him.

"No transportation?" Daniel asked, shocked, "Brandon, I—"

"Save it. Do you know how bad I want issues like yours right now? At least you have a house and multiple vehicles. You have a supportive husband and possibly kids for you in the future!" Brandon shouted, "I have nothing. Nothing except for working for your ass. I'm only ten minutes late and for you to do that to me? My rapist could somehow be found not guilty and get revenge by killing me for all I know."

"Bills? Man, I'm living in a hotel because my anxiety can't handle living in an apartment where I was raped against my will. Yet you're bitching about a nice house, with an amazing husband, and a damn good job while making me feel like shit? I'd love your problems right now. I'm trying to prove that a straight man raped a gay man. You're mad about how fortunate you are? That's really a slap in my face," Brandon then got up and walked out of the office, "Have a safe drive home, Daniel. See you Wednesday."

Brandon grabbed his items and went to get in Zach's car feeling frustrated. He slammed the door by accident and put his seatbelt on.

"Brandon, oh my God, I'm so sorry. You know you could've called me." Zach sympathized.

Brandon sighed and shook his head as he held back tears, "Can you take me to the grocery store? I'm out of food."

"Of course." Zach nodded his head and began to drive down the street. Brandon tried to calm down and forget about it all, but he was now infuriated. It wasn't right what Daniel did to him.

By Friday afternoon, he had purchased his new car. Brandon, Zach, Lewis, and Stacey all took a ride to lunch together to celebrate. He and Daniel made amends, and they promised to have tension on the next Monday morning no longer. Brandon's living situation was going to have to stay the same for a little while longer until he graduated, but he didn't mind. The old car was transported to the junkyard, and he had a great payment plan for his car notes, thanks to his friend's aunt. He'd just have to hope that the bad luck didn't return for the following year on that day.

Chapter 30: Graduates

Brandon couldn't wrap it around his head. The day finally came where he had completed the first four years of a milestone to achieve his dreams of becoming a lawyer. He had spent the night with Zach in his new apartment that was close to where they were hoping to go to law school. Brandon was still living in the hotel and was looking into moving into the same apartments. It would be a great day, and Brandon promised himself to try his best not to have anything to trigger him.

It was going to be a celebration. Brandon had made straight A's for his entire semester despite having to go through so much. Zach and Stacey had to keep telling him that he deserved it, but he was still in shock that he'd pulled it off. While he still had studying to do for the admissions test, he gave himself the weekend not to study and enjoy his accompaniment. His high school friends all flew in to be a part of his celebration, which made it even better for him.

Brandon and Zach had their gowns on and were looking in Zach's full-body mirror. They were standing side by side with grins on their faces.

"Zach, this is happening. We really did it!" Brandon enthused.

"I know! We worked so hard for this," Zach smiled and turned to face him, "However, no one else deserves this more than you do. I'm so lucky to be your new friend. You've helped me so much, and I am glad to have met you."

"Dammit, Zach, I don't want to cry!" Brandon chuckled and hugged him. It felt great to be in a friend's embrace. To be hugged and held for a good reason and not to let out cries of pain. He couldn't have made it this far without him, and Brandon hoped he knew that. While Brandon would've loved to be able to do more for him, he always took the time to give his gratitude for all Zach had done for him and continued, "I love you."

"I love you, too, friend. We've got this." Zach smiled.

"Are we all riding together?" Brandon asked and turned back to straighten his gown.

"Yeah, Lewis is picking everybody up. I told him to just come here for the both of us."

Brandon nodded and smiled at him. They looked in the mirror for a moment in silence before they both took a deep breath in and out. Brandon rubbed Zach's back and then went to sit down on the couch. He reached for his phone and checked his messages. Madelyn, Tori, and Xavier had arrived at their families' homes and were going to meet him at the graduation to collect their tickets.

"Both of my parents and sisters flew in last night," Zach smiled.

"That's awesome," Brandon grinned, "Have you seen them yet?"

"We all had dinner together last night. It was great to see them as usual. They all finally admitted that I was right to even do undergrad out of state," Zach laughed, "I had quite a battle to fight for them to agree."

Brandon laughed and shook his head, "Well, even though we just met in August, I'm happy they allowed it."

"I was local until this year, actually. I needed to get out of that crazy state, but yes, I'm so glad because I don't know where I'd be without you." Zach told him wholeheartedly.

"I feel the same," Brandon smiled back at him.

Suddenly, they were just looking at each other. Neither spoke any words, and the silence took over the room. At that moment, they had forgotten about everything. There was no Shane, no stress, no anxiety; it was only Brandon and his new fantastic friend who he was beyond grateful for. Brandon had never met anyone who had such a caring heart. They began leaning in closer to each other with their bodies shifting to face each other. Zach was the first to take the opportunity to tip in further.

Before either knew what was happening, they heard a phone rang, and it startled them both. Their foreheads clashed with each other hard, and groans came from their mouths. Brandon quickly reached for his phone on the table and looked to see who was calling without looking at Zach. He immediately answered it.

"Hey, Richard." Brandon tried to sound normal so that his brother wouldn't question anything.

"I was calling to see where I'm getting my ticket?" Richard asked, "Should I meet you at the hotel or at the venue? I know you're going to be busy."

"How about you just come to my friend's house right now? You can give everybody else their tickets for me too." Brandon suggested.

"Yeah, who's all going?"

"Madelyn, Tori, and Xavier all flew in. So you'll see them somewhere. I'll tell them to look for you."

"Alright, cool, I'll be over in ten minutes. You're at Zach's?"

"Yeah, I'll text you the address mow."

"Okay," Richard responded before he hung up. Brandon didn't make any eye contact with Zach as he texted his brother the address. They both sat in silence for a long time, not knowing what to say at all. Neither of them understood what they almost did. It wasn't what Brandon needed or wanted at all. He was caught up in the moment; love wasn't on his mind. Brandon had gotten rid of those thoughts a long time ago.

Brandon sighed as he tried to calm his fast-paced beating heart. His head wasn't much help either. His whole body felt this confusion about it all. It was complicated, and Brandon couldn't deny that. He wanted to throw up suddenly. To run far away and never see Zach again, but at the same time, he didn't ever want to let go of him. Brandon took a big swallow and looked up at Zach, who was playing with his own hands. He wanted to know what he was thinking. Did he have feelings for Brandon? Was the kiss going to mean anything to him? Or was it just going to be one of those "in the heat of the moment" things?

"Okay, neither of us can deny what just almost happened." Brandon was the first to speak.

"I wish we could, but that wouldn't be mature of us. Brandon, right now, I don't know how I feel about you. You're like my best friend and everything, but anything past that, I'm not sure." Zach honestly told him.

"You're...You're my best friend, too. Even saying that scares me, and we both know why. I just don't want to be an ass and get your hopes up for what could take me years. You deserve someone who's comfortable in their skin and not just some leftover human being."

"You are not anyone's leftovers. Especially not his. God, why can't gay people help each other without feelings?" Zach groaned, "I thought I was better than this! I'm sorry, Brandon. I'll understand if you want to go throw up or never want to see me again."

"Neither of that is going to happen, I can assure you. First, I promised myself not to throw up. Second, I guess I…I almost wanted it?"

"You're not ready, though," Zach reminded him.

"I know that. I hate the thought of love in that way." Brandon paused and sighed.

"I do not expect anything different than that. As a matter of fact, it would concern me if you did want that from anyone. Not just me. You have to heal and not think about this. About love or dating, for that matter. Focus on you, and don't worry about me. Alright?"

Brandon nodded his head, "Thank you so much."

"Don't mention it," Zach smiled and stood up, "I'm going to go to the bathroom, your brother should be here to get the tickets, and we should be heading out when our friends get here."

"Yep, that's right!" Brandon chuckled and hugged him. Zach then left the room, and Brandon watched him go. He frowned and realized that maybe Zach did like him in that way. There had to be some feelings deep down that they both knew not to act on anytime soon. His biggest worry was ever leading him on. That'd make him feel like an ass.

His thoughts were interrupted by the familiar knock on the door, "I got it, Zach," he called out as he opened the door. His brother was there with a big smile on his face and returned it giving him a big hug. Brandan gave the tickets and saw him out.

Twenty minutes went by before Stacey and Lewis were pulling up to the apartments to pick them up. They got in the back seat of Stacey's car and headed off to the ceremony. This was when Brandon got thoroughly excited about everything. The moment was finally here. He and his friends went inside the building to the area they were told to go and joined the rest of the graduates. About four hundred graduated that day, and Brandon would be the first line to go across the stage. Zach would be in the third row. Brandon mingled around talking to different people and tried to keep his mind off of him. That was his promise to himself, to not think about anything worrisome.

He was finally laughing again. Telling jokes with his classmates and taking pictures. Zach wasn't by him the entire time, but he did keep an eye on him. He made sure that Brandon stayed alright and didn't have any anxiety. Graduation was exciting to him, of course. However, he wanted nothing to trigger Brandon. Zach also knew that he was really missing Shane. He didn't know how much different their celebration would've been, but he was going to do his best to give Brandon a much-deserved celebration.

An hour had gone by before they were told to get in two lines outside of the doors. Brandon's heart pounded with excitement. He was in the line, anxious to see the big stage. There were two administrators in front of the doors who instructed them one last time on what to do when they walk in. When the doors were finally opened with the graduation song beginning, Brandon was one of the last people to go in the gymnasium to the roaring crowd. The loud cheers and claps filled up the room's atmosphere. He gazed around the entire room as he walked with a huge, genuine smile on his face. It was invigorating and felt surreal to him. His eyes were making it difficult for him not to start crying. This was only the beginning.

Brandon finally made his way around to his chair and stood up until everyone else had made it to their seats. He could see where all of his friends had sat since he was one of the last groups to walk inside. His high school friends, co-workers, and older brother could all be seen from the crowds cheering him on. The dean instructed everyone to sit down after they were all in and began talking.

"Hello, I am Wanda Simmons, and I am the dean of the Kingsborough Community College. I welcome you to the class of 2019 graduation ceremony!" The dean began. Cheers and applause soared in the room again before she continued, "The students who will be walking across the stage here shortly have been some of the most admirable people that this college had the privilege of knowing. To the students, I say congratulations. I may not know everything you've been through to get here, but please allow this to be your celebration. May you take this day to acknowledge all of your accomplishments. I hope every one of you goes onto your desired universities and career choices and live your life to the fullest."

Throughout the ceremony, there were many speeches and music playing. The college had an honorary guest speaker as well. Past graduates were there to encourage everybody as part of the college's success stories. Brandon looked around the room as everyone listened. He was so glad to see his brother, friends, and bosses all in the audience. That was his support system, along with Zach. They were the reason that kept him going when he didn't think he could any longer.

The time had finally come where they were letting students walk across the stage. Brandon would be the third person to walk across the stage to receive his degree in Political Science. The names began to get called up, and the two people ahead of Brandon walked through.

"Brandon Andreas!" The dean called out finally. Tears came rolling down Brandon's face as he began walking across. They were tears of joy, relief, and a special one saying that he did it. He shook the dean's hand and smiled for their picture. When he looked at the crowd where his support was, his heart broke from the noticeable faces not supporting him: his parents and Shane. He quickly shook off his thoughts and proceeded to go back to his chair, not to hold up the line. Brandon cheered loud when he saw his friends walk across as well.

Brandon's loudest cheer was for Zach. Seeing him was just as special to him. That made him cry more, knowing that they both really achieved their goals. He got the tissues out of his pocket and wiped his eyes. Zach made eye contact with him once he got off of the stage and smiled at him. Brandon returned the smile and also gave a wink. This was the first time that Brandon had felt free in months. To have a sense of happiness in life again was beyond words for him. He needed it so badly. He missed it. What was once a familiar feeling was now abnormal to him.

"I am now happy to present the 2019 graduating class of New York Community College!" The dean announced. Cheers roared in the room again as everyone stood up. The graduates turned their tassels from the right side of the caps to the left side.

Brandon really did it. He had made it to graduation and was beyond proud of himself. After everything was over, he went to his brother and former high school classmates, where he was surrounded in a group hug.

They took many pictures together and laughed. Zach looked over from where he was by his own family and smiled at how happy Brandon looked.

Pure, genuine happiness was what Brandon deserved.

Brandon then went over to his three bosses, who all grouped hugged him too.

"I couldn't have done this without you guys," Brandon mumbled.

"We are so proud of you, Brandon. Everyone knew you would do it." Gina told him.

"Three to four years until you're working aside us as a lawyer instead of the receptionist." Daniel smiled.

"The next few years will fly by, we promise," Destiny added.

Later on that night, Brandon, his brother, his high school and college friends all went out to a dance club to celebrate. They laughed, shared stories, and celebrated each other's accomplishments.

"I also need to point out that my other great friend, Miss Madelyn, had also graduated with her engineering degree last week!" Brandon announced.

"Oh, that's right!" Xavier grinned. Everyone then proceeded to cheer for her as she gave Brandon another hug.

"Thank you!" Madelyn chuckled, "I am so ready to start my career. I'm very excited."

"I say this is the perfect time to make a toast," Tori announced as she raised her glass.

"Let me do it," Richard requested as he stood up, "All three of you have worked really hard to get here. Whether I know your struggles or not, I am proud of the three of you for not giving up. I know that I can rest easy knowing that I can eventually call up Zach and Brandon when I am in trouble. A free lawyer to bail me out? I'll take advantage of that!"

"I wouldn't be too sure of that!" Brandon teased him, which made everyone laugh.

"Shut up. I'm being nice to you for once and saying nice things. Anyways, all of you deserve it so much. I'm proud and honored to know you guys, and I wish everyone the best in their careers," Richard then raised his glass, "To the class of 2019!"

"Class of 2019!" Everyone echoed around the table as they clinked their drinks together. Of course, Brandon only had soda in his glass. He didn't mind that the others drank.

For the rest of the night, everybody enjoyed each other and danced the night away on the dance floor. Brandon and Zach both allowed themselves to enjoy the night and to be present. Starting the following week was back to studying for the most critical test ever: the LSAT. Zach, Brandon, Stacey, and Lewis studied nonstop both together and separately to prepare for it. As a graduation gift, Brandon's test was paid for by his bosses. He was grateful that they believed in him so much. That made him study even harder to make everyone proud.

They all took their tests at separate locations and met up afterward for dinner. The weeks of waiting were painful. Nobody knew what to expect, but they all knew that they did the best they could. Brandon put down Zach's address on his application since he wasn't sure if he'd still be in the hotel. Once Zach had received the scores in the mail, he texted Brandon to come over after work immediately. Brandon told Daniel that he received the scores, and he let him leave early to see.

Brandon made it to Zach's apartment as fast as he possibly could. They sat on his couch and stared at the envelopes that had their names on them. Brandon's body shook with anticipation as he looked at them. They must've stared at them for a half-hour without saying anything. Both of them were freaking out.

"Who first?" Brandon asked.

"Please go first. I can't take it!" Zach nervously admitted.

"Zach—" Brandon tried to protest.

"Brandon…"

"We do it at the same damn time."

"Okay, fine!" Zach laughed. The two friends picked up the letters and finally opened them up. They both immediately teared up as they looked at their scores. Brandon made a 168-180, which translated to one hundred percent, while Zach got a 164-167, a ninety-eight percent. Without saying anything, they swapped letters to make sure the other wasn't visualizing the wrong numbers.

"We did it!" Brandon choked out in tears.

"We actually did it!" Zach sobbed. They held onto each other yet again. There were no words that could describe what they were feeling. After all of Brandon's struggles, that was the day that all of it finally felt worth it.

He had another reason and validation to keep fighting to make all of his dreams come true.

Chapter 31: Looks Just Like You

Many things had changed in a year's time for him. Brandon and Zach had successfully completed their first year of law school. They both were able to pass the first and second-semester class loads. The classes weren't a walk in the park, but they did it. Getting used to a routine was the hardest part. Their studies were on Mondays, Wednesdays, and Fridays, and they were nearly all day long. Since their classes had to be picked for them in the first year, they only had one class together. The following year would be much better as they could pick courses themselves. Their friends, Stacey and Lewis, had the same situation.

All of his friends, bosses, and older brother continued to be his amazing support system. They were all there for him whenever he needed to vent, cry, or just have a distraction from everything. Brandon had never wanted to quit anything nearly as much as he wanted to quit law school. At the same time, each day gave him more reasons to keep pushing. Brandon's high school friends and Zach all hit it off very well as he was now a part of the friend group. Zach, Brandon, Tori, and Xavier were the ones that hung out together the most. Madelyn had found a job in engineering in California, so she decided to stay out there. Madelyn and Brandon were always texting each other, too. Richard never let a full week go by without checking on him. To say that Brandon was grateful for the people in his life was an understatement.

He didn't need him. That's what Brandon had to keep telling himself. Shane was in the past until he had to face him in court. New York was a big city, so there were little to no chances of running into him anywhere. He found out that he'd been bailed out around Christmas by his mother and father. It terrified Brandon. At any moment, he could run into him and not know what to do. It wasn't fair. Shane was completely guilty, yet he was able to get free. As if the world didn't give a damn about what he had to go through. The one year anniversary of the first rape was the worst. That was the one day that he had to miss classes because he just couldn't pull himself together.

Brandon could still see his face from that day very clearly. He remembered him yelling at him to shut up with those demon eyes that became familiar. The way he was aggressive with Brandon's body holding him down and doing whatever he needed to get his own satisfaction. How Brandon desperately wanted to move after it was over but couldn't find the strength to do so. The nightmares were frequent, and the images were just as clear. He spent many sleepless nights both at the hotel and at Zach's house in his arms. There were other days where he would be fine and smiling ear to ear. Some days would just trigger his anxiety so bad, and the panic attacks would be awful. He ran out of work many days, going straight in the bathroom into a fetal position on the floor.

It could be a TV show, a song, even a shirt that reminded him of Shane. Brandon could be riding around the city or just simply getting groceries and just walk past what was Shane's favorite snack to eat all of the time. This was so difficult for him just to keep a straight face and not break down right in front of everyone.

Brandon came from home to his job to get an update on his restraining order against Shane. He still hated that it was his reality. To have everything change so suddenly for him was always a hard thing to grasp. He made it to his workplace and headed straight up to Daniel's office.

"I finally got it done," Daniel told him and held up the paperwork giving it to him.

"Okay, great," Brandon nodded as he looked through it and then went to scan it, "Was it the same officer who's working on my case with us?"

"Yeah, Officer Jones is wonderful."

"I'm just glad that Shane didn't try to do anything to me while it was expired. I really tried to do it sooner," Brandon sighed.

"You're still safe, which is the most important thing, Brandon. Even if he did, they could have gone through your case and seen that one was in place."

"I know, but they wouldn't have been able to hold it against him, could they?"

"I don't think so, but everything is filed for a reason."

Daniel sat back down at his desk, and Brandon sat on the other side. He watched his boss update his file in the system. It was still interesting to see him, Gina, or Destiny work on any case file and help in any way he could. The day that Shane was finally given a lawyer scared him all over again. Kory Jopkins was the name of his lawyer. He and Zach spent hours looking up records and reviews of the man.

"I can't believe they gave him a good lawyer. He has four out of five-star reviews on every website. I am so scared and screwed," Brandon whined. Daniel stopped working on what he was doing and looked Brandon straight in the eyes. It took a minute before Brandon realized what he'd said, "Oh yeah, you're way better!"

"I still sign your damn paychecks. Watch your mouth," Daniel warned.

"I assume we'll work out a payment plan later next week?" Brandon asked.

Daniel turned away from his computer and looked as if he didn't understand what he said. "Payment plan for what? I'm not charging you for this."

"Daniel, shut up. I'm going to pay you." Brandon rolled his eyes.

"You are a broke ass law student who's still living in an extended stay hotel room."

"I've been looking into apartments, you dick."

"I know how much we pay you. You're broke, Andreas."

"I should've picked Gina to be my lawyer."

"As your favorite boss, I wasn't going to let that happen. So, I'm not charging you. Repay me by passing your bar exam after graduation."

"That sounds abusive," Brandon groaned and stood up, "I'll see you in the morning. How's the other receptionist doing?"

"I like her. Obviously, no one is as good as you, but she gets stuff done," Daniel explained, "So be ready for a busy day tomorrow."

Brandon chuckled and shook his head, "Alright, that's good."

He then made his way back to his car and drove down the street. Brandon called Zach to say that he was headed to the grocery store, and then he'd be right over. He got a good parking spot and made his way inside. Usually, Brandon didn't pay attention to anyone and minded his own business getting whatever he needed. When he was almost finished, he checked the list on his phone to see if he had forgotten anything. He wasn't paying attention to where he was going, and he accidentally bumped into someone with his cart.

"I'm sorry, sir, it was my—" That was when Brandon's heart dropped. It couldn't be him. There was no way that Shane was in the same store as him. He immediately started backing up.

"No, it's fine, don't worry about it." The man smiled as he turned to look at Brandon. The problem was that Brandon didn't register his voice.

He started to breathe heavily. His heart was pounding out of his chest, and everything inside of Brandon was closing in on him. The images rushed back through his mind from the nights of torture. Where he was held down by him and violated against his will, even though his brain was trying to get a grip that it wasn't him, his anxiety made it seem like otherwise. He didn't know what to do. It looked just like him: the same hair color, height, and weight. The anxiety just wanted to fight him on it.

"Get away from me…" Brandon told him in a shaky tone.

"What?" The man asked.

"I don't need to be here with you. My restraining order just got updated. I can send you back to jail!" Brandon shouted a little.

"Restraining order? Sir, what are you talking about?"

"Did you follow me here?" Brandon yelled, "Are you stalking me now that you're out?"

"What the hell is going on?" The man proceeded to shout. Being yelled at made it worse. He was startled, and he fell to the ground. His anxiety was certain that it was his rapist. He had to have been following him around the store and just happened to get ahead of Brandon, knowing where he was going next.

"Why are you touching me? I don't want you in me anymore!" Brandon shouted as tears rushed down his face. People around them were starting to stare. Brandon could feel his hands all over him again. His body was pinned down again on that bed in the apartment. Naked and exposed in his mercy, unable to go anywhere. His heart pounded out of his chest as his anxiety flared up.

"Sir, you have the wrong person, I promise! I've never seen you in my life." The man tried to tell him. Brandon could tell that this person, who he believed to be Shane, was getting nervous and annoyed. He didn't understand what was happening. This had to be Shane, who was trying to play mind games with him. Brandon started to back away from him. His skin began to crawl, his stomach started to hurt, and he wanted to throw up. The man was looking back at Brandon with full concern, not knowing what to do.

Brandon was sobbing, in a fetal position, and his cart was at the end of the aisle. People began to gather around the scene as it unfolded. Everyone looked between Brandon and the man that looked like Shane, wondering what to do. It was Brandon's worst nightmare that was coming to life. He was there in front of him, taking control of his mind without even touching him. It made him look like a damn idiot in front of this crowd of people. He was breathing hard, his head began to hurt, and he desperately needed out of this panic attack.

He slowly started to come back to reality. His body calmed down as the images of Shane went away. The tears were slowly rolling down his face. Shane wasn't there. The man whom he'd bumped into was not him, no matter how much they looked alike. He was full of embarrassment as he apologized to everyone, especially to that man. The crowd of people all went away, and Brandon returned to get the last few items from his grocery list.

After he quickly made his way through the checkout line, putting his things in the car, he drove off of the lot. Brandon never wanted to return there, but it was the only grocery store near his hotel. He decided to take the food to the hotel and to take a shower before going to Zach. The water no longer made him feel clean. It didn't matter the brand of soap or whatever body wash was used because nothing ever worked. The feeling of being ashamed never seemed to end. He felt as if everyone at his law school knew everything he'd been through just by looking at him. Brandon thought that everyone on the street, at the gas station, in the laundromat, and in the park automatically knew his pain while passing by. It was torture.

The real Shane was on the other side of New York in his new apartment that was run down. The man was still angered that he had to continue with the legal process to prove his innocence. After experiencing the hell that jail had been, the thought of prison terrified him. Why was Brandon avoiding him with a restraining order? How come his parents hadn't believed anything that came out of his mouth? Everything annoyed him. Once Shane got out of jail, he instantly went back to sex. After spending so much time in jail with all men, he was desperate for a woman's touch. Shane found very little motivation to do anything else. He had one small day job to make ends meet, and that was good enough for him.

Shane thought about Brandon often. He missed their friendship and the old apartment that they had. The one he was living in was run down, smelled like cigarettes and alcohol. He had picked up that habit in jail from a few inmates that he became friends with. At first, he hated everything about the addiction until his system craved it as much as it did for sex. Of course, he slept with a lot of the men in jail. Some were barely eighteen years old, and he didn't care. All Shane craved was a man's ass. Ever since he got out, he decided to return to women for sex. If he couldn't have Brandon, then he would have to make do.

Shane sat up in his bed and got his phone out. After scrolling through the contact list, Shane decided to dial a familiar number for some fun.

"Suzie!" Shane greeted.

"Shane Jacobs? I haven't heard from you since you were arrested!" Suzie laughed.

"I know I've missed you, but I had to get my living situation in order. How's life treating you?"

"I've never been better. My best decision was dropping out of college and becoming a stripper!"

Shane smirked once she said that, "Oh really? Do you think you could come to show me what you can do?"

"You know I've wanted to for years," Suzie responded seductively.

"I'm single and all yours, baby."

"There's no one else?"

"Never will be anyone else."

"I'm on my way," Suzie confirmed.

They hung up the phone, and Shane texted his address. He then straightened up around his place a little. He was ready. It had been ages since he had a woman under him. Shane regretted being faithful to Madelyn when she refused to put out for him. After all of that time of Shane trying to be a gentleman to her was a waste. He would have stayed banging Brandon if he'd known.

Shane went into the bathroom to fetch a condom from the medicine cabinet. It excited him to get a taste of her finally; he had figured that it was too late before now. She gave him hope to be able to get in contact with other women from his former college. He wanted to go back and finish his degree eventually, but it wasn't the right time yet. After brushing his teeth to get rid of the taste of cigarettes from his mouth, Shane made sure to have everything he needed by the bed. There was a knock at the door, and he instantly perked up.

"Well, don't you look sexy as ever," Shane complimented.

"I tried my best for you," Suzie told him.

After the door was locked, she practically jumped on Shane and attacked his lips. He immediately swooped her in his arms and kissed back forcefully. As soon as they settled on the bed, clothes started to come off. Shane explored all over that woman's body, rubbing and pinching her in sensitive areas. Moans filled the room as things heated up. Shane was finally getting his sexual desires met by a female, and it felt so good. His lips trailed down her neck and chest with small nips that made Suzie moan. Suzie's moans affirmed that he still knew the sensitive touch of a woman's body.

He toyed with her whole body, kissing and pulling her skin roughly. Shane needed to feel like a man all over again, and someone was willing to do that. The way he played with her breasts and how she pleasured him in return made it an afternoon to remember. Shane quickly got the condom rolled on and stretched her out; Suzie let out a groan once he pushed in. It wasn't about love to either of them; instead, the sexual desires were from wanting to taste each other. Shane Jacobs missed everything pleasurable that came with being with a woman. From her thighs to her perfect breasts, Shane didn't realize how much he missed it. He took his time kissing all over that woman.

Moans got louder as the thrusts sped up. They were in their own worlds and didn't care about each other. Suzie had her own desires to get met, as did Shane. Shane loved that he finally got to experience the thrill of her. They nurtured each other through the entire afternoon, even after their climax. Shane could not get enough of that sexy, mysterious woman that was in his bed. The sex buddies took turns being on top as they kissed until exhaustion took over.

Shane was the first to speak after they calmed down, "Shit, that was good."

"I've got to admit; you were pretty good."

"I need to get my groove back with women. It's been an entire year."

"A year since you banged? That's hard to believe."

"That says I'm still the best," Shane smirked.

"You're Alright, but I've had way better."

"Well, damn bitch."

"It was my pleasure," Suzie teased.

Shane chuckled and placed a hand on her butt, "In two weeks tops, you'll be begging for my dick."

"You're a little too cocky to think I'll always say yes," Suzie shook her head, "How was jail?"

"You knew I went to jail?"

"The entire campus knew!"

"Well, fuck!" Shane groaned, "It was scary until I knew everybody."

"Is it all over?"

Shane rolled his eyes, "Hell no. I'm being accused of rape. What kind of bull shit is that? This case is awaiting trial."

"Do you need a witness?"

"Yeah?"

"I can be there for you."

"You weren't there."

"Oh, you sexy oblivious man. That doesn't matter at all," Suzie then laughed at him and sat up, "All you need to do is be convincing. I'll help you. Pass me a smoke."

They lit up their individual cigarettes with Shane's lighter and took a puff. Suzie and Shane stayed silent for a while as they calmed down. Shane leaned over every once in a while to kiss in between each inhale.

He knew that she was only temporary, and he didn't care; Suzie was what he needed for the time being.

"You're willing to work with my lawyer and me?"

"Totally, it'll be a breeze to get you off the hook. So, that faggot is accusing you?"

"Yeah, Brandon is suing me."

"Was it worth it?"

"I'll let you know after trial."

The rest of the day, Shane and Suzie explored each other's bodies. The sex got better as the night went on, and they only stopped for a smoke ever so often. The truth was that Shane was afraid. He lost all of his high school friendships and girlfriend because of it all. Having Suzie there only fulfilled his sexual needs, and that had to be good enough. He was doubtful that she would be able to help him with the case, but Shane was pretty desperate to be let off the hook.

Later on in the evening, Brandon headed over to Zach's place. Zach had gotten his own apartment after he had to move out of the community college's apartments. It was a small studio in the heart of the city. The place wasn't too big, but it had a decent-sized kitchen that was to the right when walking in. The living room was big enough for one pull-out sofa bed where Brandon would crash many nights. Upstairs, which was above the kitchen, was Zach's bedroom and full bathroom. Zach would insist that his bed was big enough for both of them, but Brandon wasn't ready to even sleep in the same bed with another man yet. The only time during the night that Brandon went up, there was to use the bathroom.

He let himself in the apartments with the key fast Zach gave him. More tears were already rushing down his face as he went inside. The lights were on upstairs, which meant that Zach was home from work. He decided to sit on the couch until his friend came downstairs. The TV was on, so he grabbed the remote to turn it down. He needed to hear his thoughts.

"Brandon, is that you?" Zach called from the bathroom upstairs.

"Yeah, it's me," Brandon shouted back.

Zach came downstairs in his pajamas that he'd just got on and sat down next to him. "Everything good with the new restraining order?"

Brandon nodded his head, "Daniel said that it's active and wasn't too hard to renew."

"I know it's still hard to get something like this, but it's the right thing to do to protect yourself from him," Zach told him and rubbed his back.

"That's not why I'm upset. I'm relieved that it's finally done and that the judge agreed to renew it. Hopefully, this trial will start next year when my case is next," Brandon sighed.

"Please, do not give up and lose hope. Everything's still looking like you can have a definite win. I know it's hard to believe when given the circumstances of your case. However, you have to keep believing in it."

"I'm just tired of it. Getting so sick of the sleepless nights and the anxiety attacks."

"Did you take your medicine this morning?" Zach asked, his eyebrows furrowed in concern.

"Yes, I got them refilled yesterday. They just didn't help when I was at the store just two hours ago. I'm probably never returning there." Brandon mumbled.

"What happened?" Zach then took his hand and intertwined their fingers together. Brandon began to tell the story of what happened. Tears were dripping from his eyes again as he explained everything. Zach was hurting so deeply for this man. He was going through so much with there only being so much that he could do for his friend. The pain was still the same, but Brandon had gotten used to it. Zach also wondered who it was that could look so much like that awful man. What was his name? Were they related? Was this how Shane had planned to screw with Brandon? It infuriated him to see Brandon have to suffer for so long and hard. All Zach could do was be there for him with comfort and safety.

Chapter 32: Facing Him

He really wanted to enjoy his summer vacation. After a very full, very draining year in law school, he really wanted that break. Except, he still had to continue his healing in therapy. Brandon was entering the therapist's building going to the front desk to check-in. It wasn't long until Ms. Sharon came out to greet him.

"Hi Brandon, it's nice to see you." She greeted him.

"Hi, it's good to see you too." Brandon smiled at her. They went back to the usual room where they'd do their session, and Brandon sat down. He took in a big sigh.

"How have you been this past week?" Sharon asked to begin. She was opening up Brandon's file that she had in a filing cabinet.

"I've been feeling relieved and frightened at the same time," Brandon explained, "Ever since he's been out, it just seems like I'm scared to go anywhere. When the restraining order expired, I was scared to death. It took a couple of weeks for my lawyer to get a new one."

"You did everything that you could to avoid him. Did you take my advice to remove your social media pages and to change your cell number to make sure you are safe?"

"I definitely did. I'd removed and blocked all of his social media pages when he was arrested last year. Sure enough, people were in my messages asking me why I had removed him." Brandon groaned, "I don't know why people couldn't have left it alone!"

"Have you ever explained why?"

"No, I took my friends' advice, which was to ignore all questions. They explained to me that it was none of their business, and if anything, people could look things up online."

"I think that's great advice. In order for you to continue healing, you can't keep bringing up the past," Sharon explained.

"How is it considered my past if it hasn't even made it to trial yet? Is it really in the past when I can't even fathom touching another man yet?

I'm still obviously gay; being raped can't even make me straight. It still feels like it all happened an hour ago, even though an hour ago, I was in the shower trying to get his lingering hands off of me." Brandon explained as the tears began to fall.

"Things begin to move from present to past when you're able to say it out loud that you've been through that. Yes, you're still crying about it and having nightmares. Unfortunately, those aren't going away immediately. You can't worry about the future when it hasn't come yet. Going to trial is scary. I completely understand that. It's just that worrying about it now isn't helping you at all."

"I just keep thinking about the basic facts of my case. It alleges that a straight man raped a gay man. That just doesn't add up on paper."

"I see your point, but Brandon, your facts do add up. You've repeated time and time what happened in such detail. As a future lawyer yourself, you should know that they consider so many factors for these serious cases. Just because you are the gay man accusing a straight man does not mean that the court should dismiss your case."

Brandon took a big sigh as he looked at his therapist. He knew that she was right. Everything seemed to drain him more and more each day. Just getting out of bed seemed hard to do. There had been many days where he just didn't know how to go on. It was many nights where he'd just lie awake in his bed full of tears. Sometimes it would be torturous nights where Brandon couldn't sleep, and his face would be there staring right at him. It wasn't like he was trying to imagine him there, but that demon inside him was recreating his figure just to have Brandon afraid at night. Other times Brandon would just be in his room and startle as if someone was behind him. He became paranoid about everything he did.

"I just don't want it to seem like I've wasted everyone's time. He just wouldn't cooperate with me anymore. All that was on his mind was sex whenever he looked at me. It pains me because I wanted him to love me, not lust after me. I've spent so long trying to get him to really see me, only to have him use me? I'm hurting so bad." Brandon cried out.

"Are you able to express the pain?" Sharon asked him.

"It's as if he stabbed me in my back to only stab me again in my heart and head. All of this just to ruin my dignity." Brandon explained.

"If you saw him now and you were able to assure that you'd be safe, what would you say?" Sharon asked, and she sat up straight in her chair, "Imagine that I'm him. What do you say to me?"

"I don't know if I can…" Brandon whispered.

"Come on, try it for me." She encouraged.

"Why are you trying to end me?" Brandon began.

"Keep going; you can do this."

"What joy did you get from seeing me in pain? I was screaming, and you just kept going. Why didn't you care enough about me? When did you stop being my friend? Was it actually that night where you first…Raped me? Or was it when I agreed to be your slave without knowing that you hid it through the question of 'I've been wondering what it's like to fuck a man'? I'm trying to understand, but I can't," Brandon cried, "I needed you as my lifelong best friend. My heart yearned for you to love me, but it yawned for your friendship even more."

"Take a breath," Sharon instructed.

Brandon took in a slow and shaky breath before continuing, "I can't stop thinking about you. You were on my mind all the time, but what's changed is you now scare me to death. That monster that gave me nightmares was just some random creature called the boogie man. Now you've replaced him and became my new worst horror. Are you happy now? Is this what you wanted all along since that day we met in that high school? You just wanted me to become wrapped around your finger so that you could destroy me worse than my parents ever could?"

"Tell this man about your love. How did you feel about him?" Sharon asked. She reached into the folder and got out one of the pictures that Brandon had brought her of him. In this particular one, he was smiling and giving the camera a look that used to melt Brandon's heart no matter what was going on. He remembered that day as if it was only yesterday.

"I was in love with him…" Brandon started.

"Talk directly to him, Brandon."

"I was madly in love with you, but so afraid to say it. Yes, I did tell you many times that I loved you, but I never explained in what way. It made me afraid. Your friendship meant the world to me, and I never wanted to ruin that with my stupid emotions. The love that I had for you was way more than I had for myself. That dimpled smile of yours and such a positive attitude to keep me going. Without you, I've been struggling so hard to keep on with life."

"You did say that you did get some type of new kind of motivation to keep going for your degree. Tell him about that."

"I desperately want to prove you wrong. It doesn't matter if you didn't say it out loud, Shane. You clearly thought that my only worth was being your slut. You might've won many battles with this, but dammit, I'm not losing this war!"

"Say 'you will not own my life'!"

"You will not own my life!" Brandon echoed angrily, "My dreams will never be tarnished because of you. I will fucking move on."

"I will love myself again..." The therapist wanted him to repeat. Brandon just stared at the picture while tears still streamed down his face. He couldn't find it in himself to get it out. It didn't look possible for him to do that. All he saw within himself was someone who was worthless; that was just a waste of space on earth. The purpose of his life was hard to figure out outside of being a lawyer. He wanted to tend to others without focusing on his own needs. Brandon had been on fire for over an entire year, and he'd still instead concentrate on his friends than on him. To think that he would ever deserve his self-love ever again felt like a joke. "Brandon..."

"I can't say it," Brandon shook his head.

"Yes, you can..." Sharon told him once more. After a few more tries, she decided to give up. Brandon still felt so broken down and lost without a home. She placed the picture down on the table and guided Brandon to lie down on the church. Sharon Instructed him to pull his knees to his chest and to hug them tight. He was still burning on the inside. The hands still hovered over him no matter how much he begged for them to leave.

"I hate him!" Brandon sobbed. The pain wouldn't leave him alone. It just kept getting bigger and harder to manage. There he was, lying down in a counseling session letting his heart spill out to a picture because it was dangerous to be near him. Thinking about the whole situation was sickening to his stomach. These were supposed to be some of the most exciting and important times in his lifetime, and they were taken away.

"Let it out, Brandon. It's okay." Sharon rubbed his back, trying to calm him down.

"This seems impossible ever to be okay!"

"I know it does, but trust me, it will. You'll get through this all and be stronger because of it. Trusting is much harder to do after you've been hurt so badly. Believe me when I say that I've experienced it myself," Sharon shared with him as he calmed down, "You share your most precious and darkest secrets to the one person you think will be there forever. It kills just to know that life had other plans. You have to remember that there are other people who love you, dearly. Your friend Zach is one example of an amazing friend."

"Zach is incredible," Brandon agreed while he wiped his tears, "I don't understand why he stays my friend when I'm such a crying mess. This is tearing him down, too, and I feel so guilty."

"The last thing you need to do is carry this burden alone. Everyone who knows and loves you understands why you're like this."

"They deserve the real me back. Not this version that's such a cry baby."

"Brandon deserves to have the real Brandon back. I'm not worried about your friends having Brandon back. Once Brandon is back for you, then he'll come back for everyone else as well. I realize that you can't ever go back to the same exact person who you were before all of this. It's impossible to do so, and nobody should expect that. You also won't be able to enjoy intimacy ever again fully, but you can get to where you'll be comfortable again. You'll be finding a new sense of happiness and joy. You'll also have a stronger mindset and be able to use your personal experiences to help other men. Do you realize by looking at the big picture of this all that you can encourage men to speak out? We always hear about women speaking out. Why do you think that there are no other men in the Friday night sessions? You can turn this into a teaching moment for others."

"I want that so bad. My God, I don't think anyone gets just how afraid I am of the word sex. It's like part of me never wants to have another man in my bed with me ever again, but I also miss love and the feeling of making love. Not just sex, but true intimacy. That's what I thought Shane would eventually be for me. Maybe I'm naive for saying this, but prior to my first time with Shane, no one has made love to me. It's all been for pleasure when it comes to them. I'd been searching for it, and that's what I thought Shane would be to me." Brandon confessed.

"That wasn't real love, Brandon. It wasn't for him to make love to you despite how much you wanted it to be that."

"I can see that now. Maybe that just proves how much I didn't know about him that I really thought I did."

"Are you saying that even though you lived together, you still probably didn't know each other completely?" Sharon wanted to clarify.

"I am, yeah," Brandon sighed and ran his fingers through, "I can't believe that I'm able to admit that. I thought I knew everything. I figured that the one night stands he had was him just having the 'college experience' as people call it and that I wasn't."

"Do you now see that there's no one way to have a college experience?"

"Yeah, because my experience includes me getting raped while studying for the LSAT," Brandon bitterly stated, "Might as well include taking care of an ungrateful dying father. What happened to these years, being the best years of my life? It's all just a fun saying, apparently."

"How do you feel about your parents?"

"I couldn't care less, honestly. I have no idea where my mom is, and I don't want to. All I know is she's probably still in New York. My brother is the same way. I've never visited my dad's tombstone. There's no need to go there to tell him anything. He wouldn't care about anything that has to do with me and my life or career. If I've come to terms with something this past year, it's that he never cared for me after I came out. He thought that me taking care of him was to try to make up for me being gay."

"Was it?"

"No, but it was to try to earn his love back before he died, which I didn't," Brandon sighed.

"That's the pattern right there." Sharon realized.

"What pattern?"

"You have this mindset of 'I have to earn this person's love' because of your parents. I'm noticing it with the parents, Shane, and even Zach. For your parents, it was to have them accept you for who you are. For Shane, it was to earn his love. With Zach, it's now to have him see that you've earned his friendship and that you're worth it," Sharon explained.

Brandon sat back up on the couch and thought in silence. She was right. Brandon had always done that out of habit ever since he came out to his folks. Every time he tried to prove his worth to others, things never worked out the way he'd like. He wondered why he hadn't ever thought about it before. This wasn't some fascinating discovery, but more like an interesting realization. After wiping his eyes again, he responded with: "I think that's it. I mean, it has to be, and I've just refused to admit it."

"Which is understandable. You have to face it, Brandon. Face both yourself," Sharon paused, getting the picture back out, "While facing this man as well."

"Just hard doing so," Brandon mumbled.

"You did it today. That's something to be proud of."

"Be proud of talking to a picture?"

"Hey, it's a start. You haven't run into him, and you're not supposed to."

"I thought I did the other day, and I made a fool of myself in public."

"What happened?"

Brandon then went on to tell her about the grocery store incident. He explained how he initially reacted and how embarrassed he felt afterward. They discussed what he wished he could change if he had a do-over. By the end of the session, Sharon had given him a new homework assignment.

"I think that a lot of work still needs to be done within this next year. Hopefully, your case will be within the next year as well. You've got a long way to go, but you've come so far. Be proud of that. I'm here to guide you through this. Your assignment is to enjoy your summer break again simply. Do not take any summer classes because you earned this time off from school and studying. You will learn to love again. It will take some time, but I know you're willing to do your work. That was embarrassing, I know that you wish it'd end, and it's going to soon. He's going to be in prison for his crime, and you can go on with your life."

"I can't wait to get the legal part over with. It is so dreadful being the client and employee at the same time," Brandon sighed and glanced at his watch. There were only a few minutes left in his session. A lot still had to be worked through with his therapist as he wasn't anywhere near finished with his healing. He wasn't taking any of the sessions for granted as they were much help. Even if all he did some weeks was cry on that couch. Shane became evil, and Brandon was accepting it.

After the session was over, Brandon felt like some weight had been lifted off of his shoulders. He was ready to enjoy his summer vacation with the feeling of hope. It wasn't a lot of hope, but Brandon was accepting of whatever came from it. He told Stacey that he was headed her way to go get some lunch together. If he had learned anything from the past crazy year, it was to embrace all of the good short moments that life gave him. Brandon knew that the next year was going to be another long and dreadful one. His only wish was to have the trial over with no matter the outcome.

Brandon really didn't want it to be still dragged on longer than he'd be in law school. It was an unsettling feeling to think that he could still be waiting on his own trial while starting to get his own clients. No one knew what to expect; Brandon just knew he had to keep fighting through it all.

Chapter 33: Preparing

Another year had gone by faster than Brandon had anticipated. The year was now 2021, and it was September. Daniel had gotten notice that the trial was a few months away back in May after Brandon had successfully finished his second year of law school. He was still friends with everyone, especially Zach. Brandon had just begun his third and final year of law school, and everything seemed to just get harder for him.

His anxiety was working overtime. As the court date got closer, nightmares were horrible. He was dreaming about him losing the case, Shane getting revenge and killing him, or even worse, where his parents forced them to get married, and Shane abused him every day. Brandon was deep into searching for all of the information he could have to try to win his case. He had notes upon notes on what could go wrong and what could get held against him. As if he didn't have enough to worry about while being in his last year of law school. There was no time to waste as he still felt so unprepared no matter how many times Daniel promised him that it would be okay.

Daniel was walking out of his office headed to the break room when he saw his front desk worker typing frantically on the computer. "Will you please chill out?"

"Daniel, I don't know the definitions of being calm, not stressing, chilling out, or any other terms that aren't a synonym for being scared as shit. I can't lose this, man!" Brandon groaned.

"I know that! I rarely deal with cases like yours, but it's always scary as a lawyer who takes on criminal cases. You've seen me deal with fifteen different cases that have gone to trial, and have I lost one?"

"No…"

"Alright then—"

"You've lost four!" Brandon smirked at him.

"Focus on the positive, you ass. Eleven to four is a great ratio." Daniel fired at him.

"I know, I know. This is why I look up to you guys and not just because you're all my bosses. You're passionate about the cases you take on. Maybe I'm biased since I am an employee, but a lot of lawyers lie."

"We care about justice being served. If we don't think it can be a winning case, do we take it for the money? Not unless we are desperate for new clients." Daniel admitted and made Brandon laugh.

"I don't blame you at all. I've witnessed many crazy clients come into this office trying so hard to prove their innocence. How do you choose who to take?"

"Well, obviously, we cannot determine based on things like race, gender, and such. However, if we tell someone that we won't represent them for whatever reason, then we don't have to. We choose by the evidence given from the potential clients, we listen deeply to their story, and we look online to see where the case is at in the process. If a case is set to go to trial in a week, hell no, we're not taking it."

"Right...Wait, that's happened before?" Brandon questioned, surprised.

"Oh yeah. People are ridiculous and desperate; we are not going to trial looking like idiots. We have a 5.0 rating for our business—"

"4.2," Brandon corrected with a smirk.

"Shut up, round up like the math teachers teach you."

"You're supposed to round down when it's that low." Brandon challenged.

"I will make you take a fucking pay cut, shut up."

"I don't need that now. I'm about to look for an apartment again," Brandon groaned.

"I'm glad that you are. You were able to save up a lot by being in that hotel for the past two years."

"I know, but if that old car hadn't broken down right before I graduated, I would've had a new apartment that summer." Brandon told him, "I didn't move out because I couldn't afford it without him, but because of the trauma."

"Do you see how that was your best decision as an emotional thinker? It is good at times."

"Thanks, I rarely get complimented about that. It's always about how I should stop thinking like that, and for once, it did help me."

"That is true, and you should stop most times. Especially when you become a lawyer yourself. If you mix your emotions with these laws, you'll be fucked. Do I lie to you?"

"No…"

"Then swallow your emotions and pride. Welcome to being a lawyer," Daniel then smiled at him and proceeded to walk to the break room. "Also, stop looking up shit online. Get to studying!"

Brandon let out a sigh once his boss was out of his sight. He knew that what Daniel said was right about him worrying too much, but he couldn't help it. The case was all he thought about unless he was focused on studying for some test. Shane couldn't win. No matter how hard he'd have to fight the jury, Shane could not be excused for this terrible crime. Brandon had great lawyers and witnesses on his side, so there was no way. Sometimes it felt like Daniel didn't understand how much he wished not to have to think about it. So much was on Brandon's plate. From the bar exam that he had to get ready to take after graduating law school to making sure that he could still provide for himself, his brain never stopped working.

It would be a lie to say that Brandon didn't think about the Shane he once knew. Most days, he pushed the thoughts aside to focus on school, but it didn't work all the time. There were dreams where he'd just talk to him as best friends. He never felt afraid in those dreams because it was the man he fell for. Other nights were him getting violated by Shane repeatedly in new made-up situations that his brain came up with. He hated them all. Why would he want a good dream with Shane when the previous night was a nightmare? Why would his brain desperately want him to have visions of them falling in love when he never wanted to be near him ever again? Every morning still started with him gagging or throwing up in the bathroom, wishing for it to all end. Brandon couldn't change the past, but he really wanted to erase all of the memories.

He had to face him one last time in his life. Brandon was hoping that the trial would only take one day to complete. Things were finally calming down in Brandon's life, and the only thing left to do was to win the trial case. There wasn't a lot of information about rape trials in any of his textbooks. The issue was so taboo that it was too much to discuss in them. There were lessons and conversations in class about them.

Brandon would find himself getting nervous about what his fellow classmates would say about it. He had tried to block out his inner thoughts to stay focused and not give any emotional answers or lash out at people who wouldn't believe the victim.

The one time that happened was in the first class of the day. Brandon had nightmares about Shane the night before, and it caused him to have a rough morning. What started out as him closing up on the inside led him to lash out at everyone in the classroom, including the professor. Once the period was over, he stayed back to explain what happened to the professor and ended up telling his brutal story. He and the professor talked for the rest of that semester whenever Brandon needed someone to listen to him. Some days Brandon was yelling at his bosses, his brother, and even at Zach when he obviously never meant to. Everyone understood never to take it personally as he always apologized afterward. Brandon still confided in Sharon and the support group for help each week. He didn't want to hurt the people who supported him. All of his anger and pain was only towards himself and Shane, but unfortunately, Brandon sometimes had to let it out on others. However, Brandon quickly realized how some people were quick to put all of the blame on him. Brandon had gone from always crying to having it turn into complete anger. He got mad at himself, at other victims in the media, and at the ever so slow legal process. Shane had to be locked up behind bars. It wasn't fair that Brandon had to be more scared only because of the rights Shane had. Brandon's only right was a restraining order and to wait for the case to be next. The system didn't care to ask about his trauma. They weren't focused on what Brandon needed to heal as he had to do it for himself. At times, he just couldn't keep it all in, and he had to blow off steam somehow. That was when Brandon took up exercise, yoga, and massages.

Lewis had to convince Brandon that it was a good idea to do the massages. Brandon didn't want anyone to touch him, let alone random strangers. He didn't understand at first how letting other people feel around his back would help him. Lewis had to explain to him that it would be a way to open him up to other humans again. The first time Brandon went was the hardest. He got himself ready for the massage, leaving only his shorts on and a pair of socks. Brandon had the option of choosing between a male or female employee, and he decided to go with a man to face his fears. Lewis told him that it didn't have to be a male if he wasn't ready. However, Brandon insisted that he had a male. When it first began was the worst part. Brandon was so tense and afraid of the man he pushed him away immediately after he began to touch his lower back. It was too soon. Brandon apologized to the worker after he got dressed, and it felt embarrassing.

As time went on, he and Lewis tried different spas around New York. Eventually, Brandon was okay with the employees doing their job. It was what he needed, and it helped him more than he anticipated. They were helping him get his own body back that was stolen by that rapist. He and Lewis called it a boys afternoon outing for the two of them. They would get their massages, go get lunch together afterward and study for class. Brandon found himself growing closer with Lewis, Stacey, and Zach as time went on. He made a couple of friends in his classes, but he never really would hang out with them outside of school. It was his trust issues that kept him from others. The only people he spoke to were his professors. Brandon was never known as the shy one until life changed for him forever. Being afraid of everyone was a lot to overcome. It took Brandon a while to get used to the new school and to feel safe in it.

Well, as safe as he could feel…

His demons were still a part of him. A day never went by without them showing up. They always reminded him that he was worthless to the world. Shane's voice was always in his head to tear him apart whenever he would try to have a good day. Sometimes the demons succeeded, and other days Brandon was able to fight them off. He wanted to die on most days than to try to heal. His hope in life was so fragile that he found himself agreeing with them. They wouldn't stop no matter who he talked about them with. Brandon didn't lie and say that they were gone, but if nobody asked then, he didn't bother to bring them up. Sometimes Brandon would be arguing with them on the inside while he seemed completely fine and focused in class. The worst times were during tests. His anxiety was already terrible before each exam, and to have the demons inside always giving him hate was almost unbearable. It would still shock him to find out that he always passed the tests, even the hardest ones.

This was his passion, after all. Becoming a lawyer was what he really wanted to do with his life. Nothing else made him feel worthy or got him motivated. It didn't push the thoughts of Shane away from his mind. What it did was reassured his purpose of staying alive. He still had on a brave face during the day, while at night, he cried in his pillow, wishing for everything to all be over. The only man who could touch him most days was Zach. Something about him always felt welcoming and safe to be around. He never allowed himself to get that comfortable with his bosses as he wanted to keep some type of professionalism between them. He didn't want it to become inappropriate. They all cared about Brandon, which he knew, but it didn't feel right to just cry in their arms all day long. Brandon had started to move on from Shane. However, he didn't think that he could until the case had a ruling. He also made sure that he didn't cry about it every day. Even he needed a break from it overwhelming him.

At the end of the day, Brandon was unexpectedly called into a meeting with his bosses. He went into the break room where Daniel, Gina, and Destiny were all waiting for him. Brandon took a seat at the table and made eye contact with everyone.

"You know, for a small business, we get many clients that respect you all." Brandon complimented.

"I guess that is true." Gina agreed with him.

"You're just saying that after you mocked me this morning about our rating." Daniel rolled his eyes.

"Was I making anything up?" Brandon smirked at him. He liked it when he could push his boss's buttons.

"Whatever, we are growing is the point."

"Are we meeting to discuss this trial?" Brandon questioned.

"Yes, we are. Are you ready?" Gina asked, "We're all supporting you."

"I just don't know how I'll react when I see him. After that damn panic attack I had last year in the grocery store, I don't know what I'll do when I actually see him." Brandon worried.

"I think it'll be fine since you know that there's security everywhere. You were in public, yes, except this is now in court. A serious trial case, and if he has any common sense, then he won't do anything." Destiny assured him.

"Remember that you're bringing all of the facts while he brings the bull shit. That's always how it goes. He wouldn't even agree to settle on anything. This could've been all over." Gina reminded him.

"Yeah, but you know it wouldn't have helped my anxiety. I need to know that he's gone for good." Brandon sighed.

"What if he wins this?" Daniel asked.

"I will run away..." Brandon shrugged.

"Cute, now try again," Gina instructed.

"I will change my identity, so he won't know it's me?" Brandon tried again.

"Brandon!" Daniel yelled at him

"Okay, fine! I'll find a way to cope and move on. This will not distract me from my degree at all. As a matter of fact, it'll light another fire to get through this last year because I'm not failing this shit."

"That's more like it!" Gina approved.

"I want you to enjoy your weekend and try to relax without thinking about it. Wednesday morning is the day, and you need to be ready by relaxing." Daniel Instructed.

Brandon nodded his head, "Yes, sir. This is it."

Chapter 34: Court in Session

Brandon couldn't believe it. The day that he was going to trial with Shane Jacobs and hopefully, he'd be sentenced to prison. After two years of collecting data, fingerprints, hearings, waiting on police reports, and a booked court system, the day had finally arrived. On an early fall morning in September, and Zach had a long heart to heart conversation leading up to it. Zach eventually made him understand that this couldn't have any of his old friendship feelings involved. Due to family members hardly ever supporting Shane, and with no friends believing his side of the story, he had to stay in jail the entire time. Brandon's mind wasn't able to relax completely, but it still brought him some relief.

They arrived at the courthouse an hour early, as Daniel advised, and looked for a parking spot. He had kept his friends and Richard all up to date during the entire process, and they all wished him luck. Well, Richard said that if the court didn't make the right ruling, then he would. As if that was what Brandon needed to hear. He was already nervous and fearing for his entire life of not being believed; his brother didn't have to give him one more reason to make his nerves worse.

The number of nightmares and the frequency of his anxiety attacks that he'd been experiencing over the past couple of months were getting worse. Shane hadn't admitted to the crime, even with the police reports that were documented, and the case had to go to trial. His body shook, the butterflies in his stomach were getting worse, and he had barely eaten. Zach had to make him eat something at least once a day, even if it was only a few bites. Shane's lawyer scared him. The looks that he shot at Brandon and Daniel were intimidating, almost mean looking. Daniel said his name was Kory Jopkins, and they've had many clients going up against each other.

He startled as he felt something touch his arm, taking him out of his thoughts. Brandon turned to look at Zach in the eyes. "What?"

"I need you to stop thinking," Zach simply stated, "Everything's going to be alright. This is the last time you'll ever have to look at that vile man ever again in your life."

"I'm scared beyond words," Brandon whispered in a worried voice, "I just want today to be over with already, no matter what the outcome is. That's what I want and desire from this. It's a chance to have so much weight lifted off my chest. Why does it have to be this way?"

"I don't know, but you're going to get through this. I've got you." Zach told him.

After one last big sigh, they got out of the car and started to go inside the courthouse. Zach held his hand the entire time as they walked up the hundreds of white stairs to the building. Brandon went to find his lawyer, Daniel, who was also just arriving himself.

"Morning guys," Daniel greeted, "Today's the day. Are you ready?"

"I don't think I have a choice but to be ready. I just need this shit over with already," Brandon expressed anxiously.

"You have every piece of information in your favor, Brandon. There's no way you can lose this." Daniel comforted him.

Brandon sighed as he tried to relax, "Do you know if he's here yet?"

Daniel shook his head, "I don't think so, but I did see the lawyer when I was walking in here this morning. It was not a pleasant face."

"I feel so scared," Brandon whined.

"Brandon, I wouldn't lie to you. There's such a low chance of us losing this today. You saw every time how annoyed and impatient he was making Judge Wright leading up to this. She can't stand him." Daniel tried to cheer him up. The look on Brandon's face didn't change. He was exhausted from it all. Hopeless, drained, and weak summed up the emotions that he felt all at once. In a half-hour, he would have to put his mask on in the courtroom. Shane couldn't see him like this. It'd give him such an advantage knowing how much he had torn him down.

"Richard just texted you, wishing you good luck again. He wanted to be here, but he had business meetings that he couldn't cancel." Zach told him.

"Good, because not only is he the last person who needs to have come, he's also an idiot saying he'd 'take care of Shane if the judge doesn't.' I don't want to see him go to prison!" Brandon rolled his eyes.

He appreciated his brother so much with everything he's done to encourage him to get away from Shane. There was a reason why he was the first person to be told about this situation. He could count on him to give him the best advice no matter what the problem was. It had been that way ever since they were little.

Brandon looked around the room, seeing a lot of people who were coming into the building. He loved it whenever he got the chance to visually sit in on public cases to study the various types of cases. Today was different as he'd rather be anywhere else than suing the man he once knew and loved. He sat down on the bench next to Daniel, looking over at his suitcase full of papers.

"Help me make sure I printed everything," Daniel instructed, "Since you want to be a lawyer."

Brandon and Zach both chuckled as they sat on opposite sides of him. They spent twenty minutes going through all the information and paperwork getting them in order. Daniel was, of course, impressed with them. Especially with Brandon knowing that he'd been paying attention to all of the advice he would give him. Before they knew it, the hour had gone by, and Brandon was waiting to go on. Zach kissed him on the cheek wishing him luck and felt butterflies in his stomach. There wasn't any time to figure out what was going on with him. Maybe he was starting to have feelings for Zach. All he knew was that he had to stay focused on the most critical ruling in his life.

"In the case of Andreas versus Jacobs, please step forward." The bailiff announced from inside the room. At the prompt, the three men entered the room, going to their corner of the room. Brandon and Daniel stood at the table while Zach sat in the chair. Brandon's heart started racing as Kory Jopkins came through the doors next, shooting a daring look at him. It was as if he also had a strong hate for Brandon without a valid reason whatsoever.

"Don't pay no mind to him. He clearly hates his job." Daniel whispered in his ear, "Proof that he knows it's not going to be in their favor."

A few moments later, Shane walked in the doors into the room wearing a gray suit. Brandon's body began to tense up as he saw him. This was once his very best friend. The man that always made him laugh, told everything to, and just put a genuine smile on his face was now his biggest nightmare. That made him sick all over again just to think about it.

"Please rise. The Court of the Second Judicial Circuit, Criminal Division, is now in session, the Honorable Judge Lucy Wright presiding." Ordered the bailiff. Brandon watched as the other door opened up, with the judge coming out moments later. His heart started racing, realizing that the moment had finally arrived. He would have to try so hard to convince the judge and jury that he was telling the truth. With him not knowing Shane's game plan made him anxious with his hands sweating.

The judge sat in her seat, and the bailiff went up to her as protocol, "Good morning, your honor. All parties have been sworn in."

"Thank you, Trevon. Everyone except for the jury may be seated," Judge Wright ordered, "Trevon, please swear in the jury."

"Please raise your right hand. Do you solemnly swear or affirm that you will truly listen to this case and render a true verdict and a fair sentence as to this defendant?" After the trial members all said I do, the bailiff spoke again, "You may be seated."

"Mr. Trevon, what is today's case?" Judge Wright questioned.

"Your honor, today's case is Andreas versus Jacobs."

"Is the prosecution ready?" Asked Judge Wright.

Daniel stood up, "Yes, your honor." He then sat back down.

"Is the defense ready?" Judge Wright asked the other side.

Mr. Parkson then stood up, "Yes, your honor." Then he sat back down.

"Please give your opening statements." The judge then requested.

"Your Honor, members of the jury, my name is Daniel Hart, and my law firm and I are representing Mr. Brandon Andreas in this case. We intend to prove that Mr. Jacobs has sexually assaulted my client on countless occasions. Please find our evidence to be completely accurate, in chronological order, and in full detail. Thank you." Daniel stated.

Judge Wright nodded her head then turned to the other side of the courtroom.

"Your Honor, members of the jury, my name is Anthony Parkson, and my law firm and I are representing Mr. Shaneuel Jacobs in this case. We intend to prove that Mr. Andreas is making a false claim of the alleged performance of sexual assaults. Please find our counterclaims to be accurate information on how the incident actually happened."

With a confused look on his face, Shane turned to his lawyer in a whisper, "Allegedly?"

Mr. Parkson covered his mic up, looking at Shane surprised, "You don't know what alleged means?" Shane shook his head, causing him to sigh, "Oh God."

"Mr. Hart, your client is also an employee to you, correct?" Judge Wright asked.

"Yes, your honor."

"How long has he worked for your law firm?"

"Since June 2016. He is our secretary, and he does an amazing job."

"Four and a half years," Judge Wright started taking notes, "Have you represented him prior to this case?"

"I have not."

"I object!" Shane stood up, angrily and shouted, which caused Brandon to startle.

Everyone looked at Shane with confusion as the judge spoke calmly, "Mr. Jacobs, what exactly are you objecting to?"

"I think you miscalculated. That's three years and four months!" Shane told her.

Daniel leaned over slightly on Brandon, whispering, "Seriously?"

Brandon sighed and mumbled back, "He has dyslexia and dyscalculia; letters and numbers confuse him."

"Mr. Jacobs, I went to school, and I know my numbers. Please sit down and don't shout in my courtroom again. This is your only warning."

Brandon could see Shane's face changed to the expression that he usually had when he was proven wrong. It was a mixture of shame and frustration he'd have in class or when he got a bad grade on a test, a look of failure. Only this time, he didn't care to help him. He also knew that the Shane he knew wouldn't've lashed out like that. It was clearly the demon in control of his emotions, and that demon clearly hated Brandon.

His hands were sweating, his legs began to shake, the case hadn't even started, and he was already anxious. Whatever Shane's plan was must've been put in action because Brandon had no idea what to expect from him.

"Let's get back to the case," Judge Wright moved forward, "Will the plaintiff share their side with the court, please?"

"Your honor, my client has known the defendant for nearly ten years. They were high school best friends and college roommates up until the incident in question. The two have shared an apartment that is in my client's name only, and they split the bills evenly. They've never had a problem this big in their entire friendship. On October 20, 2018, Mr. Jacobs asked my client to experiment with him sexually, to which my client agreed to." Daniel spoke.

"He gave consent to the first time?" The judge questioned.

"That's correct." Daniel nodded his head.

"Okay, go on."

"They hadn't even agreed to continue the sexual pleasures verbally after that night. The second time that they had relations was on October 26, 2018. They were starting to have their time together until the defendant's ex-girlfriend showed up."

"So were they together at the time?"

"Not that my client knew of, your honor. They had one date after their first night, but nothing was official."

"Okay, continue…" Judge Wright responded.

"The next time was also fine. Mr. Andreas and Mr. Jacobs eventually had sexual relations a few days later, and all was fine. Everything was all okay until the first night in question."

"Can you step up to the podium and explain what happened, Mr. Andreas?" Judge Wright asked.

Brandon looked at Zach, who gave him a reassuring nod and stood up, starting to speak. "Can you clarify which night, your honor?"

"The first night of the alleged sexual harassment."

"Yes, your honor. On November 2, 2018, I was in my room on my bed when Mr. Jacobs came home that evening. Mr. Jacobs had dropped off his ex-girlfriend at the airport and came back home. He walked into my room, and he had an unsettling look on his face. I didn't have time to question it before he began kissing me. Everything was fine at first; I was participating until it began to be uncomfortable for me." Brandon carefully explained, "I was only trying to possibly change my position on the bed or tell him that I didn't like what he was doing."

"Was he speaking to you in his normal voice, or was it sexual?"

"Sexual."

"Did you try to get him to stop?"

"I did, and he shouted in my face to shut up," Brandon told the judge as he tried hard not to get emotional.

"Would the defense like to respond to that?"

"Yes, your honor. My client never said anything about shouting in his face. We only talked about the night that the police were called." Mr. Parkson stated.

"Mr. Jacobs, would you like to explain your version of that night respectfully?" Judge Wright asked and looked towards Shane.

"I thought I was never going to get to speak," Shane mumbled as he went to the podium.

"Oh my God..." Brandon and Daniel could hear Zach whisper. Zach couldn't believe that Shane was acting like this in court in front of the judge. Every time Shane opened his mouth, he knew that Brandon would win the case after the evidence was all out easily. He just hoped that Brandon realized that too.

"I honestly don't remember shouting at him whatsoever. Brandon never once told me to stop. He just kept moaning my name that special way he did when I was treating him right." Shane began to smirk at Brandon. Brandon just sighed while Zach and Daniel looked at him like the fool that he was.

"He never once tried to pull you off as he claims?" Judge Wright asked him.

"Why would he? He liked me on top of him." Brandon shivered when he heard those words from Shane as it wasn't true at all. He hated that night. Everything about it was so wrong, and it scared him. The judge looked like he didn't believe anything that Shane was saying, but Brandon couldn't be so sure. He looked over to the jury, who had similar looks for the most part as they took notes thoroughly of the case. He badly wanted to know what they were thinking. Did they believe him or Shane? Was it too early in the chance to have an opinion? Thousands of thoughts were running in Brandon's mind, even if he had a straight face on the outside. It was so frightening to him, and he didn't know what to do.

Brandon glanced over to their side, noticing a lady sitting in the other chair that was next to Shane's. It confused him as he didn't see her walk in, and he didn't recognize her at all. Was this Shane's witness? Did they pay her to be there and lie on his behalf? Brandon's heart raced faster, not knowing what to expect from her. He didn't know who she was at all. Shane's witness looked around the same age as then with brunette hair, brown glasses, and her outfit was definitely inappropriate for court.

"Do you know her?" Daniel asked in a whisper.

"Not at all. That's definitely not a former neighbor." Brandon told him.

"Mr. Jacobs, are you saying that the plaintiff liked you as the dominant one? You never once forced him?" Judge Wright asked.

"You should've heard him scream my name so pleasurably. It'd even turn you on." Shane then smirked at the judge. Everyone in the room except for the judge looked in pure shock. There was no way that he said that to the judge. Brandon especially couldn't believe it. Who was this man? Did sex really take over his mind so much that he didn't know human decency? If anything, Brandon was ashamed to admit to the court that they were once best friends, let alone temporary sex buddies. Judge Wright didn't respond to that. She just gave Shane a disgusted look before taking a big sigh. The entire room just stayed quiet until she turned back to Brandon.

"Can you please explain the next time this occurred?"

"It was December 5, 2018. Earlier that morning, I was in the kitchen when he came from his room. He pushed me up against the counters gripping my body hard, and aggressively kissed my lips. Once again, I couldn't move because he held me tight, but I didn't want it. I didn't want it at all." Brandon explained, trying hard not to let his voice crack, "His exact words afterward were 'If I didn't have to go to work right now, I'd undress you right here and have my way with you.' Then he left right after."

"Did you tell anyone at this point?"

"No, your honor," Brandon cleared his throat.

"Did anything else happen that day?"

"I was in the bathroom when he got home from work that evening. He came in there and...Had his way with me in the bathroom shower..." Brandon let more tears out, "He then told me to get out until he needed his 'high' again."

"I understand," Judge Wright nodded her head and glanced over to Shane, who had an annoyed look on his face. She didn't even call on him for any counterclaims and continued talking to Brandon, "You stated that you also received sexual harassment text messages from the defendant. May I see them?"

Daniel reached into his suitcase, getting the hard copies of the messages handing them to the bailiff, "Your honor, these are the messages exchanged between my client and the defendant during that period; as you can see, my client never responded to them. The last time he had texted back was when they had their last agreed-upon sexual intercourse prior to the first sexual harassment."

Judge Wright thoroughly looked through the papers before making a disgusted face, which Brandon determined was the naked picture Shane texted him on Christmas. "Yes, you did agree to the time at the campus, as you've said earlier. That was the last time you gave full consent from start to finish?"

"Yes, your honor," Brandon confirmed nervously.

"I assume that you never discussed using any of the purchased sexual items that he texted you either?"

"No, that never came up."

"Mr. Jacobs, you better have a strong counterclaim because it isn't looking good for you even before the witnesses are brought up to the stand. There's text messages, images, and physical evidence proving so much." The judge told Shane.

Shane just let out a groan in frustration. He knew that he was going to lose the case if the mock witness wasn't convincing enough. He called her up as she was the last female he'd slept with after Brandon. His lawyer wasn't sure if they had a chance of winning either. Somewhere on the inside, it killed him, knowing how much he'd hurt Brandon. He wanted to go back in time to have talked it out with him. The reason why he was behaving so stupid was to give Brandon a sure win. Going to prison was the last thing he wanted; being in jail had been hard enough. His hand held onto a letter that he wrote with assistance, but he wasn't going to give it until the very end. Being locked up helped him finally realize what he did was wrong and unforgivable. He was scared of the truth and of actually being attracted to men, especially Brandon. He turned to sex as his compromise, never once considering anyone else's feelings. That letter explained all of that and more. For now, he had to keep up the foolish act.

"The final time was the night that Mr. Deanes alerted the police on January 20, 2019. Christmas and New Years', he was able to get away for a few weeks. He did commit rape once before the holidays." Daniel informed the judge.

"So you escaped and went back, Mr. Andreas?" The judge asked, confused.

"I went back earlier that morning when he was at work to pack my belongings. He called me and said that he was worried about me. Once again, I was foolish to think that he'd changed back," Brandon sounded ashamed, "I never wanted sex. That was not my intention after all that he'd put me through. Yet in that pain and the stupid decision of my heart, and not my mind, the police were able to see in action him raping me, to which I have a copy of the police report from the police officer who is with us today."

"I understand that Mr. Deanes, your witness, is who called?" Judge Wright asked.

"Yes, your honor," Brandon answered.

"May I see the police report?" She asked. The bailiff then went over to Brandon's side of the room to retrieve the report from Officer Jones, who was also in the courtroom. Judge Wright looked it over for a few minutes once she was given it. She then placed the papers on her desk in front of her. To Brandon, it seemed like a really long time until she spoke again, "I also read the report of the rape kit. It only shows the DNA of Mr. Andreas's and Mr. Jacobs' and no one else's. This was done on January 20 as well?"

"I think it was after midnight on January 21, as I had to wait for a couple of hours," Brandon explained.

"Okay," Judge Wright responded, "If there is no more evidence to present, I would like to move onto the witnesses."

Judge Wright waited a moment to see if there was anything else. She then continued, "Prosecution, you may call your first witness."

Chapter 35: Court Ruling

"Thank you, your Honor. I call to the stand Mr. Zach Deanes," Daniel announced.

Zach got up and went up to the stand glancing at Shane as he went. He hated everything about that man and wanted him destroyed for everything he did to his friend. Looking at his fake witness made him sick to his stomach. She surely didn't belong in this trial. What could she possibly contribute to this situation? Zach looked at Brandon again, and he could tell that he was still afraid under his mask. No matter what happened with the verdict, Zach was going to be there through his healing process. He was never leaving him.

"Will the witness please stand to be sworn in by the bailiff." Judge Wright requested.

"Please raise your right hand. Do you swear to tell the truth, the whole truth, and nothing but the truth?" The bailiff asked him.

"I do," Zach obeyed.

Daniel walked up to stand in front of Zach at the podium, "I understand that you were the one that alerted the police station about the night in question?"

"Yes, that is correct." Zach nodded his head.

"Did you know about what was happening before the night in question?"

"I knew about the first time they had sex. Mr. Andreas informed me that Mr. Jacobs had sexually assaulted him numerous times on the day of his father's funeral," Zach informed the court.

"Were there other people involved in the incident?" Daniel then asked.

"No sir, it was only Mr. Andreas and Mr. Jacobs."

"Were you in the house on the night of questioning?"

"I was at the house, but in my car. I drove behind Mr. Andreas once he had texted me prior to the last incident that he was going." Zach sighed, "I couldn't convince him to not go in that place. There was no way that Mr. Jacobs was going to cooperate with him and just have a conversation. I begged Mr. Andreas to turn around and not go in and still file a lawsuit against him. However, in a way, a good thing came out of that."

Brandon and Daniel looked confused as the rest of the jury did. That prompted Daniel's next obvious question in mind, "What was good about it?"

"With Officer Jones' police report strengthens our case that the event occurred was, in fact, a sexual assault. She witnessed how the defendant had Mr. Andreas tied up against his will and violated him in so many ways that night. God knows I wish that I was able to stop him by myself. However, with more eyewitnesses, especially from policemen who were so amazing, it strengthens our case, proving that he committed this crime." Zach carefully explained, "Also, she could go to jail herself if she'd lied."

"That depends on the situation, but in some cases, that is correct." Judge Wright confirmed with a nod, "You may continue, Mr. Hart."

"Thank you, your Honor. Mr. Deanes, did you say anything to the parties involved in response to what you witnessed?" Daniel continued.

"I did not get a chance to see Mr. Jacobs at the station. However, I have obviously spoken with Mr. Andreas as we're friends. I have been with him throughout this entire legal proceedings." Zach spoke.

"One last question for you. Do you know why the incident or behavior occurred?" Daniel finally asked.

"I can't say exactly, but it seemed like ever since Mr. Jacobs and Mr. Andreas experimented, he formed an addiction to having sex with a man. It most likely got to the point where the craving for it took over, and it tainted the personality in him. During the time that Mr. Jacobs' ex-girlfriend was in town, they didn't have sex…"

"Meaning Mr. Andreas and Mr. Jacobs?" Daniel asked for clarification.

"Yes, I think that during that time, he must've missed it, and that's why it turned aggressive and uncomfortable for Mr. Andreas," Zach stated as he looked over at Shane again, who had his head down. He continued, "I believe that he has some type of sexual addiction towards both men and women that Mr. Andreas wasn't aware of it."

"No more questions, your honor." Daniel turned to the judge.

"Thank you, Mr. Hart. You may be seated," Judge Wright ordered. After Daniel sat back down, she sighed, looking at the other side, "The Defense may cross-examine the witness."

Mr. Parkson went to where Daniel stood to look Zach in the eye. Brandon felt nervous as the intimidating man went up to him. It was as if he was scared for Zach since he didn't seem to be fazed by it at all. Daniel patted his back as he took a big sigh. Zach would have to be very strong in order to handle this man. Not that Brandon had any doubts.

"Mr. Deanes, what is your relationship with the plaintiff?" Mr. Parkson asked.

"We met as classmates in college," Zach stated, "That was in August of 2018."

"What was your relationship with Mr. Jacobs?"

"Every time we passed by each other, we did speak. I knew him because of the college gossip and obviously through him being Mr. Andreas' roommate." Zach explained.

"Would you say that you were jealous of Mr. Jacobs?"

Zach blinked in confusion at his question. He didn't know why that question was asked, and he saw the look on Brandon's and Daniel's face, which meant they thought the same thing. It was a weird question that had nothing to do with the case. He didn't know where that was supposed to lead to. "Pardon?"

"Are you or were you ever jealous of the friendship between my client and Mr. Andreas?" Mr. Parkson asked again.

"Absolutely not! I was never jealous of their friendship, and I didn't realize that they were roommates until Mr. Andreas told me." Zach answered, feeling annoyed. However, he kept his composure and professional tone in his voice. He didn't know what game they were trying to play on him, but he wasn't going to fall for it.

"Do you know that if you called the police for a false report, you could get in trouble?" Mr. Parkson tried again.

"Officer Jones specifically stated in her report that she saw your client, with her own eyes, raping Mr. Andreas. Other policemen were also there, I may add."

"How many?"

"There were three total officers. Officer Jones talked to Mr. Andreas at the crime scene while the other two arrested Mr. Jacobs."

"How do we know you weren't trying to bait my client?"

"Why would I have to do that when he has this addiction? If anything, his love for intercourse has been shown in text messages, and Mr. Jacobs' inappropriate sexual comments towards Judge Wright further proves that to be true."

"Well, yes, they were uncalled for. I'd like to formally apologize for my client's misbehavior today," Mr. Parkson sounded defeated, "No more questions, your honor."

Brandon looked back over at the jury, who were all expressionless, and taking notes. He was still nervous that they wouldn't believe his case and side with Shane. Even though his counterclaim sounded extremely weak, they could still rule in his favor. He shared a similar annoying look between Zach and Daniel once Zach sat back down in his chair. They all knew that it was all to stall time, except they couldn't figure out what for. Whatever it was, the plan wasn't working for them.

"Prosecution, you may call your second witness." Judge Wright announced.

"Thank you, your Honor. I call to the stand Officer Linda Jones." Daniel looked over to where the officer sat.

Officer Jones got up from where she was and went to the stand, taking her seat. She adjusted her outfit, looking over at Shane before she got sworn in.

"Will the witness please stand to be sworn in by the bailiff." Judge Wright requested.

"Please raise your right hand. Do you swear to tell the truth, the whole truth, and nothing but the truth?" The bailiff asked her.

"I do," Officer Jones responded.

Daniel went back up to the podium and immediately began questioning her, "Officer Jones, I understand that you were assigned to my client's case when your station was alerted that night?"

"That is correct." She confirmed, "We received a call from Mr. Deanes at about 6:45 that evening. He was reportedly panicking and spoke urgently about the current situation between Mr. Andreas and Mr. Jacobs. He could only manage to get out that his friend was in danger. Those were his exact words. The emergency dispatchers immediately alerted the station, and we arrived in under three minutes."

"Did my client explain the scene you witnessed correctly?"

"Yes, he did. Officer Garrett and I had to break into the apartment since the door was locked, and we heard muffled screaming from the bedroom. Mr. Jacobs had ripped off Mr. Andreas's clothing, tied him to the bed, and was aggressively penetrating him."

"Did Mr. Jacobs cooperate during his questioning at the station?" Daniel asked.

"Absolutely not at all. He used foul language, resisted his arrest, and got very out of control during questioning. It took us three separate occasions that night to try to get him to answer questions." Officer Jones explained.

"Was there anything valuable that he told you guys when he did finally answer?"

"Not necessarily; Mr. Andreas explained the situation so much better than he did as he's shown today in the trial. We determined by our investigation that Mr. Jacob's claims weren't really making sense. Mr. Andreas gave the exact testimony today as he did to us two years ago. There's no way he's lying. Mr. Jacobs, on the other hand, I don't believe at all, and neither did my colleagues."

"When or have you spoken to Mr. Jacobs' witness?"

"I've never seen her before in my life. No idea who she is."

"No more questions, your honor." Daniel turned to the judge.

"Thank you, Mr. Hart. You may be seated," Judge Wright ordered. After Daniel sat back down, she looked over the other side, "The Defense may cross-examine the witness."

Mr. Parkson stood up, going back to face the officer, "Officer, we appreciate your time here. My client stated that he was humiliated when you arrested him. Is it true that you took him outside while he was still exposed?"

"We sure did," Officer Jones responded instantly, "The police department doesn't require the people we arrest to be clothed. Act like a fool; then you'll be treated like one. We gave him the jumpsuit once we arrived at the station before we questioned him. Or, before we had attempted to question him, I'll say."

"Has my client ever been arrested before this incident?"

"No, he's never had any criminal records prior to this."

"So, why now?" Mr. Parkson arrogantly questioned.

"Pardon?"

"Why put my client through the system now for a misunderstanding?"

"I can assure you that this is not a misunderstanding. Mr. Andreas's screams of help were very clear that he didn't want to be there."

"Sometimes, aggressive sex can be a misunderstanding to the eyes, officer." The lawyer challenged.

"I'm sorry, but you weren't there. I know what I saw, and I don't lie in my reports, especially with difficult cases such as this one," Officer Jones fired back, "As I was trying to say politely, Mr. Andreas was heard crying and hollering when we broke into the house and went into that bedroom. Mr. Jacobs might've muffled it as he tried to keep his mouth covered, but it was evident."

Brandon, Zach, and Daniel all listened in shock at Shane's lawyer and the police officer's conversation. There was no way that this lawyer was professional with her. Everyone in the room stayed quiet as the two lashed out.

"Is it possible that you confused moans as a cry for help?"

"Mr. Jacobs was moaning, yes. Mr. Andreas was not," Officer Jones then turned to the judge, "Your Honor, he was crying in tears. We could easily tell he was begging to be free. I'm not sure what type of sexual activities that this lawyer enjoys, or Mr. Jacobs for this matter, but Mr. Andreas didn't look like it was pleasurable for him."

"I don't know if I hate Shane or his lawyer more," Zach whispered to Brandon and Daniel.

"Trust me; this is usually his strategy when he's losing. Their witness won't help them either. We got this," Daniel confirmed positively.

"No more questions, your honor." Mr. Parkson finally announced a few minutes later.

Officer Jones walked past Brandon's table rolling her eyes and mouthing, "Unbelievable."

"Defense, you may call your first, and to my knowledge, the only witness." Judge Wright ordered.

"Thank you, your Honor. I call to the stand Susan Kayson." Mr. Parkson announced.

Brandon watched as Shane's witness went up to the stand. Susan was dressed in a black suit with a skirt that was inappropriate for court. Her brunette hair was down to her shoulders, and she had a lot of jewelry on. He started to tense up again, anticipating what she could possibly say. Where did they find her? Why hasn't she been at the other court dates if she really wanted to pretend to be a witness? He sighed and shook his head, knowing that Shane was taking this case as a joke. He felt Zach rub his back as a sign of support, and they shared a look.

"Will the witness please stand to be sworn in by the bailiff." Judge Wright requested.

"Please raise your right hand. Do you swear to tell the truth, the whole truth, and nothing but the truth?" The bailiff asked Suzie.

"Sure, whatever. I just want this to go fast." Suzie responded out of boredom.

With that, Brandon just groaned, knowing that she was there to waste everyone's time. He didn't think this lady could say anything valuable to the case. Just as when he felt he could relax, he heard the first question.

"Is it true that when you dated Mr. Jacobs, the plaintiff forced you to break up with him so he could have him?"

Brandon's eyes went wide open, and he looked at Zach in shock.

"Yep, he knew that with me in the way he'd never get a chance with Shane. All I was doing was enjoying my time with my amazing boyfriend, and he couldn't stand it." Suzie proclaimed.

"So, you've never done anything to make Mr. Andreas want to get rid of you except that you dated Mr. Jacobs for a brief period?"

"That's what happened," Suzie then folded her arms.

"So, you break up with him; they get together, why do you think Mr. Andreas would make this up? I mean, he was able to run you away. You'd think he'd be happy." The lawyer chuckled.

"Hey, I guess he realized that Shane wasn't good enough in bed for him. Maybe he no longer wanted it, and knowing how amazing Shane is, he'd try to do better to bring this selfish man satisfaction. When he failed to, he set him up to call it rape."

"That's not true, your honor," Daniel stated.

"Go on," Were the only words that Judge Wright spoke, ignoring Daniel. Brandon was starting to worry. Everything was false. Shane never mentioned that he was dating anyone when he asked. That's why he was so excited to see Madelyn come into town. If it were true, Shane would've told Madelyn that he had another girlfriend. He would've told Brandon.

"Did you ever speak to Mr. Andreas?" Parkson asked.

"I did, and I was nice. Something that I rarely am. Shane introduced me to him one month into our relationship, and I figured why not try to be nice. The guy was hot, still is," Suzie then winked at Shane, who then returned the wink infuriating Zach, "I figured that I might as well make friends with his best friend."

"How did that go?"

"He immediately was nasty towards me, threatened to harm me, told me that Shane belonged with him and I was in the way. I couldn't believe it. Shane had told me amazing stories about their friendship, and to then be greeted with rudeness and threats was unbelievable."

Brandon's heart was beating fast out of his chest. He was already upset, but now it had turned into fury. Whoever this no good blonde-haired lady was, she knew nothing about him. His body started to shake, and tears welled up in his eyes that he refused to let free. These were Shane's true colors, and he had to believe it. All he could do was stay silent and listen to this terrible testimony tear him to pieces, and be the key that lets Shane free.

"Do you have any proof of written communication between the two of you?" Mr. Parkson asked.

"I have received emails from him using his work email," Suzie told them.

"That you do," Mr. Larkson confirmed and gave her a quick smirk.

"Let me see them," Judge Wright requested. Mr. Larkson went back to his corner and gave Shane a smirk as he got the falsely printed emails to hand to the bailiff. Brandon tried his hardest not to burst into tears begging for his innocence. He looked at the jury, which gave Brandon no expression on their faces in return. Were they seriously going to believe this? He saw the judge thoroughly look them over and heard her hum. After she looked them over, she gave them to the bailiff, "Have them confirm the alleged email address and domain."

Daniel looked over the images and immediately shook his head in disbelief. The opposing lawyer either helped them make the images up, or he did it himself. "Your Honor, these are fake emails, and the username isn't my client's. The domain isn't ours either. Mr. Andreas does have a work email, but this is not it. For starters, they misspelled my law firm, and that is not the initial of my client's middle name."

"Mr. Andreas, what does your middle name start with?" Judge Wright asked, "State your full government name."

"D, your honor," Brandon spoke in a shaky voice, "Brandon Dustin Andreas."

Judge Wright handed the bailiff the box of tissues on her desk. Brandon took a few of them, thanking him, and wiped his eyes. He started to feel weak and useless at this point and didn't dare look at Shane.

"I am working tirelessly in this company. I'm getting the opportunity to learn so much, and I love it. I love having bosses that are willing to give me insight into my future career, your Honor. I'd never mess that up! Not with anything like this!" Brandon claimed and looked at Shane with fury, "I can't believe you. Why? What do you want from me?"

The room became silent as Brandon tried to calm down. Tears were rushing down his face as his entire body shook. He couldn't believe how far Shane kept going to make people fall for his sick lie. It angered him, made him feel weaker, and he never wanted to show his face to the world again. Shane was officially his worst nightmare.

Mr. Parkson smirked before turning to the judge, "No more questions, your honor." In his mind, he'd just won another case for his client. This mock witness was all they needed to win it all. Brandon was ruined for good.

"The Prosecution may cross-examine the witness." Judge Wright announced.

Daniel walked back up to the stand looking at the pathetic mock witness in the eye. He knew just how to get her to crack for good. "Ms. Kayson, you stated that you'd met my client prior to this situation beginning. What day was that?"

"I can't remember dates, man. That doesn't matter anyway." Suzie chuckled.

"I think it is important. Can you please try to remember?" Daniel tried again.

"I guess three years ago in October, why does that matter?" Suzie questioned.

"I find that interesting because in October of 2018 was when Ms. Madelyn Rhodes, the lady that my client claimed to have been the defendant's girlfriend, was in town," Daniel stated, glancing at Shane.

"We broke up before that," Suzie explained in an unconvincing way.

"Is that so?" Daniel arrogantly asked, looking at the papers he brought with him, "My client provided me with text messages between the two of them way before he got curious. Do you happen to go by the names Carly, Olivia, or Trina by any chance?"

"Maybe I do," Suzie answered, uncertain of what else that she could've said.

"I do not see Suzie or Susan in these texts. Your Honor, if I may read?" Daniel asked the judge, and she gave him a nod, "September 9, 2018, Mr. Jacobs started the conversation, *'I'm getting lucky tonight, man. Sorry for the noise in advance!'*, he included a winking face. My client replied, *'Do you even know her name, Shane? Last time you didn't.'* He texted back, *'Yes, mother, Carly Morgan.'* Are you sure you don't go by Carly?"

"I don't recognize that one," Suzie answered quietly.

"Around two weeks later, September 21, 2018, Jacobs texted *'Brandon, my bad about last night. I had another date with a chick named Olivia, and we had sex on the first night! I'll be home later.'* Is that you, Ms. Kayson? Could Olivia be your nickname?"

"No, it's not,"

"Are you the 'Totally sexy Trina!' that he was really excited about on October 1, 2018?" Daniel asked finally and saw Suzie silently shook her head.

"Susan, what the hell?" Shane shouted angrily from his seat.

"Mr. Jacobs, keep quiet!" The judge hollered.

"Your Honor, members of the jury, this proves that she knew nothing about this case and was never the defendant's girlfriend or one of his one night stands. At least, not before he was arrested. She is a fraud to this case who wasted everyone's time here, and I refuse to let her have the desperate spotlight that she craves any longer," Daniel finished proudly, "With that in mind, I have no more questions, your honor."

Brandon and Zach looked amazed at what Daniel did just then. He got the mock witness to crack. Brandon just couldn't believe it. He finally felt the relief that he needed. It didn't mean that he won the case yet, but the lies were off of his back. This meant that he could start feeling at ease.

"He's good," Zach whispered to Brandon, amazed.

"My boss is amazing." Brandon shook his head and wiped more tears away. When Daniel returned to their table, he winked at him, then turned back to the judge.

"Any other evidence or questioning that anyone would like to do, please say now. I'll give you sixty seconds," Judge Wright announced. Everyone stayed quiet for a while, and Brandon looked at Shane. He could tell he had something on his mind, and if that day was the last time they'd see each other, he needed him to say it now, even if it'd hurt him worse.

"Shane..." Brandon urged slightly.

That was all Brandon needed to say before he saw Shane sigh and went up to the podium.

"Your Honor, I would like to apologize for my behavior. I don't know when I lost myself," Shane mumbled as his eyes started to water up, "I have something to say to Mr. Andreas, but I wrote it in a letter. Well, to the best of my abilities. May I?"

"Would the plaintiff's lawyer be willing to read the letter?" Judge Wright asked.

"Yes, your honor, I will." Daniel agreed.

"Will the defendant give the letter over to the plaintiff?" The judge requested.

"Yes, your honor," Shane then looked at his lawyer, giving him a nod. He got an envelope out of the suitcase handing it to the bailiff. The bailiff took it to Daniel, who looked at Brandon.

Brandon took Zach's hand, taking a deep breath, "I'm ready."

Daniel opened the envelope and began to read.

Brandon,

You know I'm not good at words because of my dyslexia. Letters and numbers still confuse me to this day. These are all my words; someone is just going to help me write them and have them grammatically corrected. I miss you. I miss us as best friends and roommates. Those were the best three years of my life. Well, three years and however many months until I became the monster you needed to get away from. Please know that I'm not mad about it and I'm actually happy you got away. You never deserved me. Madelyn never deserved me. No one deserved to deal with my stupidity for the rest of their lives.

Why did you like me when I was always an idiot? I'm not just talking about romantically, because I was too dumb to realize your true feelings, but as friends. What made you decide to stick with me for so long? I was the lucky one, not you. I didn't deserve either of you, and clearly, my parents were right; I'm only a piece of shit. Three last few years made me realize how important you were to me and how much I needed you. Without you, I'm now useless. Guess my dumb ass should've thought of that once I heard you crying. I've reflected too late.

Please believe me when I say I really didn't know. Saying this seems ridiculous now; I know it is. The first time we had sex felt so different from when I started doing those horrible things to you. My feelings couldn't explain it, and I can't dare put it on my dyslexia. What I did is inexcusable, and I am so sorry. I should've talked to you. I shouldn't have pushed you aside to impress Madelyn. None of that matters as I'm probably spending life in prison.

I just don't want to go to prison. Can't we drop this and try to work it out for real this time? I understand if not. Thank you for believing in me when nobody else could. Thank you for being the shoulder to always lean on when I clearly stopped returning the favor. The truth is that I was scared of my emotions, so I hoped that my actions spoke for me by asking for sex. I just regretfully took it too far, and I never wanted to admit that. Hate isn't even the word I want to use as I've lost the very best friend I'll ever have in life.

You're going to be an amazing lawyer. I know you'll have a man who won't treat you like I did. He'll love you, value you, give you things that you probably wanted from me, and more. I'm sorry that I ruined you; that I ruined sex for you. Please try to heal from me. Move on, and give love another chance. Do it for yourself as you deserve that. You need to heal from your parents and me. I understand if you don't want to keep in touch with your mom, I obviously didn't. My wish for you is a new beginning with a successful career, an amazing husband, and maybe even children. You deserve this.

Once again, I'm deeply ashamed and sorry.

Sincerely,

Shane Jacobs

Brandon looked at Shane as his boss finished reading the letter with tears streaming down his face. The bailiff came over with more tissues, to which he took gratefully, trying to calm down. Zach embraced him from behind, rubbing his back, trying to soothe him as well.

"Really?" Brandon finally managed to get out, "It took you this long to finally say what I've needed you to say three years ago, Shane? Oh, my God!"

"Brandon, I'm—" Shane tried to speak.

"No! You're done talking to me; it's my turn," Brandon shouted for the first time, "I hate you! I hate you so much it's unbearable, Shane. Do you not realize how much I've needed my best friend? You put me through pure hell when I was already burning, and now that you're facing prison, you want to work it out? After you've brought this random woman to court to try to say that I was forcing you to have sex with me? I'm done with you. Never talk to me again in life no matter what the ruling is!"

Brandon took a moment to try to slow his breathing down as all of his emotions came in full force. He was angrier, devastated, hurt, annoyed, feeling exposed, and ashamed all over again. Zach didn't care about anyone else as he immediately embraced Brandon, letting him calm down. He cried hard, silent whimpers escaped his mouth, and he had difficulty breathing. Brandon felt like running away, never to be seen again. The fresh feeling of being touched by him even though they weren't next to each other came back. It was horrible.

"This has been an exhausting case; I have to say. Both the prosecution and the defense have now rested their cases. The attorneys will now present their final arguments. However, I think instead of trying to convince if the defendant is innocent or guilty because I'm taking this letter as him pleading guilty, I want to base your argument on what the punishment should be. The prosecution may begin." Judge Wright stated.

"Thank you, your Honor. Members of the jury, today you have heard testimony about the now proven rape incidents that have occurred between my client and Mr. Jacobs. I would like to remind you of some important information that you should consider in your decision. These facts include the exchanged text messages, the police report that stated how he didn't cooperate with anyone, how Officer Jones even took time out of her busy morning to testify on our behalf, and the way that he acted in court these last couple of years. I would like to see the ruling to be fifteen to twenty years. My client would also need a restraining order against him just in case that after Mr. Jacobs serves his time, he'd try to contact him again." Daniel proposed.

"Defense, you may proceed with your closing argument."

"Thank you, your Honor. Members of the jury, today you have heard testimony about the rape incidents that have occurred by my client towards the plaintiff, Mr. Andreas. I would like to remind you of how young my client is. Yes, he's made a huge mistake that cannot be undone, but it wouldn't have happened if the plaintiff had said no. Figuring out who you are can be quite the journey, and I admit that it was unfortunate how my client decided to go about it. I would like to propose for him to serve the minimum required of fifteen, if not less." Mr. Larkson requested.

"Members of the jury, you have heard all of the testimony concerning this case. It is now up to you to determine the punishment deserved for Mr. Jacobs. You and you alone are the judges of the fact. Once you decide what the proper sentence should be, you may return and give the verdict." Judge Wright ordered, "You are excused."

The judge and jury exited the room while the bailiff escorted Shane, the fraud witness, and Mr. Larkson to a separate room. Zach, Brandon, Daniel, and officer Jones went to the lobby, and they all hugged Brandon.

His eyes were red from crying so much, but he was relieved about it all. There was noise all around him, and he assumed that people were looking at them. He just didn't care. After getting that letter from Shane and knowing that he wouldn't have to suffer as much was all he needed at that moment.

"I can't believe it," Brandon breathed out, "I can't believe that they believed me, that he apologized, that I possibly won. This is a miracle."

"You've had all of the facts on your side, Brandon," Zach soothed him, "I'm so proud of how you fault in there."

"I agree; it was so amazing. You may not feel proud yet, but you will be. He's going to be locked up for so long I know it." Daniel added.

"I couldn't have done it without all of you. Especially Officer McKern and Officer Jones, I owe so much to you." Brandon looked at Officer Jones.

"It was our pleasure, Mr. Andreas. You deserve so much for having to deal with this. I won't say that it was a pleasure, but an honor to testify on your behalf." She said.

They found an area to sit down and wait. Brandon immediately had to text Richard the good news and smiled at his response.

"I am very proud of you for going through with this. I'll be in town hopefully soon. If not, then definitely for your graduation. You're stronger than you think."

Brandon sighed, feeling so much weight being lifted from his heart. It wasn't completely gone, but it seemed like everything that he needed from this case he was going to get. He looked over at Daniel, who patted his shoulder. Brandon felt so lucky to have him.

"All we have to do is wait for them to decide. It shouldn't take more than a few weeks." Daniel explained.

"Great, the waiting game continues." Brandon groaned.

"Yes, but you still won this case. The most important thing is knowing that they believed you. This will be over soon." Zach promised.

"I hope so," Brandon sighed.

The next few weeks dragged on. Brandon was starting to get worried as time went by. He would go to work and school, with that being the only thing he'd think about. He didn't let his grades slip through the cracks, however. Brandon knew not to give up now. Shane was going to prison. That was all that mattered to him. Some nights were harder than the others. The nightmares came back, his anxiety went back up, and the panic attacks continued. He couldn't help it. Zach went with him to the weekly therapy sessions as well. Sharon had to help get him together and calm him down on some days. All of his bosses gave him personal time off to try and keep the stress off of him.

Once the day had finally arrived a couple of weeks later, Brandon was ready. He was scared but ready. Zach, Brandon, and Daniel all rode to the courthouse together. His nerves were high, and he barely slept the night before. It wasn't that he felt exhausted, but his mind kept thinking about the final process.

"This is ridiculous," Brandon sighed as he and Zach walked up to Daniel.

"I know, but it should not take long. Fifteen minutes max." Daniel promised

They sat around talking until they were called into the room. Officer Jones wasn't able to make it that morning, but she sent her well wishes through Daniel. Brandon held onto Zach's hand for reassurance and to help calm him down. Once their case was called, they made their way inside. Shortly after, Shane and his lawyer came back in, not saying a word.

"All rise," Announced the bailiff. Everyone stood as the judge came into the room. She went back to her seat, and then the jury came next.

"Have you reached a verdict?" Judge Wright asked.

The jury foreperson stood up, "We have your honor."

"What do you say?"

"We, the jury in the case of Andreas versus Jacobs, find the defendant guilty as charged. We believed everything that the plaintiff accused the defendant of, and his behavior was unacceptable in court. Based on the DNA results from the rape kit, it was clear Mr. Jacobs' DNA from all of the nights in question. Mr. Jacobs was going to be found guilty as charged even if he didn't admit to the crime." The jury person stated.

"Thank you, Jury, for your service today. Mr. Andreas, I hope that you seek the help that you desperately need to start healing from this. My suggestion is to start or continue counseling if you've been going, and I hope you can find real healing. I am also granting your request for a permanent restraining order against Mr. Jacobs, as well as one hundred thousand dollars for pain and suffering. I wish you luck. I hereby sentence the defendant to twenty years in prison. The hearing is set for two weeks from today. Court is adjourned." Judge Wright hit her gavel on the sound block, and the case ended.

Brandon saw Shane leave the room once the bailiff placed handcuffs on him. They looked at each other in the eyes for a quick second, and Brandon saw an empty soul that was once filled by Shane, his former best friend. That was the last time that he ever saw Shane Jacobs.

Chapter 36: Healing

Brandon headed into the therapy room, following behind Zach and Sharon. He wanted him to join him to help explain how everything went in court. Brandon was so relieved that the most significant part of his case was finally over. That lifted so much weight off of his shoulders that he didn't realize he bore. Shane was gone, and he could move on with his life. Brandon was now free. His body could belong to only him again.

"How did it go?" Sharon first opened up the conversation.

"I think that it was interesting, to say the least. I'm so proud of Brandon," Zach smiled at him.

"I couldn't have done it without you. You held me down when I didn't think I could do anymore," Brandon thanked him wholeheartedly.

"As you know, this man is such a fighter. To see him stand up to that man and prove that he was guilty was so incredible." Zach praised him.

"I didn't doubt that for a second," Sharon smiled, "As a student lawyer, I knew that he would be able to pull through."

"I just feel so lucky and grateful that everyone from the beginning of this whole court process has stuck with me. My friends, who I now consider my family, bosses, and the police department, were always helpful. I was able to do this because of everyone else around me." Brandon admitted.

"What are you feeling now?"

"I feel free. To be honest, I understand that I'll never be the same man that I was before this. I know that I'll never fully heal, but I have to cope with it all. It's like this massive amount of weight was finally lifted off of me, and I can breathe again."

"Do you still love him?"

"No," Brandon shook his head honestly. It was the very first time that he had answered it without hesitation, "I can't even love who he used to be anymore. It took me a long time, but I have to realize that he stopped loving me enough to put me through hell. The man he became since the first rape over two and a half years ago was no longer there. I had to realize the hard way to let him go."

"That's so good to hear you say that. How are you doing emotionally?" Sharon then asked.

"I'm hurting everywhere emotionally. That's because he tried to break me down all the way again. He succeeded and then tried to apologize for it. This man was lying under oath to try to save his own ass. Him doing that made me so angry and so damn sick to my stomach because he knew how to get me acting a damn fool crying in that courtroom. It felt good to see him defeated, but he put me through so much."

"What was the outcome?"

"I won the case," Brandon started to cry tears of joy, "He eventually admitted to everything through a letter, and the judge took it as him confessing the truth. He was sentenced to twenty years in prison."

"Brandon, that's amazing news. Do you realize how much of a blessing that is? Whether or not you believe in a god, that is such a blessing. You did it!" Sharon told him.

"I know it doesn't look like it, but I am so happy. All of this was so worth the long wait knowing that justice was on my side. Hearing that ruling made everything I went through while waiting for this trial to take place worth it."

"Your story can be an incredible testimony for so many men and women that victims can be believed. Every time I asked you what happened, you explained every single detail the same without leaving any information. That alone is so impressive as many people can't."

"I had to. Practicing law has taught me to carefully listen to every time a client tells you their story. If a lot of details change each time they tell it, then they are harder to believe," Brandon explained passionately, "No matter how tough it was to make sure I never left out a single detail about what happened. I know what happened. It's my body, and I couldn't let that man get away with it so easily just because I forgot a tiny detail."

"Zach, how did you feel about all of this having been with him this entire time?" Sharon questioned Zach.

"I was aggravated and pissed to see that man lie as if it didn't matter. Brandon didn't see that every time he or his lawyer was speaking, eye-rolling and groaning were coming from the other side of the room. That was from both the defendant and his lawyer." Zach answered.

"I definitely didn't see any of that going on. It doesn't surprise me one bit. All I saw in him was hate. How the fuck did he think I was going to that little apology letter of his? That was all manipulation." Brandon commented angrily.

"Why do you think it was manipulative?" Asked the therapist.

"It wasn't like we hadn't been in court together all the times leading up to trial trying to settle it. Well, I still wanted him to go to prison, but we had to see if he would. Apparently, it's part of the process," Brandon groaned before realizing what he said, "I mean, I know it's part of it. I'm studying to be a lawyer. What am I thinking?"

"We understand, Brandon. You're just thinking emotionally right now. Do you have a copy of the letter? I'd like to see it."

Zach nodded his head and got out his printed copy. "We didn't ask for the original one; luckily, they uploaded it to the case website."

"My boss was able to print it out for me," Brandon explained.

Sharon was quiet as she read through the entire thing. Brandon saw her in deep thought as she read through it carefully. He wanted to know what she would suggest. Every time that he would read, it made him upset and angry. What Shane had written in that letter was all he was waiting to hear him say three years ago. Brandon would have talked it out with him and figured out what to do without getting the police involved. He always knew what he did was a crime, and if Shane had talked to him, then they wouldn't have had to go through that. He lost everything by saying yes.

"What he wrote would've given you so much closure two years ago. This letter was his last tactic to get him off the hook for committing the crime. He actually had some nerve to do this," Sharon sighed and shook her head, "I've seen this happen many times, and some victims fall for it even years later. To know that you didn't let this fool you is great. This is how you know that you've proven to have healed so much already."

"Yeah," Brandon sighed.

"I think you need to respond one day," Sharon suggested.

"What? I'm not his prison pen pal," Brandon looked at her like she was crazy. He didn't understand why she would suggest that after all that she knew. Why would he go back to that?

"I'm not saying that at all," Sharon clarified immediately, "I never want you to ever get in contact ever again, no matter how many years later. I'm saying this for your healing. You could bring so much healing to yourself by responding to this letter and then ripping it up into pieces. Not just ripping it up, but burning it in a fireplace afterward. Until you do that, your thoughts about him will never leave your mind. No, I'm not saying you'll forget about him ever in your life. I'm not saying that you're going to be magically healed forever. What responding to a letter does is allows you to put every emotion onto paper, allowing even more weight to come off of your shoulders so that you can be free."

"I guess that makes sense. My only fear is I'll only write 'I hate you, I hate you' all over again like a five-year-old. As if I'm masking it all because I'm afraid of others."

"The only people who need to see this letter are me, you, and Zach. No one will have to have an opinion about it because it's not going on the internet. Even if you type it up on the computer, I do not want you to post it to Facebook necessarily. The world doesn't need to have a say in your healing, Brandon. I have never shared anything we talked about with anyone else. This HIPAA agreement prevents me legally from talking to others besides your family and Zach."

"I know that, and I feel good that it's in place." Brandon sighed and wiped his eyes.

"You know I'm a vault when it comes to our friendship. Whatever you say stays between you and me." Zach promised him.

"Which is why I'm grateful for you. I don't deserve you as my best friend."

"Yes, you do, Brandon. I'm the undeserving one. What could I have done to deserve such a badass friend who never gives up even when he desperately wants to?"

"I wanted to give up every single day." Brandon reminded him.

"I don't believe that," Zach shook his head with a smile.

"Zach, every day was a struggle just to open up my eyes in the morning. I didn't want to live anymore, knowing all of the possible outcomes of the trial. It was hard to get up to go to class. Even though this is our last year, it's still hard. My mind is still going to be afraid until he is officially in prison. Anything could still happen." Brandon explained as more tears rolled down his eyes.

"Nothing is going to happen. He could get in worse trouble if he ever comes near you. You are incredible, Brandon Andreas. I am not kidding when I say that you are my hero. Going to trial was your biggest fear, and you've conquered it."

"What if the judge overrules the verdict and finds him innocent somehow? I can't take it," Brandon cried. That's when Zach's heart broke all over again. Zach looked at Sharon, who looked just as surprised that Brandon had asked that question. Even with the verdict, Shane still had him completely scared of the possibility that he'd get revenge. He didn't know what to say. It was something he had to take in for himself.

After a moment of thought, he finally found the words that needed to be said. "I promise you that isn't going to happen. The justice system, as crazy as it may be, takes these cases seriously. I know that, you know that, and Daniel knows this. That man is convicted and should be on his way to prison if he hasn't gotten there already. He's never going to be near you ever again. Not in this lifetime or any lifetime. What he did to you was awful, and he will be paying for it for the rest of his existence."

"I just want to heal. If he is gone forever from my life, then why am I still afraid?" Brandon questioned.

"That's because you just went to trial last week, Brandon. You hadn't seen him in a couple of months since the last court appearance, and you've been healing from this. Look at how far you've come since three years ago. That's incredible progress, Brandon. You're now done with him. There are no more court appearances, no more judges, and no more waiting. This time last year, you were worried that it'd go on past our graduation." Zach reminded him.

"Yeah, you were." Sharon smiled, "All you have to focus on now is the bar exam next summer. How does that feel?"

"God, that feels amazing," Brandon chuckled, "I really cannot believe that I'm still standing. However, I still feel his grip. His hands are forever on me, and I can't shake them. Hopefully, I can erase some of the feels off as time goes by, but it'll always haunt me from time to time. I can't just forget what happened."

"While that is true, you still don't have to let that ruin your whole life. You have to make it part of your life's testimony, owning your truth, and say, 'I made it through this.' You have to say that because you truly did. That's not a lie because you won this case." Sharon explained.

"I hope that when I get cases that go to trial, I won't break down in court as the lawyer." Brandon worried.

"You definitely won't. Brandon, we've studied cases like this in our classes, and you always pull through. Professor Dorn even told you how impressed he was to see that you did so well on those assignments. That was last semester, remember?" Zach reminded him.

"Can I just say that it has been a pleasure to witness how your friendship has grown over the past two years? Zach was there since the first group meeting. That's such a special friendship." Sharon grinned.

"I love him so much. He's the best thing that has happened throughout all of this. I really don't think I would've done this without him," Brandon shook his head with a smile, "I know he's tired of me being sad."

"I don't know if I'm tired of it, but I definitely want to see you happy. It is unfortunate that I couldn't have met you sooner to have known the original Brandon, but this Brandon is so much stronger. I can hardly wait to see what lawyer Brandon is like." Zach smiled back at him.

"Which brings me to this question. If Brandon in 2021 could speak to Brandon in 2018 when this all started, what would be the advice?" Sharon asked.

Brandon sighed as he thought for a moment. He had a million things to say to that man, and he didn't know where to begin. That had never crossed his mind before thinking about his past in that sense. To sum it all up made it that much more difficult. He had so much to reflect on with Shane.

"I would probably start by saying, be careful. Yes, you have this entire future planned out about him even if you're not together in the end. Yes, you can help your friend out, but it'll leave you hurting in the long run. You don't know him like you think you do, and you need to be very careful. Having sex with him will make him forget everything about you. He won't know your signs anymore. That man won't know when you're shutting down anymore. All he will see you as is a sex toy to play with whenever he wants to. Don't fall for that to save yourself." Brandon thought out loud.

"Would you tell him that he needed to move on?" Zach asked.

"He wouldn't have listened. Especially if this was a conversation post-sex." Brandon shook his head.

"What about before that?" Sharon asked.

"He would've been in denial. This is his very best friend we're talking about. Anyone else who he went to school with, maybe. Maybe not from his group of friends who he ate lunch with in high school, but the casual friends, yeah." Brandon nodded his head.

"What about me?" Zach questioned.

"I don't know because we were just getting to know each other. You were always attractive to me. Yet, I knew that you were in a relationship, and I respected it. I'd tell myself to cherish your friendship obviously and to never take you for granted." Brandon told him honestly.

"I am glad that you guys weren't trying to hook up or anything before this. That would've made things so much more complicated, if I may ask, and I know you're not ready, Brandon, but is this a possibility?" Sharon hinted.

Brandon and Zach had big blushes on their faces. He just admitted that he found him attractive. It wasn't a regret, but he did set himself up to be asked that. He wasn't ready. His body was still healing from the past while he desperately needed to move on with the future. When he thought about Zach, things seemed complicated. The last thing he wanted was to ruin their amazing friendship. At the same time, he was everything Brandon imagined having for a lifetime partner.

"I don't know, honestly. This man means so much to me, and I don't want to date him just because we're both gay. I have thought about it, and I think it could be a possibility," Brandon answered.

"I feel the same way," Zach nodded his head.

"We've never told anyone else that we almost kissed once," Brandon explained.

"When was this?" Sharon asked.

"Oh, goodness, I don't remember…" Zach sighed and tried to think.

"May 2019, Zach. The day we graduated undergrad school." Brandon reminded him as he turned to face him, "We were filled with excitement about the day. Remember we had put our gowns on, smiling from ear to ear looking in that mirror of yours. I don't remember what got into us that we almost kissed. Luckily my brother interrupted at the right time by calling me."

"That's right," Zach nodded with a slight chuckle, "This is also why you are going to be a great lawyer. Your memory is so awesome and in some ways detailed."

Brandon gave a small smile and rubbed the back of his neck. "I guess that's one of the good things my mother taught me before I came out. She would say no matter what, you should always remember the details. Maybe not the tiniest of details, but enough to make sure that you're believable."

"Have you spoken to her since your father passed away?" Sharon wondered.

"I obviously see her around town from time to time. She doesn't make any move to try to speak with me, and I'm done begging. If she wants to be alone and miserable because of who I am, then I have nothing for her. I took care of her dying husband, and she still didn't give a damn," Brandon gave a sarcastic laugh, "If moms know their kids, then obviously she knew something was wrong with me. Did she care enough to ask? No."

"You really lost your best friend and parents in the same year," Sharon sighed.

"I sure did," Brandon nodded his head as more tears fell from his eyes, "I just had to keep pushing. If I had let that stop me, then I wouldn't be graduating next year in 2022."

Sharon then took out a flashcard packet that was on her desk and looked through them. She found the cards that she needed and gave them to Brandon.

"Fighter, survivor, warrior, motivated, and passionate." Brandon read out loud.

"These are the words of how I describe you. This is how I've always thought about you since we first met. The words that you describe for yourself aren't the truth. I think Zach would agree that these fit you better?" Sharon smiled.

"There aren't enough words in this universe to describe him, but these will have to do perfectly." Zach smiled in agreement.

"I'm giving you a lifelong assignment for whenever you feel bad. Say each of these words, starting with 'I am.' I'd like you to do it now." Sharon instructed.

"I am a fighter. I am a survivor. I am a warrior. I am motivated. I am passionate." Brandon spoke out loud.

"This creates confidence just by speaking it into existence. You will heal, Brandon. You've been healing and doing a fantastic job. Do not give up, please." Sharon looked into his eyes, "You are worth it."

"I promise that I'm not giving up. If anything, this is my start to move on officially. I don't want him in my life ever again. He's in prison, and I know that he isn't going to survive it, which makes me sad for him but relieved for me. Not really sad like it'll get me upset or anything, but he ruined his life because of his sex addiction." Brandon clarified the last part.

"I think he's coming back," Zach grinned, "Brandon is returning, and he's so amazing. Part of him will never return, and everyone who loves you understands that. However, we want your happiness to be restored. That's what everyone is expecting. This is always, unfortunately, going to be a part of you. Yet you'll use it to help so many other people. Especially men because we hardly speak up."

"I hope so," Brandon sighed.

Zach then took his hand and intertwined their fingers together, "I'll always be with you, alright?"

"Alright." Brandon smiled at his best friend. He didn't know where life would take him, but he was glad to know that he'd always have a friend in Zach.

Chapter 37: Officially Lawyers

By the time June had come around again, Brandon and Zach had successfully graduated from law school. Their friends, Lewis and Stacey, had also graduated. Brandon was at Lewis' house with his friends, and they were all laughing and talking.

"I can't believe we did it. Just imagine if we had listened and had taken that year off. Fuck that idea." Brandon laughed.

"I know, man. We've accomplished everything in time, too. We can do so many things. Are we still opening our own law firm?" Lewis asked.

"We should do that. The four of us would be a damn good team." Stacey nodded her head.

"I would love that. The thing is we need a lot of money first. So, my bosses are letting Zach and I join their law firm!" Brandon announced, and everyone cheered. Zach and Brandon looked at each other with a smile and chuckled.

"That's incredible!" Lewis smiled.

"Thank you guys," Zach smiled, "Daniel, Destiny, and Gina are all so amazing. I figured that they'd want Brandon for obvious reasons, but I wasn't expecting an offer."

"You're welcome, by the way," Brandon smirked at him.

"Wait, you suggested that I join the team?" Zach asked and looked at him, surprised.

"Why wouldn't I? You're amazing, Zach. I'm sorry that I couldn't convince them to hire all three. They only allowed me to pick one, and I had to go with him." Brandon told his friends.

"I understand completely. We weren't expecting that in the first place." Stacey smiled.

"I wasn't either, and I'm not jealous. We've got each other through these hard years, including Brandon's case, but we have to do something on our own too." Lewis agreed.

"Oh, I feel so special!'" Zach laughed and hugged Brandon.

"You need to come with me to work Monday morning. That's when we start," Brandon informed him.

"Oh, my God!" Zach grinned.

"Damn, you guys aren't sick of each other yet?" Stacey made a sarcastic remark.

"Who said we weren't?" Brandon fired back playfully. Everyone laughed and kept talking.

On the outside, Brandon was trying hard to become happier while fighting off his inner demons. The nightmares were still happening even if they weren't as frequent. That man had officially been gone from his life for nine months, and Brandon still had moments of anxiety and fear. As a result of that, Brandon was put on depression medication by his doctor. Despite all of that, he was still trying to push it away to focus on the positive. He was over the constant tears, and the panic attacks were happening less. The thought of love still scared him, and sex was still out of the question. He had gone back to noticing attractive men, but that was as far as it went. There weren't many conversations around that either. He would discuss other's love lives, but he was off-limits.

Brandon would get hit on from time to time. It flattered him and feared him at the same time. He had so many classmates that he became friends with. There were obviously a few men and women who were clueless about his sexual orientation that would ask him out. He just didn't know how he could ever trust again. To trust anyone with his heart that wouldn't break it or turn out to be another disappointment. Brandon didn't know what he wanted in a man anymore. Well, he knew that he needed to be gay. Not straight nor bisexual. He couldn't even allow himself to date someone who was questioning their sexuality. He remembered when Madelyn had told him that, and Brandon knew she was right. They had to be gay in order for him to agree to a date. It felt like he was excluding and being too picky, but he had a reason to. The dating apps were too scary, and the hookup apps were obviously out of the question. It was a good thing that he wasn't in any hurry.

"Brandon, do you have any wants for your first case?" Lewis asked him, which brought him out of his thoughts.

"I don't know. I told Daniel to surprise me since I trust him. You wouldn't believe the types of cases they get in their system. Being the receptionist was so fun, and it was funny to read the case inquiries," Brandon laughed and shook his head, "A lot of them tend to be defendants who are asking to get a lawyer. If a plaintiff needs one, then we get notified usually through the NYPD."

"Was that how yours got chosen?" Stacey asked.

"No, I went to them myself. The police department offered to have them get me one, but I said that I knew someone. That next day I went into work, checked their schedule, and saw that it was fully filled up, and Daniel told me to block out his lunch hour and put the 'new unknown client' in." He explained.

"Basically, you told them that you needed a lawyer without saying that it was you who needed it?" Lewis guessed.

"Yeah, pretty much. Everything worked out in the end, so it wasn't a big problem."

"The judge even asked at the trial if he worked for them. That was luckily fine." Zach added on.

"Wait, you still went to work the very next day after the—?" Stacey questioned with a surprised look on her face.

"I sure did. Zach, how much sleep did I get that night—well, morning?" Brandon turned to look at him.

"It had to be only for three hours. We left the police station and went straight to the hospital for you to go do the kit. That alone took a couple of hours to do. Then we went to my old apartment. You immediately went to sleep and woke up with your alarm clock pretending to be rested." Zach recalled.

"I did what I had to do," Brandon sighed.

"This is why everyone says you're strong, Brandon. No matter what, you refused to give up mentally. Even when it was tough to keep going."

"It's no surprise to say that I almost did when the car broke down. I mean, that day was just the start of everything going downhill even further."

"You've made it through is what matters."

"As for you two," Brandon turned to Stacey and Lewis, "I forbid you from joining one certain law firm."

"We know, and we don't want to. His ratings are so good, though." Lewis said.

"I know, Lewis." Brandon glared at him.

"Sorry."

When there was a knock at the door, Stacey went to open it. They had ordered pizza and wings for their gathering. She set the boxes down on the kitchen table and went to get some plates while everyone else washed their hands. Brandon and Lewis sat down on one side of the table while she and Zach sat across from them. Everyone got their slices and wings then began eating.

"I feel like we should go on vacation or something before we start working," Lewis suggested.

"Gee, Zach, what can we do for our forty-eight-hour vacation?" Brandon enthused with sarcasm.

"I have an idea! How about we go out of the country? Surely we can get back in time for Monday." Zach said with the same sarcasm.

"Shut up," Lewis laughed, "I forgot, okay?"

Brandon chuckled, "I'm just messing with you. They wouldn't mind me taking a vacation first. Daniel just told me that we have to go in next week to set up our individual offices."

"Our own offices too?" Zach excitedly repeated.

"Yeah, Raymond and Kyle were never there because they were opening their own location. So, we get theirs, and it's the same size as Daniel's office." Brandon said.

"That's awesome."

The friends enjoyed the rest of their night talking and playing games together. They had a good time remembering their time in college and law school. The only thing that was refused to be brought up by name was Shane. No one cared about him anymore, especially not Brandon. He was the past. There wasn't anything to miss about him either. Brandon had to forget all of the good times they shared because it didn't mean shit anymore. The memories would only make him upset, and he didn't need that. He didn't care how his life was in prison, whether he was ruling the place or getting beaten to death. Shane's parents had gotten in contact with him and hated Brandon for going through with the lawsuit. It got so bad afterward that he had to get a permanent restraining order against them too.

He understood why they hated him. It had to be hard to see their only son end up in prison because of his best friend. Zach didn't allow Brandon to feel guilty because it wasn't his fault. Brandon loved Shane. Why would anyone think that he'd make up something so serious knowing that he was studying law himself? For a while, it did give him anxiety. It was the situation with his parents that made Brandon realize that he should never deal with anyone with the last name Jacobs ever again.

Monday morning came faster than he'd anticipated. Brandon was at the apartment that he'd gotten not too long after his trial had ended. It wasn't too far from where Zach had gotten his. It was just a two-bedroom, two-bath apartment that was only about an hour from where he worked. His old apartment was closer, but why would he want to be near that area ever again in his life? He took a quick shower once he woke up that morning, packed his lunch, and ate a quick breakfast. Brandon was so excited. All of his struggles had paid off, and it was finally his first day at his dream job. It felt surreal. There were no more classes to attend, no more papers to write or tests to study for, and all of the doubting professors had been proven wrong about Brandon. This was finally his moment.

He sat down at his kitchen table and took his first swallow. It was probably going to be a slow first day to get everything set up in his office, but he was still excited. To have his own office in the building that he'd worked at for years was an honor within itself. Brandon wasn't going to take anything for granted. His phone dinged with a text notification from Zach ten minutes later, saying that he was around the corner from him and to be ready to come out. Brandon didn't text back so that Zach could focus on the road. The last thing they needed that day was for him to get into an accident on the way. Other texts started to pop up from his brother and friends, wishing him luck on his first day.

"I would hate to see you fuck up your first day after spending so much time getting your degree!" Richard texted with sarcasm.

Brandon laughed and rolled his eyes before replying, *"Thanks for the boost of confidence, you ass. I'll be fine!"*

"I can't wait to hear about your first day! Love you, text me tonight if you're not busy." Madelyn had texted the night before after he had fallen asleep.

"I wouldn't be here without you. I'm definitely going to call you tonight." Brandon sent back. All of his friends were wishing him luck, which made his nerves go down. He was finally starting to get his happiness back again. There were also messages in the group text that he had with his college friends. They both wished Zach and Brandon good luck on their first day and suggested dinner that night if they weren't exhausted. Times like that morning reminded him that he was still loved despite all of his inner scars and pain. The demons were still trying to ruin him. Each monster was spewing nasty things trying so hard to break him down, but he couldn't allow them to take over that day.

Once Zach had arrived, Brandon got a text saying that he was out front waiting. He took one big sigh and collected his items, then got in the car.

"Good morning," Brandon smiled at him.

"Good morning to you too! Today's a big day." Zach smiled back.

"We've had a lot of big days."

"I know, but still. This is a special one for us. Do you think we're getting assigned cases today?"

"Knowing Daniel and Gina, yeah, probably. They've been waiting for this day where they could pass some of the responsibility to me."

"This will be interesting."

"We got this." Brandon smiled. Zach nodded his head as he focused on the road. The New York streets weren't as bad as most mornings. There was still traffic, but it wasn't as heavy. Zach proceeded to drive with one hand on the wheel, with his other rested on the console. Brandon was still texting on his phone when he decided to put his left arm on the console without looking. When he realized that Zach's arm was also on it, they looked at each other and gave a small smile without either saying anything. They could only look at each other for a short second at a red stoplight, but Brandon felt butterflies in his stomach from it.

Was he falling for Zach? He wasn't ready for that. Brandon couldn't even answer it in his own mind. All he knew was that Zach made him feel safe. No matter what the problem, he knew that Zach wasn't going to judge him for anything. He didn't want to ruin that. Brandon didn't even know if Zach still liked him in that way. That day wasn't the day to figure it out. They were able to get to work on time since there wasn't much traffic. Brandon and Zach looked at each other and smiled.

"Let's go," Brandon said eagerly.

Once they got inside, Daniel and Gina were waiting for them in the break room.

"Welcome you to the introductory magnificent start day of your new careers!" Daniel enthused, and Brandon raised an eyebrow.

"You made that up on the spot," Brandon stated.

"I sure did but shut the hell up," Daniel clapped back with a smile still on his face.

Brandon rolled his eyes before he hugged him. There were not enough words in the world to thank all of them, especially Daniel. Not many people were lucky enough to have one boss who cared for them, let alone three. They were more like his friends rather than colleagues. He then gave Destiny and Gina hugs too. Everyone in that room was now his team. Brandon thought that it felt a million times better than joining any sports team.

"Since you're now on salary pay, you no longer have to clock in. You just go straight to your offices and get to work. There are no shifts, but you're not going to find much time to be away from here during the week. Sometimes you will be here on weekends as well. No more set schedules for you." Daniel said.

"We understand," Zach nodded with a smile.

"That's good," Brandon smiled.

"That being said, you will be mentally stressed out, but you cannot show it to your clients. To them, you're the professionals who can handle it. You automatically have every answer in the government and court system, and there's no way you'll lose their case." Gina laughed, "I give you both a year before you hate this career."

Everyone laughed along with her, and then they got to business. Zach followed Destiny and Gina to his office while Daniel led Brandon.

When Brandon opened the door to his room, he got emotional. The walls had been repainted, and the floors had new brown hardwood. There were a couple of bookcases to the left when people first walked in, and the desk was straight ahead. He had both a desktop and laptop as the other lawyers had in theirs. His nameplate was already there, which read "Brandon Andreas, Attorney at Law" on it.

"This is surreal, man." Brandon laughed as he sat down in his new desk chair. He looked around the room, feeling speechless. The day that he dreamed of turned out to be better than he could've imagined.

"I can't explain how proud we are of you. Especially me, man, you've been through so much. I knew before you ever told us that something was wrong, but you had that mask on that you used to smile. You were hurting, and I couldn't figure out why. Then you didn't say anything, so it was inappropriate for me to invade you like that," Daniel sighed, "I wish I'd asked then."

Brandon shook his head, "There wasn't anything in the world that you could've said that day that would've made me speak up. I was still in so much shock and stress that I hadn't even processed the fact that he raped me. Then I had to deal with a mother and father who didn't love me and yelled at me before I came to work. Daniel, I did not step out of my room unless I needed to use the bathroom or go get food. God knows I wanted to talk to him before anyone else, but I never had the opportunity. He was gone."

"What did you do after it happened the first time?"

"I completely froze. Your body knows what happened before your brain has time to register it. So when Monday morning came around, I just forced myself to do what I needed to. Also, it didn't help getting yelled at by my mom for bullshit."

"You made it through, though. That's all that matters." Daniel smiled at him and gave him a tissue from the box of tissues on the desk. Brandon wiped his eyes and then signed onto the computer. "Go in the system; I've picked out the case for you this morning."

"Cool," Brandon nodded his head. He navigated through the company system and located his first case.

"I am going to be listed in this case as a second lawyer, but I'm only your mentor. This is all for you. No training at all; you've seen me and the others in action for years. You need no assistance. Thursday, I got in touch with Officer McKern, and he's going to come in after your vacation to work with you and your client."

"My client…" Brandon repeated in amazement.

"Your client." Daniel smiled at him.

"Let's do this, then."

Brandon proceeded to open up his case file and read through the information. He was going to represent a plaintiff who was held at gunpoint in their home during a robbery. There was contact information, the claim of items that got stolen, and information on the date that it occurred.

"I can handle this," Brandon nodded his head.

"Welcome to your first day of being a lawyer, Mr. Andreas." Daniel smiled and patted his shoulder.

This was it. After his vacation, he was going to prove that he would be a great lawyer. Brandon felt nervous about it being his very first one, but he was going to be okay. He had a fantastic team behind him and Zach, who was also getting his first case in the other room. It was now his turn to start having justice be served for others.

Chapter 38: A Fresh Start

Another half a year went past quicker than Brandon had realized. He was still on his first case, and he had a decent, trustworthy relationship with the client. Brandon gave it his all as he would try to practice presenting the information at home in his mirror. Daniel and Destiny would also assist him when it was necessary. His first court date as an official lawyer went pretty well. Zach also had a case that was off to a good start. Neither could explain the satisfying and rewarding feeling of being in their dream careers and doing a good job so far. Brandon had so many things to be thankful for, and Zach was a big one.

During that time, Brandon had finally begun thinking about dating. With his therapist and friends' help, he could get himself mentally prepared to start thinking about love again. It was still scary to him, but Brandon couldn't keep denying his feelings for one certain gentleman. This man had become a rock for him. Someone who kept him going when he desperately wanted to quit. They would spend hours on the phone together whenever he couldn't sleep. He made Brandon feel safe, loved, and cared for. He made him believe in himself again. This was someone who stood by him when Brandon couldn't understand why. This person became very special in his life, and he could no longer ignore the constant butterflies that resided in his stomach. He didn't know what to expect, but he would understand if he got rejected as this person may not feel the same way about him.

Brandon walked into work with his heart pounding. He didn't want people to see him walking in with them as he made sure to be the first one there. Once he was in his office, he placed them on his desk, turned on the computer, and got signed in. Brandon then went into the break room to put his lunch bag in the refrigerator and started making the morning coffee for everyone. He was nervous. It took everything in his body to not back down from taking the next step in their friendship. All he knew for sure was that he loved his man as a friend first. No hard feelings would occur if he didn't get a yes. After he took the first sip of his coffee, he heard the new front desk worker walk into the room.

"Good morning, Brandon." Cyndi smiled.

"Hey, how are you this morning?" Brandon asked.

"I am pretty good. Last night I didn't get much sleep because of homework."

"Oh, believe me, I know all about that better than anyone else here. Well, except for Zach. How are your classes?"

"I know you do. They're fine right now, my last test went well, and I got an eighty-one percent on it."

"That's awesome! I'm delighted to hear that. Let me know if you need help."

"Thank you very much; I will."

Brandon smiled and nodded at her, then went back to his office. He pulled out his phone and went to the lawyer's group text to let everyone know he was there. Brandon then got on his computer and checked on his three cases to see if anything got updated. His email was filled with new messages, so he decided to read through them.

Daniel came into the room thirty minutes later and closed the door behind him, and sat down in one of the chairs on the other side of Brandon's desk.

"It's still fucking weird sitting like this. It's like completely backward," Brandon chuckled.

"Yeah, I know it does, but you deserve it," Daniel said before noticing the flowers, "He's going to love them."

"I just hope I'm not making a big mistake. Zach means so much to me beyond words could explain."

"I knew this was going to happen the day you introduced me to Zach at your graduation from grad school. You looked at him differently than you did with anyone else. There's no way he's going to reject you because he feels the same way."

"Are you sure? What if he says no?"

"First of all, still let him have the flowers. They are not fucking cheap. I should know as I just bought some last week for my husband for date night."

Brandon laughed slightly and shook his head, "I know; these were the best I could find with my ideal price range."

"They look nice. Second of all, I think you're worrying too much. He isn't going to say no."

"What if I'm making a mistake and he's moved on from me?" Brandon questioned.

"Are you going to hate him?"

Brandon shook his head, "I could never hate him."

"Will you still be able to be coworkers and best friends?"

"Absolutely."

"Will it make you feel awkward?"

"Asking my best friend out is already going to feel awkward."

"Then you're going to be fine."

Brandon sighed as he looked at the flowers. He knew that Zach would understand that he was taking a brave decision to get back into the dating scene, but he didn't want him to just say yes out of pity. He definitely didn't need to have feelings for another man and have it turn out to be one-sided again. It was scary for him to go down that path again. Brandon also only told Richard and Daniel that he was going to do it. It felt embarrassing for him to make a big deal out of his nonexistent dating life. His brother became his wingman giving him advice on how to ask people out. It'd been years since he wanted to ask someone on a date, even before he and Shane moved in together. In college, the guys would ask Brandon out, not the other way around.

Zach was busy in his office for the majority of the morning. His client had stopped by to give more information about the case. Brandon had a busy morning and tried to make a few phone calls to the police department, working with Officer McKern to get all that he needed to update his own clients' files. There was never a dull moment being a lawyer. Brandon made sure to be the lawyer that cared more than just about the money in most cases, and Zach was the same. He always searched for whatever information he could on laws to make sure he knew every strategy that he could use in court. Whether or not he believed if his client was innocent. Having been the client on the other side helped him empathize with his clients. He didn't share a lot about his own trial battle, but he would always say that he understood. Besides, all of the information about his case forever lived online.

Richard kept texting him throughout the morning with positive messages to keep him encouraged and confident. He didn't want to push Brandon if he still wasn't ready or decided to back out, but he also didn't want the past to be the reason that made him stop. Brandon had many months to think about it. The thought really started to be in his mind somewhere at the beginning of the year. He and Zach continued to spend so much time together even after work. They never slept in the same bed, but there were many sleepovers. Zach always made him happy and safe. Zach was the one man who never judged him or made Brandon feel like he complained too much. The more that Brandon thought about it, the more Brandon knew that it was the right choice. Brandon found himself thinking about Zach nonstop. No matter what was going on, thoughts about him put a smile on his face. There were no thoughts about the future. He didn't know what it could lead to in the future; Brandon could only focus on that moment.

Around lunchtime, he went into the lunchroom to warm up his food. Zach was already there eating. He was wearing his dark gray suit that had a left front pocket. Zach always made sure that he was well put together from head to toe. His pants were slightly folded at the bottom, and his shoes were still shiny. Brandon had never seen him when he wasn't in a good fashionable outfit. It was definitely another thing that attracted him to Zach. Even back in undergrad college, when they met, it made him stand out from everyone else.

"Busy morning?" Zach asked when he saw him walk in.

"I guess you can say that," Brandon shrugged as he got his lunch out, "I've had crazier mornings. What about you?"

"Yeah, pretty much the same. Something about my case isn't adding up, but I'll figure it out."

"Do you think that your client could be guilty?"

"I mean, what else am I supposed to think when so much information seems to be missing? I don't want to say guilty automatically, but there's still so much I feel like I don't know."

"That's what I feel about this third case I just took on. He's trying so hard to prove that he didn't break into the bank at gunpoint, but it's all over the fucking news. I'll do what I have to."

"Oh my God, we're really turning into those kinds of lawyers."

"What the hell did you expect by joining a criminal law firm?"

"I didn't necessarily ask to join this team," Zach smirked.

"You're very welcome," Brandon teased.

"No, on a serious note, you're right. There are going to be many crazy cases. Some will feel like a waste of time." Zach sighed as he continued to eat.

Brandon continued to eat as he thought about the words he was going to use. He didn't know what he was going to say. He had a lot of time to come up with something; it's just that he didn't know if anything was right. He wanted to make sure that Zach knew how he felt.

"Well, right now we need money to pay off student loans," Brandon sighed, "I still owe the community college money as well."

"What a wonderful welcome to the workforce," Zach said with sarcasm.

"It's such a joy having that over your head. We'll get through it."

Zach smiled as he looked at him, "I'm loving this newfound confidence coming from you, Mr. Andreas. It's really great."

Brandon chuckled and blushed, "I like it too."

Brandon felt the butterflies in his stomach start up again. There was something about the guy that made him even happier than before. His only hope was to give him the great first date that he deserved if he accepted. Brandon knew about Zach's dating life during the chaos of the trial. They were further apart, but it never ended as he would hope. The men that he went out with never appreciated Zach like Brandon knew he deserved. Either they would slow up late to the date, not pick him up on time, or turn out to not be what he was looking for. All he wanted was to see him happy. Brandon was hoping to become the man who could.

"I can tell something is in your mind today. What is it?" Zach questioned.

"I don't know. I guess I'm just thinking about my cases." Brandon lied.

"You're not a good liar when it comes to me. I know you too well." Zach laughed and shook his head.

"I'm not lying!" Brandon defended himself.

"Andreas…" Zach warned.

"You'll find out later today!"

"Fine, I better." Zach chuckled as he finished his lunch. He then cleaned up his area and then stood up, "I have calls to make. See you later."

Brandon gave him a nod as he watched him walk away. He knew that he was ready. That was something about that man that made him so happy. He was ready for that happiness. By the end of the day, Brandon had wrapped up his work early to prepare himself. He gave himself a quick pep talk before picking up the flowers. Brandon walked outside of his office and locked the door behind him. Once he got to Zach's office, he took a deep breath before he knocked on the door and put a smile on his face.

"Come in," Zach called out. He was just about to call it a day as well.

Brandon walked into the room and smiled at him. He could see the smile on his friend's face that he loved seeing. He walked up to his desk and looked at him.

"Are these for me?" Zach asked.

"Yeah, they are."

"Well, they're stunning. Thank you, but why?"

Brandon sat the flowers down on the desk and looked him in the eye, "I've been thinking about you so much. Zach, you are an amazing friend to me, and there's no secret that I love you so much. You've been through a lot with me when you didn't have to, and I appreciate it."

"Well, that's what we do for each other," Zach told him, but Brandon could tell that he was confused.

"Yes, and we always will. However, I think it's time for me to be completely honest about my feelings. I'm going to be slow with it, and I think it starts with this," He then paused before Zach interrupted him.

"Wait, are you asking me on a date?" Zach asked with a surprised expression on his face.

Brandon laughed slightly and continued, "Yes, Zachary Deanes, would you like to go on a date with me?"

He saw Zach start to grin as he nodded his head, "Yes, Brandon Andreas, it would be an honor to go on a date with you."

"Well, I know we wanted to see that new movie that came out last week. What about dinner tonight and then we go see it? I'll pick you up."

"I think it's a perfect way to end my week."

"See you in a couple of hours then." Brandon smiled and hugged him. He then walked out of the room and closed the door. When he turned to walk away, Daniel was there smiling, "Did you have to eavesdrop?"

"Yes, I sure did, and to that, I say congratulations." Daniel patted his back, "Don't fuck it up."

"I really hate you." Brandon groaned.

He went back home to get ready for the date. Brandon was a little excited about it despite being so nervous. He got his clothes out, setting them on the bed. Brandon had decided on a black t-shirt, dark blue pants, and black tennis shoes. Since it would be a chilly night in New York, he also put on a light brown jacket. He took his shower to try and calm his nerves. Afterward, Brandon collected his items and headed over to Zach's.

He received a text from Richard wishing him luck and that he was proud of his brother. It made him smile big as it was always great to have his support. Brandon took a breath in and out before he left his house. After he got in his car, he double-checked to make sure he had his wallet and cards with him. It'd be an embarrassment to not have them with him after going through so much within himself to give him the conference to ask Zach out. He wanted everything to go right. After turning on the radio, he drove directly to Zach's place and rang the doorbell. Brandon put a smile on his face as he waited for the door to open to reveal his date. Zach came out in a buttoned-up dark red shirt with a white undershirt, blue jeans, and white tennis shoes. He had styled his hair differently from what he had at work, and Brandon loved the cologne that he smelled from him. At that moment, he understood how lucky he was to be going on a date with him.

"You look amazing," Brandon complimented.

"Thank you, and you do too." Zach smiled at him and locked his door. They headed back to Brandon's car, and Brandon opened the door for Zach to get in, "Thank you." Brandon then got back on the driver's side and drove off the parking lot.

"I can't believe this is happening," Brandon laughed.

"I can't either!" Zach smiled, "Although, I'm so glad that it is."

"Me too," Brandon said with a smile on his face.

"Can we not talk about work tonight? I want to enjoy just us being together." Zach asked.

"That was the plan all along. You're right about us working so much to the point where it's the only thing we end up talking about."

"I love my job, but I can't talk about it twenty-four seven!"

"Exactly," Brandon agreed.

The ride only took about fifteen minutes to reach their destination to the restaurant that Brandon had chosen. It was a small upcoming restaurant that had received many great reviews from its customers. There wasn't a waiting list when Brandon had called to make his reservation, and they were friendly on the phone with him. Zach and Brandon went inside the building and walked up to the hostess.

"Reservations for Andreas party of two, please?" Brandon requested.

The hostess looked up the name and led the way to their table. Brandon pulled out the chair for Zach and sat down after he did.

"I love this place so much. I brought my parents here a few months ago, and we all loved the food." Zach told him.

"Then I was lucky to have picked this place."

"Indeed, you are!"

"Please get anything you want. Don't worry about the price."

"Alright, I will." Zach nodded his head.

The waiter came up to the table after a few minutes had gone by. "Hi, my name is Randy, and I will be serving you tonight. Can I get you gentlemen started with something to drink?"

"I'll have iced tea, please." Brandon requested.

"I will have regular lemonade," Zach ordered.

"Coming right up. Do you need more time to look at the menu?" Randy asked.

"Yes, please, thank you," Brandon smiled.

Randy smiled back and walked away. After they looked over the menu, they decided what they both wanted to eat. The waiter came back with their beverages, and the gentlemen placed their meal orders. On the outside, Brandon was freaking out over the date. He wanted everything to go right and to make it perfect. He was just mesmerized by how amazing his date looked. There was also a part of him that was very nervous and anxious about the date still. After all that he went through with that special man staying by his side, he wanted him to know how much he cared. He also wanted to show how serious he was about this. Brandon wouldn't ask just anyone out after his big and traumatic life event; the man had to mean something so special to him.

"As my best friend, I think that I'd know everything about you, but I feel like there's so much I could learn. Especially about your childhood. What was that like?" Brandon asked.

"Growing up in a Republican conservative state was never easy. Ohio avoided talking about sexuality and the LGBT community for so long. In many ways, they still do because it's still such a red state. People didn't talk about it in high school; my mom and dad didn't really understand how their only son could be gay. There were three girls and one boy in the household. I just did what my father did, but I was never interested in sports. I think fashion was always more of my interest, even as a child. Being the only boy, people obviously thought that caused me to be gay, but obviously, it isn't true." Zach shook his head.

"I always knew that you liked fashion. It was definitely noticeable when I met you that you. You always had good fashion tastes, and you still do." Brandon smiled.

"Thank you very much," Zach blushed, "I just loved both the law and fashion world. There are so many designers that I love, even though I can't afford most of them. My favorite is Ralph Lauren."

"Was your second dream career in fashion?"

"Yes, I loved watching fashion shows with my sisters and mother. We still talk about them all the time."

"That's cool. I'm more into sports, and of course, the judge shows. I think baseball, football, and basketball are my three favorites. That's what my brother and I bonded with while growing up. My dad liked that we were similar to that. He just really hated me for being gay."

"Even though you had things in common?" Zach asked, surprised.

"Oh yes, it overlooked everything else for both of my parents. Growing up in a typical conservative Christian home was hard for me. They wanted Richard to hate me too. He actually got permission if he wanted to be shit to me that he could." Brandon shook his head.

"I'm so sorry to hear that."

"Believe me; I always knew that their hatred towards me was illogical. Are you religious?"

"I don't believe in a god, but I think there's some afterlife." Zach shrugged.

"I feel the same." Brandon nodded his head, "I guess I hope my dad is at peace wherever he is."

"Do you ever think about him?"

"I do, but I never allow myself to think about him for too long. There's nothing for me to care about. He died hating me, so why waste time?"

"I hate that you have to live this hard life of yours."

"I know, but I've made it through."

"Yes, you have, and I'm so happy for you."

"I'm just ready to have a lot of happiness in my life now."

Zach smiled and placed his hand on top of Brandon's. Even though this dating thing was still frightening to him, Brandon knew that he was going to feel safe with Zach. When he looked him in the eyes, the strong connection that he'd been feeling for so long was still there. It still made him want to run away, not knowing if he was making a mistake, but his intuition telling him to stay was much stronger. Brandon just hoped that Zach would be the one who would bring him that happiness.

Their food arrived ten minutes later, and they began to eat. Brandon kept an eye on the time so they wouldn't miss their movie that was afterward. They both enjoyed the conversation laughing together and sharing more memories and stories from the past. Brandon insisted on paying for the entire meal as he was the one who asked him out. Zach was very flattered by how Brandon was acting towards him. Brandon was turning out to be everything that he was looking for in a man. Neither wanted to get caught up in thinking about their future and stayed focused on the present. They cuddled up in the movie theatre with Zach's arm over Brandon's shoulders with Brandon slightly leaning on him. There was laughter throughout the entire movie as they shared popcorn and had individual drinks. Everything was perfect, and Brandon felt relaxed for the rest of the night. When Brandon dropped him off at the end of the date, he walked him to the door. Thru exchanged a few words, and Brandon went in for a kiss on his cheek. Even that was enough to make the butterflies in Zach's stomach go crazy.

It was a successful first date.

The next few weeks were crazy busy. There was no time for many dates, but they managed to go on a few on some weekends. On one Saturday afternoon, Brandon was over at Zach's house watching TV while Zach was making them lunch. They hadn't made the relationship official, and Brandon was ready for that.

After they ate, Brandon helped clean the table. "That was really good, babe."

"You think so?" Zach smiled.

"I know so," Brandon smiled at him. He carried his dishes over to the sink, washed them, and loaded the dishwasher.

Brandon then went back to the living room with Zach. He grabbed Zach's hand and faced him. They were both smiling at each other, not saying anything. Brandon was the first to make a move pulling him closer, and he wrapped his arms around his waist while Zach wrapped his arms around Brandon's neck. Brandon was the first to lean in to initiate their first kiss. When their lips finally pressed against each other, it felt as if they finally found their own home. Everything that Brandon was questioning was officially being answered in that living room. Nothing else mattered. Neither of them wanted to pull away until they needed air.

Everything went silent for a couple of seconds while their brains registered that the moment had finally happened. Brandon's heart was beating fast, and his mind was going a mile a minute. He did it. He finally kissed someone, and it felt so perfect. He blushed from ear to ear, as did Zach.

"That was amazing," Zach said softly.

"You don't know how long I've waited to do that," Brandon admitted.

"I feel the same way," Zach smiled.

"I have one important question."

"What is it?"

"Zach Deanes, will you give me the amazing honor and become my boyfriend?" Brandon asked while looking into his eyes.

"Yes, Brandon Andreas, I would love to become your boyfriend." Zach grinned. They then hugged each other tight and sat down on the couch again. Zach found something to watch on TV and cuddled with his new and amazing boyfriend. He was beyond proud of how far Brandon had come and was happy to be in a relationship with him.

Chapter 39: Out of Love

The following few months passed by, and their relationship was going great. They made a mutual promise that no matter what happened to the relationship, they'd forever be best friends. Brandon and Zach were just having fun without making it too serious. Brandon had fallen in love with the perfect man. Brandon thought that Zach was everything he didn't deserve at all. Zach was funny, loving, gentle, and, most importantly, patient with him. Everyone at work knew about their relationship, but it never interfered there. They both knew that their professionalism had to remain.

Their relationship wasn't perfect at all. Brandon hated to admit that his past still came up from time to time when they'd argue over some things. Whether it was over personal space, being late to something, or just out of frustration with life, sometimes it only caused small conflict. Zach also understood that Brandon was still in a battle with his demons. It felt like they would never go away, and although Brandon had accepted it, Zach always wanted to help get rid of them somehow. Most of them had disappeared in time, but Brandon understood that not all of them would go away. It was something that he had to live with for the rest of his life. Everything else seemed to be going great. Every day gave Brandon another reason to fall deeper in love with his boyfriend.

Things took time before the relationship between them got serious. They made sure to keep the foundation of their friendship healthy. Zach and Brandon still laughed and talked as friends. It wasn't all romantic.

Brandon was at home watching TV in deep thought, waiting for Zach to arrive. He loved Zach, and he was so attracted to him. The more that he would think about his boyfriend, the more he fell for him. The topic of sex still hadn't been brought up, but they were at the point of making out. Brandon loved how Zach would be in his arms with him giving passionate kisses. Everything was starting to feel more and more comfortable for Brandon. He was beginning to feel like a man again.

Brandon wasn't just emotionally attached to his boyfriend; he was obviously sexually attracted too. He just needed enough time to be ready for that as it still scared him. Sharon had been a big help in talking to him about the subject. He was so grateful to have a therapist that didn't care about his sexual orientation and that it never got in the way of his session.

That night, though, he was ready. As much as it was scary for him to trust another man with his body, Brandon knew that he wanted Zach. His boyfriend didn't just have a fantastic personality, but also an amazing body. Brandon loved his boyfriend's muscular toned body, how some of his outfits showed what a good looking man he was. Brandon understood that he was beyond lucky to call him his boyfriend. It was so nerve-wracking to talk to him about it, but Zach was gentle and open with him when they finally had the conversation. The night had finally come, and the couple decided to make it a date night and enjoy each other. That way, even if Brandon decided not to, then it would still be a good romantic night for the couple. Once Brandon got home from work, he took a shower, got in comfortable clothing, and cooked dinner for them. There was soft music playing on his iPad, and he had turned his electric fireplace on.

Zach let himself in with the spare key that Brandon had given him. "Hey, honey, I'm here."

Brandon smiled as Zach walked up to him after washing his hands and kissed him on the lips. Zach could feel how nervous and tense Brandon's body was just from that one touch. He understood that he was trying to be brave for both of them, but Zach was more worried about his mental health that night more than anything else.

"You look amazing." Brandon complimented.

"So do you," Zach blushed, "I also love how you've made this place intimate."

"I wanted tonight to be special for us…"

"I see that. Once again, I just want to remind you that we don't have to do that if you change your mind. Spending time with my boyfriend is amazing enough." Zach told him seriously.

"Thanks, babe, but I know that I am. There's something about you that makes me want you so bad. I'm in love with you, Zach Deanes, and now I'm ready to make love to you."

"I understand that, but the last thing you should do is force yourself," Zach said seriously as he took his hands and intertwined their fingers, "This is such a major step for you, babe. I'm truly honored that you trust me with this; I feel fortunate. You have no idea. Although, please, if you ever get one small sense of doubt tonight, please let me know. I need you to promise me."

"I just want you to feel the love and appreciation that you deserve. You're so special, Zach. You mean so much to me, and I—"

"Brandon, you don't know how much I love you. I can wait for you."

"I just miss feeling normal," Brandon confessed.

"I know you do, Brandon. It kills me that you don't feel completely normal, but having sex to try and get your feeling of normality back will not help you. It could hurt you."

"I haven't had sex in almost four years, baby. Part of me misses it."

"That's completely natural because you're still a human being, Brandon. Your desires for sex is expected, but what does your heart say?" Zach asked him and placed his hand on Brandon's beating chest.

"My heart loves you. It keeps telling me never to let go of you. That I have to make sure I work out any problems that may happen between us because I can't ever let go of you. It's been saying that since our first argument as a couple. However, I'm not saying that I'm ready for sex because I think you'd get tired of waiting and leave me. I'm really ready for sex because I know it's part of my healing. I'm ready to make love because I'm so attracted to you. We both know that if I wasn't ready, we'd still be avoiding that discussion we had about this. Zach," Brandon paused with a chuckle, "I know that the time is now. If I don't commit to this, then I did all of this mental work today for nothing. I even prayed, and you know I don't believe in God. Not after what I've been through, but I'm ready."

Zach's heart melted as he heard Brandon talk like that. It was amazing to know how far he had come. Zach wanted the night to be just as special for him. This was important to both of them. The pain and suffering had ended, the worries had gotten better, and Brandon was finally getting back to being happier. Zach had imagined this day for a while. He often wondered how Brandon would ever get to that milestone in his healing. At times, there was a lot of worrying that it'd never happen. To see Brandon finally even consider sex was amazing within itself.

Zach placed another soft kiss on his lips and whispered, "No matter what, I've got you."

Brandon smiled at his boyfriend and then went over to the kitchen stove and checked on the food. He then put it on their plates while Zach opened up the champagne pouring some into their glasses. They sat across from each other and smiled.

"Cheers to a new beginning, babe," Zach spoke softly.

"Yes, a new beginning," Brandon agreed as their glasses clinked. They each took a sip of their drinks and began to eat. Brandon had cooked something new for the night. The meal was grilled salmon and shrimp. Brandon had begun cooking more often over the past year; it was another way for him to cope with his anxiety. The smell of food cooking just calmed him down for some reason, and Zach really loved how he cooked. Whenever Brandon had a minute to himself at home, he discovered his love for the kitchen. It allowed him to be creative and to unwind from stressful days at work. Cooking served as another therapeutic activity as he found himself doing it often.

"This is really good, babe." Zach complimented the food.

"I definitely tried my best to put my own spin on a recipe I found online today."

"You found this today and learned it?" Zach asked him, impressed.

"I mean, I don't want to brag." Brandon smiled.

Zach chuckled as they continued to eat. They both hummed to the music that Brandon had on in the background, just enjoying the night. After they ate, Brandon cleared up the plates and then joined Zach back in the living room. Brandon held out his hand once the next song started to play, which was a slow song.

"May I have this dance?" Brandon asked with a grin on his face.

"You definitely can," Zach blushed as he grabbed his hand. Brandon took his hand while he wrapped his other arm around his waist. They began to dance to the music slowly and sang along. Brandon felt safe with Zach. When he looked into that man's eyes, he saw safety—a person who could become his forever home. There were sparks in those eyes that he had never found in any other men. It was as if he'd finally found his true soul mate. There were a lot of things that he had in common with him, a lot more than he had expected to have. Brandon loved his lips. Brandon loved his laughter. Brandon loved his touch.

Brandon twirled him around during the song, and they both laughed from having a good time. Thru shared a quick kiss on the lips as they continued to dance. Each kiss got deeper than the last one. By the time the song had ended, they were kissing passionately, holding each other tight. Moans escaped their mouths, and Brandon's heart skipped a beat. He knew what was about to happen.

It was time…

Brandon pulled away from the kiss and took in a deep breath. He looked at Zach in the eyes and gave a small smile, to which Zach returned. Brandon led the way to the bedroom, and they began to kiss more. Zach laid down on the bed and pulled him on top. Brandon kissed him slowly as he ran his hands all over his boyfriend's body. Zach had his hands on Brandon's back, rubbing against his shirt. They didn't need to rush. This was about falling in love in the most resounding way they could. It was about trust and healing those deep and sensitive scars that were invisible on Brandon. Zach was allowing Brandon full control and simply followed his lead. Moans started to fill the room. The skin to skin connection felt surreal to them. It was as if they were finally breaking down Brandon's hardest wall barriers one by one, neither being in any rush.

Brandon began to kiss down Zach's neck. It was an arousing sound for Brandon to be taking his time and still be able to give pleasure to his boyfriend. Brandon started grinding his hips against Zach's. Everything felt like a dream. Was this really finally happening? There were a lot of terrifying questions in Brandon's mind as he was pleasuring him. The demons were still there attacking him. They were trying to tell him that he wasn't good enough, he'd never feel confident in sex again. He couldn't help but wonder if he was failing with his actions. His hands roamed over his boyfriend's body, touching places that he remembered were sensitive to men. Some areas he made sure that to touch would drive him crazy. Brandon wanted Zach to remember that night of pleasure from his neck to the most intimate place as much as he would. He loved to tease as it was one way that he was able to enjoy sex. Also, knowing that the man he was with was anticipating his mouth spiced things up. Things got progressive as the night went on.

"How are you feeling, babe?" Brandon whispered. He didn't want to make the night be all about him as Zach's feelings also mattered.

"I feel good," Zach affirmed. He then kisses down Brandon's neck giving him the same treatment. Brandon moaned as he tried to relax. Zach was gentle with him. He made his way down the same path that he took, pleasing him while being careful. While Brandon was loving everything that was happening to him, he was still subconsciously afraid. While Zach had that trust, he was still learning to trust himself. The anxiety still had him on edge, worried about the possible bad outcomes. The way that his boyfriend nibbled on his ear. Every touch that he made was special. Brandon gained relief as Zach made love to him. It wasn't about sex at all. It was about Brandon taking more control of his body back and reintroducing himself back to being sexual. Zach understood that even without them ever saying it.

Zach removed the rest of Brandon's clothing and threw them on the ground. He rubbed his hand over Brandon's private area, which caused Brandon to gasp and jerk a little. Zach went back up to kiss his neck to try and relax him. He felt how Brandon had tensed up, and he felt bad.

"I'm sorry, baby," Brandon moaned and rubbed his back.

"It's okay; we're going at your pace," Zach promised. Zach then captured his lips in another kiss. Brandon didn't want to mess up after coming so far. He was so gentle and loving to him. His boyfriend didn't care how long it would take that night. Zach wanted Brandon to feel safe and loved. They kissed for a few minutes before Brandon gave the okay for him to try again. His body felt relaxed again. Zach sucked the top of the member slowly.

Brandon couldn't remember the last time someone had made love to him. Not sex, but actual love. Brandon was getting comfortable within his skin again in milestones, and he was grateful to have an amazing boyfriend to share this one with. More importantly, It was good to have someone who could show him love again and how to enjoy it without any guilty feelings. The inside of his mind started to overthink. They were exploring each other at their most vulnerable moment, especially

Brandon's. Finally, his nerves calmed down, and he began to enjoy the pleasure more. The aura of the past was fading away, and the love of his sweet boyfriend replaced it.

Zach eventually stopped and went back to kissing his boyfriend hard. They flipped back over, and Brandon picked up the condom and rolled it on himself. Neither were ready to go unprotected. Brandon's hands worked on stretching Zach out carefully, not wanting to hurt him at all. Brandon eventually pushed into him, slowly feeling him. Although it was scary, it was also refreshing for him. He loved how his boyfriend felt around him and how with each thrust felt like he was returning to normal. They gained more pleasure as time went on.

There was a lot of faith that Brandon had given Zach with his heart and vulnerability. Zach cherished that wholeheartedly and didn't want to mess it up. Even though he was mindful of that, Zach still allowed himself to be present at the moment to be pleasured. Their climaxes happened around the same time as they settled down from the thrill. Hundreds of thoughts were floating through their minds, especially Brandon's. It was relieving to have finally had sex. He wrapped his arms around Zach, and they both remained silent for a couple of minutes.

"How was it?" Zach finally asked to break the silence.

"I had fun. It was frightening at first, and I had to embrace myself mentally, but I think I liked it." Blains said.

"I'm proud of you, babe. You're healing so much more now that you've gotten through your first time."

"I give you all of the credit for helping me get here. This has been a long storm, and I'm finally free."

Zach smiled when Brandon said that. Helping Brandon was never about taking any of the credit or eventually getting in a relationship with him. He would've been there anyway as a friend. They talked for about an hour before drifting off to sleep, knowing that they can make it out of any storm together. Brandon had won back his body.

Epilogue

Zach's and Brandon's relationship continued to grow after that night. Once they both had saved up enough money over the following several years, they finally decided to move in together and eventually got married. They had a decent sized house in New York, had several trusting clients, and Brandon loved working at the same law firm. This was everything that he had hoped for in his life, and he wouldn't trade it for anything in the world. Brandon didn't think that he'd ever see the day where he could finally have his happiness.

It was a typical Tuesday morning, and Brandon had decided to take a week off since he had finished a case that drained him out emotionally. His client was never cooperative with him, and he had struggled while trying to do the best that he could. This was still the most rewarding thing he'd ever done in his life. Zach was the one to convince him to take time off to relax. Brandon tried to protest against it but eventually gave in. He had made coffee for his husband and kissed him before he left for work. Since he had nothing to do, Brandon decided to go out for a drive in the city. It was a beautiful day in New York, and he wanted to take advantage of it. He finished his breakfast and then got clothes on.

Brandon drove by many places around the city, such as his first college that he went to. It was hard to move around the campus and remember that he went to classes and visited friends who lived on campus. Zach was one of them who he remembered visiting. When he saw one of his former professors, he decided to go up to her. He parked his car and went up to her.

"Hi, Professor Baker!" Brandon greeted.

"Well, isn't this a pleasant surprise to see one of my favorite former students!" Professor Baker smiled delightedly.

"How've you been?"

"I'm great! How about yourself?"

"I'm doing good. Just very glad to be done with law school and settled in my career and life."

"That's great to hear. I get so happy when I see students become successful in their careers. Did you start your own law firm?"

"I actually decided to join the law firm where I was the receptionist at," Brandon explained, "I just couldn't let go of that business."

"You deserve it, you know? No one worked as hard as you did."

"Thank you, that means so much to me. I was going through so much when I was in your classroom. It scared me not knowing where my life was headed."

"What do you mean?"

Brandon sighed and looked down. He began to talk a little quieter so no one else would hear, "My roommate was raping me."

Professor Baker's face immediately went into shock when she heard that. She embraced him in a warm hug without caring who saw. Even though Brandon had healed tremendously over the past few years, it still hurt him. There was always going to be something that triggered him about it. Tears began making his eyes swell up as they stood there in silence. Neither of them cared who saw. Brandon quickly wiped his eyes before anyone could see.

"Why didn't you tell anyone at the college?"

"I was too ashamed at first. He was my best friend, so I thought that we would've worked it out, and he'd apologize. Neither of that happened."

"Did you decide to report?"

"I did, and it went all the way to trial. Thankfully, I won the case, and he was serving fifteen years in prison."

"Was serving fifteen years?"

"He was beaten up severely after two years. I saw in the file that it had happened," Brandon told her.

"How do you feel?"

"I think it was hard at first, but it also brought me so much relief at the same time. It was like a guilty relief of knowing he got what he deserved. There's no more anticipation of what's going to happen after the fifteen years were up. He was my best friend until then, and although

I believe in second chances, I gave him multiple chances. If he had given me an honest apology, I wouldn't have reported him." He admitted.

"You've survived it, and that's what is most important. I'm not sure what I'd do in your situation either. Who did you get to represent you?"

"I picked one of my bosses, now a colleague, to represent me," Brandon smiled, "Zachary Deanes was one of my witnesses as well as a police officer. I'm now happily married to Zach."

"I am so happy to hear that. How are you now?"

"I am better. I'll never completely heal, but I'm at peace with everything."

"That's understandable. Well, it was great to see you. I have to get to my classes but have my number," Professor Baker gave him her email address and personal number, "I would love to keep in touch."

"I will definitely keep in touch with you," Brandon smiled and gave her his business card and personal email, "Great seeing you, too."

They parted ways, and Brandon continued to walk on campus for a while. There weren't many people around that morning, and it was a very sunny day. After an hour of getting some exercise, he drove out of the campus and made his way to the cemetery. He had never visited the cemetery before, but he decided to be the bigger person and see his father's tombstone. Something about moving forward was still on hold until he finally was brave enough to do so. It was his therapist's idea to go visit, and of course, Brandon fought it for so long. Why should he visit the man when he didn't care about him? What good could it do to have Brandon stare at this plot where his coffin was buried underneath it? However, he knew that his husband and therapist wouldn't suggest anything to hurt him.

He drove through the Calvary Cemetery, looking for his area. Brandon had asked Richard what his tombstone number and where he was located. It felt weird that it was his first time visiting, but Brandon had been stubborn. Once he got to his spot, he just stood there looking at it. "Harold Andreas, July 2, 1961 - January 18, 2019" was written on it. There weren't any flowers meaning his mother hadn't visited in a while, and that made him feel a little better. He figured that there weren't any chances of her coming that day either. However, there was no way of knowing for sure since they didn't talk anymore. She just never tried to get in touch with him after the fallout and funeral, and Brandon didn't care. He was done trying to prove his worth to anyone. Brandon still wanted to speak to his father.

"Hey dad, it's your unwanted son finally ignoring your wishes not to visit you. You knew I'd eventually come. I gave you eight years of peace; I think that's fair. No, I don't think you'd care to have an update on my life, but you're getting one anyway," Brandon began, "To start, I'm officially a lawyer. I finished law school five years ago, and I love it. Despite all that was going on in my life, I didn't let it stop my learning from getting my degree. You know, that's one thing you taught me when you did love me was never to quit your biggest goals and aspirations. Richard and I both took that to heart, which is why he's a movie star, and I'm a criminal lawyer."

"I tried, dad," Brandon began to cry after he took a pause, "I really tried to follow the doctor's orders to help with your cancer care. I went from class to your house to feed and bathe you to having to rush in to do a four-hour shift at work. It was hard, and I soon didn't have a safe home to go to at night. I'm not going into detail because I know you wouldn't care anyway. Since I'm not straight like Richard, I know you don't give a shit. That's okay, though. You guys stopped caring about me after I came out. It felt like I never got a break, and I had to get used to it. Whatever curveball that life threw at me, I just had to suck it up and deal with it. You were my top priority, believe it or not. I came on days when nurses refused to show up. I came when I didn't even have to and checked on you. Hell, I was your nurse while getting prepared to study law. All of a sudden, Richard does the same for only three weeks before you went into the hospital for the last time, and he's a hero? How is that fair, dad?"

"Dammit!" Brandon cried out in frustration, "He didn't truly want to fly in that year. I had to convince him for a whole month to come and see your dying ass. Be fucking grateful for me! You're already dead, so it can't kill you!"

They never got the chance to have the conversation before his father crossed over. He didn't think that he needed it, but now that he was there alone on his knees, Brandon realized that he did. It probably would've ended like every other deep conversation he tried to have with him, but at least he would've tried. It wasn't necessarily a regret for him, however. Maybe it just wasn't meant to happen for some reason. Brandon had to come to terms with that after the trial. He couldn't focus on grieving, which he knew wasn't healthy either. Visiting the cemetery was his chance to do just that finally. Zach was the only one who knew that he was going to do that. His husband wanted to go with him and had promised to stay in the car, except Brandon realized that he had to do it alone.

"I didn't think I'd survive without you growing up. You taught me so much about being a man, and believe me, I listened. I still love you, dad. I still love mom, and I feel like I'm obligated to for so many reasons. She's just not allowed in my life again until she needs me medically. Even then, I'm not sure if I will become one for her too. I can't put my husband through that. Yes, I'm married to a man—the love of my life. Our wedding was beautiful. I just wanted you to know that. Richard was the best man. He's also married to his longtime girlfriend, Alison." He then stood back up, "I hope you're happy and at peace wherever you are. Maybe I'll see you again one day."

With that, Brandon went back to his car and drove away. It needed to be done. Something else was weighing heavily on his heart that week. It was the letter. Even though it was going to be hard, Brandon figured that it was best to get through all of his deep, emotional scars in one day. He went through a fast-food drive-thru and made his way back to the house. Zach wasn't going to be home for a couple of hours, which he needed. No one needed to be there while Brandon did this. He went into the bedroom, getting his notebook and a pencil, and sat down at the kitchen table. Brandon ate his food first to keep it from getting cold and then got to the task. After a long deep breath, he began.

It took him many breaks in between Either he couldn't calm down from his tears and anxiety, or he just had trouble finding the right words to say. There was a determination to finish that letter in one sitting. He had thought about it for so long that he didn't want to prolong and procrastinate with it. After all, this was going to come straight from his heart. Every emotion was going from his body onto that paper.

Zach came home at the end of the day. Brandon had finished the letter, and Zach saw him on the couch asleep with the papers on his chest. For a moment, it worried Zach because he didn't know what happened. He placed his briefcase down on the floor and went to wake him up.

"Babe," Zach shook him gently, "I'm home."

Brandon yawned as he woke and sat up. He kissed his husband on the lips and smiled. "How was your day?"

"I just had a bunch of paperwork to do. Are you okay? It looks like you've been crying."

"I am, I just had a very healing day, and tears were involved."

"You did? What happened?"

"I finally went to the cemetery." Brandon explained, "It was time for me to visit my father for the first time."

"I didn't know that you were thinking about doing that," Zach said, feeling proud. He took his husband's hands and sat down next to him.

"I just needed to do it without anyone knowing. It was for me to finally get what I needed to say for years off of my chest. I was lucky that my mom didn't show up. That would've caused a problem."

"I can't stand her. It's good that you got rid of her."

"Thank you for your understanding," Brandon sighed.

"Of course. Let's talk about something good. Did you know Madelyn and her husband Michael, are visiting this weekend?"

"I know, I'm so excited to see them. It's good that she found someone. She deserves it."

"Yeah, she does. Maybe she's pregnant."

"I would love to raise our kids together," Brandon grinned and kissed him again.

"Me too, babe." Zach smiled as he kissed back, "Did you do anything else today?"

Brandon nodded his head and gave Zach the letter, "I finally wrote it."

Zach looked confused, not knowing what he meant at first. Once he glanced at the first page, he saw his name at the top and realized. "I forgot that you were supposed to do this."

"I never forgot it. It just took me time to finally pull through and get it done."

"Let me change clothes, and we'll read it and talk about it." Zach went into their room and changed out of his suit. He was eager to see how far his husband came. Even though he obviously could tell how much he had healed, the letter was going to give him more clarity. Brandon snuggled in his arms and began to read out loud.

Shane,

There are so many things that I never got to say to you. I can't let myself spend days and days trying to put into words all we went through. I knew there was something so special about you the way we met. I can remember it clearly. Do you remember who greeted who first? It was you. I was so afraid to talk to you, knowing you were on a few sports teams and doing all of these activities. As you know, Madelyn and I were already friends since elementary school. Little did I know that being boy crazy would lead to high school jealousy.

Looking back, I was always so stupid. Madelyn was always my friend first! Why would you be able to get in the way of that? I was willing to get rid of her as my best friend for a boy; for you. Yet, we can leave that as "high school drama" without the drama because if you know me, you'd remember that I wasn't about to create it. The craziest part is you did know me. You knew me better than I knew myself. Better than Richard even, and he knows everything. However, that's how special you were to me. So somehow you mean to tell me that you NEVER knew that I fell for you? That just seems full of shit.

You didn't miss me. You missed owning my body, but you were trying to sugar coat it by saying that you did. I now see your tricks better than ever before. Shane, you made it very clear that the main reason was to save your own ass from prison, where you belonged for the remainder of your life. You were too late to apologize. It took you two years too long to write this letter to me. That was definitely a plan to help get your charges dropped. I know the game! I was in college to study this game, and I'm so glad I didn't fall for it.

It did hurt that you were beaten to death. That was such a shock to read that in the system. I was devastated beyond words, and it took me weeks to get through the depression. Maybe even a couple of months. You had to have known that I wanted the complete opposite for us. I was foolish enough to want to become yours forever. Someone that you fell in love with and not in lust with. We lived together, and it's scary to realize that I still didn't know you until then. It had me in complete denial. I should've begun mourning you the next day after you wanted to experiment. I should have kept Madelyn away from you for the right reasons. At the same time, maybe it needed to happen in order for me to fall in love with my soul mate, Zach. I proposed to him, and now we're expecting our first child in a few months. Our surrogate is in her second trimester

I love myself again. I can trust myself again. Now, I have the responsibility of protecting my daughter. In a way, I do thank you for this. Without you, I wouldn't be as strong as I am now. Yes, I'll forever hurt because of you but what you did is no longer part of my identity. The rape is my past, my anxiety is my past, and I'm now in the future without you happily. I hope never to see you in any afterlife because you don't deserve another chance.

Your former sex toy,

Brandon Andreas

Zach's mouth was wide open when he finished that letter. It was better than Zach had ever imagined. He finally understood Brandon's history with him on a more profound level. That also killed him even more for his husband. Without saying anything, Zach embraced him in a warm hug, and they sat in silence. Nothing else needed to be spoken at that moment. Brandon didn't feel the need to cry anymore. He had already done enough crying for the day. If anything, he was proud of himself for being able to write it.

"I'm so proud of you, babe. You're right, we are soul mates, and I couldn't be happier to be your husband," Zach finally said.

"Thank you; I don't know what I'd do without you."

"Likewise." Brandon smiled and kissed him.

Brandon decided to keep the letter and to copy it on the computer. He did, however, burn the handwritten version as the therapist suggested. It was healing, and it was freeing himself from the burdens of his past. He placed the letter in the fire pit in their backyard, and they watched it crumble into ash. Brandon had healed. He had grown.

Brandon had survived.

About the Author

Sean Gold is a young, black, gay man with a disability. His desire is to enlighten, inform and support others in his hometown of St. Louis, Missouri, and beyond. He is an advocate for people with disabilities, a public speaker, and has one Microsoft certification for web design. In 2020, Sean was elected as president of the disability-owned nonprofit organization, Coalition in Truth and Independence. He considers his faith, family, and friends the most important things in his life. His physical disability is Cerebral Palsy, and he has had a Tracheostomy Breathing Tube since he was only one and a half years old. Even though he's nonverbal, it doesn't get in the way of his love of creative writing and storytelling.